"Once again, O.R. Melling weaves her visionary web
of soul-searching explorations, some of them credibly
chilling. They will not disappoint her readers."
Eugene McCabe

"*Every once in a while you come across an extraordinary book,
the book you give to friends and say, 'you have to read this.'*
People of the Great Journey *is just one of those books.
Magical, mystical, romantic, heartbreaking, and full of humour,
this is a book of essential truths and eternal mysteries."*
Michael Scott, author of *The Secrets of the Immortal Nicholas Flamel* **series**

"*Innovative, ambitious and courageous."*
Carlo Gébler

"*By turns thrilling and chilling, but above all fundamentally
wise, this gripping account of one woman's spiritual journey
is an utterly compelling example of an esoteric testament
destined to become a classic. Highly recommended."*
Herbie Brennan, author of the *Faerie Wars* **Chronicles**

PEOPLE
OF THE
GREAT
JOURNEY

PEOPLE
OF THE
GREAT
JOURNEY

O.R. MELLING

HAY HOUSE

Carlsbad, California • New York City • London • Sydney
Johannesburg • Vancouver • Hong Kong • New Delhi

First published and distributed in the United Kingdom by:
Hay House UK Ltd, Astley House, 33 Notting Hill Gate, London W11 3JQ
Tel: +44 (0)20 3675 2450; Fax: +44 (0)20 3675 2451
www.hayhouse.co.uk

Published and distributed in the United States of America by:
Hay House Inc., PO Box 5100, Carlsbad, CA 92018-5100
Tel: (1) 760 431 7695 or (800) 654 5126
Fax: (1) 760 431 6948 or (800) 650 5115
www.hayhouse.com

Published and distributed in Australia by:
Hay House Australia Ltd, 18/36 Ralph St, Alexandria NSW 2015
Tel: (61) 2 9669 4299; Fax: (61) 2 9669 4144
www.hayhouse.com.au

Published and distributed in the Republic of South Africa by:
Hay House SA (Pty) Ltd, PO Box 990, Witkoppen 2068
Tel/Fax: (27) 11 467 8904
www.hayhouse.co.za

Published and distributed in India by:
Hay House Publishers India, Muskaan Complex, Plot No.3, B-2,
Vasant Kunj, New Delhi 110 070
Tel: (91) 11 4176 1620; Fax: (91) 11 4176 1630
www.hayhouse.co.in

Distributed in Canada by:
Raincoast, 9050 Shaughnessy St, Vancouver BC V6P 6E5
Tel: (1) 604 323 7100; Fax: (1) 604 323 2600

Text © O. R. Melling, 2013

This book is a work of fiction. The use of actual events or locales, and persons living or deceased, is strictly for artistic/literary reasons only.

The moral rights of the author have been asserted.

A catalogue record for this book is available from the British Library.

ISBN: 978-1-78180-207-6

Printed and bound in Great Britain by TJ International, Padstow, Cornwall.

MIX
Paper from
responsible sources
FSC® C013056
www.fsc.org

For Patrick Black,
who has walked me through the darkness many a time

And in memory of my precious friend, Dr Nena Hardie,
Gus an coinnich sinn a-rithist

CATEGORY: INNER SPACE FICTION
For there is never anywhere to go but in.
Doris Lessing, *Briefing for a Descent into Hell*

*The mystery of primordial images is deeper, their origin
more remote, their cave more hid, their fountain less
accessible than those suspect who have yet dug deepest.*
C.S. Lewis, *Selected Literary Essays*

*Here it is, again setting out on the most perilous of
adventures, the adventure of being what we are, human
beings for whom their humanity is a conscious choice.*
John Moriarty, *Invoking Ireland: Ailiu Iath n-hErend*

ACKNOWLEDGEMENTS

This book took many years to write, so there are many I need to thank for succour along the way: as always my amazing daughter, Findabhair, and the Whelan family; the early readers – former editor Meg Masters, New York writer Rachel Gallagher, Frank Golden, Eve Golden-Woods, Martha O'Grady, Kate Mullaney, Martina Brady-Arbuckle, and Helen Murphy; Fr Joe Walsh and the priests and brothers of the Franciscan Abbey at Multyfarnham, Co. Weatmeath for an artist's residency; Srs Miriam and Barbara of the Luisne Spirituality Centre, Co. Wicklow; Martin Duffy and Annette Peard of the Irish Centre for Shamanic Studies; the Moon Women of County Wicklow (Sherron, Kathleen, Pam, Sara, Charlie, Maura, Deirdre, Siofra); Cáit Branigan for the experience of a Celtic Sweat House/An Teach Allais; Vicky Heslop and writer Kate Thompson for horsey knowledge and advice; Professor Dáibhí O'Cróinín for correction of my Irish; poet Niels Hav for Danish correction and translation; Sylvain Despretz for long talks about Thaddeus Golas; United States Holocaust Memorial Museum; Rigpa Fellowship, California; the Findhorn Foundation including the Findhorn ecovillage and Isle of Erraid; Gerard McGrath of McGrath/McGrane for legal advice; Jenny Sherwin and the Wicklow Arts Office for a research grant; the Arts Council of Ireland for a travel grant; Joe Murray, computer angel; my wonderful agent, Marianne Gunn O'Connor; my editor, Mary Tomlinson; Michelle Pilley, Julie Oughton, Amy Kiberd, and all at Hay House UK who restored my faith in the publishing industry.

Special mention goes to Panchen Otrul Rinpoche, my teacher, and Venerable Tenzin Choeden (Margery Cross) at Jampa Ling Tibetan Buddhist Centre, Ireland, for a place to write, work, and meditate.

And whispered thanks to Na Daoine Maithe.

FOREWORD

ALPHA

It began with a journey to the Outer Hebrides with my dearest friend, Dr N. At last, a suitable setting for a depiction of the Work! I have taken my time to write of it, for personal and professional reasons. Please understand that this presentation is fictional. It is not "true" in the factual or scientific sense. The characters, in particular, are my own creation, and do not represent persons living or dead. But I agree with the late great Anthony de Mello that the shortest distance between a human being and the truth is a story. And the tale was written, in the words of Gottfried von Strassburg, twelfth-century author of *Tristan*, as "a labour out of love for the world, and to comfort noble hearts".

O.M., 21 June 2013, Ireland

CHAPTER ONE

THE CALL

Long before she arrived at Dunesfort House, where the events recorded here took place, Olwen knew she was approaching extraordinary territory. It began with the letter.

Dear Writer of Fairy Tales,
I may misperceive of what you intend, but it seems to me that you write of matters pertaining to the world of the immortal spirit; that world of which the arts are but a reflection. Perhaps, like Alice, you might wish to pass through the looking-glass and explore the source of your work?
Rose
Director, Dunesfort House
Isle of Lewis, Outer Hebrides
Scotland

It felt more like a summons than an invitation. Enclosed with the letter was a single-page leaflet advertising a week-long residential course called "The Great Journey". There was no mention of what the course specifically entailed, only a black-and-white photograph of a great house overlooking the sea and a mission statement:

Humanity is experiencing the titanic struggle of death and rebirth. The contractions are under way — blood and violence, upheaval and uncertainty, pain and suffering. Yet the baby will be born. The long dark age of greed and aggression is coming to an end: a new age dawns. As midwives to this great event, we are called to heal our own wounds and awaken. At Dunesfort House, we use ancient wisdom and visionary practices towards this end... and this beginning.

Olwen was immediately caught by the words, as well as the image of a baronial mansion on the edge of a cliff. The course took place in mid-summer. She would have finished the last edits on her new book by then. The fee was manageable with the help of her credit card. All she needed was the slightest of nudges to confirm her decision.

That came when a friend rang from Toronto. Dr N was planning a trip to Barra in the Outer Hebrides for a gathering of her clan. Would Olwen like to join her? The two women had travelled together before, most recently around Ireland, where Olwen lived, to visit megalithic sites.

The coincidence was too big to ignore.

"Synchronicity!" said Dr N, a Jungian psychologist, when she heard the story.

"A big word for magic," agreed Olwen.

CHAPTER TWO

THE HIGH ROAD

It was getting late. They had crossed the northern hump of Scotland and were driving south towards Ullapool. Conversation in the car had dwindled. The road was narrow, continually twisting and turning, rising and falling. Dark mountains and forests shadowed their way. Again and again the coastline broke into lochs of choppy waters and moonlit cliffs. There was no other traffic. They had opened their windows to let in the balmy air and the sweet scent of peat smoke.

Dr N was driving. She changed gears as the road began another steep rise.

"You take the high road and I'll take the low road," Olwen sang softly, *"and I'll be in Scotland afore you."*

"The low road is the Path of the Dead," Dr N remarked.

"Really?" Olwen shivered.

"That's why he'll get there first...and why he and his true love will never meet again on the banks of Loch Lomond."

Olwen gazed out the window at the night. She had pushed her seat back to make room for her long legs. At forty-nine, she was often mistaken for a decade younger. The mane of auburn hair was partly responsible, any hint of grey dyed away, as well as the genes of her long-living mother; but there was also an irrepressible vitality and youthfulness that fired her speech and manner. The amber eyes had plenty of laughter lines at their edges, and her mouth was full-lipped and generous.

"It does seem a bit like we are on the Path of the Dead," she murmured. "All these ferrymen carrying us across the waters."

They had taken numerous boat trips over the past week, beginning with the longest from Belfast to Troon. After exploring the Highlands, they had taken the ferry from Scrabster to Stromness in the Orkney Islands and then several smaller ferries within the Orkneys themselves. They were now on the last leg of their journey. They would stay overnight in Ullapool and sail the following morning to Stornoway on the Isle of Lewis.

Dr N frowned. In her mid-sixties, she had silver-grey hair cropped neatly to frame elfin features and sharp, intelligent eyes. She threw Olwen a sideways glance.

"Are you having second thoughts?"

Olwen grimaced. "Would you sign up for a mystery course in the middle of nowhere?"

"No," Dr N said honestly. "But I'm not you. My adventures tend to be interior. You, on the other hand, are more daring in the outer world. It makes sense. That kind of curiosity feeds your work."

"So I tell myself." Olwen bit her lip. She was about to say more when she was distracted. "What's that?"

In the ditch to their left, small almond-shaped lights were blinking on and off: then, suddenly, on the road ahead, a great stag. He froze in the beam of their headlamps. Antlers branching, magnificent and male, he straddled the lane, poised for fight or flight.

The two women were stunned.

"Aisling," Olwen said softly. Vision.

Dr N reduced her speed and dimmed the lights. "Think small. Submissive." The car inched forwards. "The fawns and does are in the ditch."

Would there be room to pass? Would he charge them?

With a great shudder of his haunches, the stag moved sideways into the verge. Still towering over the road, he held his position as they crawled past him. Even when they were a safe distance away, he continued to fill their mirrors, framed by the starry sky behind him.

They drove on in silence.

The following day they were on the Isle of Lewis, lost in a wild and lonely landscape. Beyond the capital of Stornoway, the countryside looked barren, almost treeless, with only scatterings of crofters' cottages and black-faced sheep. Stark mountains brooded over vast tracts of bog. The few road signs were in Scots Gaelic. *Achadh Mór. Gearraidh na h-Aibhne.*

They stopped for a picnic on a deserted beach. A flock of gulls slept on the white sand. The sea glittered a pristine blue. When they attempted to paddle in the water, it was so cold it scalded their feet. Retreating to the blanket, they ate salmon sandwiches and sipped hot tea from a flask.

Olwen had been quiet the whole morning. It was her turn to drive. She had suggested they go sightseeing instead of heading directly for Dunesfort House.

"Will we have a look at the Callanish Stones?" she said now, as they finished their lunch. "Everything I've read says they're more incredible than any of the circles we saw in Ireland."

Dr N agreed readily, but as they returned to the car she rested her hand on her friend's arm.

"If you've changed your mind about the course, you're more than welcome to join me. There'll be many in-laws and outlaws at the gathering. It's not as if anyone will notice."

"I've already paid the fee. It may not be refundable. I can't afford to throw away money like that."

Dr N's look was sympathetic. "Why don't you make your final decision when we get there? I'll give you my honest opinion of the place. I'll be able to view it objectively as I'm not involved. You know the old Hebrew saying, 'A stranger can see what's wrong in the first three minutes.'"

Olwen's relief was huge. "Great idea! I trust your instincts more than my own. You know me. Rose-coloured glasses. I see what I want to see, hear what I want to hear. It can even override my baseline paranoia!"

They both laughed.

"But I still want to see Callanish," she added.

"Me too," said Dr N.

Their first sight of Callanish was a shock. Nothing they had seen in Ireland had prepared them for its scale and majesty. Both the size and number of the stones were overwhelming. They were almost fifty in all, with the tallest near the centre standing sixteen feet high. A spacious avenue led to an inner circle surrounding a ruined burial chamber. Three shorter rows of stones radiated outwards from the centre. The megaliths dominated the windswept landscape. Overhead arched an expanse of sky.

The site was so immense, the two women felt as if they had it all to themselves, despite the groups of tourists that came and went. There was no loud talk or laughter. The stones inspired a muted awe and respect.

Dr N consulted her guidebook. "They're dated anywhere from 3000 to 1500 BC. Completed over generations. The stones themselves are ancient. Three billion years old!"

"But why here?" Olwen wondered. "Why such a huge monument for a small population? Could it have been a place of pilgrimage? A ritual centre to which people travelled?"

Dr N continued reading. "The Vikings used to raid the islands and ruled here for a time. The original name appears to be 'Tursachan', and a suggested translation is 'place of sadness or suffering'".

"Place of Sadness," Olwen repeated softly. "Place of Suffering."

Dr N wandered off to the Visitor Centre adjacent to the site, but Olwen chose to remain among the stones. She walked aimlessly, musing on their presence. These were the grandmothers and grandfathers of all the megaliths she had explored over the years. Ancient spirits of stone, millions of years old.

Removing her sandals, she went barefoot in the grass. The folds of her cotton skirt brushed against her legs.

Eventually she grew aware of a new arrival to the site. He was a striking young man with lightning-white hair that fell to his shoulders. Everything about him exuded the confidence of a male in his prime. An image of the stag on the road flashed through her mind. He wore the black-leather gear of a motorcyclist, with heavy boots, gauntlets, and bulky jacket. His look was Scandinavian, Teutonic. *A Saxon lordling. A Nordic prince.* There wasn't a woman on the site who wasn't aware of him.

He removed one of his gloves to stroke the tallest stone that towered over the central circle, the one Olwen thought of as the king-stone. She shuddered slightly as if his hand had stroked *her.* Amused at herself, she prowled the perimeter, keeping him always in her sights. A small harp-shaped case was slung over his shoulder, like a quiver of arrows. After a while, he sprawled on the grass, legs stretched out to bask in the sunlight. His leather-clad body glistened like a pelt. The harp rested on his lap. When he caught her watching him, he stared back at her with a careless grin. It was as if he had thrown down one of his gloves in front of her.

Strolling over, she hunkered down beside him, trying not to laugh. It was an old game. His features were a series of sharp angles, cleft chin, and high cheekbones.

"Will you play?" she asked, indicating the harp.

"*Ja,*" he said with a shrug.

Unzipping the cover, he drew the wired-string harp out of its case. He took a few moments to tighten the strings, and then began to play.

She remained crouched beside him, eyes half-closed. The music rippled around her and over the stones. An old Scottish air, perfect for the place, it stirred her blood.

When the tune ended, he raised his sunglasses. Wintry blue eyes regarded her.

"*Go raibh míle maith agat*," she said, thanking him in Irish.

He was surprised. "*Gaelisk?*"

She nodded. "You?"

"*Dansk.*"

Her mouth twisted wryly. The strange repeating patterns of her life. She had once loved a Dane. Now she saw the faint trace of crow's feet at the corners of his eyes. He was older than she had first imagined, more like thirties than twenties. He, in turn, was staring at her lips. The invitation was evident. It seemed a fair reward for the gift of his music.

She leaned forward, intending a light kiss, but his lips swooped suddenly to capture hers. She was caught off guard and lost her balance. As she fell against him, his arms grasped hold of her and his tongue forced her mouth open. He sucked on her breath. For a moment she forgot where she was. Then she pushed him away, though not harshly. She couldn't help but laugh. With a wave of her hand she indicated the obvious. They were in a public place.

Another careless grin. Another shrug. He would have continued regardless.

Her own grin was rueful. The difference in age. *Too bad*, she reflected as she walked away from him. *Too bad I stopped.*

Dr N was waiting for her in the car park.

"The Centre is closed," the older woman said. "I forgot everything shuts here on Sundays. Strict Sabbatarianism."

A motorcycle roared to life behind them. The young man sped past with a beep and a quick wave of his gloved hand.

Olwen watched as he disappeared down the road, fair hair streaming in the wind.

"Did I miss something?" Dr N asked, eyebrow raised.

"Another stag."

"You and your young men."

"They just appear out of nowhere."

"And you don't ask for it?"

"All the time."

It was late afternoon when they began their ascent up the winding road that bordered the craggy coast. Olwen was following the map that accompanied her receipt for the course. She had grown pensive again.

"What on earth am I doing?"

"Do you want my professional opinion?"

"Not if you're going to charge for it."

They both smiled. It was an old joke.

"We look for new answers when the old ones we are living with – or living by – no longer serve us."

"That makes sense," said Olwen. "A 'turning fifty' thing?" The sky had darkened. It began to rain; one of the many sudden showers that kept assailing them. They were travelling along the edge of a cliff, with the sea to their left. The road ahead wound ever upwards, every corner blind. She slowed to a near crawl, praying she wouldn't meet other traffic.

"If it's any comfort," Dr N said after a while, "I can't think of a single dangerous cult that was run by a woman."

"One of the chief deciding factors," Olwen admitted. "Female director. I also liked the way she used her first name only. Very informal and friendly."

They had reached the top at last. The road moved quickly away from the cliffs to cross a wild moor. And there in the distance, rising darkly through the veil of rain, was Dunesfort House.

CHAPTER THREE

THE CASTLE

Standing on a promontory overlooking the sea, Dunesfort House was an immense and mazy structure. Turrets and towers protruded from stone walls. Mullioned windows glinted over iron balconies. Tall chimneys rose above varied levels of slated roof.

"Wuthering Heights," Olwen said, in awe.

"Or Manderley," Dr N suggested.

The rain had stopped by the time they approached the house. The road veered away from the front entrance, leading them through an archway into a courtyard at the back. Gravel crunched under the tyres. At the centre of the courtyard stood a small fountain rimmed by a stone bench. To their right was a long greenhouse fronting sheds and stables. To their left rose the house. Row after row of shuttered windows gazed down like lidded eyes.

Olwen shivered as she stepped out of the car. The atmosphere was gloomy. The only sound was of rainwater sluicing down the drainpipes.

"I always knew you'd be delivering me to an institution one day," she said to her friend, but the attempt at humour fell flat. The air was oppressive, heavy with damp and the smell of seaweed. She didn't take her luggage from the car. "Remember, if I say I forgot something in Stornoway, we're out of here like a shot."

"Understood," said Dr N. She was about to say more when she let out a little cry. "Good God, is it a broch?"

She hurried over to inspect the circular tower that cornered the house. A glass conservatory curved in a half-moon at its base. Higher up were deep-set windows. It was massive in size, apparently much older than the rest of the building that had been constructed around it.

"There's no mortar!" Dr N exclaimed, pointing upwards. "Can you see? It's held together by the sheer weight of the stones. Brochs were the first Scottish buildings, before the Romans came. They're ancient. This restoration is amazing. It must have cost a fortune!"

Under normal circumstances, Olwen would have shared her fascination, but history was the last thing on her mind right now. She walked through the archway and around the side of the house to find the front door. Dr N followed after her.

Here, the house took the full brunt of the wind that came in off the sea. There was no lawn or garden, only an expanse of grass and stony ground that ran to the precipice. A grey sky hung over an equally grey sea capped with white breakers. In the distance a squall lashed the water with needles of rain. The house itself stood stolid and unconcerned, its sheer bulk enough to withstand the elements. The spacious glass porch was warm and dry inside. It smelled of greenery, with plants in ceramic jars and shelves lined with wellington boots of every size. Mounted beside the oaken door was a ship's bell, polished to shine.

"I'm beginning to envy you," Dr N remarked.

"Hmm," said Olwen. She was a little overwhelmed.

She rang the bell. It was a while before they heard footsteps within.

A big stocky countrywoman answered the door. She had a broad smile, weathered features, and strong dark-brown eyes. As Olwen met her frank gaze, she found herself thinking of bog pools in the wilder regions of the Irish mountains she had hiked. Though the woman appeared to be well into her seventies, she exuded great energy.

"Rose?" asked Olwen.

A quick shake of the head. "The Director is nae here at present. I am Morag Macleod, the housekeeper." The Scottish burr thickened an already earthy voice. "You may call me Mrs Macleod or Morag, whichever is fine. I don't mind. Do come in. *Fàilte romhaibh.* You are very welcome to Dunesfort House."

Olwen was already relaxing as she stepped into the hallway. Responding to the Scots Gaelic, she thanked Morag in Irish.

"*Go raibh maith agat.*"

"No thanks are needed," Mrs Macleod said quickly, but her voice was warm. "*A bheil Gàidhlig agad?*"

"I'm afraid not," said Olwen. "Irish only."

"*Is teanga álainn í.* I speak all the Celtic tongues."

They were ushered into a parlour off the main hall. It was cosy and private, with a small marble fireplace, antique furniture, and a wooden sideboard covered with photographs.

"You must stop for tea," Mrs Macleod said to Dr N. "I have fresh scones just out of the oven." And to Olwen, "You are the first to arrive. My brother Ruairi will take in your bags. He's working in the stables at the moment."

"No worries. I can manage myself," Olwen said.

"And please don't go to any trouble on my behalf," Dr N added. "I'd like to get on the road. I have a B&B booked."

"Nonsense," came Morag's brisk reply, to both of them. "It is all in hand."

When the housekeeper left the room, the two women grinned at each other.

"We know who's in charge here," said Olwen.

"She's wonderful," Dr N agreed. "Salt of the earth. You can bet the house runs like clockwork."

Neither sat down. Instead they moved around the room, inspecting its contents. Olwen scrutinised the photographs on the sideboard: different groups of people in front of the house, no doubt the participants of other courses. They showed a wide range of ages and races. She studied their faces. Were these the kind of people she would like?

Dr N was admiring the artwork on the walls. The paintings and photographs were mainly of the Hebridean landscape, along with portraits of crofters and fishermen.

"Extraordinary!" she exclaimed. "Come look at this!"

She was staring at an ink engraving of the Callanish Stones. The title underneath the image was "TURUSCHAN CALLERNISH", with a smaller subtitle, "as seen under the influence of spirits". The stones were depicted as giants; some holding pitchforks, and others, musical instruments. Winged demons hovered in the air above them. In the foreground were two children: a boy sitting on the ground and a girl standing beside him. Both had horns and tails. At the centre of the stones, a skeleton was emerging from the ruins of the burial chamber.

"Bizarre," said Olwen. She felt uneasy.

They were still looking at the engraving when Mrs Macleod returned, wheeling a tea trolley. Both jumped back guiltily.

"It's a canny picture," the housekeeper remarked.

"I expect there are a lot of stories about the Stones," Olwen said.

"Oh aye."

Olwen walked Dr N to the car. The evening had grown brighter. The sky shone with a dusky glow. Twilight came late this far north.

"Will you be all right?" Olwen asked. "Make sure you drive slowly on the cliff road."

"Don't worry about me, I'll be fine."

Olwen had just taken her luggage from the boot, when a man

stepped up behind her. Startled, she let out a yelp.

Dark mournful eyes regarded her from lined features. He wore a forest-green mack and muddy boots. The smell of hay and horses lingered around him.

"Ruairi?" said Olwen, remembering Morag's mention of her brother. "How do you do? I'm Olwen Mellory. I—"

He nodded curtly, took hold of her bags and, without uttering a word, trudged towards the back door of the house.

"Not like the sister," Dr N remarked. "You'd better follow him."

The two women hugged goodbye. "Enjoy your clan," Olwen said. She bit her lip nervously.

"You'll be fine," Dr N assured her. "Morag is wonderful. Go on inside."

But Olwen stayed by the arch until the car disappeared in the distance. Her last link with the world severed, she was abandoned to her fate.

Drama queen. Don't be such a wuss.

Following after Ruairi, she entered the house through the back door. There was no sign of him. She hesitated in the corridor, looking left and right. To her left, the passageway curved around the wall of the broch where it intruded into the house. To her right was a long hall with a row of doors on one side facing the tall windows that overlooked the courtyard.

She was still deciding which way she should go, when Mrs Macleod found her.

"Let me show you to your room, *dawtie*. You can rest awhile before supper at half seven."

"Oh thank you. I'm hopelessly lost already!"

Olwen was overjoyed to discover that her room was in the broch. Her first thought was of Rapunzel, but as she climbed the winding stairwell into the tower, she decided Alice in Wonderland was more appropriate. There was something to see on every side. Narrow windows looked over the courtyard and the landscape beyond, but there were also niches in the thick stone walls that held plants, old books, stuffed animals, and ornaments. She stopped to admire a white statuette of the Madonna and Child. It was an unusual rendering: the Madonna, tall and slender, dressed like a medieval queen, and the Child held aloft on her shoulder rather than in her arms. The base of the figurine said *Our Lady of the Isles.*

"It's a copy of the great statue on the Hill of Rueval in South Uist," Mrs Macleod told her.

"I thought the Outer Hebrides were Protestant?"

"The north is Protestant. The south is Roman Catholic."

"Like Ireland."

The housekeeper nodded. They continued upwards. Olwen noted that neither of them stated her religion or enquired about the other's. Like Ireland.

Halfway up the broch they reached a landing with an oval door.

"That takes you onto the second floor of the house," Morag said, before continuing upwards to a third and final floor.

They were on a circular landing with three doors.

"As you can see, there are three suites up here." The housekeeper took a ring of keys from her pocket. "They all have bonnie views, though one looks ower the rooftops to the loch." She stopped at the door with a golden number three. "This is yours. The White Room."

It was a spacious room, with two large windows looking south and east, and a fireplace in between. The walls curved gently to the shape of the tower, their white wallpaper embossed with a pattern of green leaves. The carpet was white, too, and the lace duvet on the queen-sized bed. The other furniture, of a honey-coloured wood, included a wardrobe, dresser and dressing table, a roll-top desk and captain's chair, and a chaise longue covered in white and gold damask. The big armchair by the fireplace was a deep green velvet with silver-threaded cushions.

"Fabulous!" breathed Olwen.

It was beyond anything she could have imagined for the price she had paid. Her bags looked like shabby orphans abandoned in the middle of the floor.

"I'll leave you to settle," said Morag. "You'll hear the gong for supper. The dining room is off the main hall. Turn left when you leave the broch and the corridor will take you there."

As soon as she was alone, Olwen kicked off her shoes and danced around the room.

We're in the money, the sky is sunny,

Old Man Depression, you are through!

A quick inspection of the bathroom produced more sounds of glee: cream-coloured fittings, a tall ceramic vase with fresh orchids, and an old-fashioned bath on a plinth of yellow tiles. There was also a modern electric shower. Any reservations about Dunesfort House had evaporated. She only wished Dr N could have seen the room.

Unpacking her laptop, she searched for an outlet to plug it in. The acceptance letter had included a request not to bring any kind of technology such as computers and mobile phones. It was a rule she had no intention of obeying. The screen flickered to life with a reassuring hum. Though it was ludicrous to hope for an internet connection in the middle of nowhere, she tried nonetheless. Of course not. Reaching for her handbag, she tried her mobile phone.

Searching, searching, searching. No network coverage.

Her isolation was complete.

The room was warmed by radiators, but a fire had also been lit. Olwen fed it more turf from the wicker basket by the hearth. She began to peruse the bookshelves. There was no logic or order to the books' arrangement. Novels and academic works stood next to children's books. Her excitement grew as she scanned the titles. *Le Milieu Divin* by Teilhard de Chardin. *The Stormy Search for the Self* by

Dr Stanislav Grof and Christina Grof. *Dreamtime* by John Moriarty. *What the Bee Knows* by P.L. Travers. R.D. Laing's *The Politics of Experience and The Bird of Paradise.* Olaf Stapledon's *Star Maker.* Shirley MacLaine's *Don't Fall Off the Mountain. The Universe in a Single Atom* by His Holiness, the Dalai Lama. Alexandra David-Néel's *Mystiques et Magiciens du Tibet* and *Les Enseignements Secrets des Bouddhistes Tibétains.* There were many books by Herman Hesse, one of her favourite authors. Also works by another favourite, Doris Lessing: the complete set of the *Canopus in Argos* series and *Briefing for a Descent into Hell.* In fact, there was no book here that didn't appeal to her.

Choosing randomly, she flipped through *True Hallucinations* by Terence McKenna. A bookmark had been inserted and a passage highlighted.

> *The Other plays with us and approaches us through the imagination and then a critical juncture is reached. To go beyond this juncture requires abandonment of old and ingrained habits of thinking and seeing. At that moment the world turns lazily inside out and what was hidden is revealed: a magical modality, a different mental landscape than one has ever known, and the landscape becomes real. This is the realm of the cosmic giggle. UFOs, elves, and the teeming pantheons of all religions are the denizens of this previously invisible landscape. One reaches through to the continents and oceans of the imagination, worlds able to sustain anyone who will but play, and then one lets the play deepen and deepen until it is a reality that few would even dare to entertain.*

Who had marked the passage and why? Was she meant to read it? A vague paranoia scraped the back of her mind. But what were the odds she would pick that particular book? Then it occurred to her that others might be similarly marked. Sure enough, *The Lazy Man's Guide to Enlightenment* by Thaddeus Golas had a dog-eared page and a section underlined by pen.

It's an interesting mental exercise to turn the whole game upside down: the problem is not how to free yourself from the mass level, how to get enlightened. The real question is: If you are a completely free and self-determined being, how did you lock yourself into a body to play games on the material plane? How did you get yourself and others to agree to this game? How did you get it to be compulsive?

She chose a few more books. Some had bookmarks, dog-ears, and notes in the margins, but others had none. Mystery solved. This was someone's personal library, possibly extending throughout the house. Rose, the Director's?

Olwen abandoned the bookshelves to rummage through her suitcase for her stash of treats. With a chocolate bar clamped between her teeth, she climbed onto the bed and pulled her computer onto her lap. Opening her journal file, she typed a quick line.

4 June 2006. Dunesfort House, Isle of Lewis, Outer Hebrides.

After a moment's thought, she wrote a single sentence.

I am meant to be here.

Then she shut the computer down again. She needed to get settled. By the time she had put her clothes away in the wardrobe and dresser, her toiletries in the bathroom, and her cosmetics on the dressing table, she was exhausted. It had been a long day after a long week of travel. She climbed under the duvet. A wave of loneliness washed over her. She thought of the lover only recently left behind.

It's over. He's gone. Move on.

Had she dozed off? She grew vaguely aware of a vehicle arriving in the courtyard below. Shaking herself awake, she listened to the sounds in the depths of the house. Doors opening and closing. The low murmur of talk. The other participants? She had declined an initial meet-up with the others in Stornoway, as she had wanted to travel a little longer with Dr N. Now she was wondering if that had been wise. They were making friends without her. She was the odd one out.

A glance at her watch told her it was a half-hour before supper. She had definitely fallen asleep. She scrambled out of bed to get ready. What would she wear? How did she want to present herself? She tried on various outfits, growing more anxious by the minute. She should have asked Morag if supper was formal or not. Given the setting, it might be. In the end she chose what she felt most comfortable in: a long-skirted summer dress and a chunky necklace and bracelet. The jewellery was handcrafted by an artist friend.

The gong sounded as she was applying the last of her make-up. A quick brush of her hair and she was done. She met her eyes in the mirror. Was that fear or excitement?

She stepped gingerly towards the door.

CHAPTER FOUR

I DO NOT LIKE THEE, DR FELL

Olwen stood in the doorway and peered inside. The big dining room looked almost empty. No more than twenty people. The tables were of various sizes and oddly shaped, reminding her of jigsaw pieces. Many were empty. A wooden sideboard along the wall displayed a generous buffet with casserole dishes and soup tureens on hotplates. Some of the diners were already seated and eating. The rest were queuing, waiting to serve themselves. As she surveyed the crowd, the words "professional" and "suits" crossed her mind. They all seemed middle-aged or older, both men and women. She was the most brightly dressed amongst them. Her jewellery suddenly seemed garish. The only other splash of colour in the room was the floor-length curtains that covered the windows on the far wall. They were a dark green velvet threaded with gold.

No need to be self-conscious. You're an artist. You dress as you please.

Joining the queue, she felt another wave of anxiety, her usual reaction to buffets. Would there be enough food? So often there were those – usually men – who heaped their plates with no regard for the hungry people behind them. She craned her neck to look ahead. Were there empty dishes already?

The woman in front of her glanced back. Olwen grinned apologetically.

"Sorry. I'm fighting the urge to elbow my way in. Survival instinct.

The perils of coming from a large family."

The woman regarded her gravely. Olwen noted the expensive glasses.

"Sounds like an issue to bring to the Work?"

Olwen was taken aback by the remark. The clipped English accent made it all the more offensive. She glared at the woman without responding. The other raised her eyebrows and turned away.

When she reached the buffet, Olwen piled her plate angrily, barely noticing that there was plenty of everything. Still fuming, she waited until the woman took a seat and then chose a table as far away from her as possible.

Great. Gathering resentments already.

The three people at Olwen's table were well into their meal. There was no room for introductions as the two men were engaged in an intense discussion, while the woman seemed to be ignoring them as she concentrated on her food. After a few minutes, Olwen gathered that the men were talking about Mary Magdalene.

"She represents the ultimate underdog, the fallen woman, the lowest of the low amongst sinners, redeemed by God to become his favourite."

The speaker had handsome features and dark hair with silver streaks. Though he didn't wear a collar, Olwen dubbed him the Priest. His accent was Oxford or something close, what she called "toff".

"A sexier version of the Prodigal Son," the other man agreed.

This one sounded vaguely Scottish. His skin was badly pockmarked, but he looked distinguished, and his voice had the intonations of someone accustomed to lecturing. She named him the Professor.

"But she wasn't a prostitute!" Olwen said eagerly. She loved this kind of conversation. "That was an invention of the Church, in the Middle Ages, to undermine her position as Christ's right hand. The Bible says only that she was a woman possessed by demons and that after Jesus cured her, she joined him. She was an apostle, possibly even his wife."

"There's no need to deny her background," the Priest responded sharply. "It's judgemental to see it as demeaning, when in fact it heightens the sanctity of her redemption."

"And please tell us you are not referring to that loathsome potboiler," the Professor added.

Olwen's face reddened. "I'm not making a moral judgement. If it's biblically or historically incorrect, it's wrong to insist she was a prostitute just to suit your theory or create a symbol. And there's plenty of textual evidence to back what I'm saying without any need to resort to conspiracy theories or bestsellers."

The atmosphere at the table grew chilly. Olwen regretted that she had spoken so freely. It was typical of her to jump into the deep end without checking if she was talking to friend or foe. More often than not, she found herself out in the open, drawing fire. Was that a glance of approval from the woman? But why, then, didn't she open her mouth?

Because she has more sense.

The two men exchanged glances and changed the subject, speaking of people they both knew. Olwen lowered her head at the snub and ate in silent rage. At least the food was good. Excellent, in fact.

One of the far tables burst into applause as a serving girl wheeled in a dessert trolley. There was loud banter in Scots Gaelic and Scottish-accented English.

Oh, why didn't I sit with them?

When the trolley reached her, Olwen pointed to the chocolate cake and the chocolate mousse.

"One of each," she said.

"Oh aye," said the serving girl with a cheeky grin. Barely out of her teens, she had red hair and freckles. "Will I lash on some cream?"

"Gobs of it."

The other three at the table eyed Olwen with surprise. She stared them down.

Comment at your peril.

She was well into her second dessert when the gong rang out.

"I thought we didn't start till tomorrow," said the Priest.

"I noticed a fire was lit in the Meeting Room," the Professor replied.

"Rose must have something to say to us," said the woman, speaking for the first time.

Olwen caught something in her tone at the mention of the Director's name. Was it mirrored in the men's faces? Awe? Surely not fear? Though she had vowed not to speak another word, she found herself asking, "Have all of you been here before?"

They nodded.

"Is this your first time, then?" the Professor asked.

"Yes."

More glances exchanged, as if that settled something, but they were curious now.

"How did you come to the Work?"

"What are you bringing to it?"

She heard the capital letter and the same kind of phrasing that had been used by the woman in the queue. A shared jargon meant a shared belief system. *Oh no.* What had she got herself into?

"I was invited," she said shortly. "So I came."

Before they could question her further, Olwen moved quickly to follow those who were leaving the room. She was eager to meet Rose. What she thought of the Director could well determine whether she would stay or leave.

The Meeting Room was a great hall that somehow managed to seem intimate. A fireplace stood at one end with a mantel of dark wood elaborately carved. A large gilded mirror hung above it. The floor was covered with a rich brown carpet flecked with green. The tall windows were shuttered against the night. Music filtered quietly through speakers mounted high on the walls: the gentle sounds of cello and flute. The high ceiling was lost in the shadows of the dim lighting.

The other participants were settling into chairs that had been arranged in a circle in the middle of the room. Olwen delayed joining them by going to the fire to warm her hands. Did they all know each other? Was she the only stranger? Her heart sank.

What am I doing here?

The carvings on the mantelpiece only added to her unease. Wild faces peered out from a tangle of vines: horned fauns and satyrs with wicked grins. Backing away with a shudder, she retreated to the circle.

There were only two chairs left. No doubt one was for the Director who had yet to arrive. Looks were cast in Olwen's direction as she sat down. Most were friendly, but she was unable to respond. She had gone deep inside herself.

But it wasn't long before her attention was caught by the peculiar design of the chair. Made of the same golden wood as the furniture in her room, its shape was not unlike a lotus flower. The round seat was wide enough to allow a person to sit cross-legged. The back formed an elegant wave that included support for the arms. The solid base had rollers. Olwen curled her long legs around them.

"There are two levers underneath." The woman beside her leaned over to explain. "The one on the left raises the chair to suit your height. The one on the right brakes the rollers."

A simple thing, the design of a chair, but it brought home to Olwen two startling truths which she had already begun to suspect: an immense fortune lay behind Dunesfort House and behind that fortune, a formidable will. She was still coming to grips with that realisation when the Director entered the room.

The shock was like a physical blow.

Rose was a man.

CHAPTER FIVE

THE MAGUS

Her first impression was of a tall grey figure. His face was remote and stern, scarred on one cheek. He leaned on a cane, his left leg moving stiffly behind him. She was reminded of the French Canadian depiction of *le diable*. In their folk tales, the Devil always appeared as a mysterious gentleman who walked with a limp, because of the one cloven hoof he couldn't transform. Her aversion was immediate and acute. She sensed the violent nature behind the evident restraint; the tense arrested muscles of a caged panther.

He didn't sit down, but took up position behind the one empty chair. From the advantage of height, he appraised the circle, taking each in his gaze. When it came to her turn, she was far from comfortable under the stare of those icy-blue eyes. She fought to keep her expression neutral. She didn't want him to see the state she was in. But her unhappiness was obvious and she saw that he saw it, before his glance moved on.

How long Rose spoke or what he said, she couldn't be certain. His words were barely audible over the roar of blood in her ears. The discovery that the Director was a man – and one she suspected was dangerous – revealed another truth about Dunesfort House. *Nothing was as it seemed.*

Schedules were passed around the circle. Through a confused blur, she took in the list of activities: Meditation, Mythic

Journeying, Celtic Sweat House, Breathwork, Soul Retrieval, Spirit Boat, Firewalk, Labyrinth. Many of the items were a mystery to her. The thought of new and radical experiences with people she didn't like or trust was nightmarish. With sudden clarity, she knew she couldn't stay.

By the time Olwen had made her decision, Rose was winding up his talk.

"Look to your dreams tonight. Ask to see yourself, who and where you are, here at the beginning of your journey."

When Rose left, the others remained in the room to chat with each other; but Olwen jumped up to run after him. Arrangements had to be made. She wanted to leave as soon as possible. But on stepping into the hall, she found the corridor empty. She listened for footsteps or the tap of his cane. The old house creaked and rustled, but gave no clue to which direction he had gone. How could he move so fast with a lame leg?

Hurrying down the passage to her left, she knocked on various doors. All stayed shut and silent. She tried turning a handle. The room was locked. So was the next. She ran through the corridors, expecting to come upon him at every turn. It was like a crazy dream. She knew she was acting compulsively, but she couldn't stop herself.

At last a doorknob turned in her hand. She peered into a small windowless room. It was painted white, with blue tiles on the floor. A massage table stood against the wall. There were shelves stacked with towels, scented oils, and body brushes. The faint scent of incense hovered in the air. A wooden statue of the Buddha smiled benignly. She felt a mild reproach in the room's stillness. She was an intruder here. At the same time, she calmed down. There was nothing more she could do that night. First thing tomorrow she would tell the Director she was leaving.

....

It took Olwen a while to find her way back to the broch. When she reached her room, she was more than relieved to be greeted by the sight of her own things. To her pleasant surprise, she also found that her fire had been stoked and her bed turned down. Two ceramic jars were warming the sheets. *Mrs Macleod.* The housekeeper's thoughtfulness eased Olwen's fears, but didn't change her mind. She put the schedule on the desk. Gave it a cursory glance. The course might have been interesting.

But not with these people. Especially that man.

Tired and dispirited, she couldn't face packing so soon after unpacking. She would do it in the morning. As she prepared for bed, she chose flannel pyjamas over a satin pair. She needed to feel safe and secure. Pulling the duvet around her, she turned on her laptop. She clicked on the Thunderbird mailbox where she stored her correspondence. All of William's emails were still there. Her finger paused over the delete button. She couldn't do it. Not yet. The shadow of failure hovered over her. She closed the mailbox and opened her journal. The words she had written earlier seemed to mock her.

I am meant to be here.

She shut the computer down.

There were several things she had to do before she could sleep. Though her door had a key to lock it, she wasn't satisfied. She jammed the captain's chair under the handle. Now she turned out the light to test the darkness. Too much. It would drown her. She opened the shutters of both windows. Moonlight and starlight brightened the gloom. One window looked out over the night landscape and the sea beyond. The other overlooked the courtyard and outbuildings. The fountain plashed quietly.

She was almost there.

Popping a sleeping pill, she nestled under the duvet. *One hundred. Ninety-nine. Ninety-eight. Ninety-seven.* Somewhere around sixty she began to drift. Somewhere near thirty, she grew vaguely aware of sounds rising up from below – hushed voices, footsteps, doors opening and closing. A large vehicle crunched over the gravel in the courtyard. What was happening?

Some part of her urged her to get up and investigate, but she was already falling into the soft dark of sleep.

CHAPTER SIX

FIRST NIGHT: AT SEA

She was swimming in a warm green ocean. It was tropical, Asian, somewhat polluted and murky. Her belongings floated like debris in the water around her. Was it a shipwreck? A disaster at sea? She spied her ship in the distance, an outline on the horizon. Striving with all her might, she swam towards it, trying to catch up.

But it was too far away.

With a sudden burst of energy, she exploded from the water in a shower of spray.

Now she ran across the surface, leaping over the waves.

CHAPTER SEVEN

DOWN THE RABBIT-HOLE

Olwen woke to sunshine on her face. Blearily she grabbed for her watch on the bedside table and let out a groan. How early did the sun rise here? Her room was in the southeast corner of the broch. It was flooded with light.

She padded across the floor to look out at the landscape. There was the road she and Dr N had taken to arrive at the house. It meandered across a vast grassy moor. To her right were the cliffs that dropped to the sea loch and beyond them, the sea itself. The water shone a pale blue, flecked with white foam.

A movement closer to home caught her eye. Below her, on the flat of rough lawn that surrounded the house, was a lone figure. With a start she realised it was Rose. His movements were slow and stylised. Some kind of martial art. How was he able to do it? Where was his cane? She continued to watch him, standing back from the window in case he saw her. He avoided leaning any weight on the left leg, which sometimes called for an odd, bird-like hop. At one point he raised his lame leg and both arms at the same time, like a crane about to take flight.

Olwen turned away, uneasy about spying on him. Then a twinge of paranoia. He knew where her room was. Had he chosen that spot so she would see him?

Oh yeah, like I'm usually awake at this hour.

It really was too early to be up. She considered climbing back into bed, but she had to pack. A jolt of anxiety. Would there be problems leaving? Would she get her money back? She needed to contact Dr N. There must be a house phone. She would ask Morag.

A shower helped to waken her, but she was craving coffee. She pulled on blue jeans and a white T-shirt, but didn't bother with make-up or jewellery. There was no longer any need to make an impression. She would soon be gone. As she packed her bags, she fought off feelings of failure and regret. Was she doing the right thing? It wasn't like her to give up so easily. *You're almost fifty. Life's too short to spend with people you don't want to be with.* When the gong rang for breakfast, she didn't respond at first, but she knew she couldn't put it off forever.

Time to face the music.

She heard the talk and laughter before she reached the dining room, rising above the rattle of dishes and cutlery. A wave of anger surged through her. They were all enjoying themselves. Everyone except her. The smell of freshly brewed coffee wafted into the hall. She was too tense to eat, but she would grab a quick cup before confronting Rose.

Olwen stood on the threshold, bewildered.

What the–?

Was she dreaming?

Everything had changed, changed utterly. The dining room was filled with strangers. She was looking at an entirely different group of people! There was no sign of the woman who had annoyed her in the queue, or the two men she had argued with; nor the friendly woman who had shown her how to use the lotus-chair. Now she recalled the sounds she had heard in the night.

What was going on?

The velvet curtains had been drawn back, and the high arched windows looked out on an expanse of sea and sky. The dining room was bright with morning light. There was no buffet. The freckled, red-haired girl was waiting on tables, along with another young woman, dark-haired and sleek. The room was full.

In a daze, Olwen spotted an empty place near the window. There were two others seated there: a handsome middle-aged man and a frail old lady. As Olwen made her way towards them, she caught snippets of other languages in the conversations around her.

When she reached the table, the man stood up to greet her with old-fashioned courtesy. It was something her father used to do whenever women entered the room and it snapped her out of her stupor. She guessed the man to be about her own age or a little older. His beauty was startling, not least because of his ebony colour. He wore casual but expensive clothes. And though she was tall, he was taller still, well over six feet, with a commanding, almost military stature. He put out his hand – a firm, warm grip – and his smile was wide and toothy.

"Jack Elphinstone. Pleasure to meet you. This is Elsie Goldfarb. Have you eaten? Will you join us?"

His voice was a rich baritone. Was that a Canadian or American accent?

Her own voice shook a little as she introduced herself.

"Yes...I'd like that...if it's...?"

The old woman was studying Olwen with the sharp eyes of a bird. She was at least eighty, well dressed, with coiffed hair and a plethora of gold jewellery.

"Feel free, honey." The accent was pure New York. "It's always good to meet new blood. Dr Jack and I know each other so well there's hardly anything left to say."

He's a doctor.

Dr Jack held Olwen's chair as she went to sit down.

"Jesus, don't," she said quickly. "I'm too uncoordinated for that lark. We'll be here all day."

The other two laughed. She was beginning to relax.

"We've been telling our dreams," Elsie informed her. "You should always trot them out when there's a shrink in the company. Free consultation."

A psychiatrist.

"Except that Elsie is much better at interpretation than I," said Dr Jack.

"I don't remember dreaming last night," Olwen admitted, "but I tend to get some pretty hilarious ones. My subconscious is a stand-up comedian."

"Really? Do tell." His grin was mischievous.

The pull toward him was magnetic. His looks would have done it alone, but the way he regarded her, with the full attention of a professional listener, was irresistible. She wanted to lie down on a couch and tell him her life story.

"Let her get her breakfast!" said Elsie, bird-eyes moving from one to the other.

The red-haired girl brought a menu. There was plenty of choice, right up to a full Scottish breakfast with kippers and blood pudding.

"A little bit of everything?" Olwen murmured to herself. Her appetite had suddenly returned. She ordered fresh fruit salad, scrambled eggs, toast and coffee. "Okay, I'll tell you one of my favourites," she said, getting back to their conversation. "It was the night before I got married. I was in an aeroplane, walking up the aisle. Around my neck was a toilet-seat ring. Like a yoke for oxen."

Elsie's laughter was almost a screech. Dr Jack had just taken a sip of his coffee and nearly spat it out.

"And you went ahead with the marriage?" he asked, eyebrow raised.

"We're not going there," she replied.

Elsie grinned. "I had a dream something like that many years ago. I was crossing the border into another country, carrying a big knapsack on my back. I was called into the customs office. An official ordered me to open the bag. And what was curled up inside? Chaim, my poor husband. Go figure."

When they had stopped laughing, Elsie insisted that Dr Jack repeat his dream from the night before.

"Well, as Rose always suggests, I made a mental note before I slept to ask if I could see myself where I am right now. I also added that I'd like to see where God is in my life, as I've been feeling disconnected from the Divine lately." Dr Jack was already chuckling before he continued. "When I described my dream to Elsie, I thought I had only got a response to the first item. There I was, a circus performer on a unicycle, juggling all kinds of things – electrical appliances, books, vegetables, ice cubes, and strange objects I'd never seen before. I was in a panic as I juggled, aware that if even *one* went astray, the whole show was over." His grin was wry. "A no-brainer, that one. I can't argue the fact I'm doing too much as usual and juggling – struggling – to stay in control. But my dear amateur psychologist friend here was quick to point out that the second request was also covered in this image. No wonder I'm disconnected from the Divine. I'm too busy playing God myself!"

They were still laughing when a young Japanese girl arrived at their table. Slight and petite, she was quixotically dressed in Harajuku fashion with black combat boots and a frilly polka-dot dress. Her hair was dyed pink. Dr Jack introduced her as Suzume Oshiro from Tokyo. In contrast to her flamboyant style, her behaviour was painfully shy. There was something fragile and wounded about her. Olwen was reminded of one of her daughter's friends who had spent most of her life being shunted between two warring parents.

"All the fun is at this table," Suzume said to Dr Jack in a little-girl voice.

"You are welcome to join us if you wish, Suzume San."

She shook her head. "There is no room for Christy."

"Are you sayin' I'm fat?" came a voice behind her.

Christy Bird introduced himself to Olwen after he had greeted the others. Middle-aged and paunchy, he had a round open face, merry eyes, and a shock of thin hair combed over his bald patch.

"You're Irish!" Olwen was unable to hide her surprise. A Dublin working-class accent was the last thing she had expected to hear.

"I am," he said with a cheeky grin. "And ye needn't sound so shocked. Even Northsiders have been known to latch on to this New Age touchy-feely shite."

"No...that isn't...I..."

They were all laughing at her now. She threw up her hands in surrender.

"I'm from Bray," she told him. "But I grew up in Canada."

"Ah, that explains the accent."

"What do you mean?" said Dr Jack. "She sounds Irish to me."

"Me too," agreed Elsie.

"Go way out of that," said Christy. "She's one of you lot."

"Don't you be calling me a Yank," Olwen warned him.

"I'm Canadian," Dr Jack pointed out.

"And I'm from New York," said Elsie.

There was more laughter all round, but when Suzume and Christy left, Olwen frowned at the other two.

"Do you all know each other? Am I the only one who has never been here before?"

Dr Jack glanced around the room. "I know a good few, but not everyone."

Elsie nodded. "Same here. But nobody looked as lost as you did, hon, when you came in."

"That wasn't just because I'm new. It was the whole group change. What happened to the others? Did they leave en masse?"

"*What?*" said Dr Jack and Elsie together.

Their faces changed from astonishment to curiosity as Olwen briefly described the previous evening. While she didn't go into details, it was obvious she didn't regret the change-over.

"That explains the last-minute arrivals," Elsie said to Dr Jack.

"What do you mean?" Olwen asked.

"We were all due to arrive yesterday or today," Elsie explained. "As usual, most of us knew well in advance that we were coming. Our invitations arrived months ago. But there were some on the bus – and then more when we got here – who said they had received last-minute calls."

"And they came anyway?"

"Oh yes," Elsie said. "There isn't one of us who wouldn't drop everything to come when we are called."

"Within reason," Dr Jack corrected her. "There are times when family, work commitments, or health can make it impossible. But we certainly come if we can."

"The others obviously didn't suit you, dear," Elsie said to Olwen.

"*Me?*" Olwen sucked in her breath. "What do you mean? Why would...What's it to do with me?"

"Well, you're the only one left standing. You must be a key player and the others as useless as tits on a bull."

Olwen's unease was growing exponentially. Old horror movies flashed through her mind. The kind that involved chosen ones and sacrificial lambs.

The Wicker Man. Rosemary's Baby.

They could see she was upset.

"You mustn't feel responsible," Dr Jack assured her, misunderstanding her distress. "No one takes it personally. Most of us have been doing this for years. We trust what happens. It's the nature of the Work."

Again, the capital letter. Shared doctrine. But there had been no hint of a religion or belief system in the brochure. Was she being naïve?

Elsie patted her hand. "Talk to Rose. He wouldn't want you to be unhappy."

Olwen shivered. Dr Jack was about to add something more when Christy and Suzume returned. The young girl looked as if she might die of embarrassment, but Christy nudged her forward.

"Quick question for ye," he said to Olwen. "You wouldn't happen to be the writer O. Mellory would ye?"

Olwen nodded. Suzume's face lit up.

"She's read ye." Christy grinned. "You're one of her favourite authors."

Olwen was suddenly as bashful as Suzume. It was unnerving to meet one's readers in a social setting. There was always the chance of disenchanting them by being a complete idiot.

Suzume struggled to overcome her shyness.

"Your translator travels to bookshops for gatherings where we talk about your stories and characters. Some of us dress up, especially as fairies."

Olwen was delighted. "I didn't know that! How wonderful! Thank you for telling me." She was also secretly pleased that Dr Jack looked impressed.

Before more could be said, the gong rang out. Everyone finished what they were doing and began to file out of the room.

Elsie pushed back her chair. Dr Jack stood up quickly to help her rise. She beamed him a smile of thanks. Olwen was the only one who hadn't moved. Her mind raced. Was she staying? Was she leaving?

Dr Jack leaned towards her.

"Are you coming?"

She bit her lip.

"Give me a moment. I need to think."

CHAPTER EIGHT

THE CIRCLE

The tall windows of the Meeting Room looked out over shining vistas of sea and sky. The circle of chairs was an elongated oval stretching the length of the floor. Dr Jack sat next to Elsie. His face beamed when he spotted Olwen at the door, and he waved her over to the empty seat beside him. She was reminded of school days and best friends keeping seats and she hurried over to join him.

Rose arrived last. When he took the only chair left, it immediately became the dominant position in the circle. Everyone turned towards him.

In the light of day and with new companions around her, Olwen was able to regard him with a calmer eye. He was dressed all in black. There was something haggard about him, like a crow in winter. She guessed him to be in his late fifties or early sixties. His features were ascetic, emphasising the intensity of the wintry blue eyes. He didn't raise his voice when he spoke. He didn't need to. And there was a faint trace of an accent which she hadn't caught the night before; Scandinavian or German. Did he deliberately mask it? Once again, his gaze surveyed the circle as he addressed them. When it rested on her, she stared back defiantly.

"Now that you have arrived," he told them, "you have left behind your ordinary life, that with which you are familiar, both consciously and unconsciously. The doors of perception stand open. You are invited to enter. Be prepared to confront realities different from the one that keeps you thinking as you have always thought, perceiving as you have always perceived, feeling and behaving as you have always felt and behaved. This is the nature of the Work you have come here to do. *Transformation*. That is the name of the game. Nothing more, nothing less. Make no mistake about it, it will not be easy."

Normally Olwen would have liked this kind of talk, but she was unable to separate the words from the speaker. She still distrusted the Director, still sensed the latent violence in him. And there it was again, the capital letter on "Work", indicating a body of belief to which she wasn't privy, though apparently the others were. Why, then, had she been invited? What part was she expected to play? This wasn't like the artists' colonies she occasionally visited, or her weekend yoga retreats. This wasn't a disparate group of strangers briefly united by a common interest or activity. Something much deeper was involved, and somehow it seemed to hinge upon this man.

"Everything that happens is good," Rose was saying. "Everything that happens is gold."

The word *cult* wormed its way through her mind. She was being assailed by misgivings. If she hadn't met Dr Jack and Elsie at breakfast, she would already be on her way. Was it wise to change her mind so blithely?

"We'll begin by introducing the circle," Rose announced. "Some of you know each other, but you have not all shared the same sessions and there are new people also. Please state your name and tell us why you are here, perhaps a little about yourself and what you hope to achieve this week. After the introductions, there will be a short meditation session followed by a mythic journey. You'll be guided through each. Let us begin."

One by one they introduced themselves. Some were eager to talk, others less so. Some spoke at length, while a few said little more than their names and their reason for coming. The group was too large for Olwen to register all the personalities at once, but she had already begun the process of discrimination, noting the ones who had caught her interest and whom she wanted to meet.

The French scientist was certainly the most glamorous. Thirty-something, wearing the latest Parisian fashions, Euphémie Cadot looked more like an actress or a model than an interstellar physicist. She was a beauty, with her bob of black hair, heart-shaped face and dark red lips; but more fascinating were her comments on scientific materialism and her desire for the romantic truths of the universe.

"Science select for *athéisme*, or at least *agnosticisme*. You speak a belief outside this, you come under suspicion and have difficulty with position, grant, collaboration. *Toujours*, I keep my thought inside. But to be alone this way in work and always to be careful, it is not good. One time a magazine show a pyramid from a questionnaire to the science community. The very low of the pyramid – I mean to say, the people in small position at work – they admit belief in God or some thing not material. *La plupart*, the most part of the pyramid, they say they do not believe. *Mais, c'est très intéressant*, the very top – *la crème de la crème* – the best of all the scientist, these too, believe. Like the great Einstein!" For a moment she smiled, then her smile faded. "But they can say, because they are on the top; while I cannot, because I am not. *Pas encore*," she finished, with a little smile. "Not yet."

Tenzin Dawa was one of the younger participants, in his early twenties. He came from Dharamsala, the colony of Tibetan exiles in northern India, but had lived most of his life under duress in Tibet. He wore faded blue jeans with cowboy boots, and a T-shirt adorned with the image of an Asian singer called Sa Ding Ding. His shoulder-length hair was pulled back in a ponytail. In courteous tones, without any apparent bitterness, he made it clear that he was not there by choice, but as a favour to someone he loved and respected. It was over two years since he had left his monastery in Tibet and put away his robes. No longer a monk, he had finally got permission to travel to America where he hoped to live and work. But he had promised his former teacher and lama that he would come to Dunesfort House before he embarked on his new life.

There was another Irishman in the circle, Roy McCabe, dark-haired and craggy-looking. He was a youth worker in the inner city of Belfast, after years of peace work and politics in Northern Ireland. Sitting next to him and possibly his partner – or so Olwen imagined – was a statuesque Scotswoman with a mane of golden-brown hair. Her name was Una McKinnock and she openly declared herself a pagan witch. There was an older, very elegant lady from southern India named Savitri Bhatt. She wore an orange-and-red sari of shimmering silk. Her long black hair, peppered with silver, fell to her waist in a single braid. Beside her was Brother Aguerre, a plump middle-aged Franciscan friar from the Basque country. His brown habit was tied with a belt of white rope, and he gestured with his hands when he spoke. Olwen also noted Penny Li Jau, the Malaysian environmentalist, and Harry Rhymer, the former British soldier who was now working as a gardener in a spiritual community in northern Scotland.

Some of the participants spoke of their intentions for the week, either obstacles they hoped to overcome or dreams they wished to manifest, but most, including Elsie, simply stated that they had come for "healing". Olwen was surprised by this as the various individuals sounded healthier and saner than most people she knew. Dr Jack's comments made her smile.

"Well, what can I say, I'm here for the ecstasy." His grin was wicked. "I'm too old to take drugs, so this is where I get my out-of-body experiences." The circle laughed along with him, but then he grew serious. "My desire and ambition is, of course, greater. I seek nothing less than union with the Divine."

Olwen's eyes widened at his last remark, but she didn't have time to assimilate it. It was her turn to introduce herself. She was suddenly flustered. Though she was well used to speaking in public, this was somehow different. With a mild shock she realised that she desperately wanted this circle's approval. Would they accept her as one of them?

Everyone was waiting for her to speak. Rose leaned forward slightly. Her voice shook a little.

"I'm Olwen Mellory, a writer, mostly fairy tales and fantasy. I was born in Ireland, raised and educated in Canada, now back living in Ireland for many years." She bit her lip, paused a moment, then pressed on. "To be honest, I don't really know what I'm doing here. Always ready for an adventure, I guess. And who knows, I might get a book out of it."

The words were no sooner out of her mouth than she felt a wave of dismay. Her face burned. *Idiot.* She had sounded so flippant. What could they possibly think of her? And why did she care so much?

A few more spoke after her, but Olwen didn't hear them. She had retreated into herself, questioning and berating. It took her a few minutes to realise that everyone was moving about and levering their chairs into reclining positions. Someone had dimmed the lights. Incense tinted the air.

"We will meditate for twenty minutes," Rose announced. "Then the drums and drones will sound to begin the mythic journey."

Olwen was familiar with meditation from her yoga classes, but had no idea what the second practice entailed. Had she missed the instructions? She quelled a pang of anxiety and the urge to ask. *Go with the flow.* The others around her were already sitting cross-legged or lying back with their eyes closed. She quickly sorted herself into a half-lotus position.

Gentle sounds issued from the speakers overhead. Monks chanting *om.* She closed her eyes. All her muscles relaxed. She began counting her breaths, in and out. *One, one. Two, two. Three, three.* Her mind grew still. A little smile formed at the edges of her mouth. She lost track of time. Surely it was only minutes before Rose spoke again. His words seemed to echo from far away.

"You are about to journey in your mind's eye beyond everyday reality into the world of the imagination, into the Dreaming. Let the beat of the drums be your wings. The scientists among us will confirm that a monotonous beat or sound can stimulate brain waves into the theta range. While beta waves are associated with ordinary waking consciousness, theta waves are related to creativity, vivid imagery and states of ecstasy.

"A few words about shamanism which is at the core of this practice. The word itself is generally used to refer to the oldest religions found all over the world. Shamanic practices vary by culture and time period, however Mircea Eliade, in his exhaustive study *Archaic Techniques of Ecstasy*, showed that there are common themes and understandings.

"There is a three-fold division of worlds or realities. The Lower World is earthy and underground, inhabited by the spirits of plants and animals. It can be found in caves, under the sea, in jungles and forests and is usually reached by travelling in your mind through tunnels, wells, or deep holes in the ground. This is where you find your animal guide who will accompany you as a protective spirit. A literary version of this motif is the white rabbit who leads Alice down the hole into Wonderland.

"The Upper World presents itself as ethereal, full of light and air, existing in high places. It might involve ice, crystal, or glass. This is where you meet spirit guides, angels, bodhisattvas, mythic archetypes – all the higher celestial forms who are committed to helping the human race evolve.

"The Middle World is our own reality as seen through the third eye or with mystic vision. When we journey through our own world we can view past lives, engage in out-of-body travel, meet our ancestors, heal parts of our body, heal others, and so on. Most importantly of all, concerning the Work we do here, is the fact that we can move through time. In particular, we can journey into our past to moments when we experienced trauma. Then and there we can be what Alice Miller calls an 'enlightened witness' to our own suffering. Returning to the present, we may well discover long-buried memories of a beneficent presence who supported us through the worst of our experiences. The core truth here is that reality is malleable and even the past can be changed."

Despite her negative feelings towards Rose, Olwen couldn't help but be captivated by what he was saying. The ideas were radical and exciting. His voice was mesmeric, inspiring images, thoughts, and even colours and sensations.

"If you are new to shamanism, you must use this first journey to enter the Lower World and find your animal guide, then establish a bond with him or her. You will know instinctively to whom you belong. You may find yourself asking, 'Is this real or am I making this up? Is this just my imagination?' When this happens, try to surrender to the mystery. Most people do not question the inner workings of their watch or computer. They simply use them. Try to cultivate the same attitude towards this experience. Trust the process. See what happens."

As Rose stopped speaking, new sounds issued from the speakers. There seemed to be countless drums, echoing each other like peals of thunder. And behind them came the steady drone of uillean pipe chanters and Breton bombards. The effect was overpowering. Olwen's heart began to pound. Her breath quickened. Something was happening.

Something *wonderful*.

CHAPTER NINE

RUNNING WITH WOLVES

She was in a forest of tall pine, very Canadian-looking, walking along a gorge that overlooked a river. The cold grey waters rushed along at a terrific speed. Remembering Rose's descriptions of the Lower World, she looked around for signs of a cave or tunnel. What if she couldn't find her way in? What if she didn't have an animal guide? The forest was strangely still. No birds sang in the trees. No creatures came into sight.

This is ridiculous. It's all just my imagination. Active daydreaming.

On a sudden impulse, she turned round and hurried back along the gorge. There it was: a magnificent waterfall streaming into the river. Without stopping to think, she plunged through the curtain of water. Her body shuddered involuntarily as she felt the icy shock. She could hardly breathe. A cave of wet, glistening rock stretched in front of her. Though some part of her kept arguing that she was making it up, she was thrilled to the core of her being.

It's like writing. No, like magic!

The drums and drones echoed around her, resounding from the walls of the cave. They seemed to urge her on. She raced down the tunnel, splashing through puddles. When she came out on the other side, she found herself in a wintry landscape. The ground was covered with snow. The trees and bushes glittered with frost. A frozen lake lay before her. Her breath streamed in the air.

She wasn't alone. Moving slowly through the trees, almost invisible because of their colour, was a pack of white wolves. They were coming towards her.

Olwen felt a shiver of fear, but she would have been disappointed if wolves hadn't come. She was expecting them. Mellory was her mother's maiden name. She had chosen to use it because its lyrical sound suited a writer of fairy tales. Her patronymic was Whelan and she had always known that its Irish origin was O'Faoláin, from the Old Irish word "*faol*", meaning "wolf". All her life she had felt an affinity to the wolf. She had never liked the way it was depicted as evil in European folk tales, preferring instead its honoured role in Native American stories. The moment Rose had mentioned finding an animal guide, she knew who and what she was hoping for.

"I'm so glad you came!" she cried as she threw her arms around the lead wolf's neck.

The others barked joyously around her. She laughed and wept as she hugged them all. There was a lot of jumping and licking and friendly nips as well. Sometimes she found herself on all fours, furred and fanged, a sister wolf of the pack.

The playfulness lasted for a good while but eventually the mood changed. The pack formed a circle to pen her in. Red tongues lolled. Chests panted with excitement. Golden eyes transfixed her. The alpha female's voice rang in her mind.

"What are you doing here?"

Olwen began to repeat what Rose had said about finding an animal guide, but she had only uttered a few words when they barked to cut her off.

"What are you doing here?" the leader asked again.

Olwen frowned. Was it a trick question? She began to tell them about Dunesfort House, but now they started to howl. Wrong answer again! She bit her lip, thought hard, and began to speak of her life: the new book she had finished, her doubts about her work, the empty nest after her daughter left for college, the man who was gone, yet another failed love affair, her precarious finances, her fear of ageing as she faced her fifties. They didn't interrupt this time. Some even cocked their heads as they listened. She felt the emptiness yawn inside her. Tears pricked her eyes. Her voice faltered.

The lead wolf's gaze was sympathetic, yet the question was asked a third and final time.

"WHAT ARE YOU DOING HERE?"

The words seemed to be writ large and mythic, as if resounding across the universe to pin her where she stood.

"I...I...don't know," she said at last.

Olwen had barely uttered her answer when the drums and drones burst into her consciousness. She had left the sounds back in the tunnel, but now they were battering her ears, like someone banging on the door, demanding to be let in. They were calling her home. She cried out her farewells as the wolves disappeared in a blur of white snow.

And a deep silence descended.

Olwen shifted in her chair, reluctant to open her eyes. Her legs were cramped. How long had she been sitting in the half-lotus position? She stretched slowly. Heard others moving around her. She had actually forgotten that she wasn't alone!

With a sigh, she opened her eyes, just in time to catch Rose staring at her. He looked away quickly. Had he been watching her? The thought was disturbing. And there was something vaguely familiar about his hungry gaze. Like one of the wolves in the pack.

The lights in the room brightened. Everyone straightened their seats. Rose stood up to address them.

"There will be no lunch or supper today as we will fast for the Celtic Sweat House this evening. A midnight feast will be provided afterwards. May I ask for a show of hands from those who will be new to the experience?"

Olwen was relieved to see she wasn't the only one. At least ten hands went up.

"The Sweat House is a purification rite found in many cultures," he explained, "including the ancient Celts and Norse. In this modern era, it is more commonly known as a First Nations practice. As its name indicates, the rite involves intense heat and sweating. Una McKinnock, our resident Wiccan, will hold the ceremony and lead us through it. Loose and light clothing is recommended for those who choose to wear it."

Elsie leaned over to Olwen.

"Most of us go naked," she whispered gleefully.

Olwen was thankful she had brought a swimsuit.

"You have the rest of the day to prepare yourselves," Rose finished. "I would suggest that you maintain silence and solitude. Walk in nature or take quiet time in your room. Think about your intentions for the week. Perhaps write them down. What has brought you here? Why did you respond to the invitation at this particular time in your life? What do you hope to transform in the crucible? What is the dream of your soul?

"Keep in mind the nature of the Work that we have come here to do. It is not for the faint-hearted. This is a call to rigorous self-examination. Our society is addicted to the need to avoid pain of any kind. It encourages us to use anything that will keep us from being fully conscious – alcohol, drugs, television, sex, work, shopping, gambling, sport. On an individual level, this causes loss of soul and authenticity. On a communal level, it results in aggression and insatiable greed, the two forces that threaten all life on our planet. Thus the Work we do here is both personal and communal. *Heal yourself, heal the world.*"

Olwen muttered to Dr Jack, "A reading list might have been handy."

"Someone likes to be in control?"

"Don't start. I already have a friend who shrinks my head."

They both laughed. Rose frowned over at them. Others were rising from their seats and leaving the room. The first session was over.

Olwen returned to her bedroom. Her luggage stood ready, awaiting her departure. It seemed aeons since she had awoken that morning with the intention to go. She began to unpack again, happy with the distraction. She was uneasy and fearful about what lay ahead. A purification rite. Intense heat. And no food till midnight!

She was already hungry. If she had known they were going to fast, she would have eaten more breakfast. She took a bag of chocolate-covered raisins from her stash of treats. Nibbling away, she switched on her laptop, opened her journal file, and began to write. She described her journey to meet the wolf pack, detailing every aspect. She was amazed at how much had happened in such a short time. She could recall sounds and smells as well as images. Was it simply her imagination? It had all seemed so...real.

What am I doing here? The million-dollar question. No coincidence the She-Wolf kept asking, even as I tried to dodge the ball. Why am I here? In this life? On this planet? What is my purpose? My mission? What does my soul want to achieve? What's my wish list? What do I want (demands Freud)?

First off the top of my head, I'm thinking a marriage that works. That lasts. My soul mate, in other words. But what kind of dream is that for a forty-nine-year-old? An absurd romantic notion left over from my youth?

Success in my work? Yes, I would like that, please. More recognition, and let's not forget money. Art for art's sake and money for godsake. I'm sick of struggling. The thought of growing old and destitute terrifies me.

And yet, and yet...some part of me is appalled when I demand these things. They are the desires of my ego, not the dreams of my soul. Deep down I really and truly want something else.

What is it?

She stopped. Took a deep breath. Started again.

I want to deal with the demons inside me. I know they're there – unconscious forces working away to undermine me, destroy me, ruining my efforts to enjoy life. Even as I sink into despair, I feel my Higher Self calling from the depths of my being: there is a larger, more conscious way to live!

My life's work is writing. I feel reasonably sure about that. I have the ability to create stories and I love words and images. But there's more. Writing came out of my childhood and how I survived it: the kind of books that nourished me. Those books – all fairy tales, all fantasy, all magical – kept me alive, kept my soul intact.

Sometimes I think I'm not a true writer because the stories don't flow out of me like they do for so many of my writer friends. I have to brood in the dark for ages before anything comes. And then, when I have finally grasped a vision, there is the hurdle of writing it. I hunch over the keyboard, crippled, scratching out sentences that do no justice to the shining thing I glimpsed.

As for my personal life...it has been both sad and wonderful. Songs of joy and catastrophe. I've travelled, married, worked all kinds of jobs, published a few books, loved a few men, reared a beautiful child. But now I am at a crossroads: a world-weary woman in search of her soul.

It's not enough to write another book or travel to another country or find another lover. I want something more, I need something more, to satisfy the hunger inside me.

I believe in destiny. I know there is something I am called to do.

What is it?

What am I doing here?

Olwen stopped writing and walked to the window that looked over the landscape. There was a flurry of movement on the lawn below. A small pit had been dug some distance from the house and a bonfire was being built beside it. Men were arriving with wheelbarrows of wood, large stones, bottles of water, buckets, and jugs. A long table was set up nearby. One of the men was Morag's brother, Ruairi. No, wait, there were two of them, like peas in a pod. Identical twins! There were a few others from the circle, including the Ulsterman, Roy McCabe. A woman was directing them, Una, the Scotswoman who had called herself a witch. She appeared to be in charge. Quickly and quietly, the group constructed a framework over the pit, made of boughs lashed together. Layers of heavy blankets were laid over the frame and then a final great canvas. By the time it was finished, the structure looked like a giant tortoiseshell. The pyre of wood for the bonfire was only a few feet away.

Olwen was struck by an odd notion. She felt as if she were looking out the narrow window of a prison tower to view the preparations for her execution. Her sight wavered a moment and she saw the platform on which they would behead her. *Adulteress.* Or was it a tall wooden stake surrounded by faggots where they would burn her? *Witch.*

She backed away from the window. Returned to her laptop.

God, I'm starving.

Rose said we should think about our intentions for the week. What will I bring to the fire, to the Sweat? I'll translate that into my own language. What are my hopes and dreams? Transformation. That's a word he used more than once. Yes, I would like that. I'm falling apart. I'm losing cohesion. But it seems too general a desire. Too abstract. What do I want specifically? True love? Soul mate? Fame and fortune? Love and money?

She closed her eyes and waited in the stillness.

Why are you so sad these days?

She caught her breath. Waited for the answer.

The magic has abandoned me. I no longer believe.

She gasped as her first hope, her first dream, rose like a bubble from the cold depths of her psyche. She typed quickly, breathlessly.

I want to return to the magic that I used to believe in, the true heart, the true source of my work. I want to see fairies.

She was about to sit back triumphantly, when a second thought surfaced: the little silver trout that had breathed the bubble. Her hands hovered over the keyboard, fingers trembling.

In the dark night of the soul, on the borders of the country where the ego dissolves, desires for love and money, even purpose and work, are trivial and mundane. I strive to catch true sight of my Self. There! A small figure on a ladder that leans upwards into the stars.

Her heart beat wildly, she could hardly breathe, as the second hope, the second dream, leaped from the depths and into the air – silvery, wet, and luminous.

I want to see God.

CHAPTER TEN

THE CRUCIBLE

The gong for the Celtic Sweat House sounded at sunset. Olwen headed downstairs in her bare feet, wearing a blue dressing gown over her one-piece yellow swimsuit. She was only mildly self-conscious; she was not ashamed of her body. Full-figured, she kept in shape with yoga and gym, dancing and hill-walking.

The others were gathered in the front hall. It was strange to see everyone half-dressed. There was a quiet, bashful air over all.

"Aren't we an odd bunch?" Dr Jack said, when he joined her.

He wore a brown cashmere dressing gown and open-toed sandals. His eyes sparkled with mischief.

"An adult pyjama party," she said, laughing, "or…" and she stopped. A reference to suburban orgies seemed inappropriate.

A grin flashed across his face but he, too, chose not to go there.

When Elsie arrived, she linked her arm in Olwen's.

"We'll be together on the women's side. If I pass out, don't make a fuss. I'll come round again. Whatever happens, don't let them carry me out."

"You can faint from this?!"

There was no time for Elsie to answer. The gong had sounded again. An expectant hush fell over them as they filed out the door. The ceremony of the Sweat House had begun.

The sun was sinking into the loch, setting both sky and sea

aflame. It was a splendid backdrop to the fire dance Roy performed when they gathered in front of the porch. He was stripped to the waist, revealing an astonishing array of multicoloured tattoos that covered his torso. *The illustrated man.* His eyes were outlined with kohl, as dark as his mane of black hair. He twirled a long staff that burned at each end, creating fiery circles and spirals of light in the air. In a final flourish, he threw the flaming stave over his head and spun around before catching it again.

Everyone roared their approval. Olwen smiled to herself as she imagined him tossing his baton at the head of an Orange Parade.

When Roy finished his dance, he led them to the Sweat House. The bonfire was blazing. Sparks flew into the air like a swarm of red bees. Brother Aguerre, in denim overalls and white undershirt, tended the fire along with Harry Rhymer, the ex-soldier. The grey-haired monk had the strong arms and big hands of a man accustomed to labouring on his friary's farm. He worked silently, without looking around. Harry, on the other hand, was quick to smile and laugh, greeting them as they arrived. In his late twenties, he was well-built and good-looking despite the baldness that accented his large ears. He and Brother Aguerre used pitchforks and shovels to turn the rocks they were heating at the heart of the fire. At a table nearby, Savitri Bhatt, the older woman from India, and Penny Li Jau, the Malaysian environmentalist, were folding towels and cotton sarongs; while Christy Bird unpacked crates of bottled water and stacked cups and basins.

It was obvious that the helpers weren't going into the Sweat House, as they were all fully dressed. Olwen wondered why she hadn't been offered the choice. Did she really want to do this? *Could* she do it? Wouldn't she rather observe from the sidelines, making notes as a writer should?

The Sweat House looked like a dark mound, ancient and mysterious. Its mouth was formed by lifting a flap of canvas and blanket. Una McKinnock stood by the entrance. In a green cloak embroidered with pentacles, she was the Gatekeeper, the High Priestess. Her golden hair glimmered in the firelight. She held a sprig of holly in one hand and a spray of oak in the other.

"Welcome to *An Teach Allais*," she cried. "Please divide into queues of male and female. We will enter one by one into the womb of the Mother Earth. The women will go first, moving *deiseal* – sunwise or clockwise – to take up the western side of the House. The men will follow after and take up the east."

Una removed her cloak and handed it to Roy. The flamelight flickered over her naked body, pale and beautiful. Spiral tattoos wound in a chain up her arms and over her shoulders.

Everyone began to disrobe. Many went nude, but not all. Some of the women wore bathing suits or light dresses and some of the men had opted for shorts or trunks. Discarded clothes were placed on the table.

The women lined up to follow Una into the Sweat House. No one spoke. The only sound was the snap and crackle of the burning wood. The evening air had grown cool with the twilight, but a great heat emanated from the fire.

Suzume sidled up to Olwen who stood staring into the flames. The girl wore a white cotton slip.

"Japanese bathe naked in public," she said softly, "but I cannot."

"Me neither," Olwen whispered.

Her misgivings were growing. She clutched nervously at her dressing gown and didn't follow Suzume into the line. It was Penny Li who came to reassure her. In her early thirties, the Malaysian woman was small and fine-boned. Her dark eyes seemed much older than her age. Olwen could see the grief in her delicate features.

"You do not have to go in," she said. "If you wish, you are welcome to join the Guardians of the Fire. We assist the others in their ceremony and this makes us a part of it. At the same time, let me tell you, it is completely dark inside the Sweat House. No one can see you. The experience is very private."

Olwen thanked her sincerely. It was all the encouragement she needed. Slipping out of her dressing gown, but not her bathing suit, she was the last woman to enter.

It was pitch black inside the mound and cold as the night. The smell of damp earth filled her nostrils, along with traces of the women's soap and perfume.

"Please keep moving." Una's disembodied voice sailed through the darkness. "Go around the pit from left to right. The men will come next."

Firelight spilled into the tent as Olwen crawled away from the entrance. A deep pit yawned in front of her. She moved around it, following Una's directions, to join the shadowy forms sitting cross-legged on her right.

"Over here!" Elsie hissed from the far side.

But there were too many bodies to climb over. Olwen settled in the middle of the tent, on the border between the men's and women's sides. The ground was cold underneath her and she wished she had brought a towel to sit on. She was already beginning to feel crowded and trapped.

The men began to enter. As more and more arrived, Olwen's claustrophobia increased. Would there be enough room? Would there be enough air? They had to squeeze closer to fit everyone in. The soft skin of the women pressed against her. Musky male odours came wafting over.

At last they were all in.

Roy's voice called through the opening.

"Prepare to welcome the first of the Old Ones!"

A shovel was pushed into the House, bearing a rock that glowed like a red jewel. It gave off great warmth.

"We welcome the first of the Stone People amongst us," Una responded.

Her body was silhouetted by the light from the entrance. Beside her were bundles of herbs, a small cauldron with a ladle, and a wooden flute and panpipe. She grappled the rock with metal claws and placed it in the pit, sprinkling herbs over it. The scent of lavender and sage filled the air.

Moments later Roy called out again.

"Prepare to welcome the second of the Old Ones!"

Again and again he called out, and again and again Una answered, until the pit was lined with hot stones. Though the ground was still cool, the air was now very warm. When the last rock arrived, the door was closed. They were plunged into darkness.

"This Sweat is held in honour of the Moon," Una declared. "There will be three rounds of the Cauldron, in keeping with the sacred triads of the Celtic nations. The Stone People, the Old Ones, were brought by Roy from the Giant's Causeway in County Antrim. They are basalt, over fifty million years old, born in the fires of an ancient volcano, now returned to the fire to bring us vision."

With every sentence she spoke, Una ladled water onto the stones. Loud hisses and clouds of steam punctuated her words.

"The first round is the Cauldron of Warming. Let your blood heat. Let your heart beat. Let your body tell you what it needs to say. What you need to hear."

She began to chant in Scots Gaelic. Her words fluttered like bird wings in the darkness. More herbs were sprinkled over the rocks. The air grew pungent with rosemary and thyme. More water was splashed. More hissing erupted. More clouds of steam bloomed. Time was drawn out in waves of heat and gasps of burned breath.

Olwen's skin felt scalded. Her face was red-hot. A film of sweat rimed her limbs and torso. Somewhere in the faint and swelter, she grew aware of the pain that was rising inside her body.

"Whatever comes up for you," Una said in the darkness, "bear witness to it. Face your demons. Face your pain."

Then she began to sing. Some of the women joined her and a few of the men. It was a song to the Great Mother with a simple refrain. Olwen opened her mouth in an attempt to participate but no sound came out. She was wracked with pain. Every part of her body seemed to be twisted and torn. Moans escaped from her throat, though she tried to contain them.

Somewhere in her agony, she grew aware of a male version of her cries echoing from the other side of the House. Was it the elderly man from Belgium who had an artificial leg? What was his name? Thomas Tillman. She had noticed him, dressed in shorts, supported by the men in line as he waited to enter the mound. His metal limb had been removed.

"He's a big shot," Elsie had whispered to her. "Billionaire. Bankrolls a lot of what goes on here."

Olwen couldn't help wondering about him. With all that power and money, why would he put himself through this ordeal?

And why would she?!

'Cause you're a fucking masochist, that's why.

No, it's more than that. Tests of strength and character. Pushing the envelope. Facing one's fears. The hero's journey.

Yeah, right. Bloody madness.

And why should not old women be mad?

But why so much pain? What was happening in her body? She didn't think it was from the heat itself. None of the others, except for the man who mirrored her, appeared to be suffering this much. The Sweat had to be calling it up, as Una had warned; drawing it, like a poison, from the marrow of her bones, from the memory of her cells.

How long she endured it, she had no idea but the time came when she knew she could bear it no longer. She couldn't breathe.

Her bathing suit was like a vice, constricting her lungs. She was about to ask to be let out when Una announced that the first round was over.

The flap was lifted. Fresh air rushed in with the stream of light.

"Those who want to stay inside are free to do so," she told them. "Water will be brought in. Those who would like to go out are welcome to leave. You'll be called back for the second round."

Olwen had to stop herself from scrambling over the other women.

Get out and stay out!

You wouldn't survive another round, never mind two!

She burst from the mound, head first, born into the night. Weak and dizzy, she trembled like a damselfly newly born from the wreckage of its former self. The air was deliciously dark and cool. She swallowed great draughts of it. Then she began to laugh, hiccuping with joy and relief. She staggered forwards. Kind hands steadied her. A cup of water was placed in her hands. She raised it to her lips, slurped noisily. So cold. So refreshing. Sinking to her knees, she pressed her face into the earth, inhaling the wet green scent of grass, the thick brown scent of soil. All her senses were heightened. She lay on her back to gaze at the night sky. *What is the stars? What is the stars?* They danced before her eyes.

After a while, she sat up and looked around. Other bodies lay scattered on the ground, pale and damp. The Guardians of the Fire moved among them, offering water, towels, and kind words. The Sweat House, like a great humped creature, was still spitting out humans. She watched Thomas Tillman emerge, thin and hairless, his bare chest almost skeletal. He crawled slowly, one leg propelling him forward, the other a short stump in the air.

Harry moved quickly to help him up.

"That is enough for me, I think," Thomas said quietly.

"Well done," was Harry's response. "Outstanding, sir."

Those near Thomas applauded him. He smiled shyly.

Elsie had followed the old man out. She leaned against Savitri who helped her drink from a cup, like a mother with her child. Not far from them, Christy was taking care of Suzume. Her white shift was soaked and clung to her body, her hair plastered against her skull. Christy wrapped a bath towel around her and tucked her under his arm. Where was Dr Jack? Olwen could see no sign of him. Nor of Rose. Did the Director join the ceremony? He wasn't there earlier, when she had entered the House. It seemed he preferred to remain aloof.

"Would ye like a splash?"

Roy stood in front of her with a basin of water.

"Work away," she said.

As the icy water poured over her, she let out a cry of shock and pleasure. It was like being drowned in a sea wave.

"Fantastic!" she cried, panting for breath.

"Good on ye, girl."

Moments later, he offered the same to Thomas who had retrieved his titanium leg. The elderly man consented and let out a whoop as he was drenched. When Olwen nodded to him in admiration, he nodded back with a proud smile.

By the time Una announced the second round, Olwen was ready for another go.

The House was roomier now. Many had dropped out. Would that make the Sweat easier? More hot stones were added to the pit. More herbs were burned. More water ladled. More songs sung. Waves of heat engulfed the darkness. Groans of protest broke out on all sides.

"This round is the Cauldron of Vocation," Una announced. "What are you called to do? What are you called to face? What is your mission? Why do you walk the Earth? Why are you here?"

With fewer people around her, Olwen was able to lie flat on the ground. She was desperate to escape the heat. Any hope she had entertained that it would be easier the second time was quickly dispelled. The pain in her body was back with a vengeance. She pressed her face to the earth now churned to mud.

Una invited them to chant with her. Many voices rose up, but Olwen was incapable of joining them. All she could utter were sounds of anguish. And once again, she heard the echo of her cries among the men. Whoever shared her pain was still in the tent. Not Thomas, then.

"Call out your intentions for the week!" Una urged them. "The Old Ones will hear you. The Moon will bless you."

Everyone began naming their hopes and dreams. Elsie's voice quavered above the rest as she cried out for forgiveness. Olwen was startled. What could the old woman have possibly done? Dr Jack called for an end to his bouts of despair and for guidance on his spiritual path. Despite the sorrow in his voice, he sounded strong. And so, too, did Elsie, and all of the others. Olwen's heart sank. She was still prostrate on the ground, barely able to speak.

She whispered her secrets to the earth.

I want to see fairies.

I want to see God.

Her bathing suit felt like a boa constrictor, squeezing her to death. In a sudden fit, she stripped it off and flung it aside. All the women around her were already naked, and at this point she was beyond modesty or any kind of decorum. Una had begun to tell stories, fairy tales of the Western Isles. They seemed to involve a lot of blood and battles. Olwen couldn't concentrate enough to hear. Time was stretching into eternity. Would she ever see the outside world again? Was she forever exiled from air and sky?

At last the round ended, the flap was lifted, and she was free to leave once more.

Olwen clawed her way out, oblivious to the fact she had left her swimsuit behind. The night had grown darker. There were fewer people around. Roy stood ready with another basin. She waved him over. In a state of rapture, she stood naked beneath the stars, relishing the sluice of icy water. Christy handed her a towel, and a sarong to wear. Drawn to the bonfire, she gazed into the flames. She was thrilled to be alive.

The third and final round was called. She smiled to herself as she hurried inside. She would see it through.

"This is the Cauldron of Knowledge," Una told them. "The last round that brings it all home. The end of the hero's journey is the triumphant return. Whatever treasure is won, whatever vision gained, we offer it to the community for the good of all. *Heal yourself, heal the world.*"

The last hot stones entered the House. The last of the water was poured, again and again. The steam was like a dragon exploding in the darkness, whipping its fiery tail around them.

Olwen collapsed again. She was now resigned to the truth: her body carried a huge store of pain. Outside the Sweat, she found ease and relief but no sooner did the heat strike her than she was nailed once again. Was this the prize? Was this what was sought? This knowledge of pain? But what was she to do with it? What use could it be to others? How could she spin this dark thing into gold?

Una began to play her flute. Everyone knew the song and they all joined in.

Oh you take the high road and I'll take the low road,
And I'll be in Scotland afore ye,
But me and my true love will never meet again
On the bonnie, bonnie banks of Loch Lomond.

Everyone, that is, except Olwen, who could only utter tortured noises. Elsie's high-pitched notes trilled like a lark. How was she able to do it? And there was Dr Jack's rich baritone. She hadn't seen him since the Sweat began. He had remained inside between the rounds. Could he be the man who mirrored her? The heat was burrowing into her body like a living thing, a cruel parasite. The pain was unbearable. She thought she would go mad. Slowly she crept to the wall of the tent and prised open a crack in the canvas. Pressing her face against it, she sucked in the cool air. No part of her felt shame or guilt for cheating. Here was another discovery at the dark heart of the mound: she would do anything to survive.

As the song ended, Una made a request.

"I'd like the men to sing to the women to ease their suffering."

The voices of the men rose up like a choir. Olwen found herself carried on the buoyant surge of sound. Dr Jack's fine tones rang out above the rest and she allowed herself to think he was singing especially to her.

Be strong, my lover, my mother, my child, my wife,
Be brave, oh daughter, the joy of my life...

To her surprise, she suddenly recognised Rose's voice in the mix. He *was* in the Sweat House! His voice was resonant and melodic. All the men sang with fervour and care. The pain in her body eased. She sat up.

"Now let the women sing to the men to lighten their burden," said Una.

Even as the men had, the women sang with all their hearts, weaving their messages in and out of each other's. Olwen licked her lips. She really wanted to sing, especially to the man who had echoed her pain, whoever he was. Though her voice cracked at first, as soon as she began 'Blackbird' by the Beatles, the other women recognised her song and joined in.

"Thank you," the men murmured when the women had finished. "Beautiful. Thank you."

A short while later, Una chanted a farewell to the Moon and the Stone People and declared the Celtic Sweat House over.

Olwen felt a rush of triumph as she left the mound for the last time. She had passed the ordeal by fire. A good number had made it to the very end. Elsie looked tiny and utterly drained. As she crawled from the tent, Harry wrapped her in a blanket and carried her away. Tenzin Dawa had stayed inside throughout, as had Euphémie, the French scientist. Her naked body was slender and perfect. The young Tibetan offered her a sarong. His smooth chest gle⸱ ⸱ned with sweat above his white cotton trousers. They smiled at each other. The sarong moulded itself to Euphémie's damp body and she looked all the more beautiful. She raised her arms to the sky.

"*Magnifique!*"

When Rose exited the tent, Olwen suffered a moment of disorientation. She expected to be revolted. She had assumed his body would be white and sickly. But he was lean rather than thin, toned and muscled, and his skin was tanned. What did disturb her were the scars. They covered his torso and limbs in jagged pale lines. Worst of all was the lame leg, twisted like a piece of bog oak. What could have happened to him? Her stomach lurched as a thought struck her. Was he the man who had matched her pain?

She turned away from Rose to be confronted by another startling image. Dr Jack stood naked by the fire. Eyes closed, he smiled in ecstasy as Roy emptied a basin over him. His muscles shone ebony-black in the firelight. The broad chest was matted with dark curls.

Olwen's gaze was still roaming over his body when he opened his eyes and caught her. His grin was wide and cheeky. She could only grin back. There was no use pretending. He admired her in turn. She had yet to collect her clothes, and her body was still rosy and beaded with sweat. She found herself pinned under his look. As much to shake him off as to release the tension, she made a thrust with her hips. He laughed. Turning away, he accepted a sarong from Roy. She laughed, too, and went to fetch her dressing gown.

Una was the last to leave the Sweat House. She stood tall and tattooed against the shadow of the mound, eyes flashing, the pagan Priestess.

"Let us feast in the name of the Moon and what we have done in Her sight!"

The midnight meal was a fairy banquet. The dining room was transformed. White lace covered the tables. Crystal glass, bone china and silver cutlery glimmered in the candlelight. There were green salads and summer fruits, glazed salmon and trout, cheeses, cold meats, and baskets of bread. On the sideboard were tureens of soup and an array of desserts.

Olwen was one of the last to arrive. She laughed to see so many in their pyjamas and dressing gowns. Elsie wore big fluffy slippers; she was bright-eyed and animated, chirping like a bird. Everyone was in high spirits. Olwen herself felt loose-limbed and elated. She had taken a hot shower and her skin glowed like a young girl's. She, too, had slipped into something comfortable: rose-coloured trousers of a soft material and a silk wraparound blouse.

"You look like you belong on a cruise ship in the 1940s," Dr Jack remarked.

He wore brown corduroys and an open-necked shirt.

"Spacious cabin, moonlight on the ocean," she agreed. "Call me Vera or Lynn."

They joined Elsie at their usual table. Olwen let out little moans of pleasure as she ate. Everything had such vivid flavour. All around her, others were making the same noises, along with bursts of laughter and lively chat. People called out to each other from table to table. It was like a wedding party. Olwen glanced around. The only one missing was Rose.

"That was you who started the Blackbird song, wasn't it?" Dr Jack asked her.

"Yep. I love it. Reminds me of my favourite Irish poet, Padraic Fiacc. *I am the blackbird of the ruined nest who sings.*"

"Ah," he said, regarding her thoughtfully.

"Don't," she warned.

He lifted his hands in surrender.

"I'll be ready for my bed after this," said Elsie, as she tucked into a plate piled high with food. "I'm *farmutshet.*"

Olwen climbed naked under her duvet, exhausted and happy. It was a long time since she had felt this good. Every part of her gloried in the triumph of the challenge she had met. Her last image, before she fell asleep, was of Dr Jack, standing naked by the bonfire, gazing at her. But he wasn't looking at her body. He was staring thoughtfully into her eyes.

"Ah," he said.

CHAPTER ELEVEN

SECOND NIGHT: NIGHT MARE

She was riding a dark horse over the wild landscape of Lewis. It was twilight. The first stars flickered overhead. The sun was drowning in the sea to the west. The wind blew her hair and kissed her skin. A cold kiss. She was naked, riding bareback, no saddle or reins. She kept her seat with a tight grip of her thighs.

In the distance rose the jagged silhouette of a fortress perched on a cliff. She turned her steed's head to race along the precipice. Below, the waves crashed against the rocks. As she approached the fortress, she saw a light shining in one of the towers. A lone figure, dressed in a white gown, stood in the high window, gazing outwards.

She threw back her head and let out a cry. The horse sped faster. It was only in the last moments, as they passed the castle, that she realised they were heading for the edge of the cliff. She shouted at the horse to stop, even pummelled it with her fists. But the creature's eyes rolled white with terror, and it didn't stop.

The horse leaped from the cliff, legs still moving, as if to race on the dark sward of air. She was thrown backwards, arms and legs splayed like a starfish, as she plummeted towards the cold waters below.

"Jesus!"

Olwen woke with a start and gasped for breath. Her room was lit by moonlight. She was naked under the duvet and drenched with sweat. Did she have a hot flush? Or was it the aftermath of the Sweat House? She went to take a quick shower. As she towelled herself dry, she recalled fragments of her nightmare. A dark fortress on a cliff. A terrifying plunge into the sea. Then she remembered the black horse. And riding it naked. Her mind suddenly turned to Dr Jack. She shook her head.

Cliché queen!

But the horse was a mare, not a stallion. Being a horsewoman, she knew.

She heard sounds in the hall, outside her door. Pulling on her white dressing gown, she went to look. The corridor was empty. But she heard whispers in the air. Where were they coming from? The other two rooms in the broch were occupied by Euphémie and Tenzin Dawa. Padding barefoot into the hall, she stopped at each door. Not a sound from within. The whispers continued to beckon her, rising up from the stairwell. She hesitated on the landing, then hurried down the steps. The air had grown chilly. A shiver ran up her spine.

She found herself wandering on the second floor of the house. Most of the bedrooms were on this floor, along with the Common Room where people played pool. She was still following the whispers. They were like a trail of breadcrumbs, or Ariadne's thread leading her through the labyrinth. But the corridors were empty and all the doors were closed and the rooms, silent.

She roamed like a ghost through the dim passageways, but she was on the right track. The whispers had grown louder. She didn't stop to ask herself how she could have heard them high in the tower. She simply felt compelled to find their source.

At last she spied an open door ahead of her. Light spilled into the hall. Murmurs echoed softly. Her heart beat faster as she drew near, but she wouldn't admit she was afraid.

She stood on the threshold. At first she wasn't sure what she was looking at. Much of the room was in shadow. The only light emanated from the big canopied bed. Did it come from the sleeping beauty who lay there? Or from the two men who leaned over her? With a start, she recognised Suzume. The girl was still and white. Like a corpse. What were the men doing in her room? Were they the source of the whispers? Both were chanting in a strange tongue.

This isn't right. They shouldn't be here.

Olwen opened her mouth to object, but all she managed was the squeak of a mouse. Still, the men heard her and she nearly choked when they looked up. Their hands hovered above Suzume as if they were about to strangle her.

Why is Dr Jack here with Rose? Are they in this together?

Rose barely acknowledged her presence before he returned his attention to the sleeping girl; but Dr Jack smiled.

"It's all right," he assured her. "We're just doing some work here." Then he said to Rose, "She's quick. A good sign." When he spoke to Olwen again, his voice was warm with approval. "Well done! So soon! But don't go outside just yet. Wind and water. Beware of these things or you might not get back."

She was shivering, as if struck by a cold blast. Something was very wrong. The two men were almost transparent. She could see the pattern of the wallpaper through them. And when she looked down, she too was barely visible.

Again she uttered the tiniest of sounds. Then, turning on her heels, she ran. Waves of shock and terror assailed her. She kept plucking at her dressing gown and pulling at her hair, but she couldn't feel a thing. There was nothing real to touch. Bursting through the door of her room, she came to an abrupt halt at the edge of her bed.

There, beneath the duvet, lay her body. Fast asleep.

....

"*Jesus!*"

Olwen woke with a start and gasped for breath. She was naked under the duvet. Her heart pounded. On instinct, she pinched herself savagely.

"*Ow!*"

She lay still and alert, listening hard. The wind buffeted the walls of the broch. The last of the fire sighed and collapsed in the grate. No other sounds. No whispers. She climbed out of bed and pulled on her white dressing gown. The satin felt cool against her skin. Holding her breath, she unlocked the door and peered into the hall. Nothing. Not a sound.

It was just a dream. A nightmare.

She walked to the window and looked out into the night. What was that in the distance? She backed away from the window, denying what she saw. Her terror was primal. Glancing towards the bed, she half-expected to see her body lying there. But the bed was empty, the duvet turned down. She was truly awake.

She ran to slap on the light switch. The view outside her windows went black. She would have closed the shutters as well, but she was afraid to go near them. She wanted, needed to convince herself that she had seen nothing.

But as she scrambled into bed, the image rose in her mind's eye: out in the cold uncharted night, a rider on a dark horse galloped along the precipice. She huddled under her duvet, listening to the wind as it battered the broch. Who would ride at this hour? In the cold and the dark? Her eyes closed fitfully. Behind the wind, she heard the sea as it broke on the rocks. And drifting into an uneasy sleep, she heard the echo of Dr Jack's words.

Wind and water. Beware of these things or you might not get back.

CHAPTER TWELVE

WHATEVER HAPPENS IS GOLD

Olwen woke early as the first rays of sunlight struck her face. Stretching under the duvet, she was surprised to discover her white dressing gown twisted around her body. Hadn't she gone to bed naked after the Celtic Sweat House? Images of the experience flashed through her mind. The bonfire under a starry night. The red glow of the stones in the dark tent. Dr Jack in all his glory. It had been an incredible experience, one she had yet to assimilate. She hurried to the window to see if the mound was still standing. The covering had been removed, leaving only a skeletal framework. The cold stones lay in the pit. All that remained of the fire was a circle of ash.

Beyond the ruins of the Sweat House, Rose was doing his morning exercises. He was not alone. Others moved in unison behind him, following his lead. Elsie was there in a purple tracksuit, still sporting her jewellery. Harry and Penny Li arrived late but were soon in step with the rest. Savitri was all in white, in kurta pyjamas. Her long braid trailed down her back. Beside her, Roy wore black karate trousers, having discarded the jacket to go bare-chested. In the light of day, his tattoos were clearly visible. Olwen started when she recognised the images that marked his chest and back: they were taken from the famed murals of the two warring communities in Northern Ireland. He had spoken of his work as a reconciliation officer "before peace broke out". Were the tattoos a memorial? Or had he shown them to the people whom he had fought to reconcile?

A figure in the distance drew nearer. It was Dr Jack, jogging along the road that led to the house. He wore a grey tracksuit and a towel around his neck. He slowed down as he approached the others, but didn't greet them. Instead he stopped to do a few stretches nearby.

There was something both casual and intimate about the way they all behaved with each other. Exactly how long had they been together? Each of them, like her, had been invited by Rose. But how did he choose? What were his criteria? Until now, she hadn't questioned how he found her. She simply assumed he had read some of her work or come across her website. Thinking about the "how" only begged the bigger question of "why".

Why me?

Uneasy, Olwen spread out her yoga mat to begin her own morning routine.

The dining room resounded with breakfast chatter. Olwen saw immediately that a new feature had been added. One of the tables held a placard that said SILENCE PLEASE. A lone person sat there. The young Tibetan ate his bowl of porridge with eyes lowered, oblivious to the rest of them. Though he didn't look unhappy, she felt a pang of motherly concern for him.

She had decided to sit at a different table that morning; but there were no empty places except the ones near Tenzin Dawa and she wanted to talk. Both Elsie and Dr Jack smiled when she joined them.

"I saw you looking around for another place to sit," Elsie said mischievously. "Are you sick of us already?"

Olwen laughed. "Nothing personal. I just don't like getting caught in routines."

"Spoken like a true Sagittarian," Dr Jack said, with approval. "Always on the move. Always looking for new experiences."

"How–?" she started and then stopped.

He grinned. "Takes one to know one."

"You're just in time," Elsie said. "I've got a big dream to tell. I was lying on a table, or maybe it was an altar. I wasn't human. My skin was transparent, made of a silky kind of light. I should be so beautiful. I had no features, no eyes or mouth, but inside me was a silver skeleton. Well, not a skeleton like ours, but a lot of ribs and ridges. There were other beings standing around, looking down at me. They were studying me or maybe they were tending to me. As I lay there, I tried to make sense of what I was. Was the light coming from me? Was this who I really was? Or was this what I was trying to become? I woke up all *verklempt*, tears on my face."

"Wonderful!" said Dr Jack. "Not surprising after the Sweat."

"I love big dreams," Olwen said. "You wake up *knowing* that something huge and important lies at the heart of things."

"Oh yes!" Elsie agreed, eyes shining. "What about you two?"

"I was hard at work all night," Dr Jack said wryly. He poured himself another cup of coffee. There were dark circles under his eyes. "Found myself back in the psych ward of my old hospital in Halifax. The most stressful post I have ever had. Between it and the maritime weather, I jumped at the chance to move south to California."

"And you?" Elsie asked Olwen.

"I must've been sleeping the sleep of the dead. I don't think I had any dreams last night. If I did I can't remem–"

Olwen stopped as an image flashed through her mind. A naked figure on a dark horse. Her face flushed with the intensity of the memory. She ducked her head and focussed on the omelette that had been placed in front of her.

But Elsie's sharp eyes had caught her. "Oh I think you do remember and I'm guessing it's a doozy."

"No holding back," Dr Jack insisted. "We're all about truth at this table."

"Oh, bloody hell," said Olwen.

She described the night ride and the black horse and her plunge off the cliff into the sea. Elsie was already howling with laughter before Olwen was halfway through. Dr Jack's grin could not have been more wolfish.

"Any stabs at an interpretation?" Elsie asked him, wiping her eyes.

"In my professional opinion, I should pass on this one," he said gravely.

"Fuck off," Olwen mouthed at him. "The horse was a *mare!*" she said to Elsie. "I should know. I ride."

"Jungians say that a woman's animus relates to a man's anima," was Elsie's response, in between snorts.

Olwen was about to protest further when she suddenly sat up. "Wait, there was more!" Her voice echoed with wonder as the memory flooded her mind. "It was incredible. It felt so real."

She recounted the experience of wandering through the house like a ghost and finding Rose and Dr Jack in Suzume's room.

Elsie turned to Dr Jack. Her tone was admonishing. "That's where your dream came from. A distorted mirror. What did I say about working at night? You need to put salt at the four corners of your bed to keep you in!"

Dr Jack shrugged. "I go when I'm called. How can I not? I'd say we went to you as well, by the sounds of your dream."

"You're both joking, right?" said Olwen.

Surely they didn't mean what she thought they meant? But neither was smiling and Dr Jack did, indeed, look exhausted. She was about to question them further, when the gong sounded.

"Hey ho," said Dr Jack, "it's off to work we go."

Olwen gulped back the last of her coffee.

There was a discernible buzz in the Meeting Room. Everyone was in high spirits. The Sweat House had clearly bonded the circle. Olwen found herself smiling at various people she now felt closer to: Una, Roy, Suzume, Penny Li, and Thomas.

When Rose entered the room, there was a hint of a smile on his stern features.

"It was a great success," he declared, looking around. "The *chi* of the group feels purer. Let us thank Una for the gift of her wisdom."

The circle applauded, bursting into whoops and cheers. Una stood up to bow, and extended her hand to include the Guardians of the Fire and the rest of the company.

When they had settled again, Rose explained the day's schedule. There would be two sessions of Breathwork, one in the morning and one in the afternoon, to take place in the Trance Room on the ground floor of the broch.

"Many of you are familiar with deep Breathwork. For those of you who are not, there is no need for concern. You will be partnered with someone who knows what they are doing. Everyone will be divided into pairs, taking turns to be Breather and Watcher. The Breather lies on a mat and inhales and exhales deeply and rapidly for as long as possible. Trance music will be played to support and accelerate your efforts. My only advice is this: do not hold back. Let go of your habitual tendency to control. Leave yourself open to be surprised."

"Fasten your seat belts," Olwen murmured.

"As for the Watchers," Rose continued, "your role is to provide a safe environment for your Breather. You are to be attentive, alert and responsive, yet non-intrusive. Contracts will be made between each pair. Agree to hand signals for items such as assistance, water, need for the rest room, and so on. It is important to keep verbal communication to a minimum, as it interferes with the process. Of course that does not preclude shouts, screams, cries, and so on from the Breather. On the contrary, these are typical of the experience and are to be encouraged."

"Good God," said Olwen under her breath.

Elsie, beside her, reached out to squeeze her hand.

Rose went on, "A Breathwork session generally takes from three to four hours. Though you may deem yourself finished, you may not leave the room until a facilitator releases you. This is for your own sake. Bodywork is usually necessary to release trapped energy arising from the experience. In this matter, I can only ask that you trust the process. You will have your choice of the four facilitators available; and no one will touch you without your permission.

"Once you have been approved to leave the room, you will be taken by your Watcher to the conservatory where you will find materials to help you depict your experience – paint, clay, inks, chalks, and the like. Please resist the urge to talk. There will be an opportunity to debrief in smaller groups after supper this evening. Check the bulletin board in the dining room to see which group you belong to and where your group will meet. May I strongly recommend that no matter how you feel after your Breathwork, you attend your small group. If you need help, the others will be there for you.

"Finally, keep in mind the core truth of the Work: *whatever happens is good, whatever happens is gold.* For example, there may come that very human moment when your Watcher fails you in some way. If such a thing occurs, try to integrate the experience. Consider where it belongs in your own history, your own story. Understand, here and now, that you are about to leave your comfort zone. It is the nature of the Work."

Rose paused briefly to allow them to absorb his words.

Oh God, oh God, oh God.

Then he consulted his clipboard.

"Here are the facilitators who, along with myself, will oversee the sessions for the day."

Many of the circle looked eager. Olwen wondered if they were hoping to escape the ordeal.

"Those who will join me today are Tenzin Dawa, Euphémie Cadot, and Elsie Goldfarb."

When Elsie's name was announced, she let out a little squeal of delight. Friendly laughter rippled around her.

"Congratulations," said Dr Jack.

Not a way to escape. Some kind of honour?

"And here are the pairs of Watcher and Breather. Decide amongst yourselves who will do the morning session and who, the afternoon. I would recommend that anyone new go first. It will prevent you from prejudging the experience."

As Rose read out the various partners, Olwen suffered a strange sensation. Many of the couples made sense to her, in fact she could have guessed them – Christy and Suzume, Una and Roy, Harry and Penny Li. Most of them were already sitting together and, if not, were only one or two seats away. Nor was she really surprised when Rose called out her name along with Dr Jack's. At the same time she found herself more than a little disturbed. What did it mean? Was there some significance to the pairing? How and why were they matched?

"The first session begins in an hour. Loose, light clothing is recommended. Eye shades will be provided, but you may prefer to use a scarf or blindfold. Lunch will be served at the usual time. However, as the second session occurs immediately after, it is recommended that those breathing in the afternoon either fast or eat lightly. Refreshments will be available in the conservatory. That's all there is to say for now. We will meet again in the Trance Room in one hour. May I suggest that you take this time to prepare yourself in some quiet way."

Olwen turned quickly to Dr Jack. "I don't care what he says, I'm not going first. I want to see what happens before I jump."

Dr Jack grinned. "I was the very same. *Show me the merchandise.* Do you know where the Trance Room is?"

"Ground floor of the broch? Through the big doors? I'm curious to see it. Is it round?"

He nodded. "I think you'll like it. I call it 'the Womb.'" He glanced at his watch. "I'll meet you there in an hour or less."

Then he hurried off.

Olwen was disappointed. She had wanted to talk with him about what would happen and how they would work together. There was no chance to speak with Elsie either. The old woman was surrounded by well-wishers.

"I'm thrilled he feels I can do it. At my age!"

"*Mais oui*, but of course you can," Euphémie declared. "You are the best of us!"

Back in her room, Olwen helped herself to a chocolate bar as she considered what she would wear for the sessions. She changed into track pants and a short-sleeved T-shirt. An image of herself kicking and screaming flashed through her mind. *No way, José.* She opened her laptop and stared at the screen. Her mind was a blank. She was too anxious to write. Closing it again, she left the room and headed downstairs and out of the house.

What was she afraid of? The unknown? The demons in her psyche? Deep in thought, she wandered through the courtyard and behind the greenhouses to the outbuildings. They included stables, a small hay barn, and coops for chickens and geese.

The farmyard smells were earthy and reassuring. As a child she had loved to visit the old Riverdale Zoo. She had always wished she lived in the countryside rather than the city. As she grew older and travelled around Canada, she had looked for work on farms and ranches, eventually learning how to ride. When she returned to Ireland, she owned a horse for a time. But her heart was broken when he died, and she couldn't bring herself to buy another.

The stables were empty. She was surprised by how spacious they were, as they apparently housed only two animals. The loose boxes were large, light and airy. Had the horses been turned out to graze? Or were people riding them? An image flashed through her mind. A rider on a dark horse in a moonlit landscape. Did someone from Dunesfort House ride at night?

She was startled by a noise behind her. One of Morag's brothers, but which one?

"Good morning," she said. "Ruairi?"

"Calum."

Eyes grey as the loch met hers, then he ducked his head and moved to get past.

"*Tá brón orm*," she said, apologising for being in his way.

The Gaelic brought him up short. A shy smile broke out. He touched his cap in acknowledgement and shuffled away. She was reminded of the old bachelor farmers in Ireland who were generally terrified of women. On an impulse, she called after him.

"If you'd like a hand at any point. I mean, to muck out or even groom the horses. I know my way around."

He paused to consider her words.

"Aye, there might be some work for ye. I'll let ye know."

"*Go raibh maith agat*," she thanked him.

He shook his head, as if to ward off her gratitude, and hurried away. She returned to the house with a jauntier step. The little episode had reminded her of her strengths. *Always ready for an adventure. Always ready to work.* Whatever lay ahead, she would and could do it.

CHAPTER THIRTEEN

BREATHE

Olwen waited for Dr Jack outside the door of the Trance Room. There was a brief moment when she thought of running away, but she ordered herself to stand fast. When he arrived, she was reassured by the fact that he looked relaxed and happy; not like someone about to face something terrible.

The Trance Room was an experience in itself. She saw immediately why he called it "the Womb".

The great round room took up the entire ground floor of the broch. The high windows near the ceiling were tightly shuttered. The ceiling itself disappeared into shadow, with dim lights like stars. The upper part of the wall was naked stone, painted blood-red. The lower half had padding of the same colour. Some kind of protection? The floor was covered with a matting of brown hemp. Black gym mats, evenly spaced apart, radiated outwards from the wall like the spokes of a wheel. Stacked beside the mats were woollen blankets and large bean-bag cushions. There was another pile of bean bags heaped in the middle of the floor.

Despite the room's size, it felt strangely intimate, like a hermit's cave. The air was tinged with the scent of ancient stone. Olwen was reminded of the megalithic cairns she had explored.

"A womb or a tomb?" she remarked to Dr Jack, as he led her to a mat.

"I also call it 'the Trance Mission Room,'" he said with a grin.

"*Riddley Walker!* I loved those books."

"Me too."

She was beginning to feel easier.

Dr Jack made himself comfortable on the mat. He rolled up the blanket to use as a pillow. He was wearing grey track pants and a black T-shirt that stretched across his chest. His feet were bare.

Olwen sat on one of the bean bags beside him. Following his lead, she had left her shoes at the door. As well as the cushions, other items were provided – a box of tissues, a big bottle of water, some plastic cups, and a basin.

He showed her the different hand movements he used to indicate what he needed.

"Most importantly," he said, and he emphasised his words, "I don't want *any* interference of *any* kind. Unless I specifically ask for it. And if I ask for help, I want Rose. No one else. If he's busy, I'll wait. Got that?"

She nodded. But her brief moment of ease had fled. She bit her lip.

"You'll do fine," he assured her. "You're not alone here. The facilitators will keep an eye on you."

"It's not me I'm worried about!"

He laughed. "All the more reason to relax. I'm an old hand at this. See you on the other side."

He tied a black scarf over his eyes. She thought simultaneously of a buccaneer and a man standing before a firing squad. She wanted to say so, but didn't. He was already moving away from her, going inside himself, preparing for what lay ahead.

Olwen looked around the room. The low hum of chatter subsided as the last of the Breathers lay down. Some had brought pillows from their room and arranged the blankets as if they were in bed. Many wore scarves or kerchiefs over their faces, while others donned eye masks. There was an edgy excitement in the air. She felt it shiver up her spine.

When all the Breathers and Watchers had settled, Rose entered with his facilitators. Dressed in white, the four fanned out to greet the Breathers, moving from mat to mat. Olwen was reminded of nurses tending the sick, but also of commanders reviewing their troops.

Dr Jack removed his kerchief and sat up as Elsie knelt beside him. The two hugged without speaking. When the old woman got to her feet, she rested her hand on Olwen's shoulder.

"You look after my man," she said, with a wink.

Only then did Olwen realise the truth. These two were a pair. How could she have missed it? Like the other "couples" they were always together and had a deep and affectionate rapport. Had they agreed to split up for Olwen's sake? But Elsie had been surprised to be named a facilitator. That meant it was Rose's doing, not theirs. Olwen was perturbed by the thought, but she had no time to dwell on it. Rose himself had come to see Dr Jack.

He went down on one knee. The two men embraced like comrades-in-arms.

"I expect you to go further," Rose said to him, "for Olwen's sake. You are her first."

"Of course," said Dr Jack.

Rose turned to Olwen. The icy-blue eyes appraised her.

"You are about to see things beyond the range of your experience to date. Are you ready for it?"

She was taken aback, more by his intensity than by his words, but she managed to stammer the same response as her partner.

"Of...of course."

"Good."

When he left, she turned to Dr Jack.

"What was that about? Does he think I can't do it?"

"It's just his way. Don't worry about it."

The other two facilitators came, in turn, to wish the doctor well. Tenzin Dawa was formal and polite, but Olwen could see he was pleased to have been chosen for this duty. As for Euphémie, she threw her arms around Dr Jack in a cloud of French perfume.

"You will be *magnifique* as always!"

Olwen suppressed a stab of jealousy. *My Breather.*

Left alone again, Dr Jack was about to replace the black kerchief when he changed his mind. Putting it aside, he lay back on the mat and closed his eyes.

"Don't you need–?" Olwen began.

"No," he said, without opening his eyes again. "You'll see better without it."

Rose was striding around the room, issuing last-minute instructions.

"Watchers, take care of your Breathers. Your presence in this session is as crucial as theirs. Conclude all agreements now. Minimise talking once we begin. There will be plenty of noise along with the music, even shouting and screaming, but these blend with the experience. Remember: no Breather is finished until a facilitator says so. Once your Breather has been cleared, you will bring them through the far door that leads into the conservatory. Now Euphémie will read something to get things started. I wish you well, all of you, on your journey ahead. Be of good courage!"

"This is from a book by Anaïs Nin, *mon auteur préféré*," the Parisienne announced. "The book is called *The Seduction of the Minotaur.* I read the piece like *un petit poème.*"

> *There is that within us*
> *which wants us to expand*
> *with the flow of life,*
> *to occupy points*

ever farther removed
from the quiet centre
of the vortex of living,
to become flowing selves,
free and at home
with our essential condition.

As Euphémie finished, the music began. It seeped through the room, strong and powerful, an orchestral sound that slowly increased in volume. The room darkened. Over the two doorways, the exit signs glimmered an eerie green.

Rose called out his last words.

"Watchers, you are here to witness, not intrude. Breathers, you are here to work. Breathe until you are surprised, then breathe some more. Breathe for your life! *BREATHE!*"

Olwen leaned forward to watch Dr Jack. His effort was tremendous. Eyes closed tightly, he inhaled and exhaled with steady force. His chest strained against the black T-shirt.

The music grew louder. Speakers were mounted high on the walls. Olwen thought of them as gargoyles gushing sound into the room. She was drowning in it. An urge crept in to lie down herself. She resisted it. She was a nurse on duty. She had to watch her charge.

The music was building towards a crescendo. Percussion instruments took the lead. Voices sang in a foreign language. Arabic? Hindi? There were drums and a harmonium and people clapping to the beat.

Olwen had to stop herself from breathing faster.

You're a Watcher, not a Breather.

Dr Jack's chest was heaving. He gulped mouthfuls of air. The inhalations and exhalations grew more aggressive, even violent. His face looked skewed and distorted.

Watching him anxiously, Olwen was overcome by a sense of déjà vu. Then she remembered: the times she had looked after her child when she was sick, bathing her forehead, watching her breaths. Hour after hour, tending the small body under her care. There had been no question of falling asleep or shirking her duty. All her love for her daughter had kept her awake and on guard. She would watch over Dr Jack with the same dedication.

Other Breathers had begun to weep loudly or cry out in anguish. Olwen looked up at the sound of Suzume's voice. The young woman was screaming in terror and pain. It was shocking to hear. In a gut-wrenching flash, Olwen knew the girl had been raped.

She returned her gaze to Dr Jack. He had stopped deep breathing, and lay still and silent. But his face had changed. He looked wounded, vulnerable. Tears clung to his eyelashes. One trickled down his cheek. Where was he? What painful memory was he reliving? Suddenly, in a way she wouldn't have thought possible, she saw his features transform from a grown man's to that of a child. The tears began to fall in earnest. Her heart tightened. Tears gathered in her own eyes. He was so clearly present, that little boy, in all his innocence and pain.

The tears flowed freely for a while and then came the struggle to suppress them. Dr Jack clenched his fists. His face worked with emotion. With titanic effort he forced the grief back, damming the floodgates.

The music changed again. An eruption of hot, volcanic sound with a Caribbean beat. He began to flex his muscles. His movements were sensuous and erotic. Olwen felt the blood rush to her face. He turned onto his stomach. His body began to rise and fall. The slow, deliberate gyrations were unmistakable. His back arched under the tight T-shirt. Olwen tried to breathe normally. The room was very warm. She poured herself a cup of water.

Now he lurched into a kneeling position as his features contorted with rage. The veins in his neck bulged. He raised clenched fists as if to fight. A low growl erupted from his throat. It seemed to start in his gut, rise up through his chest and then strangle in his gorge. He swallowed and tossed his head. Another growl rose up. It was as if something alive, some ferocious creature inside him, was trying to claw its way out.

Olwen was terrified. What if it got free? She looked around for Rose. He and Tenzin Dawa were piling cushions around Thomas. The old man was thrashing about on his mat, mute and raging, his stump rising and falling with the contortions of his body. *Elsie?* She finally spotted the old lady lying beside Suzume, holding her in her arms. Christy lay there also. The two clasped the girl between them as if she were their child. All three rocked back and forth together as Suzume sobbed her heart out.

That left only Euphémie. All jealousy forgotten, Olwen stood up to wave her over. She nearly wept with relief when the Frenchwoman came running.

It wasn't a moment too soon. Still kneeling on the mat, eyes clenched shut, Dr Jack began to roar.

Euphémie moved quickly to pile a barricade of bean bags around him. She signalled to Olwen to get more. Olwen raced to the pile at the centre of the room and dragged back as many as she could.

Dr Jack began to punch the cushions with mindless fury. The violence was primal, murderous. Olwen was appalled. When he sprang to his feet, she let out a cry. How could they contain him? She looked around wildly for more help. Rose hurried towards her, leaving Thomas cradled between Savitri and the young Tibetan.

Now Rose and Euphémie took turns, holding up cushion after cushion as Dr Jack punched and kicked. But he wasn't satisfied. With a roar of frustration, he flung himself against the padded wall. His body bounced off and struck the floor, missing the mat. Olwen heard a bone crack. Horrified, she stared at Rose and Euphémie.

Neither moved to act.

Dr Jack clambered to his feet. Again he charged the wall. Again he fell back, hitting the ground with a crash.

Then again.

And again.

"*Stop him,*" Olwen mouthed to the two facilitators.

Rose drew her aside.

"What was your contract? Did he say to intervene if you felt it was necessary?"

She wanted to lie. Reluctantly, she shook her head.

Rose's features were impassive. "We must honour his request. It's his choice. His battle. Let him see it through. The psyche knows what is required, what he needs to do. We must trust the inner healer."

Euphémie had already left to tend another Breather and now Rose left too, leaving Olwen to watch alone.

Again and again Dr Jack charged the wall. She wanted to make him stop. Every part of her ached with the powerlessness she felt before his need to do this. She thought of all the women who loved warriors: men who were driven to fight, for good or ill.

With dawning horror, she watched as he was slowly broken. His body shuddered from invisible blows. He fell to his knees, face raised in anguish. But even in defeat, he didn't yield for a moment. Terrible and awesome to behold, he roared his defiance to the end. Then he collapsed on the mat, as if he were dead.

She held her breath. What was she to do? A gesture of his hand told her he wanted a blanket. She hurried to obey, covering him gently. Eyes still closed, he gave her a brief smile. She moved quietly around him, tidying up their area. She felt as if she had been through the wars herself. He was breathing quietly and appeared to be asleep. *What next?* Sitting down on her cushion, she let herself relax and looked around the room.

It was a vision of hell. On every side, Breathers were going mad. It was as if, like Dr Jack, something had been unleashed inside them. Some appeared to have taken on the characteristics of animals – barking like dogs or howling like wolves. Others seemed to be possessed by demons, their faces grimacing grotesquely. Many were coughing and spitting into basins. Many more were weeping and crying out loud. Some begged for mercy. Others screamed in agony. The music seemed to encourage the bedlam: a dark driving sound that was cacophonous and discordant.

And all the time the Watchers stood or knelt or sat, guarding, helping, protecting, assisting; and the facilitators also, hurrying here and there, like medics on a battlefield.

Despite her fear and revulsion, Olwen realised she was thrilled. The atmosphere in the room was electric. She had to admit she loved it. For she sensed another reality behind what she saw; the truth of what was really happening. Here was the base-line of existence. The eternal struggle of life and death. In fact, the eternal struggle of life against *whatever* strove to diminish it. This was deep diving into reality. Being fully human and fully alive. This was the mythic hero's journey.

She had no idea of the passage of time. There were no clocks on the wall, and they had been instructed not to wear watches or jewellery.

Eventually the music changed again. Now it soothed and refreshed. Most of the Breathers grew quiet. Some wept or moaned in low tones, but many appeared to fall asleep. Some were getting bodywork from the facilitators. The first few had been permitted to leave; their Watchers leading them out, with arms around waists or hands on shoulders.

Dr Jack lay still. Arms folded on his chest, he had pushed the blanket away. He looked like a corpse. No, something colder still. A stone effigy of a knight; the kind found in chapels or in underground tombs. His features were exquisite, as if carved from obsidian. She gazed on him with awe: a king among men.

His breathing was slow and shallow. There was hardly any movement in his chest. At one point it seemed to stop altogether. Concerned, she leaned over him, like a mother bending over her child in the cot. A warm breath bathed her face. He was alive, so. Before she could draw back, his eyes opened. They shared a long look. It seemed for a moment as if they might kiss, but neither moved.

His lips widened to a smile. He mouthed his words.

"I'm finished."

He was about to stand up, but she shook her head. With both hands, she pressed him gently back on the mat.

"Not till Rose clears you."

The Director was busy, but Olwen kept an eye on him until he was free. Then she signalled him over.

By this time Dr Jack was sitting in meditation pose. He looked peaceful and serene, like a Buddha.

Rose studied him for a while. Then, putting aside his cane, he began to work on Dr Jack's shoulders and back. He kneaded and pummelled him mercilessly. It wasn't long before the doctor was roaring again.

Olwen's palms grew sweaty. Would there be more violence?

Rose pressed a knee against his back and leaned in hard.

"Let this one go, Jack," he urged him. "It's time. Let it go."

To Olwen's surprise, the doctor suddenly fell apart. Like a broken toy, every part of his body folded in complete surrender. His shoulders shook. Sobs tore through him. He buried his face in his hands.

"Lie back," Rose ordered him softly.

Dr Jack obeyed without resistance.

"Will you hold him with me?" Rose asked Olwen.

She knew what he wanted her to do. She had seen the other Watchers and facilitators do it. And she understood what it meant: Mother and Father comfort the Child. But the thought of being locked in such an intimate embrace with Rose repelled her. She thought of calling on Elsie to take her place, but the old woman was with someone else. And so, too, was Euphémie.

It was Olwen or no one.

With a curt nod, she stretched out beside Dr Jack, even as Rose lay on the other side of him. The doctor's features were a mask. He was far away. Rose wrapped his arms around him. Olwen did the same with some trepidation, knowing that Rose would grasp hold of her. She suppressed a shudder. But when his hands touched her, she was pleasantly surprised. His grip was strong and reassuring, incredibly so, as if iron not bone was under his flesh.

Between them they held Jack tightly, rocking him with gentle motions. He started to weep and the more he wept, the closer they held him. His face was pressed against Olwen's. She felt his tears mingle with her own. Despite her attraction to him, there was no sense of the sexual in this embrace. She held him as a mother would hold her child, with a perfect wordless love.

She began to sing to him, the lullaby she used to sing to her daughter, the same lullaby her own mother sang to her.

Go to sleep, my baby.
Close your pretty eyes.
Angels up above you
Peeping at you dearly from the sky.
The same old moon is shining,
The stars begin to peep,
And now it's time for my little baby
To go...to...sleep.

Dr Jack grew quiet. Rose loosened his hold, and the three gently disengaged. Despite the intimacy they had just shared, Rose's features were as stony as ever.

"You may take him out now," he said to Olwen.

She helped Dr Jack to his feet.

"Well done," Rose added, nodding to both of them.

Then he retrieved his cane and limped away.

CHAPTER FOURTEEN

TE MORITURI SALUTAMUS

Olwen guided Dr Jack into the conservatory. It was like entering a secret garden. Fresh breezes wafted through the open windows. Ceramic figures and faces peered from a profusion of plants. Chairs and small tables were scattered throughout the greenery, some already in use. There was a worktop laden with art materials.

Dr Jack chose paints and brushes and settled down near a window.

"Would you like something to eat or drink?" she asked him.

He looked drained and exhausted. His voice was barely audible.

"Green tea...some fruit?"

She found the counter where jugs of iced water had been set out, as well as supplies of coffee and tea. There was plenty of fruit, along with bowls of mixed nuts and an assortment of biscuits, chocolates, and cake.

Olwen brewed tea for Dr Jack and chose various fruits. For herself, she poured a big mug of coffee and heaped a plate with chocolates. When she brought the tray over, he glanced at her snacks with a wan smile.

"Was it rough on you?"

"This isn't about me."

"Yes it is. You, me, all of us."

His eyes were red. He looked lost. She was feeling raw herself.

Her emotions were all over the place.

"Would you like a hug?" she asked.

"Yes."

He wept as she held him. It gave her the strength not to fall apart herself. She was still on duty. They stayed holding each other as more Watchers and Breathers settled around them.

"Thank you," he whispered in her ear, before breaking away.

He was soon absorbed in his painting. He had chosen several brushes and one large tube of dark red acrylic. Using broad strokes, he lashed the paint onto the paper. A whip cutting into flesh. Or perhaps a knife. The paint splattered and dripped like blood. There was fury and passion in these wounds, and a tale of great pain.

After a time, she got up to get him more tea and fruit. As she passed some of the others, she glanced at their artwork. The images were stunning. There were many, like Dr Jack, who made abstract or geometric shapes. Others were creating detailed tableaux of people and animals, both real and mythical, misshapen and magnificent.

All of the Breathers looked devastated and many of the Watchers, too. She couldn't help but wonder: was it wise, what they were doing? Or were they just traumatising themselves all over again?

She thought of her own session that lay ahead. She was quaking inside. But she also felt a rising excitement. Where did the Breathers go? What happened to them? What did they see? In the Trance Room, she had felt as if she were left standing on the dock...or the launch pad. The Breathers had obviously gone on some harrowing but amazing journey. Though utterly terrified of what awaited her, she had no intention of bowing out. She would not be left behind.

Some time later, Euphémie came into the conservatory to announce that lunch was being served. Dr Jack had just finished his third red painting.

"I won't eat right now," he told Olwen. "I'd rather go to my room."

She studied him anxiously.

"I've done this many times before," he assured her, managing a smile. "It looks worse than it is. You'll see. Thank you so much for being such a wonderful Watcher. Tell Elsie I said you're as good as she."

"I'm definitely taking that as a compliment."

In the dining room, Olwen took her usual seat beside Elsie. The talk in the room was muted. There were many more tables with signs that said SILENCE PLEASE. Watchers sat with their Breathers, in some cases helping them to eat. Suzume looked as pale as porcelain, with purple shadows under her eyes. She leaned against Christy as he fed her soup with a spoon, her small mouth opening and closing like a baby bird. If anyone approached them, Christy shook his head.

Olwen had arrived late as she had gone to her room beforehand to freshen up. Though the food looked inviting, she took only a cup of camomile tea. She knew others were fasting for a more powerful experience. Regardless of her fear, she wasn't about to short-change herself.

In for a penny, in for a pound.

She glanced at the empty chair beside her and then at the door.

Elsie patted her hand.

"He's fine. I checked on him. I hope you don't mind. Old habits die hard."

"No, I'm glad you did! This is all so new to me. I was debating on whether I should go look for him or bring up his lunch or something."

"Don't worry about him eating. There's always food for latecomers. And the next session is two hours away."

Elsie finished her soup with a loud slurp and tucked into a wedge of Stilton. There was high colour in her cheeks and her eyes shone.

"You look radiant," Olwen said. "Is it that good to facilitate?"

"Even better than Breathing! Who would believe it? That was my first time. I had no idea it could be so good." She put her hand to her heart. "You're there at the centre of everything."

"Like God?"

Elsie thought a moment. "Not if by that you mean an outsider in control. We're a deep part of what's happening. We swim in the stream of energy that flows around the room." She shook her head. "I should say this better. Being at the heart, you can really see where everyone is and how they are. We're not caught up in the intense bonding between Breather and Watcher. That's how we can tell when someone is finished. It's like looking at a painting or hearing a song or a story. You know by instinct if it's over. If it's... resolved.

"And it takes your breath away – do you like my pun? – to really *see* the inner healer at work in the psyche of the Breather. You see it all over the room: the beauty and the sense of it, and the patterns and themes repeated and enacted. Every Breather's experience is his or her own, but we see something universal as well. To serve this process, it's humbling and exhilarating at the same time. The ego bows before the Divine and you are filled with gratitude and a strange freedom. It reminded me of something Savitri once said about the liberation of duty, fulfilling your *dharma*, what you are called to do in a day or in a life."

Olwen tried to absorb what Elsie was saying, but her mind couldn't settle. Images of the session kept invading her thoughts: people writhing in agony, screaming and crying, spitting and retching. She felt the weight of the Work, like the great stone structure of Dunesfort House itself, overshadowing her small self. Threatening to annihilate her.

"I need air!"

She stood up so quickly she knocked her chair over. Flustered and apologetic, she caught Elsie's look of sympathy before she fled the room.

Outside the house, Olwen gulped down waves of fear and suffocation. Did she really want to do this? In the depths of her subconscious, dark things were moving. Did she want them to surface?

I'm beginning to remember.

She hurried back into the house and up to her room. Grim and determined, she changed into jeans and a T-shirt and pulled on her boots. She needed to work.

Once again, she found the stables empty. Who took the horses out? Morag's brothers? Other members of the staff? A pair of denim overalls hung on a hook inside the door. She pulled them over her clothes. There was a red kerchief in one of the pockets which she used to bind up her hair.

Calum was nowhere to be seen, but she didn't need to be told what to do. She knew how to muck out. She was soon forking and shovelling to her heart's content. The earthy smells of straw and dung were comforting. She settled into a rhythm, working effortlessly. Her body grew warm. Having finished the first box, she started on the second. She would need fresh straw from the barn, and where was the muck heap?

She was almost done when Morag's brother arrived. He stood in the doorway and grunted with surprise.

"Calum?" she asked uncertainly.

"Ruairi."

She stopped to wipe her forehead with the back of her hand. Curls of hair had escaped from the kerchief to cling damply to her skin.

"Calum said I could help. I know my way around horses. I..."

He was gone before she could finish.

"Right," she muttered. "Note to self: Ruairi's not the friendly one."

She was shovelling the last of the droppings into the wheelbarrow when he returned. He had brought fresh straw.

"Great!" she said happily. "But where do I put this?"

She grinned to herself as he trudged off with the manure. Though he hadn't uttered a word of thanks, she sensed he was pleased. More importantly, so was she. She spread the fresh bedding. Her spirits were high. The horses would be happy as well. Might she get a chance to ride them? She would ask Morag the next time she saw her.

Job done, she returned the overalls and kerchief to their place. She was about to leave the stables when Rose and Calum arrived in the yard, on horseback. Instinctively, she withdrew into the shadow of the doorway, though she could still see them.

The two horses were beauties, a dark gelding and a grey mare. Calum was on the mare. He dismounted first and moved quickly to help Rose get down. The Director thanked him, and retrieved his cane from where it hung on the saddle like a sword.

"I'll groom both," Calum said.

"No, I have time," Rose answered.

They were coming towards her.

Olwen had no choice but to step from the doorway.

Rose stopped in surprise. Calum gave her a little smile.

"I...I just did a bit of work," she said.

Her face was red. What was she thinking? It looked as if she had been spying on them! Mortified, she hurried away.

Back in her room, Olwen took a shower and changed her clothes. She chose a cotton T-shirt and the soft pink trousers she had worn after the Sweat House. Mindful of what she had seen that morning, she removed her make-up and applied plenty of moisturiser, as well as deodorant. As a final touch, she braided her hair in a single plait to keep it out of the way. She looked good after the physical work, healthy and glowing. How would she look by the end of her session?

There was still some time before it began. She was in no hurry to go into the Trance Room. Grabbing a chocolate bar from her stash, she opened her laptop.

One last shot of chocolate before I face the firing squad. Jaze, I'd smoke a fag if I had one! Truth? I'm terrified. But I'm also excited. I think something amazing is going to happen. I can feel it in my bones.

I wish I could talk to William about it. I know what he'd say. "Go, girl, go. You can do it. You are the woman!" He always got a kick out of my "enthusiasms" as he called them. Of course I ignored the reason why. He preferred to observe life through the lens of his camera, rather than to live it. He was a bystander by nature. But that was one of the things I liked about him. He was a quiet soul, content with a cup of coffee and a crossword puzzle. So different from the kind of men I usually end up with.

She stopped writing. There were tears in her eyes. Chalk up another failure in a long line of failed relationships. Why were so many women able to find partners and live with them, year after year, with reasonable success, some even with enviable happiness, but not her? What was wrong with her? She wasn't bitter. At least, not most of the time. She remembered her former lovers with affection. Sometimes even her ex-husband. In time, if not at first, she could even see where the break-ups were as much her fault as theirs. She didn't spend long in the blame game. She liked to move on quickly.

A broken heart sends the exile on her journey again.

From deep in the bowels of the house the gong rang out. Olwen typed a last sentence before she left.

Do not ask for whom the bell tolls.

CHAPTER FIFTEEN

SONGS OF JOY AND CATASTROPHE

The air in the Trance Room was clean and fresh. The high windows had been opened to let in the sea breezes. The mats were fresh, too, and there were new basins, blankets, bottles of water, and tissues. Olwen smiled to herself. The amazing Morag and her staff. Dr Jack was already in their area, arranging the cushions. He waved her over with a big smile. He looked well recovered from his ordeal, full of life and energy.

She glanced around the room. All the Breathers looked well and happy, resurrected from the wreckage of the earlier session. Even Suzume, though still a little pale, was stepping lightly around Christy, offering him a cup of water and shaking out his blanket.

"We who are about to die salute you," Olwen said to Dr Jack, before she settled down on her mat.

"Die consciously and you need never do it again."

"Thanks. I'll keep that in mind as I bleed."

They discussed their contract for the session. Olwen was happy to use the signals he had shown her earlier.

"If I need help," she told him firmly, "I want one of the women, preferably Elsie. If neither are available, Tenzin Dawa will do. The little lama seems to have come into his own. But *under no circumstances* are you to call Rose."

Dr Jack frowned. "I know you're not a big fan, but even the others would agree he's the best at—"

"I don't care. He gives me the creeps. I don't want him near me when I'm vulnerable."

Dr Jack didn't look happy.

Olwen felt a stab of doubt and suspicion. Was she in control of her own session or not?

"Do you trust me?" he asked her.

She responded frankly: "I can't answer that question right now. I don't know you well enough, even after this morning."

"What do your instincts tell you?"

She paused to consider his question.

"You're a good man. Unlikely to harm me."

"Right then," he said, taking a breath. "Would you trust me enough to call the shots if it looks to me like you seriously need help and nobody else is available except Rose? Would you take him then?"

Another stab of suspicion.

"Is this a set-up? Are you determined to make me work with him? Like facing what I hate or something?"

"No, it's not like that. It's just...I've been doing this work for a long time and if there's one thing I've discovered it's that there are no coincidences. Whenever I'm determined to avoid someone or something, I inevitably end up facing that very thing or that very person. I just want you to be prepared for that."

His tone was honest and straightforward, and his words made sense. She knew what he meant. She had had the same experience herself many a time.

"Are you referring to Murphy's Law?" she said wryly.

"I guess I am. Trust the Irish to be clued into the invisible workings of the universe."

She couldn't help but laugh at that.

"All right," she said finally. "If it looks serious – and I'm talking dire emergency here: the magic words are *I need help* – and no one else is around, I'll take him. But only as a last resort. Got it?"

"You couldn't be clearer."

With the matter settled, Olwen pulled on her favourite woollen socks from Donegal and lay back on the mat.

I can do this.

The four facilitators entered the room and began their rounds.

Olwen sat up again as Elsie hurried over to clasp her face and squeeze it tightly.

"You will do beautifully, *bubbeleh*, just see if you don't."

Tenzin Dawa smiled serenely as he murmured his best wishes. Euphémie glided over, wafting cologne, to kiss her on both cheeks.

"Bonne chance, chérie, et bon voyage."

The Parisienne lingered a moment to share a laugh with Dr Jack. Olwen felt the inevitable surge of jealousy; then caught herself and grinned.

Rose arrived last. She struggled to keep her features neutral, but couldn't stop herself from stiffening. He went down on one knee, as he had done with Dr Jack. He didn't touch her, but he seemed very near. Too near. The intensity of his gaze was unsettling. He was searching her features. What was he looking for? Some weakness? Some flaw? She glared back at him.

He nodded, satisfied.

"Journey well, Olwen."

She had brought a silk scarf to put over her eyes. As she tied it tightly, she felt a thrill run through her. Whatever was about to happen, it would be something new, something she had never experienced before. Her own craving for adventure and novelty steadied her.

The first strains of music began: Tibetan prayer bowls and cymbals and the low drone of a harmonium. Tenzin Dawa walked slowly around the room as he read his chosen poem by Nyoshul Khenpo Rinpoche.

Rest in natural great peace
This exhausted mind
Beaten helplessly
By karma and neurotic thoughts
Like the relentless fury
Of the pounding waves
In the infinite ocean of samsara
Rest in natural great peace.

The music was so loud, so intensely present in the air that Olwen felt it inside her. She breathed deeply and rapidly, the way Dr Jack had done. Before long she felt a tingling sensation shoot through her limbs. Now her arms and legs were gripped by a strange kind of paralysis. She kept breathing, but it quickly got worse, as if a vice was clamped on her body. She was about to panic when she remembered one of the things Dr Jack had told her.

Where there's a lock, there's a door. Keep breathing. Go through it.

She returned to her breathing. Deeper. Faster. Gulping in great mouthfuls of air. She imagined that she was scaling a ladder, climbing a mountain, scrambling up a cliff. Every effort, every thought was bent on going *up*. She tried swimming into the air, moving her arms in wide breaststrokes. Not fast enough! She imagined a canoe and paddled furiously, shooting the rapids of white water.

At last! *Yes!* She felt the lock break. Exhilaration coursed through her, charging every sinew. Her muscles began to twitch and spasm. *Farther up and further in.* She imagined a silver rope dangling above her and began to pull herself up.

Then a message came, as if from nowhere. A still small voice in her mind.

Surrender to win.

She let go of the rope...

Let go of her breath...

Falling into a vast and dizzying sensation...

Of falling.

But she didn't fall backwards. Instead, she fell upwards, like a lark soaring into the sky! She flew so fast and so high she shot out of the stratosphere and into space. A fiery comet.

Ahhhhhhhhhhhhhhhhh!

Her body sat up with a jolt. Her legs crossed themselves in a meditation pose, hands resting on her knees. She was utterly dazed and amazed. She was inside a network of gold and silver filaments. Light kept exploding all around her, creating and re-creating an infinity of forms. It was a cosmic playground fashioned of light: multidimensional shapes and structures, rollercoasters, wormholes, tunnels, all in motion, spinning and spiralling like Catherine wheels, bursting like geysers and spilling over like fountains. She was surrounded by light, engulfed in it, and yet, somehow, she was also part of it, an infinitesimal mote in the whole.

Suddenly a vein of light – like a giant golden straw – came speeding towards her. She didn't resist, but tipped back her head and opened her mouth wide. Cool hot silvery golden liquid light poured down her throat. Her head tipped further back, her spine arched like a bow; and her eyes rolled in her head behind her scarf as she drank in the cosmos.

AHHHHHHHHHHHHHHHH!

She had no idea how long she remained in that state of bliss; but there came a time when she was no longer in it. She was in a cavern filled with suffering souls who cried out around her. Her first feeling was guilt. They were all working so hard while she was out playing. Their pain began to affect her. She tried to shield herself from it. She began to breathe again, deeply, slowly.

She grew aware of the music. Deep drums, a dark subterranean sound, bass profundo, vaguely menacing. Trickles of fear flowed through her body. Something was coming. Something unpleasant. A chill ran up her spine. She considered calling for help, but the memory of her Watcher calmed her. She wasn't alone. She could face this.

She was inside a bubble, breathing water through her gills and looking out beyond the translucent wall at fronds wavering in the water outside. She didn't feel safe. The bubble was too thin and fragile. The shapes outside were starting to look less like underwater plants and more like snakes. Was something else moving out there? She kept staring, trying to see. Something approached. Something that wanted to get inside the bubble. To get at *her*!

Terror welled up inside her, dark and primordial. She curled up in a tight ball, shuddering with fear. Out of her mouth came a little girl's voice.

"It's coming! It's coming!"

Something huge drew near. The bubble couldn't possibly protect her. She had to flee. But there was nowhere to go. The invasion was quick and inescapable. The seal broken. The integrity of her little world compromised in an instant. The thing was reptilian in shape. Its head was huge. The skin dry and leathery. She felt a gargantuan weight bear down on her. The yellow slit of an eye blinked open. She tried to scream, but only the faintest of sounds came out. The tiny squeak of a tiny animal. The smell was overpowering. Oily, sour, and suffocating. It invaded her nostrils and her throat. A wave of nausea struck her. She began to gag and choke. She felt its mouth on her. Sucking out her heart. Sucking out her life. She sat up with a jerk, retching with violent, gut-wrenching heaves. Someone moved near her. She felt the basin on her lap. She spat into it furiously as she coughed and choked.

Another wave of nausea wracked her body. She couldn't bear it any longer. She felt weak and dizzy. In between moans, she gasped out the words.

"Make it stop. Please make it stop. *I need help!*"

Somewhere in the sickening blur, she felt her Watcher gesturing, and suddenly there was another presence beside her. At first she sensed only a rock of strength, glittering and impervious, like a meteorite.

Then Rose's voice.

"Olwen. You need only go as far as you are prepared to go. If you want it to stop, you can remove your scarf. Once you open your eyes, you will banish what torments you."

She lifted her hands to her scarf. Then paused. Something in his voice, in his tone, told her he wasn't finished. She waited to hear more.

"On the other hand, you can face it. Here and now. This thing in the depths of your psyche. With Jack and me beside you, and the strength of the circle around you, you can deal with it."

Her reaction was immediate. She curled up once again into a tight little ball, the scarf still wrapped around her eyes. She could sense the two men on either side of her, pure male energy, strong and benign. The thing she feared was nearby, hiding in the shadows, crouched at the edges of her consciousness, waiting to pounce. A dark, demonic presence. As she considered the possibility of facing it, she felt it advance. Felt the weight bearing down, a heavy suffocating mass. Her stomach clenched like a fist. She wanted to vomit. She began to choke again.

"No, no. I can't. Please stop it. I've got to get out of here."

They moved quickly to sit her up. Gently, Rose removed the blindfold. She opened her eyes.

A torrent of sound and sight rushed at her. The dark cave of the room, the roar of the music, so many people screaming and crying and writhing in agony. The atmosphere was horrific. She grabbed at the basin and heaved violently, but nothing came up. Dr Jack rubbed her back. He handed her a cup of water. She gulped it down.

"I can't do this any more. I want out of here. *Now.*"

She saw the two men exchange glances. Anger surged through her. Was she a child? Who were they to tell her what to do?

Rose hesitated, then spoke quietly. "May I ask you to stay just a little longer? You need do nothing else."

She searched for condescension in his tone, something that would allow her to defy him. But he was pleading with her.

"Please stay. You can keep your eyes open. Jack will be here with you. And I can send any of the others over to you as soon as they are available – Elsie or Euphémie or Tenzin. This stage will end soon. The music will change and something new will come. I promise you. It would be to your benefit."

She was suddenly reminded of something a priest friend had said to her long ago.

There's something to be said for sticking things out.

"All right," she agreed at last.

The two men looked relieved.

They care what I do. They have my best interests at heart. Or do they? Is it me or the Work they are concerned about?

She lay back on the mat and stared into the shadows of the ceiling above her. Her body was cold and shuddering, as if in shock. Before she could ask, Dr Jack covered her with a blanket. He motioned to someone nearby.

"More blankets!"

She was shivering violently now. Her teeth chattered. Blanket after blanket was placed over her, soft and thick and warm. Dr Jack tucked them under her till she was cocooned. She closed her eyes. A delicious heat was building up.

She dozed off.

When Olwen surfaced again to consciousness, she was surprised.

To think she had been able to sleep with all that noise around her! She felt well rested. Though she put aside her scarf, she didn't open her eyes. She was exploring the impressions of a new scenario.

She was buried in the ground, at the base of a great tree. A gentle torpor came over her. She could feel the weight of the soil above her, but she wasn't afraid. She lay still, deep in the clay, waiting to see what might happen.

Things began to emerge from her body, long strings of some sort; from the flat of her back and her buttocks and the calves of her legs. *Roots!* They delved into the soil, pushing down into the darkness, drinking the cool waters of the earth, refreshing and reviving her. She felt the creatures in the soil squirming and burrowing around her, eyeless worms and tiny insects. Another sensation: her hair was growing out of her head and twining itself around the roots of the tree. Now it pushed above the soil. Green as ivy, it encircled the tree, twining higher and higher, full of life and energy, drinking in the warmth and light of the sun.

A great sigh of acceptance.

A great sough of wind.

She hung on the tree for hours, it seemed.

Till she let out another sigh of surrender.

She opened her eyes and turned to smile at Dr Jack. He was watching her with the same intensity that she had watched him. His face wore the shape of an elaborate mask carved of black wood and streaked with daubs of vivid colour.

"You're an African god," she told him.

"Wonderful," he said softly. His teeth gleamed white inside the mask as he smiled.

"I think I'm finished."

"I'll get one of the women."

When Euphémie came over, Olwen beamed a beneficent smile. All was well with the world, the magnificent world.

The younger woman's face showed the strain of the day's work, but also her determination to do her best for Olwen.

"I like to give you *un petit massage* to see if energy is trapped in the body. May I do this, please?"

Olwen consented. She was already aware of a faint pain in her chest, like heartburn.

Kneeling behind her, Euphémie began to knead her back and shoulders. The burning sensation increased. Olwen let out a low moan.

"What is this?" the Frenchwoman asked, concerned. "Does it pain you?

"My chest," Olwen groaned. "It's on fire."

Euphémie stood up and leaned against Olwen's back, pushing with gentle force.

An impossible pressure rose inside Olwen's ribcage. She clawed at her chest to try and prise it open. The pain was mounting. Her lower back was in agony. She suddenly recognised what was happening, and reached out to grab Dr Jack.

"I'm in labour! I'm about to give birth!"

"It's all right," he encouraged her. "Let it happen. You're safe. I'm a doctor."

She wrapped her arms around her stomach. It felt swollen and bloated. Her moans turned to deep groans. Euphémie was still behind her, pushing steadily. The pressure seemed to call up an equal response inside Olwen. She began to choke and cough. The basin was there again. Would this madness never end? Was there no way out?

Her arms were still locked around her body.

"What do you hold?" Euphémie asked her.

Olwen considered the question. Another agonising pang tore through her. The answer came on a scream.

"*Me!*"

Embarrassed, she clamped her mouth shut. This had to end. She couldn't take much more.

"I want to finish," she said furiously. "I want to get out of here."

"*Je comprends*," Euphémie said. Her voice rang with compassion. "As soon as you open the arm, you may go."

Teeth clenched, muscles straining, Olwen struggled to break free of her own grip. Screeching with frustration, she fought with herself.

Euphémie continued to apply pressure at her back.

"That's it!" Dr Jack cried, urging her on. "You're getting there! Keep going!"

And suddenly she was back in the delivery ward of the hospital in Toronto where she gave birth to her daughter, as her husband shouted with astonishment.

Slowly, incredibly, she felt her arms give way. Her screams were ear-splitting. She couldn't believe she was able to screech that loud. Her body lifted in an impossible arch that sent Euphémie sprawling behind her. With a final roar of anguish and triumph, she ripped her arms apart: in her mind, a slash of red.

Then she collapsed on the mat, lips moving in an involuntary sucking motion.

"*Bravo! Très bien! Magnifique!*" Euphémie cried. "*Tu es née!* You are born!"

The Frenchwoman lay down on one side of Olwen, even as Dr Jack moved to lie down on the other. She knew they were preparing to embrace her. She sat up shakily and raised her hands to fend them off.

"*No!*"

They backed away instantly.

"What do you think in this moment?" Euphémie asked softly. "What is it your body say to you?"

The truth was simple and certain. Every part of Olwen felt it.

"I wasn't wanted."

She lay back alone, newly born and exhausted. Weeping tears of grief and defiance, she acknowledged the core feeling that had permeated her life: she was unloved, therefore unlovable.

Euphémie stood up to leave. "When she wish, she may go," she said to Dr Jack.

Olwen buried her face in her arms and wept some more.

"Would you like me to hold you?" he asked gently.

She heard the sympathy and the kindness, so freely offered.

"No," she said again. She was unable to accept it.

A little while later she sat up, wiped her face, and patted her hair. "I'm done."

CHAPTER SIXTEEN

TALES OF THE FALL

As she entered the conservatory, Olwen stopped to inhale the scent of flowers and greenery. It was as if she were using her sense of smell for the first time. She hurried to the art table to choose her materials. Though wrung-out and exhausted, she was eager to express her experience. She wanted to paint it and sing it and dance it and eat it.

"I'd like fresh coffee with lots of cream and sugar," she told Dr Jack. "And when I'm finished that, a small pot of Earl Grey with a slice of lemon. To eat, I'll have chocolates, lots of them, also some of the strawberries and roasted almonds. Oh and a few of those chocolate biscuits. Actually, bring me a bit of everything except the dried fruit."

He let out a great laugh and went to get what she wanted. By the time he had returned with a tray laden with goodies, she was almost finished her first painting.

"You did great," he said to her. "Especially for a first-timer."

"I did," she agreed. "How did it look from where you were standing?"

She tucked into the chocolates first and then the strawberries.

Dr Jack reclined in his chair and sipped on a mug of herbal tea.

"I don't know where you went at the beginning, but I sure wanted to be there."

She held up the sheet of paper covered with explosions of gold and silver paint.

"That's where I was."

She put the painting aside and began another. Washes of grey for the watery bubble and black stripes for the vegetal fronds outside. Still using black, she drew the outline of the monster in the depths. A chill ran up her back.

What is it? What do I fear in the dark?

She was soon painting feverishly, driven by a relentless muse. Dr Jack moved quietly around her, laying her paintings out to dry, bringing her a fresh pot of tea and more treats.

The first painting of the monster showed an inchoate mass. The second depicted a reptilian shape with scaly brown skin. The third showed only the yellow slit of a giant eye.

"Now I know what Tolkien was on about," she murmured.

A new painting called for thick layers of dark brown daubed with red. As soon as the daubs dried, she added the outline of her own body deep in the earth. Roots trailed from her back and into the soil. Shoots grew from her hair to rise above the surface and twine around the bole of a huge tree.

Yggsdrasil, she scrawled in a sweeping script across the page. *The Tree of Life.*

She painted Dr Jack's face in an African mask streaked with colour. As she began her last image, she found herself frowning. Quickly she sketched her body rising in an arc, arms locked around her stomach, mouth open wide in a scream. Studying the image, she made noises of disgust and dismay.

"I can't believe I'm back there again with the same old same old," she said to Dr Jack. "I did years of therapy, long ago in a galaxy far, far away. My therapist at the time is now one of my closest friends. It's pathetic to be still whingeing, 'My mother didn't love me.'"

He regarded her thoughtfully. "Do you want my professional opinion?"

"Not if I have to pay for it."

He smiled, then grew serious again. "We're never really 'done' with the primal material. We just slough off more layers every time we come to it. Jung uses the metaphor of the labyrinth for this process. Throughout our lives, if we are struggling to be conscious, we continually approach the core of our selves, our psyches, from different angles. And we get different perspectives at different times, some deeper than others. The trail can lead you all over the place, sometimes further away from the centre, sometimes nearer."

"Is the labyrinth both our life and our psyche?"

"Yes. Well put."

"Do we ever get to the heart of it?"

He paused. "I'm not sure. I don't think so. Not on this plane, anyway. But we can get very near."

"You mean, 'close, but no cigar', pardon the Freudian reference."

He laughed.

"I'm finished," she said.

Olwen was late for supper. She had spent the time beforehand lying on her bed, weeping quietly to herself. Once the thrill of the experience had worn off, she was left feeling raw and exposed, as if a layer of skin had been removed. Loud noises disturbed her. Light hurt her eyes. The last thing she wanted to do was socialise; but at the same time she could no longer bear to be alone. She finally dragged herself from the bed, ignored her image in the mirror, and trudged downstairs to the dining room.

There were more silent tables. She made her way to one of them. Dr Jack was sitting with Elsie in their usual place. He came over to her immediately.

"Can I get you anything?" he asked. "Do you want me to sit with you?"

She shook her head. Her eyes filled with tears.

He rubbed her back gently. "Just wave if you need me."

She nodded, but kept her head down. She felt cold despite the heavy sweater she was wearing. The other two at the table had also been Breathers that afternoon. Both Savitri and Penny Li looked as devastated as she. The three of them ate without speaking or even meeting each other's eyes.

The meal itself was fortifying, what Olwen called "yang" food, with plenty of carbs. She was just finishing her dessert of bread pudding when Dr Jack came over to tell her about the final session of the day.

"It starts in a half-hour. We've been divided into small groups to share our experience. Our group is meeting in the Common Room on the second floor. You can reach it from the main stairway or from the broch."

She grasped his arm. Her voice sounded desperate.

"I don't want to talk. I can't right now."

"You don't have to," he assured her. "There's no obligation. But please come. It will help. I promise. Will you come?"

She was about to refuse, when she reconsidered. It was obvious that he wanted her to go. Some part of her duty as Watcher still lingered. He might need her.

"Okay. I'll be there."

The Common Room was a rectangular hall with a great fireplace and bookshelves that reached the ceiling. Turkish rugs covered the hardwood floor. Prints and paintings hung on the walls. There were three leather sofas and an array of armchairs arranged in a square around a broad coffee table. In one corner of the room was a large pool table. In another, a counter where teas and coffees could be made. There was also an old-fashioned wooden rack with newspapers and magazines from around the world.

Olwen was the last to arrive, having wandered lost for a time through the maze of corridors. Everyone was already seated. She was happy to see that she knew most of the group and happier still that Elsie was in charge.

As usual, the various pairs sat beside each other. Christy and Suzume were on one of the big sofas, holding hands. Thomas had his arm around Savitri's shoulders. His crutches lay on the floor beside him. Savitri looked pale and drawn against the fiery colours of her sari and shawl. Olwen's other supper-mate, Penny Li, looked in better spirits. She was talking animatedly with her partner, Harry.

Head lowered to avoid eye contact, Olwen muttered her apologies as she took her seat. Dr Jack had saved her the chair next to his. He had also brought a blanket for her and he draped it over her shoulders when she sat down. She managed a smile of thanks. Though a fire was burning in the hearth and the room was warm, she felt shivery; and though the lamplight was dim, everything seemed too bright. On a sudden whim, she pulled the blanket over her head.

Great. I'm the utter nutter in the group therapy group.

She didn't care. She felt immediately better hiding inside the blanket, as if it were a tent. It gave her some distance from the group and allowed her to drift if she didn't want to listen.

Elsie asked them to say a little about who they were as well as their Breathwork experience. "Some of us know each other, but many of us don't." She also invited them to show their artwork if they wished.

Dr Jack began the sharing. Olwen heard the rustle of paper as he showed his red paintings and spoke of passion, fire, blood and war. He described being possessed by what, in retrospect, he understood to be archetypes in his psyche – warrior, shaman, lover, father, king. Some of the archetypes were easier to accept than others. When offered the crown of the king, he had tried to decline. He had never wanted to lead, or to have followers. He preferred the freedom of the lone wolf. But he was told in no uncertain terms that the king has no choice. He must lead when he is called. Those who *want* to be king are rarely fit for the job. The lover archetype was also a poet. He had devised reams of poetry, describing his beloved's hair, mouth, infectious laugh...

There was a momentary pause. Olwen sensed Dr Jack stiffen beside her, as if he had suddenly been struck by something. A suspicion crossed her mind. She had a loud and distinctive laugh. Her face flushed. She was glad she was under the blanket.

He cleared his throat.

"The poetry was beautiful. I wanted to stop the Breathwork and go to my room and write it all down, but I knew I couldn't. And of course now I can't remember a word of it."

"It may come back," Elsie said. "It's there inside you."

The shaman archetype he was also comfortable with and the words that came to him in that role were burned in his mind forever.

"Never have I not existed and never in the future shall I cease to exist. I have been every and all things."

Then the warrior. Even more than the king, he had tried to reject this archetype. He preferred to see himself as a negotiator and peace-maker. He struggled to ward off the warrior, the antithesis of his nature, though he knew it was his shadow, the part of himself he had repressed for years. When he was a kid, he was always fighting...

Dr Jack broke off abruptly. Again, Olwen was acutely aware of his physical reactions. She sensed the tension in his limbs and his desire to flee. She was reminded of the wounded child at the beginning of his session. As his silence lengthened, Elsie spoke up. Her voice echoed with sympathy, but there was also a firmness that surprised Olwen. It was almost stern.

"You don't have to say more than you want to, Jack. You know that. But weren't we just talking about the Gospel of Thomas this afternoon? *If you bring forth what is within you, what you bring forth will free you. If you do not bring forth what is within you, what you do not bring forth will destroy you.*"

"Right," he said, taking a deep breath, but still he didn't speak.

Olwen forgot her own misery as she waited, curious and attentive. She guessed that he was sorting out what he would and wouldn't say.

He spoke carefully. "As Elsie and a few of you know, my mother was a prostitute who worked the waterfront in Halifax, Canada. I was her only child, by one of her clients, an African-American sailor whom I've never been able to locate. My childhood was rough and ready in a neighbourhood that was poor, white, and Roman Catholic. I was the only black and the only bastard. I learned to fight early.

"But let's be clear here. It wasn't just a case of heroically defending my mother's honour. I was a dirty fighter. I liked to hurt, maim, and draw blood. It was the only way I knew how to deal with my anger and my pain. Or at least to ease it. Better to see it on some other kid's face, especially one who was tormenting me. But I also picked on innocents, if my mood was foul enough. That's not something I like to remember. So when I felt the warrior trying to rise, I rejected him with the full force of my will. But the more I denied him, the stronger he became, demanding to be let loose. Then came a time when I had no choice and he broke out!"

"Poor Olwen," Harry remarked. "A berserker on her first watch."

Inside her blanket, Olwen smiled faintly.

"I want to thank Olwen for being such an excellent Watcher... and the facilitators and all of you...for containing the space where my rage could be."

When Dr Jack finished, a silence fell over the group. Eventually Olwen understood that they were waiting for her to speak. She let the blanket fall back and blinked painfully in the light.

"I...I can't..." she whispered.

Elsie's voice was motherly. "Don't upset yourself, *neshomeleh meine*. Maybe you will speak after the others? Wait and see."

Olwen nodded, her eyes wet with tears.

Christy offered to go next. His painting showed two big hands, each holding a large green leaf. On each leaf lay a little baby. The drawing was crude but touching. The babies were naked, one girl and one boy, with huge eyes and laughing faces.

A plumber by trade, Christy wasn't surprised when his Breathwork journey brought him down into the sewers. There he found two babies floating on leaves. They were tiny, like Tom Thumb and Thumbelina. He picked the babies up, resting one in each palm, and tried to cradle them against his chest. They looked up at him with their big blue eyes.

"You didn't give us names," they said.

He knew who they were. He had never forgotten them. He had fathered seven children. Many of the circle knew about Bernie, his little girl who died tragically at twelve years of age of an aneurysm. But there were two others as well. Two children he might have had. One was premature at six months and died soon after; a boy who would have been the first in the family. The other came between the fourth and fifth child. She was full term but stillborn.

"The Missus was heartbroken each time and so was I." Christy's voice grew hoarse. "I'm like the old woman in the shoe. I wanted every one of me kids." He stopped to think. "They're right. We never named them. That was our way, me and the wife. Superstitious, I guess. Not until it was time to baptise them. But I'll give them names, I will. When I go back home, I'll have a talk with herself about it."

Suzume went next. Her picture was a perfect circle filled with a delicate lilac colour. There was nothing else in it. With her hand gripping Christy's, she spoke of how she had always been drawn to mystical things. As a little girl, she had dreams that were more real than her waking life. By the time she was in her early teens she could travel outside her body. All she had to do was sit in a meditation pose and slow her breathing. She loved science fiction and fantasy, and wrote and illustrated her own manga comics. She had no friends. She was too odd and reserved. One day, on her way home from school, she met a young man who was handing out flyers.

That was her introduction to the cult. She was fourteen years old. A year later, she ran away from home, travelling far into the mountains to join one of their communes.

"Renouncing my family was easy," Suzume said in a low voice. Then a sad little shrug. "People from happy families don't run away. Don't join cults."

The focus of her family had always been success, wealth and social status. Her mother had died young, an unhappy woman. Her father was stern and demanding. He never showed affection. If he spoke to her, it was to stress the need for study and good grades. He couldn't understand her spiritual needs any more than he could understand her emotional ones. He was an atheist. When she ran away, he spent a lot of money on detectives to try and find her, but he wasn't able to. It was only after the gas attack in the subways, when the police raided the compound where she lived, that she was found. The police returned her to her father. She was still underage, only sixteen years old.

He threatened to put her into a mental institution if she ran away again. She stayed with him until she was the legal age to leave. It was during that time that the nightmares began, and the headaches and suicidal feelings. She tried to kill herself more than once. When she was first taken from the compound and into custody, the police psychologist told her that most of the women in the cult had been drugged and gang-raped; but she didn't believe them. She didn't remember anything like that.

"We were a family. We did yoga and meditation together. I made friends with girls my own age. It was the first time I ever had friends. I would do anything for them, and they for me. I hate to think that terrible things might have happened to them."

Suzume's voice trailed off. Her features quivered uncontrollably. Olwen found herself thinking of a porcelain doll that had been dropped on the floor, its face seamed with cracks.

Christy put his arm around the girl's shoulders and drew her to him. She pushed her face into his chest.

"Enough," he said softly. "She has said enough."

Elsie agreed and invited the next person to speak.

Olwen struggled to stay present, to hear the stories; but there was too much to take in, too much suffering to assimilate. Her body ached with its own pain. Her mind wanted to shut down. She closed her eyes and let the images and words drift around her, like leaves in a stream.

Penny Li Jau described her grandmother's house in Malacca and the big garden where she played as a child. She loved to suck the nectar out of the *jejarum*, the needle flower, and to smell the sweet hibiscus. That was where her love of nature began. Years later she would become a botanist by profession. But what was this terrible tale she was telling? The murder of her husband in Borneo. A native rights activist, a *persona non grata* with the Malaysian authorities and the timber companies who were denuding the landscape. Penny Li met him when she was doing research in Sarawak on the pitcher plant. A quiet introvert herself, she was drawn to the passion of his beliefs and the fury of his cause. He was the son of a chieftain, educated by missionaries. Because he wouldn't leave the longhouse where he was born, she chose to live among his people when they married. She was the one who found him...not far from the house... beaten to death. It was her first real experience of evil in the world... in human beings. Not only the thugs who did it, but the men in suits who hid behind them.

"I am glad to be soul-partnered with Harry," she said quietly. "He was once a warrior, like my husband, and now he is a gardener, like me."

Harry Rhymer spoke after her. He was educated at Sandhurst and chose a career in the British Army like his father and his grandfather before him. He firmly believed, still did, that nations need armies to protect themselves and to protect the weak from tyrants and terrorists. He considered a military career a noble one, instilling character, honour and self-discipline. Iraq was his first posting. And his first experience of the nightmarish reality of modern warfare. His fellow officers and the young soldiers under him were generally good people, ordinary decent men; but Harry couldn't ignore the increasing number of civilian casualties. Or the orders from above that saw him handing over prisoners to local authorities whom he knew were practising torture and murder. Then came the rumours and finally the reports of rape, torture, and even killings committed by the allied forces. As time passed, he himself began to witness what he could barely acknowledge: his own soldiers giving in to dark urges as they cracked under unbearable pressures and strain. Worst of all was the realisation that no moral force could stop the madness once it was unleashed. You could only fight fire with fire. The day came when he drew his gun on one of his own men and told him he would shoot him if he didn't release the girl he was trying to rape.

"And I should think I would have," Harry said quietly.

Like so many others, he had returned from Iraq with post-traumatic stress disorder. He didn't go into therapy, it wasn't the done thing, not in his family, but he resigned his commission and took to the roads. He became a hobo, travelling the length and breadth of the British Isles. Purely by chance – no, he didn't believe in chance any more – purely by Providence, he found himself in a New Age community in northern Scotland.

"People who know little or nothing about Findhorn dismiss it as a place for hippies, weirdos, and drop-outs. They're always surprised to hear that two out of its three founders served in the British military."

In Findhorn, Harry found healing and a new life, working in the communal garden.

"I hardly thought I could add to this profound and undeserved happiness, when out of the blue, without warning, without even a wish or longing on my part, love entered my life. It was quite a surprise."

He let out a loud laugh.

"Not for a moment had I suspected it, all those years in Sandhurst or in the army. There was not even a hint of it, I can assure you! But there I was, queuing every day in the dining hall, waiting to greet the chap who always gave me an extra dollop of this or that, or some little treat he had made especially for me. *He* knew – and many others did too, apparently – but I was the last to cop it. Then one day I looked into his eyes and there I saw my beloved. It was the last place I had expected to find her – in a man's body!"

Another great laugh. The others couldn't help but join in, even Olwen.

When Thomas Tillman tried to speak, his throat seized up. He kept coughing and choking on his words. Savitri, his partner, fetched him a glass of water. He thanked her and drank deeply, but when he started to speak again, his voice disappeared altogether. He gave Elsie a pitiful look.

The old woman looked pensive. After a while, she spoke. "Unless it's too painful – and here I mean physically – I'm thinking you should keep trying, Tom. Some part of you is fighting to keep your trap shut, but I'll bet my bottom dollar that part doesn't have your best interests at heart. We've all got police patrolling our words and thoughts. Sometimes they're the good guys, protecting us and defending our boundaries. But other times, they're just prison guards. Give it another go. Let's see what happens."

Thomas held up a drawing done in crayon. Crude and childlike, it was a picture of a dolphin swimming in a blue ocean. Overhead shone a bright yellow sun. Thomas strained his neck and gulped at the air. With a mighty effort, he forced the words out.

"My daughter...was twenty-eight...when she died."

He looked at Christy. The two men shared a long gaze.

The death of Thomas's youngest daughter in a plane crash was the great tragedy of his life. Though it was over twenty years ago, he had not recovered from it. The loss of his leg to cancer was minor by comparison. His marriage had ended because he couldn't overcome his grief. His relationships with his other children, his son and his eldest daughter, were seriously damaged. They were bitter – and heartbroken, too, he knew – because his love for them couldn't counter his sorrow. He was wracked with guilt, but remained powerless to change.

"I know a father shouldn't say it, but Clara was my favourite. She was the one who taught me how to love. Today, in my Breathwork journey, she came to me as a dolphin, the animal she loved most in the world. She pleaded with me to enjoy my life. She promised we would meet again. She told me...she told me that she had never doubted my love for her and that my love...sustained her...in her work and in her relationships with men...she said...she said I was a wonderful father and she would have wanted no other."

He broke down and wept openly. Others wept with him, including Olwen.

There were more stories, more tales of the suffering that inevitably accompanies a human life; but she drew the blanket tightly around her to shut them out. She had heard enough. She couldn't bear any more. Leaning back in the armchair, she let herself doze off. It was only when she heard Elsie call her name that she came back to the room and the circle around her. She sat up straight, let the blanket drop away.

"Can you tell us a little about your session? Or perhaps just something about how you feel right now?"

Olwen's eyes flooded with tears. She stared at Elsie mutely and shook her head. Dr Jack leaned towards her, but Olwen raised her hand to stop him.

"Take it slowly," Elsie suggested. "A word at a time if necessary. There's no hurry. We're not going anywhere."

"I...I can't," she said finally. "Another day."

"There's always another day," Elsie agreed.

The meeting was over. Some headed for the door immediately, but others stayed to play pool or chat by the fire. Olwen was one of the first to leave. She was grateful that there was no call for hugs or other signs of affection. She couldn't have borne it. At the same time, she acknowledged that the group's respect for boundaries was an act of love in itself.

Dr Jack caught up with her in the hall. She saw the concern in his eyes.

"A few of us are going for a mindful walk beneath the stars. It'll be slow and no talking. Would you like to join us?"

She managed a smile. He was a good Watcher. A good man.

"I'm going to crawl into bed, curl up in the foetal position, and cry myself to sleep."

He studied her for a moment and smiled back in response.

"You'll feel better in the morning."

"I couldn't feel worse."

....

Back in her room, Olwen found the ceramic water jars warming her sheets.

Bless you, Morag.

She didn't wash, or brush her teeth. She hadn't the energy. Changing into her thick flannel pyjamas, she crawled under the duvet. Sleep washed over her like a dark wave, and she drowned in it.

CHAPTER SEVENTEEN

THIRD NIGHT: THE LABYRINTH

It wasn't a sound that woke her, but a sense of urgency. She sat bolt upright in the bed and stared around her room. The shadows of familiar objects looked strange and vaguely menacing. She slipped out of bed and went to the window nearest her, the one that overlooked the side of the house.

She could hardly believe what she saw. Below, on the lawn, spiralling into the distance was an immense labyrinth. Bone-white walls shone in the moonlight. From her height in the tower, it was easy to see the pattern. The way in was also the way out.

Am I dreaming?

She spun around to look at her bed. It was empty, the duvet tossed aside. She looked back at the white maze. Her fear was now a full-scale panic. She raced to switch on the light. The view beyond her window turned black like dark water.

Jumping into bed, she pulled the duvet around her.

"This isn't happening," she whispered.

She grabbed her laptop and turned it on. The familiar blue light and musical notes of welcome helped a little. She opened her journal, typed quickly.

I don't know what the fuck is going on, but I am terrified.

The wind whistled around the broch. She kept glancing at the dark window, expecting something horrible to appear.

The minutes ticked by. The suspense was excruciating.

Nothing happened.

She began to calm down.

This is ridiculous.

She turned off her computer. With every scrap of courage she could muster, she leaped out of bed, turned off the light, and ran to the window.

A huge sigh of relief. There was nothing below. Only the shadows of lawn and road and the countryside beyond.

Get a grip, girl.

She struggled to think rationally. Considering what she was doing at Dunesfort House, she had to expect this kind of thing. The immense power of suggestion. She had been dreaming beforehand: a big dream, involving a procession at night-time. The people around her had been carrying torches and they were all walking towards a walled labyrinth. When she went to the window she was only half awake. Hardly surprising she saw remnants of her dream in the night. No big deal. It all made sense.

Back in her bed, Olwen eventually drifted into an uneasy sleep.

She stood at the door of the Meeting Room. A murmur of voices could be heard inside. Now the door slowly opened of its own accord. She stepped in. A crowd of men and women were milling about. They were all elderly, with white or grey hair. At first she recognised no one. Then she saw Rose. He was on the far side of the room, shaking hands with people. Everyone was dressed in white, except Rose who wore dark blue trousers and a white shirt with a gold star on the pocket. She looked down at her own clothes. She was wearing white pyjamas. Her feet were bare.

The Meeting Room had changed in appearance. There was none of the elegance or comfort of Dunesfort House. It had a subterranean feel, like the dungeon of a castle. The walls were of the same rough stone as the broch. The ceiling arched upwards, like the roof of a church. The floor was black marble. There was no fireplace. Was she somewhere else? How did she get here?

She went over to greet a group of women.

"I'm Osiris," she heard herself say.

There was no time to say more. Rose was calling out instructions, telling everyone to sit down. He directed the women to one side of the room and the men to the other. The chairs were utilitarian, made of metal, with upright backs and no arms. She thought of the electric chair used for executions. They were arranged in straight rows on either side of a low table. The table was set up like an altar, with little stone statues of gargoyles that crouched amidst phallic-shaped cacti. She found both the statues and the plants disturbing and couldn't look at them. There was a large jug on the table, filled to the brim with a murky liquid, and a stack of small glasses beside it.

Rose stood at the head of the table. She saw he wasn't using a cane. There were other differences as well. His skin was a reddish colour, as if sunburned, and he sported a goatee. Through her mind flashed an image of the fauns and satyrs carved on the mantelpiece in the Dunesfort Meeting Room.

"My name is Rex," he announced. "Welcome to the evening's festivities. Tonight we will be Walking the Labyrinth."

His words rang with portent.

"As always, it will be a perilous venture, but I know you are ready for it. You would not have got here otherwise."

Olwen nodded along with the others. She knew she had passed earlier trials and tests to reach this level.

He began to fill the glasses from the jug and distribute them. Olwen peered into her drink. It was a brownish colour. Surreptitiously, she sniffed it. There was no odour.

When everyone had a glass, they raised their drinks high and let out a cry.

Olwen cried along with them.

"Hye kye! Iakchos! Iakchos!"

Then all swallowed the drink in one gulp.

It was sour and brackish, with a slight hint of honey. Olwen shuddered briefly at the bitterness, but felt no other effect.

Rex, who was Rose, was now handing out gold coins, two to each person. The coins were engraved with the pattern of the labyrinth. Everyone touched the coins to their eyes, then clutched one in each hand. Olwen followed suit.

Rex gave his final instructions.

"It is a confusing path, hard to follow without a thread, but if you can avoid being devoured at the heart of it, you will be led – despite its many twists and turns – back to the beginning, where you will find yourself changed. Transformed. You have been given all the tools you need. Journey well."

She was outside Dunesfort House, alone. Before her rose the great labyrinth. The white stone glittered like frost in the moonlight. The landscape all around was a dark shadow.

Is this a dream? A nightmare?

The last thing she wanted to do was enter the labyrinth. But she knew she could only wake up if she went inside. The entrance was the exit. She had to go in to get out.

Trembling with fear, she stepped in. The walls towered above her, cold and sepulchral. The ground underfoot was icy, made of the same black marble as the floor in the room. But when she moved further in, everything changed. The marble turned to grass and the walls became a high hedge of green. The night scent of damp leaves sweetened the air. The stars shone above.

She followed the path as it wound deeper inside, trying not to think of what lay at the core. What waited for her at the end of her journey.

Then a great *ROAR* shattered the night.

Her knees buckled under her as the truth struck home.

There's a monster in the labyrinth.

What was she thinking? How could she have forgotten the Minotaur? Had she lost her mind? What had possessed her to come here? She stood paralysed, trapped like a helpless animal. What could she do? Where could she go? She struggled desperately to wake up, to free herself from the nightmare, but the more she tried to wake, the more real it felt.

Another bellow rang out. The sound came from somewhere ahead of her. The beast had to be huge to make such a noise. With a squeal of terror, she turned and ran. Back the way she had come. She no longer cared about the rules or what needed to be done. She ran wildly. Heavy footfall came behind her. The ground trembled beneath her feet. A musky scent oiled the air. Her stomach heaved. She knew that smell. Sweat glands and a noisome perfume.

The monster roared a third time. It was moving fast, almost upon her. She needed to hide. She plunged into the hedge, oblivious to the brambles that tore at her skin.

Not a moment too soon, as the Minotaur stomped into view.

He was half man, half animal, with a thick bullish head, curled horns, and cloven hooves. His flat nostrils snorted steam into the cold air. His yellow eyes were small and wicked. A coarse reddish-brown hair covered his body; but jutting out below his waist were gigantic genitals, pale and grotesque.

He came to a stop right beside her. Cowering in the foliage, she jammed her fist into her mouth to keep from crying out. The musky smell was everywhere. He turned his huge head this way and that. Now he sniffed at the air. She almost fainted with horror as she recognised the truth. He was hunting...and she was his prey.

At last he started to move again, but slowly this time, dragging his feet on the ground. He knew she was near.

She forced herself to stay still. All senses alert. Every nerve end twitching, she prepared for flight. Adrenalin coursed through her. She strained to hear the slightest sound or movement. When the next roar erupted, some distance away, she scrambled from her hiding place.

Time to flee.

Away from the beast.

Into the heart of the labyrinth.

She hadn't got far when he bellowed again. The walls of the labyrinth had turned to stone once more and they trembled as he struck them with his fists. Maddened with frustration, he was on the rampage.

Heavy footsteps sounded behind her. He had caught her scent. He was coming after her! Tears streamed down her face as she ran without hope.

Dawn was seeping through the sky. As it crept over the high walls of the labyrinth, it tinted the stone a rosy hue. The night was dispelling. If she could survive till daybreak, she would be safe.

She had reached the heart of the labyrinth. The path ended at what appeared to be a doorway: a tall square of dark space. Two stone figures stood guard on either side of it. As she drew near, she was struck by a blast of cold air. She shivered violently. Bones littered the ground near the threshold. Human bones, gnawed clean. The Minotaur's lair!

She was about to turn and run again when she recognised the sentinels who guarded the door. Morag's brothers, carved from the same white stone as the labyrinth! They wore chainmail; and great wings protruded from their backs to touch the ground. Each held out a hand, palm upwards, as if requesting an offering.

Did one of them blink at her? There, he did it again! Was it the statue of Calum? Now he lowered his gaze to stare pointedly at her hands. Only then did she remember the gold coins. She was clenching them so tightly they had marked her palms with the sign of the labyrinth. On instinct, she placed a coin in the hand of each sentinel. The effect was instant. Colours bled into the white stone as the statues turned to flesh and blood. The one who had blinked at her smiled briefly. It was, indeed, Calum.

She was about to question him when a roar broke out behind her. She almost collapsed with shock. The monster had found her! Sick with terror, she faced him. He was only feet away. His stench was overpowering. The thick lips parted in an evil grin. The teeth were jagged and broken. Most horrible of all was his stare – utterly cold and impersonal. He didn't know who she was and he didn't care, yet he would make her suffer unspeakable agonies.

He stepped slowly towards her, savouring her fear.

She pleaded with Morag's brothers, begging shamelessly.

"Please help me! I don't know how I got here. I didn't choose to come. I'm no hero!"

The twins exchanged looks.

"It's not our place," Ruairi said gruffly to his brother.

"She cleaned the stables without being asked," Calum argued. "We are in her debt."

He was already reaching out for her. His great wings trailed behind him, a swan's span of feathered strength.

"If you can't fight," Calum said gently, "take flight."

"Yes!" she said, weeping with relief. "Yes!"

The Minotaur let out a screech of rage.

Olwen screamed as he bore down on her. It was Calum who stepped between them and Ruairi who caught hold of her. Wings beat the air with a thunderous noise, as Ruairi lifted her from the ground.

A monstrous hand gripped her leg. The fingernails dug into her skin. They were curled and black with dirt. She screamed again.

The hand let go as Calum attacked.

Ruairi carried her high into the air. For a moment they hovered above the labyrinth. The white walls shone in the early sunlight. At the heart of the design wrestled beast and angel. The monster clawed at Calum's wings. Olwen heard the crack of bones, saw red blood seep into the pure-white feathers.

"*No!*" she cried.

She woke with a great shout. Tiny feathers fluttered in the air. She was clutching her pillow. Leaping out of the bed, she raced to the window.

The lawn was empty. No sign of a labyrinth. A red glow suffused the sky. Sunrise. Despite the early hour, she refused to go back to bed. She was too afraid to sleep. While she was no stranger to nightmares and night terrors, this was the worst she had ever had.

I can't stay here.

CHAPTER EIGHTEEN

FEATHERS FALL AROUND YOU

Olwen woke with a start. She was curled up in the big armchair by the hearth. *What?* The last thing she remembered was crawling into bed. Did she sleepwalk in the night? Her head ached. Every part of her was sore. Her stomach felt sick. She glanced at the clock on the mantel. She had missed breakfast. She was also late for the first session of the day. A quick glance in the mirror confirmed she looked as bad as she felt. Her skin was blotchy. There were dark circles under her eyes. She held out her hands. They were shaking. She knew the signs. It must have been a long night of terrors.

Vague and menacing images crept to the edges of her mind. Some were illumined by flashes of clarity, like lightning in a horror film. A room filled with strangers. A dark drink. A bone-white labyrinth. A monster chasing her. Nothing new as far as her nightmares went, but somehow the after-effects were worse. Was it because of the Breathwork? Or Dunesfort House itself?

She took a quick shower, threw on jeans and a cotton shirt, pulled her hair back into a bun. She hadn't the time or energy to do more.

Downstairs, she found the dining room empty. The tables had been cleared and set for lunch. Her heart sank. She needed food and coffee. Strong coffee.

Mrs Macleod entered the room. She looked concerned.

"*Ciamar a thà tù?*"

"*Níl mé go maith,*" Olwen answered honestly. "*Go dona,* in fact. I feel awful."

"Sit you down." She nodded towards Olwen's usual table. "I'll bring you something to break your fast."

"You're an angel!"

Amusement flickered in the housekeeper's eyes. An image flickered in Olwen's memory. Ruairi and Calum with wings! What on earth was she doing dreaming of Morag's brothers?!

It wasn't long before Mrs Macleod returned with a pot of freshly brewed coffee and a plate of soda farls. The farls were warm, and there was a dish of butter and another of home-made jam. Olwen wolfed down the lot. Her eyes closed with relief as she drank the coffee, dark and strong. But once her meal was finished, she was faced with the dilemma of what to do next. She had already checked the schedule. The morning session was listed as "The Great Journey: A Talk", taking place in the Meeting Room. Was it a lecture by Rose or a group discussion? Either way, she was reluctant to go. Another image flared in her mind. The Director with a red face, goatee, and a gold star on his chest. He was in her dream, too!

She felt the shadow of some threat hovering over her. What did she really know about these people? Suzume had been a member of a dangerous cult in Japan. Now the girl was at Dunesfort House. Out of the frying pan and into the fire? Olwen herself had had some experience with cults when she was a teenager, hitch-hiking around North America in the 1970s. Homeless and penniless, she and her young companions, when not panhandling in the streets, often joined religious groups for food and board. But while her friends feigned interest in the Hare Krishnas, Zen Buddhists and various Christian sects, Olwen had been truly interested. She was a spiritual seeker from a very young age. As a child she had loved the Greek and Roman myths as well as the Roman Catholic rites she had grown up with. When she was twelve, she bought a statue of the Buddha and burned incense to it. "She's worshipping a graven idol up there," her mother complained to her father. "It's just a phase," was his response. And indeed it was, but when she eventually went to university her subjects included theology and comparative religion. Was it any wonder that she found herself in this bizarre neverland?

Olwen looked out the window. She felt trapped, claustrophobic. The sky had clouded over. It was drizzling rain. A walk didn't appeal. Still undecided, she made her way to the Meeting Room. She stood at the door. A murmur of voices could be heard inside. Her heart beat rapidly. She was overcome with a sense of déjà vu. This was how her nightmare began!

Turning on her heels, she hurried away. Rain or no, she was going outside. A visit to the stables would calm her down. With any luck, she might catch the horses at home. She pulled on a pair of wellies in the porch.

Crossing the courtyard, she spotted one of the twins heading into the greenhouse. Was it Calum or Ruairi? He carried a bucket. There was something odd about him. She stopped in her tracks when she realised what it was. One of his arms was bound in a sling. A cold chill ran through her, though she didn't know why.

She was standing there in a daze when Dr Jack came up to her.

"You were missed at breakfast. And at the discussion. You would have liked it. Life, the universe, and everything. 'The whole catastrophe' as Kazantzakis put it."

"I loved *Zorba the Greek*...and *The Last Temptation of Christ*."

"We have the same excellent taste."

His tone was warm, his look solicitous. She felt a pang of guilt over her suspicions. How could she even think he'd be part of something sinister?

"I had a bit of a rough night," she told him, her smile wan. "Up for a walk?"

"The legs could do with a stretch."

They left the courtyard and strolled along the road that bordered the moor. The rain had stopped, but the air was cool and damp. To their left rolled fields of rough grass and patches of rock. To their right stretched the precipice and the grey waters of the loch. Seagulls skimmed the waves or circled overhead with lonely cries.

They hadn't gone far when they came across a clump of white feathers in a mess of dried blood. Olwen stopped and stared.

"What happened here?"

"Nature," said Dr Jack.

"Good answer," she murmured.

She told him about her nightmare, that is, the parts she could remember. She was still putting the pieces together: the strange crowd in the Meeting Room, the different version of Rose, the dark drink, the monster in the labyrinth. She didn't mention the appearance of Morag's brothers; too personal somehow.

Dr Jack listened keenly and didn't speak until she was finished.

"Breathwork is a powerful practice," he said. "It brings up a lot of unconscious material. It lets us bypass the thought police, the censors that guard the borders of the deepest and darkest parts of our psyche."

Olwen let out a noise of exasperation. "I can't believe there's any more shite down there to dig up."

He laughed. "I understand your point, but will you consider this? The 'talking cure' of analysis or psychotherapy can clear trauma from the mind and the emotions; but there is a school of thought that says this is not enough. Many of us believe that the material is still held in the body, as a physiological reality. For example, there is compelling evidence to show that abuse in early childhood causes physical damage to the amygdala. This is a pre-verbal phenomenon, outside and beyond the range of words and cognition. The amygdala can flood the neocortex with primal and non-verbal memories of abuse. The talking cure *cannot* clear this. It's simply not able to. Only bodywork can clear what is stored in the body."

Olwen stopped in her tracks. A little burst of light exploded in her mind, even as some invisible weight seemed to shift.

"Are you saying that the monster is a *physical* memory rather than an emotional or psychological one?"

"Something like that. It would appear the Breathwork has released the memory from your cells so that you can deal with it. I would also suggest that the labyrinth is, in fact, your body."

Olwen gasped. Her body, her psyche, her life.

"Yes," she murmured. "*Yes.*"

He was waiting for her to say more, but she had no intention of doing so. At least not yet.

They left the road and trudged over the boggy ground. Their boots squelched in the soft earth. A hare shot out from an underground hole and dashed across the moor. With wordless agreement, they turned full circle and headed back for the house.

"It was certainly a big dream," he said, after a while. "You'll have a lot of them here. The drink you took reminds me of *Alice in Wonderland*. The little bottle that said 'Drink Me'. But it also sounds like ayahuasca or yagé, as some call it."

"Yagé!"

William Burroughs was another of Olwen's favourite authors. She had read *The Yagé Letters* which chronicled correspondence between Burroughs and Allen Ginsberg. The letters presented their very different experiences with the psychotropic drink brewed from a vine in the South American rainforest.

"Something you've tried yourself?" he asked.

"Oh god, no. I'd be far too much of a coward. Alcohol was always my drug of choice."

"Interesting that Rose was there. I like how your unconscious renamed him 'Rex'. The King."

She caught the mischief in his tone. "That kind of remark is called shit-stirring in Ireland."

He laughed. "America, too."

They were almost at the house. With a faint shiver of unease, she realised they had traced some of the pattern of the labyrinth, treading over the same ground where it had stood in her dream.

"This place is really getting under my skin," she admitted. "It's triggering off a lot of paranoia."

Dr Jack raised an eyebrow. "You mean we might be some kind of devil-worshipping cult? And Rose is a necromancer?"

"Exactly."

"How do you live with a head like that?"

"Most of the time I'm on my own...writing."

"No surprise it's fantasy."

They were still laughing when they entered the house. The gong was sounding for lunch. Olwen didn't feel like eating. She needed to rest. More than that, she needed to think and to write. She wanted to record her dream before she lost the details.

"I'm not hungry," she told him. "I had breakfast a little while ago. I'll catch up with you later. Give my love to Elsie."

And she slipped away before he could respond.

Back in her room, Olwen felt the chill creep through her body. She sat cross-legged on the bed, with the duvet around her. Her teeth had begun to chatter. She wasn't surprised. Regardless of all the therapy she had done, this particular effect had never gone away: the invasion of cold that accompanied certain memories of her childhood. But she would not react in her usual way. She would not huddle under a blanket until it passed.

She reached for the laptop. Her muscles were beginning to lock. Her breath clouded the air, as if the temperature of the room had lowered drastically. Was this the root of possessions and hauntings?

There was no doubt in her mind that she herself was changing the atmosphere around her. The cold was issuing from her own body.

Though her fingers were going numb, she typed furiously.

Uncle B was a big man, even as adults went. When I re-lived the memories in therapy, oh so long ago, finally admitting them, they didn't carry the direct experience of the senses. That smell. His aftershave mixed with his body sweat. I'll never forget the stink. And omigod, I know why the Minotaur's gaze was so horrible. That look in his eyes, that impersonal and callous appraisal. Ultimately that is the paedophile's attitude towards his victim. Though he may tell himself that he loves children, the child knows the truth. It's the same way torturers dehumanise their victims and don't see a real person in front of them. When all is said and done, the core truth is this: the child senses that, as far as the abuser is concerned, she is just something to use and discard.

"That makes sense," Olwen murmured to herself, as she finished her entry.

For the child, being sexually abused by an adult is a form of demonic possession.

CHAPTER NINETEEN

RIDE A PALE HORSE

It was a while before Olwen realised that someone was knocking on her door. She had dozed off, with her back to the headboard. Her laptop had turned itself off. In a panic, she hid it under her pillow.

"Come in!" she called, clambering off the bed.

When no one entered, she opened the door.

Mrs Macleod stood in the hallway, holding a tray with lunch. Olwen started to apologise for causing her trouble, when Morag cut her off.

"This is a bribe, *dawtie*. What do the Americans say? There's nae such thing as a free lunch."

Olwen laughed and made room on the desk for the food. The housekeeper sat in the armchair by the fire as Olwen tucked in. The soup was home-made minestrone peppered with chilli, served with crusty bread, a slab of crumbly cheese, and a dish of olives.

"Delicious," she mumbled, her mouth full.

"Calum tells me you are a horsewoman," Morag began.

"Yes, I am. In fact, I was going to the stables earlier to see if I might meet the horses but I..." An image of Calum and his wounded arm flashed through her mind. "I got side-tracked."

The housekeeper studied her a moment. Olwen wasn't able to hold the scrutiny of those dark-brown eyes for long. She turned back to her meal.

Morag continued. "Perhaps I might ask you to exercise the mare today? Calum has injured himself. Ruairi cannae ride and nor can I. We could get a man from the village, but Director Rose doesn't like to bring others onto the grounds once a circle has formed. He insists he can look after the two horses himself, but I am not happy with this. He is in enough pain and shouldn't ride at all. I'm not one to request favours but..."

"I'd love to!" Olwen burst in. "Please, it's hardly a favour, unless one to *me*. There's nothing I'd want more. And for godsake, you've been so kind to me in so many ways."

The housekeeper smiled and raised her hand.

"We will agree that we are friends and nothing is owed."

"*Cinnte*," said Olwen. "Do you have riding boots I might borrow?"

"Calum's own should fit you. We'll have the mare saddled and ready by two o'clock."

Olwen was quick to object. "I'd rather groom and saddle her myself. The best way to become acquainted before we ride."

"*Glè mhat*," said the housekeeper with a satisfied noise. "I'll make sure he hears of it."

Something told Olwen that Morag wasn't referring to Calum.

"Do you mean Rose? He isn't happy that I'll be riding her?"

Morag's smile was wry. "He is a stubborn man. The horses are his pride and joy. But once he is assured you are an accomplished horsewoman, he will rest easy."

When the housekeeper left, Olwen changed into a pair of stronger jeans and a woollen sweater with sleeveless jacket. She was in high spirits – well rested, well fed, and now a chance to ride!

There was no one around when Olwen reached the stables. She was delighted. She wanted to greet the horses on her own. They were magnificent. Their ease with each other told her they had been long-standing companions. Their names were carved into the beams above their boxes. *LORD DONN. EPONA.* Only now did Olwen see the lettering and she wondered how she could have missed it before.

The gelding was restless at the approach of a stranger. Olwen spoke in low, unhurried tones to reassure him. She gave him time to get used to her. Quietly praising him for being friendly, she stroked his nose. She could see he was intelligent, but like most thoroughbreds he was likely to be highly strung and excitable. Though he took a while, he eventually relaxed in her presence. She had passed the first test.

She went next to Epona. Mares were usually patient animals, but they could be tricky and skittish. At first glance, Epona looked obliging.

"You are a beauty, aren't you?" Olwen said softly, stroking her nose.

She stared into the mare's eyes, hoping to judge her temperament. Much of what she saw pleased her, but there was something else there as well. A gleam of mischief?

A bucket of brushes had been left outside the door. As the horse was well-groomed, all that was needed was a superficial effort; it was the handling that mattered. Olwen moved into Epona's box, keeping up a stream of friendly chat.

"What do you think? Will we get along? Hmm? Will we make a good team?"

She began with the mane, brushing it down in smooth strokes. Then she moved over the body, the hocks, and finally the tail. Her own intense joy at grooming such a beautiful creature was undoubtedly passed to the mare. Epona watched her contentedly, remaining still until the job was done.

It was easy to find the right saddle in the tack room. The mare's name was tooled into the green leather, along with a spiral pattern painted in gold leaf. And the reins were plaited with gold thread.

Olwen had never seen such gear: fit for royalty!

She had no trouble saddling Epona, but the moment of truth would come when it was time to mount. She was about to lead her out of the stable when Ruairi arrived.

His eyes widened as he took stock of Epona and he let out a grunt of approval.

"She be *foliar*," he said suddenly. "A true mare. First filly foal out of the first filly foal for seven generations."

"Like the seventh son of a seventh son?" Olwen could hardly believe what she was hearing.

"Nought can harm a true mare. Ye can take her out at any hour and ye'll be safe. She will fight off any evil that comes at ye."

Olwen was utterly thrilled and grateful to be told these things.

Ruairi handed her a pair of riding boots. Though well worn, they were finer than any she had ever seen. Handmade, of a rich, dark leather, they had their own tooled design: leaves or wings, she couldn't be certain.

"I...I'm honoured," she stuttered.

Ruairi didn't reply. He gazed at Lord Donn, who was watching over the half-door.

"They gendered many a fine foal together, before..." Ruairi broke off darkly.

Olwen felt a cold grip on her heart. A tragic tale hovered over the stables. She was unsure whether or not she wanted to hear it, but she knew she wouldn't, couldn't ask him. She thought of Rose's lame leg. Were the two injuries connected?

Ruairi disappeared as she sat down to pull on the boots. They fitted her like a glove. Freshly polished, they gave off a lovely lemony smell. It was only when Ruairi returned with the gelding's saddle that she realised she wasn't riding alone. Her heart jumped into her throat. Morag said this twin didn't ride. That meant...

Damn, I should have known!

Rose was waiting in the yard, leaning on his cane. He wore jeans and a chequered shirt. She cringed inwardly when she spotted the red kerchief around his neck.

He greeted Olwen with his usual stiffness, but his attention was on the mare. He and Epona touched noses. Then he placed his head against hers as he petted her lovingly, all the time whispering soft words.

Olwen was surprised, not only by his tone but by the language he used.

"Does she understand *dansk?*"

It was his turn to be surprised.

"You know the language?"

"Jeg taler lidt dansk."

Rose wasn't able to hide his astonishment. "I wasn't aware you had a connection to Denmark."

"Why would you be?" She took perverse pleasure in the fact he was obviously thrown. Something out of his control. She barely contained her smirk as she answered boldly, "I had a Danish lover."

"I see," he said, quickly losing interest.

He sounded dismissive, judgemental. She felt it like a slap in the face.

Sensitive to the mood of the two beside her, Epona began to fidget. Olwen walked her a short distance away and prepared to mount. But the moment her foot reached for the stirrup, the mare took a step sideways. Olwen stumbled. She swore under her breath. Here was the mischief she had detected in the mare's eyes.

"Badly done, Epona," she said sternly. "You know better than that."

Rose glanced over at them. His tone was cool.

"Wait till Ruairi comes. He can hold her for you."

Olwen felt her blood rise. Her face grew hot.

"Is she that poorly trained that she won't stand for mounting?"

It was his turn to redden. He spoke sharply in Danish, but not to Olwen. The mare stiffened, as if coming to attention, and stood stock still.

Satisfied, Olwen slipped her foot into the stirrup and took her seat in a quick leap.

"Well done, lady," she murmured in the horse's ear, adding a friendly pat.

She knew well that the mare was simply obeying Rose's command, but it was best to avoid an adversarial relationship. The move paid off. Epona let out a friendly snort and remained at a standstill.

While Olwen was busy with the mare, Ruairi had led the gelding from the stables and helped Rose to mount. The Director sat tall in the saddle, with no hint of lameness or pain.

"Will you follow me?" he asked her.

Olwen shrugged. "You're the one who knows the terrain. Lead on, Macduff."

"And damn'd be him that first cries, 'hold enough!'"

She was taken aback a moment, then realised he was finishing the Shakespearean quote she had used. She couldn't help but be amused and just a little impressed.

Before they left the stable yard, she drew up beside Ruairi.

"Tell Calum thank you...for the boots...and...I...I hope his arm..."

He returned her look without blinking.

"No thanks are needed or welcomed."

Olwen kept a loose rein as they set out. She felt Epona's appreciation in her easy gait. Agile and sure-footed, the mare moved with energetic strides. Despite the earlier incident, Olwen couldn't fault her. She was perfection in motion.

Ahead of them, the two males were a picture of unity. Moving further down the road, they began to trot and then to canter. Olwen kept pace, wishing they would veer off into open country. She assumed they had to go slow due to Rose's lameness. She was already plotting how to get away from him and ride alone, when he halted and waited for her to draw up alongside him.

"Will you gallop?" he asked.

"I'd love to. But what about your leg?

"That is my concern, not yours," he said curtly.

"Let's gallop then," she said in the same tone.

And they were off.

As soon as they left the road, a light touch of Olwen's heels encouraged the mare to canter. Epona, too, had apparently been yearning for speed, though she had shown no sign of it till now. She dropped her head and broke into a gallop. *Ag dul ar cosa in airde.* "Going with legs high", as it was said in Irish. Her hooves seemed to barely touch the earth.

When they passed Rose and Lord Donn, the gelding flattened his ears with indignation. The chase was on. Lord Donn had the advantage of power and drive, but the mare was quicker to turn. Each time the gelding drew near, Olwen would charge away in a different direction. Not even her own beloved horse had responded with such skill.

The Hebridean countryside opened before them: vast tracts of moorland speckled with wildflowers. In the distance ranged the heather-clad mountains of Harris. Knowing the land well, the horses had no trouble with the uneven ground. At one point, when they were neck and neck, Olwen glanced over at Rose. He was leaning forward in the saddle. His face shone with a fierce joy. The ascetic beauty of his features caught her by surprise.

They rode long and hard. Both horses seemed tireless. But there came a time when Olwen noticed that Epona's neck was lathered. She drew gently on the reins. The mare slowed willingly to a trot. Rose and Lord Donn followed suit and they rode side by side. Now Olwen realised that she, too, was exhausted. Beside her, Rose looked strained. He was clenching his teeth. Was he in pain? But why hadn't he called to her to slow down? She was angry with herself for being so thoughtless, but also with him for being so proud. A shadow had fallen over the brightness of the day, the joy of the ride tainted.

"We should go back," she said, in a shorter tone than she had intended.

He nodded without speaking, his face a mask.

Turning the horses, they rode for Dunesfort House.

CHAPTER TWENTY

THE HARROWING OF HELL

By the time Olwen had showered and changed, she was late for the afternoon session. A quick check of the schedule told her that something called "Soul Retrieval" was taking place in the Trance Room. She raced down the stairs. But as soon as she entered the room she saw there was no need to rush. The others were drifting in slowly, in twos and threes. Was there some reluctance to do this practice? Or was the intensity of the programme beginning to wear people down? She herself felt refreshed and invigorated after the ride. Ready for anything.

The mats were laid out in a similar arrangement to the Breathwork session, radiating outwards from the wall. But now they were arranged in pairs and there were no blankets or cushions. Beside the mats were pens and notepads, eye shades, and rattles of various kinds, including hand-painted gourds and maracas.

Olwen felt a shiver of excitement. Something new again!

Some of the mats were already occupied by their respective couples. Olwen was surprised and disappointed – not to mention, jealous – to see Dr Jack with Euphémie. Had he chosen her or she, him? At the centre of the room, Roy was checking people's names on a clipboard. She soon saw that all the new partners belonged to the same small group in which they had shared their Breathwork experience. Dr Jack was with Euphémie, Tenzin Dawa with Suzume,

Christy with Penny Li, and Thomas Tillman with Elsie. Who was left? Who was she paired with? She assumed that Rose was the matchmaker, and once again wondered what criteria he used to make his decisions. An image of a chess master carefully moving his pieces came to mind. *Magister Ludi.* But the Director was nowhere to be seen and Roy had taken over his duties. A pang of guilt shot through her. Was Rose in too much pain after his ride?

Before she could approach Roy about her partner, Savitri came up to her. As usual, the older woman wore a beautiful sari.

"We are together in this," she said to Olwen. "I hope you are not disappointed?"

"I'm delighted!" said Olwen and she meant it. She had always been drawn to all things Indian – music, food, literature, films. Though she had yet to travel there, it was on her list of places to see before she died. One of her dearest friends in Toronto was a Canadian-born Tamil. "You might be sorry yourself. I've never done any of this before. You're getting an absolute beginner."

The older woman replied with an easy smile. "In this work it is the heart not the head that matters. I have done soul retrieval many times and yet I always find it a challenge. Come, let us take our place and make our preparations."

When everyone had settled down with their partners, Roy asked who was new to Soul Retrieval. Olwen and a few others raised their hands.

"I'll give ye's a wee introduction then," he said. "You've all experienced mythic journeying from your first day here. Soul retrieval is the same with a few added extras. You'll find it easier, because you're journeying for someone else instead of yourselves. We all seem to be able to go that extra mile for others. At the same time, I'd ask ye to keep in mind that it's not you but your animal guide that's doing the retrieval and you are but their instrument."

Roy's Ulster accent lilted musically. Olwen noted that his tones and modulations were a milder version of a Pentecostal preacher.

His background perhaps? But what bizarre circumstances could have brought him to Dunesfort House? She found herself wishing that he was the Director. He was so much warmer and more personable than Rose.

Roy continued: "Soul retrieval is all about soul loss: the loss of a part of your spirit through trauma of any kind – incest, sexual abuse, violence, bereavement, accidents, disease, surgery, miscarriage, abortion, job loss, love loss...the lot. It can occur at any age, even in the womb. Assaults on the mind or body will catapult a fragment of the soul or psyche out of the body that houses it. Mircea Eliade refers to the 'rape of the soul' and talks of soul parts straying away or even being stolen.

"Common indications of soul loss are a sudden onset of apathy or listlessness, feeling only half alive, the desire to sleep all the time, depression, and so forth. Physical illness or disease can be a symptom also.

"Modern psychology believes that trauma causes parts of the personality to split off and be lost or buried in the subconscious or unconscious. Their methods of retrieval include analysis, dream interpretation, association, and other talking techniques. The shamanic view is that the split-off parts are lost to other realities or worlds which can be described and mapped. These may be fearful places like hell realms or beautiful worlds of peace and joy."

Olwen was listening, enthralled. She had always believed in other worlds, multiple dimensions and alternate realities, but here was an entirely new way of viewing them.

Roy gave them specific instructions. Partners were to lie down beside each other, touching lightly with arms, elbows or feet.

"Don't embrace," he warned them. "The body might set its own agenda, seeking lover, parent, child...or maybe even something to eat."

There was a ripple of laughter.

"I'd also suggest you exchange objects with each other, a piece of jewellery or an item of clothing. You can look for that object in the other reality to confirm the identity of the soul part. Only one retrieval is done at a time, so decide which of you is to journey first. As in Breathwork, you can use eye shades or a scarf, or simply close your eyes. There will be drums and drones to send you off. The one for whom the retrieval is being done is not to journey, but should try to remain awake and still.

"Remember to call on your animal guides. Name the person on whose behalf you're journeying and state your mission clearly. Ask your guide where and how to find the soul part that needs to be retrieved. Keep your focus at all times. As most of you know, it's easy to be distracted in non-ordinary reality. There's so much to see! Follow the advice of your guides at all times.

"For the more experienced, I'll say a word about vital essences. These are core parts of the soul stolen by malign forces or driven to impossible distances by the most extreme of traumas. To retrieve a vital essence is the work of advanced shamans. It can be perilous and calls for great skill. Because the soul part is held against its will, it must be abducted rather than retrieved. This is a mission into enemy-occupied territory or, from the psychological point of view, into the darkest regions of the shadow of the collective unconscious. You will come under attack. The danger is real. Your guide's assistance is crucial here. Anyone new needn't worry. You won't be expected to do this kind of work.

"What happens after you've located the soul part? It's not unusual to encounter reluctance. There might even be anger or resentment. Remember, it left for good reason. In some cases, the soul part has fled to such a wonderful place, it won't want to leave it. Speak gently but firmly on behalf of your partner, say how much he or she misses this part of themselves and how happy they would be to have it back. Argue your case. Explain that the person has changed and has improved or corrected whatever it was that caused the loss. Also reassure the soul part, especially if it is a child, that it will be loved and protected. Negotiate if you need to, make promises if you must. Everyone here is committed to the work of wholeness and healing, so you can confidently represent your partner in this regard.

"The bottom line is this: except in the case of a vital essence abduction, the soul part *must* agree to return. Once it does, your animal guide will help you carry it home. When your mission is completed, sit up and kneel near your partner. Blow the soul part into the heart and then the crown of the head. You might whisper, 'Welcome home', or some other friendly greeting. Then use as many rattles as you need to seal the soul part in. Finally, lie down again beside your partner and wait for the second retrieval to begin.

"There will be a few minutes' rest between retrievals. Please refrain from talking, no matter how tempting it may be. There will be time for that later. Don't break the altered state you are both in. Move on to the second retrieval, following the same process. When everyone is done, the drums will finish with a fast-paced battering to call you back. Then, when you are ready, you can write down your experience in the notebooks provided. You will present your partner with the notes you have made. You are free to read them but, again, please try to speak as little as possible. The desire to talk is actually the mind seeking escape and distraction. Stay in the depths a little longer. There will be plenty of time to speak later. The schedule is clear for the rest of the day. Take a moment now to decide who will go first. Then good luck to all of you and journey well."

Olwen assumed she would do the second retrieval as she was the beginner. But then she noticed how wan and tired Savitri looked. There were dark circles under her eyes.

"Will I go first?" Olwen asked her.

Savitri's relief was plain.

"I would be most grateful. I am anxious that I might not be able to do a good job for you, as I am feeling very low right now. I did not sleep well last night." The Indian woman looked pained and apologetic. "I do not wish to put you in this position, but I trust what happens in the Work and I know you will do well for me. After the retrieval, I will have more energy to journey for you."

Olwen nodded nervously. She had actually hoped that Savitri would decline the offer.

They exchanged items of jewellery, as Roy had suggested. Savitri gave Olwen a gold bangle engraved with a design that looked something like a wheel. She, in turn, gave Savitri the only ring she wore, a band of silver set with her birthstone of turquoise.

They lay down together, backs to the floor, touching at the elbows and ankles.

Olwen donned the eye shades provided and tried to relax. But she needn't have worried. As soon as the drums and drones sounded, she began to journey. It was as if her psyche had been yearning to do this again. Was that Savitri's perfume wafting towards her? Traces of jasmine and lemongrass. With a shock of delight, she found herself transported to another place.

It was a warm dusky evening, with the slightest touch of a breeze. The sun had just set. She was standing in front of a wooden door set in a stone wall. Beside her was a schoolgirl of about nine or ten. The girl wore a blue uniform over a crisp white blouse and white ankle socks with black patent shoes. Her jet-black hair was tied in two long braids with big blue bows the same colour as her uniform. Olwen knew immediately it was the young Savitri, even before she spotted the gold bangle on her wrist. The girl smiled shyly up at her and took her hand.

They went through the door and into a long entranceway. On either side were shelves filled with rows of shoes. Little Savitri removed her shoes and socks and put them away carefully. Olwen followed suit. Only then did she realise that she was dressed all in white, in kurta pyjamas. She padded barefoot after the girl.

They entered a courtyard filled with people of all ages. It was evidently a shrine, shaded by banyan trees and strung with coloured lights. At the centre of the yard was a marble tomb, half-hidden under a mountain of fragrant blossoms. The scent of flowers and incense was overwhelming. Olwen and little Savitri joined the queue of devotees. When their turn came, each knelt at the tomb, resting her head and arms upon it.

Olwen felt the cool stone beneath her cheek and inhaled the delicious smell of the flowers. A feeling of peace and well-being came over her. She could have stayed there forever. But the schoolgirl nudged her gently. It was time to go.

Collecting their shoes, they went out into the bustling streets of a large town. Olwen's senses were assaulted on every side. The pavements were crowded with people. The roads were blocked with gaily painted cars and trucks, rickety buses, motorised rickshaws, scooters, and motorcycles. Beggars reached out with trembling hands. Shops displayed shimmering fabrics, jewellery, and exotic ornaments. Stalls sold every kind of fruit, food sizzling in pans, sweetcakes and flowers. She knew, of course, that she was in India.

They passed a group of women working with picks and shovels. Olwen had read about India's female labourers who came from the lowest castes. In shabby but colourful saris, with cheap bangles on their wrists, they sweltered in the midday heat, breaking up rubble and carrying it away in heavy buckets. They worked long hours for the smallest of wages. Their lifespan was half that of their peers in less onerous jobs. Yet they smiled as they worked and chatted happily amongst themselves.

One of the women pointed to Savitri. The schoolgirl pretended she didn't see her and tugged at Olwen's hand to make her walk faster. The woman called out even as she elbowed her neighbour, but the other woman shook her head and told her to stop. Olwen studied the woman who had hushed her friend. She was the image of the grown Savitri, but with telling differences. This woman's features were coarsened by outdoor work; and the dullness in her eyes spoke of a life of hardship and resignation. Still, there was no sign of bitterness. She glanced shyly at her daughter with love and pride.

Olwen looked down at Savitri. The little girl was fighting to keep back her tears. Her look was rife with shame and guilt. Olwen understood immediately, not only how the little girl felt, but why she had lost a part of her spirit here.

"You're only a child," Olwen said gently. "Children can't help their feelings. They're easily embarrassed and don't know what to do about it. Your mother doesn't judge you for that. She understands. She loves you and is very proud of you. Believe me, Savitri, I know what I'm talking about. I'm a mother. Nothing my daughter could say or do would make me love her less. Will you return with me? We can talk about this together, you and I and big Savitri."

To Olwen's surprise and consternation, the child shook her head.

"We can't go back yet. There is another part you must save. I promise I'll return if you succeed."

Then the child disappeared.

And the scene changed abruptly. Olwen stood on the side of a snow-covered mountain. It was one of a range that extended as far as the eye could see. The sky was lit by a wintry sun. The icy cold was a shock. Still dressed in her light clothes, she shuddered from head to toe and her teeth chattered. What was going on? There was no sign of little Savitri. This wasn't the kind of journey Roy had talked about. In a moment of sheer panic, she realised her error. She had forgotten to call on her animal guide. She had been working on her own.

"Wolf!" she shouted at the top of her lungs. "Where are you?"

The wind howled in response. A blizzard whirled around her.

Something large and white came towards her: a sacred cow with garlands of flowers around her horns. She looked unaffected by the storm.

"Have you seen the wolf?" Olwen asked her. "I'm so sorry. I'm new to this. I've done it all wrong!"

The golden eyes of the cow shone with compassion. She breathed on Olwen, a warm green grassy breath. Olwen felt heat course through her body. Her muscles relaxed. The golden eyes continued to hold her gaze as the cow transformed into a white wolf.

"There is no need to apologise," she told Olwen. "But I could not come until you called me."

Olwen threw her arms around the wolf's neck and spoke hurriedly. "The child Savitri says there is another soul part we must rescue."

The wolf's voice deepened as she nuzzled Olwen's face. "Are you willing to go to any length? It will not be easy."

Olwen didn't hesitate. "Whatever must be done."

The wolf threw back her head and let out a howl that rose above the howl of the storm. Out of the blizzard came the rest of the pack. There were at least a dozen. The wolf barked at Olwen to climb on her back.

They raced above the storm, following a path that wound over the mountain. Below her, Olwen could see tortured shapes in the spirals of snow. Shrieks rang out. Snow devils? The wolf ran along a causeway covered with frost. It spanned a snow-filled ravine that sheered to dizzy drops below.

Now the wolf let out a bark and Olwen saw it ahead: a fortress in the clouds, constructed of glass. Or was it ice? She caught sight of a tiny figure in the window of the highest tower. In that moment she realised the truth. This wasn't the regular retrieval that Roy had spoken of. This was an abduction. She had been called upon to rescue a vital essence.

There was no time to wonder or worry about it. The fortress was surrounded by a wall. The gates were closed.

"Over the wall!" she cried.

In a fantastic leap, the wolf flew into the air. Olwen's grip tightened as her stomach lurched. The rest of the pack followed. One of the younger wolves didn't clear the height and crashed into the wall. With an agonising yowl, he fell to the ground below. Olwen felt a sharp pang of loss and knew he had died. She wanted to weep. How many more would meet injury or death? Could the same happen to her? Roy had warned that this kind of work was perilous.

They landed in a paved courtyard. It was filled with statues of strange creatures, half-human, half-serpent. Olwen tried not to look at them. Instead, she surveyed the towers that soared above her. At last she spied Savitri at a narrow window. To Olwen's surprise, the soul part was an adult, not a child. She waved at Olwen. A good sign. She wanted to be rescued. Seconds later, the window frosted over and she was gone.

They would have to storm the citadel.

"It's war!" Olwen cried, jumping off the wolf's back. "Seek and find!"

The wolves spread out in all directions, running up stairways and leaping through windows. Alone, Olwen ran to the main door. It was made of metal, engraved with disturbing serpentine sigils. The handle was an iron ring. Driven by a sense of urgency, she pulled with all her might. Time was running out. Something was coming. The keeper of the castle? Some terrible thing that bound Savitri here?

The metal ring turned slowly. She pushed against the heavy door. A rush of foul air struck her face. Her stomach heaved. Covering her nose with her hand, she stepped inside. The wolf was waiting for her, ears flattened and eyes wild. On her back was something barely human; a bloodied scrap of skin and bone with eyes half dead. Around its wrist was a gold bangle.

"Oh my God," Olwen whispered. "What happened to her?"

There was no time to talk, no time to help Savitri or ask for her consent. Quelling her own horror, Olwen climbed onto the wolf's back and grasped the soul part in her arms.

"Get us out of here!" she cried. "Back home!"

Wolf let out a howl. The other wolves poured into the courtyard from all directions. Quickly they formed a guard around their leader. When Olwen saw why, terror gorged in her throat. The statues were moving. The serpent creatures were coming to life.

The wolves ran in formation. Leaping over the wall, they raced for the causeway. Olwen glanced behind. The creatures were in full pursuit, jumping over the wall with horrible speed. Olwen clung to Savitri. From a distance came the sound of drums, battering rapidly. But the sound was faint. So far away. And the creatures were almost upon them.

"End the journey!" she cried to the wolf. "End it now!"

In a magnificent arc, the wolf leaped from the causeway into the snowy ravine below. Olwen felt the breathless freedom of the fall.

Then landed with a thump inside her body.

She was back in the Trance Room. The light was dim. The air was filled with the sound of rattles. She sat up with a jerk. Her arms were clasped in front of her, as if holding something tight. She could actually feel it, though she saw nothing there. Beside her lay Savitri, pale and still, like a corpse. The woman's eyes were closed, her features strained in anguish. Kneeling quickly over her, Olwen blew into her chest and then the crown of her head.

Instead of the gentle words Roy had suggested, she heard herself hiss, "This is for you! Take it! Hold on!"

Then she grabbed several rattles in each hand and shook them rigorously over Savitri. After a while she grew aware that she was the only one rattling in the room. Was she the last to finish? It didn't matter. She kept rattling until it felt safe to stop. Only then did Savitri open her eyes.

The older woman let out a deep sigh.

"Thank you," she whispered.

Olwen didn't respond. Drained and exhausted, she fell back on her mat. Soon her own retrieval would begin. She had to fight the urge to run out of the room. Every part of her was in shock. A phrase ran through her mind. *The harrowing of hell.* Did she do the right thing? It had all seemed so rushed and wrong. She wanted to talk with someone about it – Roy or Jack or Elsie. What had she brought back for Savitri? Was it a vital essence? But how could she have been sent to retrieve such a thing? How could a beginner be entrusted with that kind of mission?

The second set of drumming began. Despite her distress, Olwen fell into a light doze. A peaceful feeling washed over her. It was as if she were floating on a warm ocean beneath a summer sky. After what seemed a very short time, she felt Savitri move beside her. Now a pleasant sensation of heat entered her chest and after that, the top of her head. To her surprise, the heat surged through her, making her arms and legs twitch. She didn't know what she had expected, but it wasn't this. She felt suddenly lighter. Before she could stop herself, she let out a whoop and burst out laughing.

Then came the cadence of a rattle, like rain on a tin roof.

And, finally, silence.

CHAPTER TWENTY-ONE

THE MOTHER

The lights in the Trance Room brightened slowly, but Olwen still found herself blinking. There was a rustle of movement as people sat up. Despite Roy's enjoinder to remain silent, a low murmur of talk and muffled laughter rippled around the room. Here and there partners hugged each other. Some were comforted as they wept.

Olwen was relieved to see a smile on Savitri's face. The older woman looked happier and healthier than she had before the session. After returning each other's jewellery, they recorded their journeys in the notebooks provided. Olwen had only begun to write when she paused to think. Did little Savitri return? The schoolgirl wasn't at the fortress. But it was no place for a child. And she had promised to return if the other was found.

When they had both finished writing, they exchanged notebooks.

"I am not an authoress like you," Savitri said apologetically. "I do not have the facility with words to describe the experience as it deserves to be described."

"Don't worry about it," Olwen said sincerely. "Whatever you've done, I feel terrific."

Savitri's handwriting was bold and elegant.

I spent some time feeling the rhythms of the drums and the drones. I found myself wishing there was a tabla as well and thinking that I would suggest this to Director Rose. Then I became angry with myself for considering such trivial matters when I should be concentrating on the task and seeking help for Olwen.

As soon as I called out to Tiger and Cobra, they came to me. I asked to be taken to that soul part of Olwen which she needed to retrieve at this time. I climbed up on Tiger's back and Cobra wrapped herself around my waist like a belt. Tiger leaped into a giant banyan tree that touched the sky. The stars hung like fruit in its branches. I noticed Cobra inspecting the various stars and finally she began to stare at one in particular. It gave off less light than the others and I thought it might be dead or dying.

"She is there," Cobra said.

Tiger leaped onto the branch that held the star and then onto the star itself. Either it grew larger or we grew smaller, for we were able to stand on it. It was like landing on the moon. The star was barren, with no trees or vegetation and covered with a golden dust. There was a young woman sitting cross-legged on the ground. She was about seventeen or eighteen, dressed in a colourful T-shirt and denim jeans with patches. She wore a floppy suede hat over long curly hair that was reddish-brown. I recognised the younger Olwen, but was also reassured by the ring on her finger.

She looked angry, as well as sad and lonely. I asked her if she would like to return with me. She shook her head, very much the sullen and defiant teenager. I had to do a lot of talking to convince her that Olwen had changed and would look after her now. Finally she agreed, but she did not look happy as she climbed up beside me on Tiger.

"Bring her somewhere nice," Cobra whispered in my ear. "It would not be good to return just now."

I asked young Olwen if she would like to visit my home in India. She became very excited and told me she loves to travel and wants to see as much of the world as possible before she dies. Tiger brought us to Pondy and I showed her around the beach and the shops. Everything was "cool" and "far out". We stopped to eat in a restaurant and she told me she was vegetarian. I told her I was also as are most southern Indians. We had rice, dhal, bhajis, spinach paneer, and parathas. She had a good appetite and exclaimed over everything. I could see she had a great love of life and was willing and eager to try new things.

I was debating on whether I would bring her to the samadhi or not, when Cobra told me I should. She didn't mind removing her shoes and was very respectful when we approached the tomb of Sri Aurobindo and the Mother. Like me, she laid her head upon it and stayed in that pose for some time. I could see that she was affected by the sacred atmosphere.

When we left the samadhi, there was a flower seller waiting for us. I bought Olwen a string of jasmine for her hair. She pulled back her long locks into a ponytail, and I wound the jasmine around it. Tiger and Cobra insisted that they were to have garlands also. This made Olwen laugh so much she had to hold her stomach. I knew she was ready to go home. I gathered her up in my arms and asked Tiger to bring us back to the Trance Room. It wasn't long before I heard the call-back of the drums. I said goodbye to Tiger and Cobra and thanked them for their work, then I opened my eyes and sat up on the mat. Quickly I blew the soul part into Olwen's heart and head and I welcomed her home. I did not need to rattle for long. I felt the young woman had settled in. For me, it was a very beautiful and emotional experience.

When Olwen finished reading, she looked up at Savitri.

"That was definitely me," she said, with tears in her eyes. "At eighteen, I hitchhiked across Canada and down to California. You were the perfect person to bring her back. You were able to catch her interest with travel, and you made her laugh. Thank you so much."

Savitri bowed her head. "I cannot take the credit. It was my guides who advised me at every turn. As for what you have written for me..." She looked stricken. "I cannot yet speak of it. Please, will you excuse me?"

Olwen sat stunned as the Indian woman hurried away.

Roy was calling everyone's attention to bring the session to a close.

"You have an hour before supper and the rest of the evening is free. Please keep in mind a few things. Soul retrieval can trigger total recall. Memories of trauma may return with the lost soul part. Stay with whatever comes up. This is the work you have agreed to do. You are here to face and transform your pain. Don't let the soul part flee again. You are stronger now and you are not alone. Seek help if you need it. Speak with your partner or with others of the circle. We are all in this together.

"Remember also, it is not all about pain. Look out for the good stuff. You are likely to feel new energy and vitality. But don't despair if you feel no immediate changes. Some soul parts integrate sooner than others; some take their time to land. As always with this work, look to your dreams tonight. The soul part may manifest by that avenue."

Olwen was barely listening to Roy. She was locked inside herself, devastated by Savitri's reaction. Had she done it all wrong? Had she brought back something bad? Something dead? She wanted to ask Roy about it, but he was deep in conversation with Tenzin Dawa. Where was Dr Jack? She had spotted him earlier, talking animatedly with Euphémie, but there was no sign of him now. And Elsie was nowhere to be seen either. What should she do? Who could she talk to?

Olwen stumbled out of the room and literally bumped into Rose. There was an awkward moment when their bodies met. She felt a jolt run through her, as if she had touched an electric fence. She stepped back quickly. The first thing she noticed was the shadows under his eyes, then the strain in his features. Her suspicions were confirmed. Their ride had taken its toll on him. She wanted to apologise, or at least to enquire about his health, but found she couldn't. Instead, on impulse, she spoke of her concern about what had happened in the session.

Rose listened impassively as she described her journey. He didn't react to the abduction scene. When she finished, he spoke briefly.

"You needn't concern yourself. Anything you brought back for Savitri would be good. It is up to her to integrate what you retrieved. Look to your own work."

Olwen felt her face burn. Was that a rebuke of some kind? If only she had spoken with Roy. She was really beginning to hate this man.

"Thanks. You're a great help."

With a snort of annoyance, she brushed past him.

Olwen was walking along the cliff when Savitri caught up with her. The older woman wore a woollen sweater over her sari and wellington boots.

"May I come with you?" Savitri asked carefully. "Or do you wish to be alone?"

"I'd love it! I was afraid I had upset you."

Savitri laid her hand gently on Olwen's arm. "In this work, my dear, you must let each person be responsible for his or her own feelings, even as you are responsible for yours. It is what Brother Aguerre calls 'the freedom of the children of God'. I hope you do not mind me saying this?"

"No, I understand," Olwen said, though she couldn't help but note that Savitri was echoing Rose's words.

They strolled together along the edge of the precipice. The sun lingered over the rim of the loch. The water looked enamelled with the rosy hue.

"It is so beautiful here," Savitri murmured. "I like to be near the water, as I am in Pondy."

"Is that your home in India?"

"Yes. Pondicherry. On the Bay of Bengal. I walk each evening along the promenade."

"Isn't Pondicherry where the boy in *Life of Pi* came from?"

"Yes! One of my favourite books."

"Mine too!

They smiled at each other.

"In some ways, the tiger reminds me of my animal guide," Savitri said. "I wept when he left Pi."

"I did too! He reminded me of my big tomcat, Hamish."

They came to a spot where crude steps were hewn into the side of the cliff, leading to a cove below.

"Smugglers?" Olwen wondered.

They decided not to risk the steps, but sat instead by the edge.

Savitri reached into the pocket of her sweater and took out a little cloth bag tied with a string.

"Would you like some fennel seed? I use them instead of tobacco. Smoking is not socially acceptable for Indian women. Nor is it something doctors should do!"

"You're a doctor?"

"I run a free clinic in Chennai, for street women...like my mother." Savitri grew pensive. Her eyes darkened. "Some people's lives are much harder than others.'"

They chewed on the seeds in silence. Olwen was beginning to understand why an adult part of Savitri had fled so far away.

As if reading her mind, the other woman spoke quietly. "You cannot imagine some of the horrors I have seen. Some of the things I have had to do. The Work helps me to do *my* work. I already feel the strength you have retrieved for me this day."

"Was it a vital essence I brought back?"

"I believe so. When you blew it into me, I knew it was extremely important."

"But how could this happen? How could they send a beginner to do a shaman's job? I could have failed you or worse!"

"But you did not. You should have more faith in yourself, Olwen. There is such a strong life force inside you. It burns like a great fire."

Olwen felt a lump in her throat.

Savitri looked thoughtful. "Director Rose did a soul retrieval for me one time. He told me there was a part of myself that was a very great distance away. It was beyond his reach." Her eyes crinkled. "But *you* found it!"

Something inside Olwen crowed. She had done what Rose couldn't do! Was that why he was so abrupt? She laughed out loud.

"Ah, this sounds like your younger self," Savitri said.

"That's because I'm laughing from pure badness."

At supper, Olwen sat with Savitri. She smiled over at Elsie and Dr Jack, who were in different places also, sitting with their Soul Retrieval partners. A quick look around confirmed that everyone had done the same. It was as if someone had picked up the room and shaken it like a box of marbles. There was a lot of lively chat and laughter. The atmosphere was triumphant.

After supper, Savitri invited Olwen to her room. It was on the first floor of the house in the long corridor that overlooked the courtyard. Like Olwen's, it was spacious and richly furnished. The fireplace was made of Connemara marble. The soft carpet was also green, and the wallpaper was printed with a pattern of leaves. Savitri had added a few touches of her own. A multicoloured throw, stippled with tiny mirrors, covered the bed. On a table nearby were two photographs in jewelled frames. One was of an Indian man with long white hair and a beard. His handsome face reflected an extraordinary intelligence. The other was of an elderly European woman with finely sculpted features and soulful eyes.

"Sri Aurobindo and the Mother," Savitri explained. "My 'gurus' as we say in India, meaning teacher or mentor, though the word has such negative connotations in the West. You will remember the shrine from both retrievals. My parents were devotees. Lower caste and illiterate, my father was a cleaner in the ashram; but there was no job for my mother so she worked on the roads. They lived in one room nearby, while I boarded as a student. It was a great honour and opportunity for their child to be so educated. Most of their wages went to pay my way, but they could not cover all my expenses nor my fees for medical school. That was achieved through scholarships and working in the ashram office when I was older."

"Your parents must have been so proud when you became a doctor!"

Savitri's eyes filled with tears. "My mother did not live to see it accomplished – the road workers of India do not live long lives. But at least she knew it would happen. I was an intern when I nursed my father to his death. He died with a smile on his face."

Savitri chose a little stone statue from among the things on her desk. It was of Ganesh, the plump happy god with the head of an elephant.

"I would like to give this to you," she said to Olwen. "He is my favourite god. The Remover of Obstacles. I prayed to him throughout medical school. Perhaps he will be of some help to you this week."

"Oh I love Ganesh, too! How could I not, being a writer? Wasn't he the one who inspired the *Mahabharata?*"

"You know this story?!"

"I love Indian culture. Such an ancient and fascinating land. I've always wanted to go there, especially to see the River Ganges, but it just hasn't happened yet."

"I am so happy to hear this! It is settled, then. You will come to visit me in Pondy and I shall bring you to the *samadhi* and Auroville, the community founded by the Mother, and then we shall go on pilgrimage together to Varanasi and the Mother Ganges."

The two women hugged each other before parting.

Still clutching the little statue, Olwen walked down the corridor towards the broch. She was only halfway down the hall when she heard voices murmur from a room ahead. The door was slightly ajar. Another pair of soul partners sharing confidences? She didn't intend to look as she passed by, but something caught her eye and she was brought up short.

It was Elsie's room. The old woman stood in the middle of the floor, her face tilted upwards. She looked so small and frail beside Rose's height. He seemed to loom over her. Olwen's first impression was one of threat. Then she saw that Elsie was smiling and there were tears of joy in her eyes. Her hands reached out to cup Rose's face as she gazed up at him. He, in turn, was gazing down at her with a profound happiness. The intensity of their love, the depths of that intimacy, shook Olwen to the core. Mother and son? But how could that be? She suddenly felt like an eavesdropper. She shouldn't be there, witnessing such a private moment.

Stunned by what she had seen, she hurried away.

CHAPTER TWENTY-TWO

FOURTH NIGHT: THE HOMECOMING

Olwen was woken by the sound of someone calling her name. She turned on her bedside lamp and stared around the room. There was no one there. She padded to the nearest window. The shadow of the house fell across the moonlit lawn. The dark ribbon of road disappeared into the dim landscape. She went to the second window overlooking the courtyard.

Ah yes.

Below, under the light of the archway, stood a lone figure: a slender young woman in patched jeans and bright T-shirt. A floppy suede hat was perched on her fall of long hair. She leaned against the wall, arms folded, staring up at the tower.

Olwen threw on jeans and a sweater. She raced downstairs and out the back door. Her heart beat wildly as she approached the girl. The musky smell of patchouli oiled the air. The girl's features looked pale under the lamplight. Black eyeliner was her only make-up. There were streaks of purple dye in her hair. Her feet stood bare on the cobblestones.

"Ollie."

The girl didn't return Olwen's smile.

"Why did you call me back?" she demanded.

Her tone was as sharp as a slap in the face.

Olwen recoiled. This wasn't what she had expected. All she could do was answer honestly.

"I had no idea it would be you. I thought a child would return because of...well, you know...But I was thrilled when Savitri described you. I've taken the memory of you into many adventures, including this one. But I'd like more than a memory. I want you back. To live fully, I need your spirit."

The girl looked mollified, but only just. She shivered in the chill of the night air. She was dressed for a Californian summer, not a Scottish one; and though she bridled with the defiance of a teenager who had already left home, she also looked lost and lonely.

"Will you come inside?" Olwen asked her. "I can make you a hot chocolate, maybe a bite to eat? There's a Common Room with a pool table and a real fire."

Ollie shook her head. She glanced up at Dunesfort House. "It looks creepy. Is it haunted?"

Olwen hesitated before answering. "There are a lot of ghosts here," she admitted. She almost added that the teenager was one of them, but stopped herself in time. "Would you at least let me get you a sweater and maybe some shoes and socks?"

Ollie nodded grudgingly.

Olwen was reluctant to leave her, afraid she might take flight, but the girl's teeth had begun to chatter.

"Please don't go," Olwen begged her. "Please wait for me here."

Ollie nodded again, but offered no other assurances.

Olwen ran into the house, taking the stairs of the broch two at a time. In her room, she grabbed her big Aran sweater plus a pair of woollen socks and her hiking boots. With sudden inspiration, she raided her stash of chocolate. Then she raced down the stairs again. When she opened the back door, her heart sank. The archway was deserted. There was no sign of the girl. A little cry of disappointment escaped her lips. Then she spotted Ollie on the stone bench by the fountain. The girl was gazing up at the moon.

Olwen hurried over and sat down beside her. "Thanks for waiting."

Ollie didn't reply. Her lips were blue and she was shaking violently. Quickly Olwen helped her into the bulky Aran. Ollie declined the shoes, but pulled on the thick socks. She drew her legs up inside the sweater until it covered her knees and feet.

Olwen sat back, feeling a little freer to relax. She glanced up at the house. Most of the windows were dark and shuttered, but a few lights shone. Was anyone watching them?

No longer shivering, Ollie helped herself to a chocolate bar.

"Midnight snacks are cool."

Olwen agreed, and they munched together in companionable silence. Behind them, the fountain splashed quietly.

When she finished eating, Ollie produced a pouch of tobacco from the back pocket of her jeans. Inside was a piece of carrot to keep the tobacco fresh, and a packet of roll-up papers.

Olwen smiled to herself, remembering. "Show me the trick with one hand. I've forgotten how."

The teenager grinned. Pretending to drive with her right hand on the wheel, she positioned the pouch on her lap. With her left hand only, she extracted a paper, manoeuvred a wad of tobacco onto it with her thumb, and spread it evenly. Next she rolled the paper and tobacco between her thumb and fingers, and finally sealed it with a lick. The slim cigarette dangled from her mouth as she lit it with her lighter. The sweet scent of tobacco filled the air.

"Bravo," said Olwen. "Well done. Take a bow."

Ollie looked pleased. "Remember the guy who showed us?"

Olwen nodded. "Small pick-up truck crossing the Prairies. He was really nice. When the sun began to set, I asked if I could sit out in the back. It was a warm summer's evening. A soft breeze blew over the wheat fields. I could see the yellow lights of houses winking in the distance. There I was, homeless and on the road, in the dark of night, blissfully happy. I didn't want to be trapped in one of those little boxes. I wanted to be free."

"Yeah." Ollie's face shone. "All those months on the road with Carol and Ron and Tim and Linda and Peggy. We crossed Canada, hitched through Washington and Oregon, hung out in California. They said thousands were living on Highway One that summer. It was far fucking out."

"May I?"

Olwen reached for the tobacco and managed a fairly decent roll-up, though she had to use both hands.

"Do you have Prince Albert in a tin?" she asked the teenager.

"Then let him out!" they shouted together.

It was the common joke of that hobo summer when she wandered around North America with no money and no shoes.

A friendly silence fell between them. Identical smoke rings sailed through the air.

"I quit smoking years ago," Olwen told her. "Female past forty, you have to stop. Cancer city. Not to mention osteoporosis."

"You're over forty?"

"Fifty this year."

Ollie checked her up and down. "Not bad."

"Thanks."

Another pause. Olwen didn't want to break the mood, but she had to ask.

"Why did you leave?"

The teenager stiffened. She looked ready to run. Her features had cooled to a mask.

"Please." Olwen said quietly. "I need to know. I'm not angry with you. I just– "

"Not angry with *me*?" Ollie's voice rang with incredulity. Then she exploded. "And why the fuck would you be? *I'm* not the one who ruined everything. *I'm* not the asshole who totally fucked up her life. *I'm* not the big failure!"

Then it all poured out. *J'accuse.*

"What happened to law school, eh? Why did you drop out? I was going to be a labour union lawyer and fight for the rights of workers. And then I was going to go into politics, all the way to the top. First woman prime minister of Canada. I could have done it! Everyone said so! My grades were so high, I got into Osgoode Hall with only two years of university. And my time in the military, as a promising young naval cadet, offset my hippy days. Didn't Captain Franklin say I'd be the first woman captain of a naval reserve unit? I was set to reach the stars! And my personal life was great, too. Sweet Robert, so handsome, so gentle, so kind. He would have been a wonderful husband and father. And what did you do? You dumped him! And for what? A bad marriage! By my own efforts, my own hard work, I set up the perfect life for myself – law school, navy, fiancé, great future. I would have had a happy family, meaningful work, a nice house and lots of money. I laid it all out for you. I succeeded in everything I did and what did you do? You became an *alcoholic* and threw it all away! You worked at menial jobs and you married a crazy man and you wasted year after year of my life. *You destroyed my dreams!"*

The teenager's features twisted with rage and grief.

Olwen buried her face in her hands and wept. She cried for the loss of her youthful hopes and dreams, and especially for the mess she had made of her personal life. But after a while, she came to her senses. The teenager's self-loathing was not a true reflection of how Olwen felt now. She had dealt with these issues. In a long painful process, she had sobered up and then gone into therapy with Dr N, coming to terms with her past and forgiving herself.

Olwen wiped her eyes and sat up straight. Her voice rang with a calm and brutal honesty.

"It was self-destruct time, Ollie. The reckoning of the past. Yes, you built a beautiful life for yourself; and all credit to you since you did most of it alone, with hard work, scholarships, and living on your own. The fact that you could even imagine such a future for yourself, coming from where you came from, was amazing to start with. But it was a house built on sand, kiddo, and that wasn't your fault or mine. The foundations were rotten. Our inheritance was a mountain of pain that came down the pipeline on both sides – alcoholism, sexual abuse, violence, manic-depression. And just as you were about to reap the rewards of your gifts and your work, the shit hit the fan, like a time bomb set to go off. We hadn't a hope. We were lost before we began."

It was Ollie's turn to cry. She wept quietly as she rolled another cigarette with trembling fingers.

"We had a lot to act out," Olwen said quietly. "A lot to recover from. Generations of crap. I guess we didn't come here for an easy life. Those fabulous dreams...they weren't our destiny."

Ollie wiped her nose with the back of her hand and lit her cigarette. She took a long drag, blew out the smoke.

"You married that crazy artist 'cause he was like Dad."

Olwen nodded. "Handsome, Irish, charming...volatile. Fourteen years I stayed in that abusive marriage. The drinking helped me stay. But I can't blame it all on him, Ollie. He was as wounded as me and that's one of the reasons I married him. He matched me, when Robert didn't. Bob was too sane, too Canadian, too...kind. And I'll tell you now, I had some good times with my husband. We both loved books, horses, art, travel, films. And we *did* love each other, as best we could, but our drinking and our craziness meant dead-end jobs and a lot of harm inflicted on each other. Those were dark years with occasional flashes of happiness, like lightning in a storm. Though our marriage was doomed and we never managed to stay friends, it was he who went to AA first and then came back for me. I will always be grateful to him for that. I was a long time recovering, not only from my alcoholism but from what lay behind it. Step by step, some small, some big, I slowly but surely built a new life for myself.

"I returned to an earlier dream, a much older one than law and politics. Don't you remember? We always told stories, from the time we were little. I'm a professional writer now and I've published a good few books. They're modern fairy tales, like the ones C.S. Lewis wrote, our most beloved childhood author. Though I could do with more money, I'm reasonably successful. My books are in a lot of countries, translated into different languages, and I've won a few prizes. Best of all are the times my readers contact me, most of them kids. Some are suffering hard lives and they say the books help them through the dark times, the way that Narnia helped us."

She could see that Ollie was caught. Books had always played a big part in her life.

"I modelled one of my stories on *The Martian Chronicles*."

"You did?" Ollie grew excited. "Remember that time we went into the library in San Francisco and even though we were in our bare feet, they let us in? I was tired of the road and the heat and hanging out with street people. We left the others in a park and spent the whole day in the library. There was a long table and sunshine pouring through the tall windows, and we read Bradbury's book from cover to cover."

"He's a wonderful writer," Olwen said, nodding. "You can sense his benign presence behind all his work. A beautiful man, kind and humane."

Ollie smiled in agreement. Olwen could see she had softened. Now was the time to plead her case as if she had stayed in law school.

"This is a good time to come back to me, Ollie. Things are really happening for me. I've just started an exciting new series and I'm branching out into graphic novels and film. But at the same time," and here her voice grew quieter and somewhat ironic, "you need to know that 'success' for the sake of it – I mean, fame and fortune – is no longer a priority, or even a big wish. I'm on a spiritual path. I'm striving for enlightenment. God, that sounds so pompous when I say it out loud. What I'm trying to say is that I'm following my soul's journey, not my ego's. You shouldn't be too surprised. Weren't we always into spiritual stuff? Didn't we worship Apollo and Artemis when we were little, then later dreamed of being a Carmelite nun? And do you remember burning incense to the statue of the Buddha? How old were we then? Eleven? Twelve? At university, I studied mythology, theology, and philosophy, not just because it suited pre-law, but for the subject matter itself. Exploring the depths of consciousness is the ultimate adventure, is it not? Even better than travelling to foreign countries?"

Ollie was hanging on every word, no longer quick to argue or judge. Olwen felt a rush of optimism. Now she described the little house she owned in Ireland, in the town where she was born. The first home of her own; the first real security in her life, a permanent roof over her head.

"We live in Ireland now?"

She also spoke of the garden she had planted, harking back to a childhood wish to grow flowers and vegetables.

"I planted a border of bleeding hearts."

"Bleeding hearts," Ollie murmured.

Another strong memory. Walking to school when she was little, she had to pass through the slum that bordered the new low-income estate where her family lived when they first emigrated to Canada. There was a factory on the corner, a sweatshop as she knew now. She used to stare into the open window at the workers as they laboured over steaming presses. The men and women always smiled and waved at her. The next street over was a row of dilapidated houses with broken windows, sagging porches, and

yards littered with garbage. But there was one house at the end...
Though the owners were no doubt as poor as their neighbours, they
had grown a patch of paradise at their front door. The small square
of garden bloomed with flowering bushes and plants of every
kind. Best of all was the herbaceous border of dicentra – tiny pink
and red flowers shaped like hearts with a drop of blood. Each day
she passed that garden on her way to school and she would stop,
entranced; a scrappy, undernourished little girl, she would drink
in the loveliness, silently worshipping that corner of beauty in an
impoverished world.

"I've planted bleeding hearts wherever I've gone," Olwen told her.
"Like Johnny Appleseed. I buried my beloved tomcat under them.
He died in battle, but his sister Emma still lives."

"We love cats now?"

Both remembered the grandmother who had passed her virulent
hatred of cats onto her children and grandchildren.

Ollie's face closed like a clenched fist. The anger had returned,
but it was no longer directed at her older self.

"So, how's the family? Gramps and Gran? Mom and Dad?"

The question came as a shock. Of course she didn't know. Olwen
wavered a moment as she felt the stab of pain. Old wounds opening,
heart bleeding.

Ollie saw and understood. Her anger fled. She looked stricken.

Olwen nodded, unable to hide the truth. "It's been a long time.
They're all gone. Mum and Dad too."

The teenager's mouth dropped open. She let out a guttural sob,
then instantly suppressed it. Her shoulders shook in spasms as she
fought to control herself. She didn't speak. She couldn't.

Olwen reached out to comfort her, but was instantly rebuffed.
No surprise there. She had never accepted solace from any source.
It was a sign of weakness.

When Ollie finally found her voice, it sounded small and lost.

"We're orphans. Alone in the world."

"No, we're not."

Against the death of her parents, the older Olwen had a prize to offer, the secret she had kept till last. The pearl of her misbegotten marriage. The treasure of her misshapen life.

"I have my own little family. A lovely daughter. Her name is Robyn."

"I'm not babysitting!" Ollie's outburst was instant. "I spent my whole life looking after kids until I finally got out of that house!"

Olwen tried not to laugh. "You won't need to. She's a college student. I've already done all the work."

Ollie was immediately curious. "What's she like?"

Olwen grinned. "Very different from us. Real sporty. Surfing is her bliss. And she's a scientist, studying Earth and Ocean Science. Fashion is another thing of hers. She loves clothes. Always did, ever since she was little. And though she loves to dance and party, she has no interest in drugs or alcohol."

Their faces mirrored each other's astonishment.

"Is she like her father?" Ollie asked.

"Not that I can see, except for the raven-black hair. I think the stork brought her." Olwen's face lit up. "She's really wonderful. One of the most amazing people I've ever met. Kind-hearted, generous, loves animals, plans to work for the environment, has lots of friends...and except for the fact I've raised her to think she's a princess, so she sometimes acts like one, we get along brilliantly. I love her more than anyone or anything I have ever loved in my life."

"More than *me*?"

The words slipped out before Ollie could stop them. There was a plaintive ring. She looked embarrassed.

Olwen hesitated a moment before answering. She gazed into the eyes of her eighteen-year-old self and saw what she had never seen in her own daughter's eyes – the sadness of the abandoned child, adrift in the world without foundation, deeply wounded and crippled by that wound.

"No," Olwen told her, surprised at her own answer. "I love *you* more."

And in her heart, she knew it was true and also that it was right. No harm would come to Robyn because of it. On the contrary, her daughter could only benefit. For if our mother cannot love herself, how can she love others? And if she cannot love us, how can we love ourselves? Handed down the ancestral line, all the motherless children pass their wounds to the next generation until one stops and learns to love herself, passing that knowledge of self-love on to her children and their children and their children...

Olwen opened her arms. Her voice was shy and entreating.

"Come, Ollie, it's time. Let me make it up to you, not only for all the mistakes I made, but all the ones our parents made, too, because they couldn't pass on what they didn't have themselves. It's not a perfect life, certainly not the one you imagined for yourself, but it will be good and it will be fun. And I can promise you this: there are more adventures to come."

Ollie nodded dumbly, tears pouring down her face.

Olwen held her tightly, rocking her back and forth on that cold stone bench by the fountain under the moonlight.

There came a time when Olwen was alone. The only thing in her arms was her Aran sweater. She held it to her face and inhaled the musky scent of patchouli. Then she stood up to return to the house.

A long-lost part of her had come home at last.

CHAPTER TWENTY-THREE

OH, WON'T YOU COME WITH ME?

Olwen woke the next morning feeling lively and refreshed. A tune was ringing in her head. She hummed a few bars as she jumped out of bed, singing to herself.

In a gadda da vida, honey.

After her shower, she stood before her wardrobe, grimacing at its contents. Items were flung here and there with noises of disgust. Then a wail of despair.

"I've NOTHING to wear!"

Several combinations later, the floor was strewn with discarded clothing. She didn't notice the mess. She finally settled on the one pair of jeans that hugged her hips and not her waist, along with a black T-shirt that showed off her curves. Her hair was brushed vigorously until it stood out like a bush. Then a liberal application of eyeliner and mascara, followed by a dash of red lipstick and a cloud of perfume. The scent wasn't Tabu, her favourite, but at least it was strong. She stood back to survey herself critically. Something was missing. A quick search through her jewellery produced a pair of dangly earrings. All she needed now was a belt. Did she bring anything else besides those plain old leather ones?

A dive into the closet, more clothes on the floor and she found it: the silver chain belt she had bought on a whim, but never worn. Its day had come! Black high-heeled boots completed the outfit. She was almost ready to face the world.

Where's the fucking Juicy Fruit?

She rummaged through her stash of treats, but all she could find was some breath-mint gum. It would have to do. Chewing noisily, she left the bedroom, unaware that it looked as if a tornado had struck.

Still humming her song, Olwen strode into the dining room, hips swinging. She was late for breakfast and the last to arrive. Most of the men glanced in her direction. Some glances lingered. A few of the women frowned instinctively, while others raised their eyebrows and grinned. She sashayed over to her usual table. Elsie's face broke into a big smile. Dr Jack stood up with his usual courtesy. His grin was wolfish as he appraised her. She didn't sit down, but wriggled her hips and sang to both of them.

In a gadda da vida, baby
Don't you know that I love you?

"Iron Butterfly!" Dr Jack snapped his fingers. "Their best hit."
He joined in with her, both of them gyrating as they sang.

In a gadda da vida, baby,
Don't you know that I'll always be true?

Laughter broke out around the room. More voices joined the singing.

Oh won't you come with me
And take my hand?
Oh, won't you come with me
And walk this land?

There was drumming on the tables, air guitars and back-up boom-box. The younger participants nodded with appreciation. It was a great beat, raw with passion and honesty.

Please take my ha-aaaa-nd.

When the song ended, the room burst into applause along with whistles, catcalls, and howls of laughter.

"Soul Retrieval always livens things up," Elsie remarked.

Olwen flopped down into her chair and ordered a big breakfast. "I could eat the lamb of God!"

"What?" said Dr Jack.

"Irish expression."

When her food arrived, she gorged herself. "Everything tastes so good!" She slathered her toast with strawberry jam.

"There's more of you having the experience," Elsie pointed out.

"It's fucking fabulous," Olwen agreed, her mouth full. "Yum and yum!"

Her lips were smeared with jam. Dr Jack leaned over to wipe them clean, then licked his fingers.

Elsie threw them a look.

"If you two get any hotter, I'll have to take off my blouse."

Olwen was still cramming toast into her mouth when the gong sounded for the day's programme to begin. The dining room was almost empty. She slurped the dregs of her coffee and charged for the door. She was heading in the direction of the Meeting Room when Dr Jack grabbed her arm.

"We're in the Womb this morning."

Needless to say, she hadn't bothered to consult the schedule.

In the Trance Room, the high windows were open to let in the morning light. The air was fresh with sea breezes. Everyone stood around in little groups, chatting and laughing as they waited for the Director. The atmosphere was light-hearted, less formal than usual.

When Rose arrived he, too, appeared unusually cheerful.

"You have all done a lot of work these past few days. Before we set out for deeper waters, it is time to play. We'll begin with a session of drums and drones to move you into an ecstatic state. Feel free to lie down on a mat, sit in meditation pose, or remain standing with your eyes closed, whatever you prefer. After a time, music will begin and you are invited to dance."

"YES!"

Olwen's exclamation escaped before she could stop it, even as she punched the air. Laughter rippled around her. She ducked her head in embarrassment.

Rose acknowledged her outburst with a brief smile, then continued. "We dedicate this day to integrating the lost soul part. Let the body celebrate the one who has returned. A lot of you will have retrieved children, so don't be surprised by urges to hop, skip, and jump. You needn't worry too much about the consequences. We have more than enough medical staff and bodyworkers in the crowd to treat any pulled muscles or strained tendons."

He paused to allow another wave of laughter.

"The duration of the Trance Dance is up to you. Feel free to go for a walk, spend time in your room alone, or do some artwork in the conservatory. Play dough and wet clay have been added to the materials."

Euphémie let out a "yippee!"

More laughter.

Rose finished his instructions. "To enhance your focus on your own retrieved soul part and its integration, I recommend minimal interaction with others. At lunchtime, all tables will be silent. Notices will be posted to remind you. There will be plenty of time to talk later. As per schedule, we'll have a full circle sharing in the Meeting Room before supper."

Rose had no sooner finished than the mesmeric sounds of drums and drones began. Olwen grabbed a mat and flung herself on it in a lazy sprawl. She had barely lain down when it happened, like a great soft blow. There was no tunnel, no sensation of movement, no indication whatsoever that she had begun her journey: she was just suddenly far from Dunesfort House.

She was lying on her back in the sunshine, on the side of a dusty road. Her knapsack lay under her head like a pillow. Her left arm was stretched out, thumb pointing upwards. Her suede hat with the wide brim was tipped over her eyes to ward off the glare of the noonday sun. Nearby were her two friends and travelling companions: Ron, a tall black man from Kentucky, not long out of the army after service in Vietnam; and Carol, a fellow office worker from Toronto, who had set off with Olwen that summer in the early 1970s. They were hitchhiking their way down Highway One in the state of California. The coastal road skirting the blue Pacific was home to thousands of transients, both young and old.

A flat-back truck drew up. The driver shouted in Spanish and gestured at them to climb in. The Mexican workers in the back hauled them on board. The rickety old truck took off down the highway, leaving San Luis Obispo behind in a cloud of dust.

One of the men passed her a gallon jug of cheap wine. She hooked her finger in the ring on the neck, leaned the jug on her shoulder, and took a long swallow. A joint of marijuana followed. Someone strummed an old, beat-up guitar.

Do you know the way to San José?

Ollie grinned to herself.

This is the life.

Olwen grinned to herself.

I will never forget who you were.

The drums and drones began to fade. A Caribbean beat erupted from the speakers. With a shout of delight, Olwen was on her feet and out on the floor. Hips shaking, feet moving, fingers snapping and clicking, she danced up a storm. Why didn't she do this more often? She *loved* to dance! Her blood pulsed with the raw energy of youth: that energy primed to propel her into the broad vista of life stretching before her like a golden prairie.

"HOO-YA!" she shouted.

Grinning rakishly and up to no good, Dr Jack sidled towards her, doing the Harlem Shuffle.

"Glad to see you don't have white rhythm, Heavy Metal Rock Chick."

"You're doing some smooth moves yourself there, my friend."

"I'm a James Brown man."

"But of course."

They danced around each other, flirting outrageously. Olwen directed a series of bumps and grinds against him. He responded in kind, sliding his body along hers. In sync with each other, wrapped up in their own world, they were oblivious to the others around them. A few eyebrows were raised and looks exchanged, but most of the dancers were caught up in their own bliss.

Elsie swayed back and forth, arms waving in the air, while Euphémie hopped and skipped around her. Tenzin Dawa was executing the latest moves from the discos in Delhi. Suzume danced beside him, copying his footwork. Thomas Tillman stood upright, hips swivelling gently, as he leaned on his crutches.

At one point Olwen spotted Rose on the far side of the room. She had assumed he would leave once the dancing started. He didn't strike her as someone who could surrender to music. But though he didn't attempt to move like Thomas, he did tap his cane on the floor in time with the beat. She thought of Diaghilev tormenting his dancers in the Ballets Russes. There was a moment when the wintry eyes met hers, before moving on to Dr Jack. Was that a look of disapproval or did she imagine it? Her antipathy rose. Who was he to judge? An asexual misogynist who wouldn't touch women in case it polluted his aura? She threw him a glare before dancing out of his line of vision.

The music kept changing. Now a heavy samba beat, now a light dash of English folk, now a vibrant Indian air. Eventually people began to drop out, the older ones first, except for Elsie. Some headed for the conservatory and the art supplies. Others left for their rooms or to go outdoors. Many remained in the Womb, lying on the mats to be immersed in the music.

Olwen looked around for Dr Jack. She had lost him when she dashed off to skip around the room behind Euphémie, Suzume, and Christy Bird. Her clothes were sweaty. Her hair clung damply to her neck. It was time to go. She would shower and change, then head for the conservatory to do some painting.

He was waiting for her on the steps of the broch.

"Wanna play hooky?"

"I need to shower. I've been dancing for Ireland."

"Rose might catch us. It's now or never!"

That rakish grin again. Her teenaged self crowed. Open rebellion against Herr Direktor! She always liked to play with the bad boys.

"Where are we going?"

He caught her hand and pulled her towards the stairway that led to the basement. She quivered with glee. They were entering forbidden territory. Rose had made it clear that the lower floor was for staff only, off limits to the rest of them. The stairwell had iron balustrades. The steps were worn from years of tread. Olwen tightened her grip on Dr Jack's hand. The light seemed to grow dimmer as they descended.

They entered a spacious subterranean kitchen that was a strange mix of old and new. An open hearth held a great black cauldron on a cast-iron frame. Under it lay a stack of turf waiting to be lit. But it was the Stanley range cooker that heated the room. A silver kettle simmered on top. At the centre of the kitchen was a long wooden table with baskets of fruit and vegetables. Shelves were lined with foodstuffs in tins and jars. From the beams of the ceiling hung bunches of onions, garlic, and dried herbs.

The kitchen was empty. Dr Jack opened cupboards and drawers, despite Olwen's gasps and worried glances around her. When he located a wickerwork basket, he filled it to the brim with edibles. He was just closing the lid when one of the serving girls entered. It was Annie, the youngest one with red hair and freckles. Her eyes widened at the sight of them.

Dr Jack put his finger to his lips and winked. Annie smiled shyly and suppressed a giggle.

Basket under his arm, Jack led Olwen down a narrow passageway, past laundry and boiler rooms, several pantries, and a walk-in freezer.

"Red or white?" he asked, stopping at the door to the wine cellar. "He has some excellent Bordeaux."

Olwen hesitated. "Bit early in the day, isn't it?"

"Point taken."

He stopped again before they reached the back door and entered another room. It was the staff lounge. The older of the serving girls, Fiona, sat on the sofa, smoking a cigarette and reading a book. A cup of tea rested on the table beside her. She looked up in surprise. Again, Jack mimed secrecy and silence, as he pulled a rug from one of the armchairs and threw it over his shoulder. Fiona shook her head and laughed, then returned to her reading.

"Mr Charming Pants gets away with murder," Olwen remarked, as they left the house.

"Colour helps," he said, with a grin. "Decent people who don't have regular contact with other races go out of their way to make us feel welcome and not 'different'. I don't take offence – it's not like the negative racism of hatred and fear – but I do take advantage."

She looked at him, aghast. "I don't know what to say to that."

He laughed. "I know a great spot for a picnic."

CHAPTER TWENTY-FOUR

THE PICNIC

Dr Jack led her along the precipice to the smugglers' stairway she had discovered the day before. The descent was difficult and they had to go slowly. The steps were uneven, slippery with moss and bird droppings, and the cliff face provided no purchase. Seabirds circled overhead, crying out their warnings. When they reached the bottom, he unfurled the rug in a sheltered spot. The sand glistened like crushed gold. The water of the loch was aquamarine, cold and pristine in the noonday light.

"I'm taking a dip," Olwen decided.

She was still feeling clammy from her frenetic dancing. Quickly she stripped to bra and panties, glad that she had worn her peach-coloured lingerie. Not much different from a bikini. And she wasn't shy. Hadn't he seen everything the night of the Sweat House?

Dr Jack was unpacking the basket. He had taken quite a haul – fresh figs and grapes, several cheeses, green and purple olives, tins of crab meat, a slab of pâté, crusty bread, and a bottle of elderflower drink. There were also dishes, cutlery, glasses, and cloth napkins.

"I'll join you!" he said. "Great idea!"

She ran ahead of him to reach the water first. It was imperative not to hesitate. She knew what it was like to swim in the Atlantic. One had to leap before mind or body had time to object. Splashing through the shallows, she ignored the first shock of freezing water and dived straight in. The cold pierced her brain like an ice pick. Her skin burned. Her muscles cramped. She gasped for breath.

Glorious.

Surfacing, she let out a whoop of agony and delight.

He was standing on the shore, watching her. He wore black briefs. His physique was magnificent, toned and muscled, with a mat of dark hair on his chest. When he plunged into the water, he roared like a sea lion.

They didn't swim for long. There was no growing used to that intensity of cold. Instead, they strolled together along the strand, letting the sun and the sea breeze dry them off.

Olwen gathered stones, gull feathers, and sea shells to take back to her room. Talk seemed superfluous as she inhaled the fullness of the moment: sea and sand, sky and light, a beautiful man beside her.

"Shall we have our picnic?" he said, after a while.

When they returned to the rug, she pulled on her T-shirt, but didn't bother with her jeans. He put on his slacks but left his chest bare. Opening the bottle of elderflower, he poured her a glass. It tasted light and fruity. He arranged their plates of food, stopping to hand her a chunk of crusty bread slathered with pâté. A sharp, musky flavour. But when he lifted the purple grape to her mouth, she didn't bite. Taking it from him, she nibbled it pensively.

Her feelings were ambivalent. Flirting was fun, but she needed to draw the line. She nodded towards the gold ring on his finger. The thing she had been ignoring for too long.

"You're married. I don't go there. It's tacky."

He looked surprised a moment, then smiled briefly. "Sorry for the mixed messages. I forget I'm wearing it. I've been separated for just over three years."

He handed her a plate of food. After the cold swim, she ate with gusto.

"Why do you still wear it? If you don't mind me asking?"

He started to eat, pausing between mouthfuls. "It wasn't my idea to end the marriage. I wanted to keep trying. I suppose when I've finally conceded defeat, I'll take it off."

She was dying to ask more, but didn't want to pry. Instead she helped herself to another glass of elderflower. Her silence seemed to encourage him.

"Sometimes I tell myself it was a simple case of me wanting children and her not. That was certainly at the heart of most of our fights, but really there was a lot more to it than that. Darker things. Truth is I wanted to save her and I couldn't." He gazed out to sea. His tone was self-deprecating. "I needed a lot of therapy myself to recover from that madness." Then came an ironic laugh. "And did she fall apart after we split, as I predicted? Not for a minute. Her life continued unchanged and unscathed without me – designer drugs, drink, overwork, parties, photo shoots, and fun. You've probably heard of her. Mercedes Hall?"

An image of the stunning dark-skinned model flashed through Olwen's mind, followed by a twinge of dismay. How could she hope to compete? Mercedes's name was entangled with millionaires and movie stars. There were also lurid tabloid stories, though Olwen couldn't recall any mention of a husband.

"Physician, heal thyself," he said with a sigh, draining his glass.

"So, you're a fool for love." Her voice contained no judgement. "I've made a complete ass of myself so many times it isn't funny." She started to peel a fig. It was beautifully ripe. The purple skin came away easily and the juice ran down her mouth. She wiped it off with the back of her hand. "A few years ago, I took my daughter on a weekend trip to Paris. It was my first time in that divine city. I went on one of those tourist boats that go up and down the Seine. We were approaching a bridge, Pont Neuf, I think, and the guide said we had to make a wish as we passed under it. All the way up to the bridge I argued back and forth with myself between love and enlightenment. I finally settled on the higher goal – enlightenment – and was whispering the word to myself as we drew near. Then, just as the boat reached the edge of the bridge, I mentally shouted, *'Love! Love! I want love!'*"

He laughed along with her. "I see nothing wrong with that. When all is said and done, that's what we're here for: to express love of every kind. I believe our true purpose is to love and be loved."

"I like that."

He threw her a quick look. "Are you with someone right now?"

"Nope. My usual status. Just out."

He grinned, paused, and then probed some more. "Did things end well?"

"If they did, would they have ended?"

He shrugged. "Some relationships die a natural death."

She grimaced. "Natural for him, maybe."

"Ah." He waited a moment, as if expecting her to say more or to tell him to stop. When she did neither, he pressed on. "If you were to give him a label, an archetype, say..."

She laughed. "As nosy parkers go, you're an evil genius." She thought a moment. "The Reluctant Lover. My image of him is a man hurrying up escalators, disappearing around corners, hesitating and frowning, and driving off in his car."

"The idiot," said Dr Jack.

She smiled, but her tone was wry. "I picked him. What does that make me? The idiot's mate." She let out a little sigh. "I actually thought we were building something real and substantial. We had a lot in common and there was a lot of honesty. At one point he said, 'show me your worst. I promise I won't run.' And then, when the time came, and I showed him just how far down I can go into despair..."

"He ran."

"Like a yellow-bellied dog."

"Men are bastards."

"Agreed."

They laughed together.

"What drew you to him?"

"There was no one else around at the time." She stopped. "I'm *not* a bitter woman."

He laughed.

She continued. "We met at a writers' conference in Atlanta. He was the official photographer. Attractive, a great talker, very funny. I love to laugh, you may have noticed. He's Anglo-Irish, lives in London, an exciting city and only a cheap flight away. I loved visiting him. Of course the long-distance aspect suited me just fine. High on freedom, low on intimacy. He had a strong libido, like mine. Whenever we met up – once a month, more or less – the sex was non-stop and amazing."

Dr Jack chuckled deep in his throat. His eyes appraised her frankly. She looked away.

"It was the opposite with Mercedes." He sighed. "She was sexually dysfunctional, pardon the clinical description. I was well aware of this before we married. We had an unspoken agreement that I could 'satisfy my needs' elsewhere when she couldn't handle them, which turned out to be most of the time. I believed my love for her transcended sex. It was a binding of the soul. Fascinating the degree to which we can delude ourselves. Did she love me? I'm not sure any more, but I thought she did at the time, at least to the degree she was able to."

"There's the rub," Olwen murmured. "What is love?"

She drew her knees up to her chest and folded her arms around them. "I think I only truly discovered love when my daughter was born. She was the first and only person I have ever loved fully and unconditionally."

"Do you not love yourself?" he asked.

She shifted uneasily. "I admire myself." Then, after a moment, "I like myself. A good start." She frowned pensively. "Do you know that short story, the one about the child and the rocking horse?"

He nodded. "Classic Freudian."

"D.H. Lawrence, what do you expect? Do you remember how the boy heard the unspoken whisper that permeated his family home? The whisper that drove him to rock on the horse? Something about the need for money. It was the dark secret, the unspoken obsession of the family, particularly his mother's. Well, one day, when my printer was running off a manuscript to send to my publisher, Robyn, my daughter – she was only three at the time – told me it was saying: *Don't love me. Don't love me.*"

His look was sympathetic. Olwen was reminded that he was a psychiatrist, a trained listener. Only now did she realise that the atmosphere had changed between them. Where it had been charged and crackling with electric attraction, it was now a damp squib. An old ennui settled over her. The last thing she wanted or needed was a rehash of her failed attempts at relationship. She had finished eating. There were a few crumbs left on her plate. She threw them to the gulls that had settled on the sand.

He began to clear away the picnic, tossing things into the basket. There was an edge to his movements. Was he disappointed? Angry?

Though the sun was still shining, she shivered as she reached for her jeans. What on earth was she thinking? They had only just met. She hardly knew him. What kind of carry-on was this for someone her age? Acting like a teenager! She was annoyed at him for egging her on and more so at herself for responding. With more force than necessary, she pulled her jeans to her knees and stood up to hitch them over her hips.

And that was when she lost her balance.

Somewhere in the moment of falling towards him, her mind teased her with a titbit imparted by Dr N. Jungians tell of "the Fool" who walks behind us on the tightrope of life, always waiting for the right moment to jump up and down and throw us off. Tripping us up with words or actions. Shattering our illusion that we are in charge. Making us absurd.

He didn't see her falling. He had turned away to pour the dregs of the elderflower into the sand. When she landed on top of him, he thought he had been struck by something. He let out a yell. She yelped too in the tangle of limbs, her jeans halfway up her thighs, her breasts cushioning his head as he attempted to duck.

Seconds later, they were stretched out together, arms and legs entwined, laughing so hard they wept.

"The Fool knocked me over," she said, knowing he'd understand.

When they stopped laughing, a deep silence fell between them. They made no effort to separate but stared into each other's eyes. The charge between their bodies was all the greater for having been briefly cut off. The heat was rising fast.

"God bless the Fool," he murmured. Then he kissed her. A slow warm wet kiss.

There was an urgency to their love-making, as if they both felt the need to outrun second thoughts and cooler judgements. Passion triumphed over reason. An act of utter indiscretion. Irresponsible. Imprudent. Their bodies were delighted. At last, the consummation of an attraction that had begun the moment they met.

They quickly stripped each other naked. He pinned her hands to the ground as he moved over her. She opened her legs wide to receive him, locking his ankles with her own. They fell willingly into the madness, driving each other on, opening the love wound, the soul mouth, fulfilling the primal urge to join what was broken, returning to the beginning, the sacred ocean, the bliss.

She cried out first. He followed soon after. Spent and gasping for breath, they clung to each other like survivors in the sea.

"You're stunning," she said, after a while. "I nearly passed out."

He laughed low in his throat. The words every male wants to hear.

"It takes two."

But he said it as an afterthought, a throwaway line, and she heard it and he saw that she did. Before he could correct himself, she threw back her head and laughed out loud.

"You have a beautiful laugh," he said. "A beautiful mouth."

He kissed her again and again.

They eventually loosened their hold on each other, but kept arms and legs linked. He pulled the edges of the rug around them.

"Oh God," she said. "I am that woman who gets the leg-over at courses and conferences!"

They laughed some more.

"The libido wanders where it will," he said, with a shrug. "It's hardly surprising. Freud was wrong in a lot of departments, but not that one. Sex is life. Life is sex. Even the stars do it. Euphémie has a great theory on that."

Her eyebrow shot up. "Is there something between you and La Belle?"

He answered her seriously. "I've slept with no one in the circle... until now...and nor did I ever intend to, believe me. I'm aware of my nature as a sexual predator. I make a conscious effort to control it."

She snorted indignantly. "Oh, so I'm to blame? I seduced you?"

She would have said more, but he tightened his hold on her and kissed her repeatedly until she was no longer annoyed.

"You caught me off guard," he confessed. "I wasn't expecting to meet my match here. I should've known. Irishwomen are all about sex." His grin was wicked. "They make great whores."

She punched his shoulder hard. "I can't believe you just said that, though I admit some part of me considers it a compliment."

"See?" He laughed again. "I wouldn't dream of saying that to a woman of any other nationality."

"Yeah, well, you're right," she agreed. "Historically we were known to enjoy promiscuity, taking lovers under our great cloaks. 'The wild Irishwoman' as the anally retentive English called us. Then of course the Catholic Church went crazy trying to stamp it out of us. The sin of Eve, the great temptress of man. Not that they succeeded. It just went underground. Mad for it, we are," she said, mimicking an Irish brogue. "A fuckin' good ride, bejasus, that's the ticket."

Dr Jack howled. They kissed some more. Then he drew back a little to study her. That grin again.

"What outrageous thing are you going to say now?" she demanded.

"You're my first redhead."

She was caught between a laugh and a gasp.

"That's as bad as me saying you're my first black man!"

"Am I?"

She opened her mouth to protest, then closed it again. She saw that he was genuinely curious.

"I had a Jamaican boyfriend in my early teens," she said. "Very sweet and courteous. But I was a virgin and not yet into drink or drugs, so too afraid to go too far. Also his grandmother, whom he lived with, called me a lady and said I wasn't like white trash girls. She even invited me to dinner. I didn't want to let her down."

Olwen paused a moment, moving closer against him.

"The contrast when you and I...it was gorgeous. I kept opening my eyes to see. Ebony and ivory, like the song says. But there was something more to it, I won't deny it, something about crossing taboos, forbidden fruit, being conquered by the Other. Sex *and* race. It was delicious." Her grin matched his. "So, what's it like for you? I'm your first redhead but not, I take it, your first white woman?"

"I've had a few. Like you, I get a kick out of the Otherness. Also the forbidden. Acting out Ol' Whitey's greatest nightmare."

They both laughed wickedly.

"There's another side to it," he added. He held up his hand. "A white woman's body is like this." He turned his hand over to show her the pale palm. "Another side of *me*."

She caught her breath.

"You're wonderful."

"You too." He smiled. "You shine...like a star."

They had reached a state of perfect accord. They had also returned to reason. Both were solemn.

"We can't do this again," she told him. "Not here. Not this week."

"Understood," he agreed. "But I hope..."

He stopped. His look was uncertain.

She felt the same ambivalence.

"We can't know," she said. "Not now. This is a strange place and strange things are happening. We can only wait and see."

He nodded. They were already moving apart. But when she heard his sigh, so sincere, so full of regret, she had to stop herself from giggling.

"One more for the road?"

With a great laugh, he reached for her.

"Oh Irishwoman, divine wild Irishwoman."

CHAPTER TWENTY-FIVE

THE OPUS CLARIFIED

They tiptoed into the house, pausing in the hall to listen. Faint sounds issued from the Meeting Room. The full circle sharing was well under way. The two of them had already agreed that they wouldn't rejoin the group just yet. No doubt their absence had been noted, if not at lunch then certainly by now. Better to leave re-integration for the less formal atmosphere of supper time. Plus they needed to shower and change.

"I'll return these to the kitchen," Dr Jack whispered, indicating the basket and blanket.

"See you at supper," she said.

They were both snickering. He grasped her around the waist before she could leave.

"One last kiss?"

"We agreed no more!"

But the protest was mild and she yielded readily.

"Last kiss," he repeated as they broke apart. Then he winked. "Until the course is over."

She grinned to herself all the way back to her room.

The hot shower was glorious. She took her time, luxuriating in the water and the scented soap. Though a few misgivings niggled at the back of her mind, she had no real regrets. Wearing only her dressing gown, she plumped down on the bed and opened her laptop.

So, Jack is my lover. It wasn't really my intention, but I guess all that sparkage was bound to lead somewhere. Here I go again. Falling for a man who lives in another country. It can't be a coincidence. What did my dear Dr N say? Avoidance of intimacy. Love at a distance. Yeah well. What does that mean in real terms? You're supposed to ignore a handsome brilliant sexy man who's attracted to you just because he doesn't live in your neighbourhood? How does that—

The knock on her door pulled her out of her thoughts. She scrambled to hide the computer.

It was Dr Jack. He hadn't showered or changed yet. Leaning against the door frame, he looked into her room curiously.

Surprised to see him, she felt mildly irked. She wanted and needed some time to herself.

Did he glimpse her annoyance? He looked amused.

"Apologies for intruding. Rose wants to see you."

Olwen's heart jumped. A surge of panic.

"Oh God, are we in trouble? Will we be—?"

"Expelled? Sent home with a note?" He laughed. "There was some threat to that effect, unless we knock it off. I didn't bother informing him that we had already come to that decision. Just told him his patriarchal stance was absurd. We're not children."

"I don't like the man at all. He scares me."

Dr Jack was surprised. "What are you afraid of?"

She was drawn up short. What exactly was it about Rose that disturbed her?

"There's something there...something...sinister. A threat of violence."

Dr Jack sobered instantly. "I've known Rose for years. Believe me, you're in no danger whatsoever. Not in that way. I can guarantee it."

Something about his solicitude grated on her. And his assurance was odd. *Not in that way.*

"I can look after myself, thank you." She tossed her head.

"Of course you can." His eyes lit up. "And if it comes to a barney between the two of you, my money's on the fighting Irish. Get dressed. I'll show you to his office."

She made him wait in the hallway while she put on her clothes. This was no time for messing. She needed to collect herself. Despite the show of bravado, she was utterly unnerved. A private interview with Rose after she had been clearly misbehaving was the last thing she wanted. Better a firing squad!

Her anxiety increased as she followed Dr Jack to the second floor.

"What did he say?" she quizzed him. "Did you have a big row? How did he know– ?"

"There isn't much he doesn't see. But don't sweat it. You've got more power than you realise."

"What's that supposed to mean?"

He was taking long strides. She quickened her pace to keep up with him. Her mind was racing with questions, but she found herself distracted by her surroundings. There were all kinds of artwork and sculpted pieces in the hallways. She noticed, in particular, the many mirrors. One startled her so badly she jumped. Small and round, it hung at her eye level. When she first glanced into it, she thought she was looking at a man's face. Then she saw that the mirror had a long twist of hair dangling from its rim, so that anyone looking in the glass acquired a beard. The effect was both shocking and amusing. At the same time the trick was strangely familiar. Where had she heard of such a thing before? She would have shown it to Dr Jack, but he was already ahead and she had to hurry to catch up.

They reached the northern wing of the house. It had an additional storey rising above the main building. As Olwen approached the stairwell that led to the third floor, she was overwhelmed by a sense of déjà vu. A forgotten dream? She stopped to stare back at the last door on the landing.

"Is that Suzume's bedroom?" she asked him.

"It is." He looked at her curiously. "How did you know?"

She frowned, as the memory tugged again, then shrugged.

"That's my room," he said, indicating the door across from Suzume's.

The statement was neutral and didn't invite intimacy or humour. Olwen certainly didn't feel like joking. Her uneasiness was approaching panic.

"Straight up the stairs, down the hall, and turn left," he told her. "You'll see the door. It's black."

"You're not coming?!"

"I need to clean up. You'll be fine," he said, trying not to laugh.

"Bastard," she mouthed at him.

He did laugh, then, and off he went to his room.

"Fuckhead," she added as she walked reluctantly up the stairs.

There was a moment when she felt something invisible brush against her; something soft and light, like a veil, but she couldn't see anything.

The third floor passageway was dimly lit by lamps resembling torches. The stuffed heads of animals lined each side. Olwen shuddered at the sight of a magnificent stag with glassy eyes. At the end of the corridor was a tall window with a breathtaking view of the loch. To its right was an alcove housing a life-size version of the statue she had admired on her first day: a stately woman in medieval dress and crown, holding a child on her shoulder. *Our Lady of the Isles.* It was a beautiful image of motherhood and the feminine Divine. Olwen felt a wave of calm. A second later, her heart jumped as she faced the black door on her left. The entrance to Rose's quarters.

Before her will could fail her, she knocked loudly.

"Come in!" came his voice on the other side.

She tried to breathe normally.

It's not the Principal's office! And you're an adult, not a kid!

She opened the door.

Rose stood by the window, a lean figure gazing outwards. He didn't turn as she entered. She was struck by the thought that he was granting her time and privacy to adjust to her surroundings. Her first impression was a room of shadows and clutter. The heavy curtains were partially closed, only allowing a half-light. The mahogany desk held centre stage. It appeared to be of the same craftsmanship as the mantelpiece in the Meeting Room, with elaborately carved legs and clawed feet. On the far wall, the fireplace was of black marble. The mantel held an ornate clock as well as numerous framed photographs. There was a golden harp in one corner of the room and other instruments scattered here and there. He was a musician?

"Please, make yourself comfortable," he said.

He gestured towards two armchairs in front of the fire. No doubt he intended to join her there. The idea repelled her. It was too close, too intimate. She wanted him to sit behind his desk and keep things formal.

She sat down reluctantly, pushing the chair back as far as she could manage.

"Would you like a drink?" he asked. "Mint tea perhaps?"

He opened a cabinet that concealed a kitchen unit with sink and hotplate. Without waiting for her to respond, he put tea leaves, honey and fresh mint into a silver pot. He wasn't using his cane, perhaps because of the short distances. When he began to arrange a tray, she rose to help him. He waved her back.

"I can manage sufficiently, thank you. Will you pull over the little table?"

The tea was served in blue glasses with silver holders.

"This is delicious!" she said, after a sip.

He settled into the chair opposite her.

"I acquired a taste for it," he said, "when I lived for a time amongst the Tuaregs. They are like the Irish with their tea, drinking it on every occasion."

She followed his glance to the mantelpiece. Beside a tall hookah pipe was a faded photograph of a man on a camel. Most of his face was covered with a blue headdress, but she assumed it was Rose. Was he trying to impress her? He had certainly succeeded. She acknowledged the implication of great adventures beyond her own. It left her feeling a little naïve and off-kilter.

She drank her tea and waited to see what he would say.

"I would like to speak of your work, if I may," he said.

She was taken aback, it was the last thing she expected, but she managed a shrug.

"Sure, why not. Everyone's a critic."

"Would I be correct in saying that you use children's stories as a vehicle for what you want to say about life and the world? As opposed to writing specifically to and for children?"

The question disarmed her. It was a subject dear to her heart.

"Yes! In the same way as C.S. Lewis and P.L. Travers did. Travers actually hated being called a children's writer. She, like Lewis, considered the fairy tale an ideal genre for expressing matters of the soul."

Rose listened to her with an earnestness that both flattered and unnerved her.

His tone was strangely eager. "You are, I believe, aware of Philip Pullman's objections to C.S. Lewis and J.R.R. Tolkien? He argues that their work is a rejection of the material world and hence, a rejection of reality and life itself. In short, a longing for the Otherworld is...a death wish."

Though she was anticipating an attack of some kind, she didn't see it coming. His words fell like a blow. She had never viewed her yearnings or her stories in this light.

Could this be true? I can't deny that at the heart of my books is a longing for the Otherworld; and a deep desire to leave this one. How else can you leave this world except by dying? Is my love of Faerie a love of death?

Rose leaned towards her. "Both Tolkien and Lewis suffered the trauma of the Great War in their youth. Both were hospitalised. Neither of them spoke or wrote in any detail about their experiences, though Tolkien referred to the 'animal horror' of the trenches, while Lewis attributed his lifelong headaches and nightmares to that time. Both lost many of their young friends in the conflict. It's only natural that their world view would, at its very heart, reject reality. Mr Pullman lacks compassion when he attacks the two writers for their inevitable expression of the death wish; but he most specifically objects, of course, to it being presented to children. I think this is his greater error.

"I would argue that it is the unconscious identification with the death wish which explains why so many who have suffered trauma – both young and old – find solace in *The Chronicles of Narnia* and *The Lord of the Rings*."

"That makes sense," Olwen said, after a while. She spoke softly, sadly.

He paused a moment. Was that a look of sympathy? Then he continued.

"You have written articles about these three authors, some in defence of Tolkien and Lewis against Pullman. You have referred to 'my dear beloved C.S. Lewis', giving him credit for your early moral development. You have also claimed that he helped you to survive your childhood."

Olwen stiffened. "Have you got some kind of file on me?"

"I have files on everyone here. The Work is profoundly personal. How else can I choose whom to invite? I must know who comes to the circle. I must be careful of the ingredients that go into the crucible."

Anger and revulsion coursed through her. She moved to the edge of her seat, preparing to leave. He raised his hand to stop her.

"There is no need to be upset. I have breached no boundaries. All the information I have collected is in the public domain. I have read everything you have published – books, articles, papers, and reviews – and there is also your website. You give of yourself freely and generously on your blog, providing your readers with a wealth of information about your activities, your thoughts, your hopes and wishes, even your dreams. Like Theseus's thread, your blog guides the reader through the maze of your life and your mind."

Against her better judgement, Olwen sat back again, intrigued by his words.

"If you'll excuse me," he said, getting to his feet. "I have a treat to accompany our tea."

Olwen's mouth watered at the sight of the Turkish Delight, arranged attractively on a crystal plate – squares of pink rose, green mint, and yellow lemon, all powdered with sugar.

"In honour of Narnia?" she asked, amused.

Was that a hint of a smile on his lips?

"I do prefer Edmund to all of Lewis's characters," Rose said, as he returned to his seat. "Deeply flawed. Deeply human. He betrayed his siblings for his own gain, but came to understand the nature of his wrong through suffering. I think his experience with evil and inner pain made him a fuller and more complex character than his idealised brother, Peter."

"I agree! Edmund the Just. I thought he was wonderful. But my favourite character is Aravis. Also flawed, but a truly heroic girl-adventurer, straddling two cultures and destined to be queen. I wish he had written more stories about her."

Olwen was beginning to enjoy herself. She helped herself to more tea and another piece of Turkish Delight.

Rose regarded her a moment, then dropped his next depth charge.

"I take it the present group is more to your liking than the first one?"

She almost splashed the tea over her. She had actually forgotten about her arrival – it seemed so long ago – and the group she had dubbed "the Disappeared". The mention of them now was such a surprise she answered without thinking.

"Yes, I prefer this group. Especially Elsie and Dr Jack. Also Christy and Roy, because they're Irish. And Savitri and Suzume and..." She stopped the tumble of words and caught her breath. "What happened to the first group?" To her dismay, her voice quavered.

"They were sent home. They displeased you."

His tone was matter-of-fact. He watched her closely.

She struggled for composure. There was no doubt he was playing mind games with her, even as he evidently manipulated the circle, indeed everything that happened at Dunesfort House. *The Magus. Magister Ludi.* She had to keep a cool head. She had to be clever. *Ní mór don fhear beag bheith glic. The lesser man must be cunning.* But even as she sat up straight, she saw that Rose observed her efforts with approval and satisfaction. She refused to be complimented. Charm itself was a trap.

He set his empty cup on the table and leaned back in his chair. The wintry eyes continued to study her.

She nibbled on another piece of Turkish Delight, determined not to speak first.

With a faint air of amusement he acknowledged her resolve and then apparently came to a decision.

"We have spoken of your work. I would like to speak of mine. It is not an easy thing to do. Words sever and limit, label and bind, a process diametrically opposed to the essence of what we are doing here. Still, there is no other way to communicate as our race has lost the skill of telepathy."

If Olwen were a horse or dog, her ears would have pricked up.

"What's going on at Dunesfort House?" he mused. "Many words might apply: *mukti, samadhi, satori,* individuation, enlightenment, the Kingdom of God, the New Jerusalem, Shambhala, *hieros gamos...*"

He placed his fingertips together.

"The aim of all religions – and I refer to their ideal and their Source, not their use or abuse as human power structures – was and is a meeting with the Divine, in whatever form that principle might take in its cultural environment. Many paths have been created to aid the pursuit of the goal: rites and rituals, prayers, doctrine, meditation, the use of teacher plants, vision quests, and so on. The path may be solitary or communal and–"

"That's one of my intentions for the week!" she said suddenly. "To see God!"

She had completely forgotten that she'd meant to shut him out. He was speaking of her heart's desire!

"I'm not surprised," he said. "That is the goal of all mystics. However, you must understand, this is not the aim of the Work, though it is often a consequence. But I digress, one of the perils of attempting to describe the indescribable."

His frustration was evident. She watched him struggle for words. Her feelings towards him softened.

"Break it down," she suggested. "Or start in the middle and go from there. This is my stuff. I'm with you."

Was that a grateful look?

"The primary goal of the Work is healing," he said. "First for the individual and then, through association, the larger community in which the individual lives. *Heal yourself, heal the world* is the sound bite invented by one of our younger members. Dunesfort House is but one circle in a worldwide network. A great movement is being birthed on the planet at this time – a rising tide of consciousness against the unconscious forces of greed and aggression that rule our governments, industries, financial institutions and militaries. We have reached a crucial juncture in the history of our race. We have wired our planet for self-destruction. We stand on the brink of annihilation. If we do not transform ourselves we will fall victim to the inexorable law of evolution: *change or die.*"

Rose paused. Were his hands trembling?

"But I have digressed again. The various circles use different methods and even different aims to assist the change. The Work at Dunesfort House is based on energy – *chi* or *prana*. More precisely, the Work is about the release of energy. Jung once remarked that 'the shadow is gold'. The Work of our circle concentrates on the shadow – what is repressed by the individual – pain, torment, wounds, flaws, trauma, and dark secrets. Through activities like the Sweat House and Breathwork, the participants release trapped energy. It is both an individual and collective project as the release of individual energy feeds back into the circle, magnifying the healing of all in a chain reaction."

"The Work is alchemy!" Olwen said suddenly. "You're spinning gold! Energy and light out of darkness and pain. It's spiritual and psychological alchemy!"

Rose's face lit up. For the second time, she noted that he could be beautiful. Her heart tightened as she realised that his features were usually constricted, apparently by pain. Was it physical? Related to his lameness? Or was it emotional? The shadow he spoke of?

"Wonderful," he said quietly. "I knew you would be able to find the right words."

His open admiration rendered her defenceless. She was adrift, with nothing to hold on to.

"It *is* alchemy," he agreed. "And, as in alchemy, the ingredients are essential. In a kind of science that is also an art, I must choose people and match them, according to what they might achieve alone, with a partner, and in the circle as a whole."

"The first group..."

She could hardly say it.

"They did not suit you," he said, nodding. "Or at least some of them did not. Your unhappiness was obvious and, more importantly, your intention to leave. There was no time to discover who had alienated you. It was expedient to send them all away and call in replacements. My only hope was that you would find the remainder of the group acceptable as well as the new arrivals I called up in haste. I confess I arranged for you to be seated that morning with Jack and Elsie. They are two of the most experienced of our circle. I've yet to meet anyone who didn't respond to them favourably."

She stared at him, speechless. All her suspicions were proved correct. He *was* a puppet-master! He had even used the others to manipulate her. And yet...and yet...she couldn't deny that some part of her was hugely flattered. Elsie had said it on the very first day. Whatever the game, Olwen was a key player!

As if he could read her mind, Rose confirmed, "You are central to this circle. I invited you for good reason."

There was a brief hesitation before he spoke again, so brief she might have missed it except for the lowering of his eyes. Was he hiding something? She was already on guard, watching for signs of the sinister; but what he said next rang with truth.

"Threaded throughout your books are strands of 'soul stuff'. Hints and glimpses of experience with and secret knowledge of a reality or realities beyond the norm. Without wishing to be critical, I think that you have not brought this material to fruition. I mean to say that you have not yet found the vehicle to express it fully."

He leaned towards her again. There was a strange light in his eyes.

"It is *my* intention, my hope and dream, that this week will provide such a vehicle for you. Please understand that I do not mean to pressure you. I know well that, if I did, no good would come of it. I believe in the Work, and though many might think such a belief a fairy tale, I am convinced it has the potential to save the world. I wish to make it available to as wide an audience as possible, but my strength lies in working with small groups."

A wry smile crossed his lips. His tone was self-deprecating.

"I am an introvert, and I have not been blessed with the ability to write. You are an extravert. You travel to conferences, you talk to large audiences and more importantly you tell stories and are published worldwide. I am hoping that if this experience goes well for you and you are truly inspired, then you will write about it."

Olwen wasn't sure how to react. Her mind was spinning. She felt utterly ambivalent. She agreed with his assessment of her work to date. Though each new book brought her a little closer, she had yet to get anywhere near the sacred mountain of her vision, what she truly wanted to say. "When did mission become work?" one of her writer friends once asked in despair. "Writing is a prayer," another had declared.

But none of this meant she was ready to jump on Rose's bandwagon. It wasn't her nature either to follow or lead. She was a lone wolf. And she hadn't even begun to address her resentment at being used like a chess piece.

"There are a lot of people writing about this kind of thing," she pointed out.

"Works of non-fiction," he argued. "But as Anthony de Mello once said, 'The shortest distance between a human and the truth is a story.' There's also the problem that this subject matter is used too often to gain wealth and power. This is a lower aspiration, a form of sorcery. Many New Age leaders and gurus are ultimately abusive. They have not dealt with their own pain and they inflict it on their initiates and followers, even as tyrants and dictators do. The aspirations of true practitioners are noble. They seek healing, not wealth and power. Having dealt first with their own pain, they pass the healing on and wherever possible, they do so freely."

"But you charge –" she began and stopped, suddenly realising the truth.

She had paid so little for what she had received, and was well able to afford it.

"Yes," he said, nodding. "I weigh the price per person. *From each according to his means.* Those who cannot pay are fully subsidised."

A silence fell between them. So much of what he had said appealed to her. Still, her resistance was strong. She did not want to commit herself. She had responded to his invitation for a variety of reasons but, despite her initial quip about "getting a book out of it", she had at no time considered that she was researching a novel. For one thing, she was exhausted after a three-year slog on the biggest book of her career: seven hundred pages of blood, sweat and fairy tale. Just the thought of writing made her heart sink.

"I can't make any promises," she said flatly. "I'm on sabbatical right now."

He strove to hide his reaction, but the clenched jaw spoke volumes. She steeled herself. He was accustomed to being in control. Would there be consequences for crossing him?

She stood up to leave, and was about to thank him for the tea and sweets when he cut her off.

"A final matter before you go," he said coldly.

His tone brought her up short. *Here it comes.* Would he eject her from the circle, even as he had so blithely expelled the first group?

"A strong life force is inevitably accompanied by a strong libido," he said.

Her face burned. She made a noise of protest, but he continued relentlessly.

"The energy of the circle must be forged like a chain for the healing process to succeed. Couple energy creates a break in the circuit. Lovers inevitably withdraw from the world to concentrate on each other. I would ask that you put your relationship with Dr Elphinstone on hold, until the course is completed. Either that... or leave."

Olwen nodded abruptly and turned on her heels.

She couldn't get out of there fast enough.

CHAPTER TWENTY-SIX

REFLECTION

Olwen was on her way back to her room when the supper gong sounded. She had spent almost an hour with Rose. It had seemed much longer. She quickened her pace, but only to avoid meeting anyone. There was no question of facing the crowd in the dining room. The idea of talking to anyone, let alone fielding questions from Dr Jack or Elsie, was unthinkable. She needed time to recover. Time to reflect.

Back in her room, she locked the door and took out her laptop. Her hands shook as she opened the journal file. She felt cold. Was she in shock? She decided to light a fire. There were firelighters, old newspapers, and a basket filled with turf. It wasn't long before the flames rose to cheer her.

Back on the bed, wrapped in her duvet, she wrote like one possessed.

I'm absolutely fucked, no pun intended, and there's two of them in it. Jack thought it was funny throwing me into the lion's den, but was there a conspiracy? What do I know about these guys? Fuck all. Was I doubly seduced? First a picnic with sun and sex. Then the big talk – "you're someone special" – sweetened with delicious drinks and Turkish Delight. Fitting that we spoke of Edmund. Am I being groomed by a modern version of the White Witch? These people are already so far under my skin they're swimming in the marrow.

Olwen stopped a moment, her hands poised over the keys. Her fingers trembled.

Okay, I know I have an overactive imagination and a tendency (hah!) to paranoia but what's the definition of a paranoiac? Someone who has all the facts! I'm being played. I can feel it in my bones. And everyone – not just Jack and Rose – seems to know far more about what's going on here than me. It's not like I haven't seen this horror movie before. The woman wanders around clueless as the plot thickens and you almost think she deserves what she gets because she's too dumb-ass to run.

And yet...I can't deny it, my ego is pleased. It appears that I, yes, little ole me, am a key player in this glass bead game. I mean, my god, Rose actually admitted that the Disappeared were sent away because they pissed me off! Me!

She drew the duvet closer.

If only I could have recorded our meeting. There was so much to it and I'm already forgetting. So many big ideas. He talked about abusive cult leaders who inflict their own unresolved pain on the people who follow them. Talk about the pot and kettle. What about him? What unresolved pain is he acting out?

She frowned at her image in the mirror of the wardrobe across the room.

I bet it's something to do with sex. He was quick to use it as a weapon against me. Repressed homosexuality? Impotence? Sado-masochism?

From the very first day, she had sensed the violence behind his restraint. With good reason she was hypersensitive to any hint of it in men. Regardless of what Dr Jack said, she trusted her own instincts. Did Rose prey on the women in the circle? Perhaps the young men? A lot of people seemed to be in awe of him. She recalled the lingering glances cast by many, including Euphémie. The inevitable attraction of the alpha male, the man in charge, the Leader.

To even think of Rose that way made her queasy.

He did his best to appear as if he was telling me everything, but Paranoid Patty or no, my gut feeling is usually right about these things. He was holding something back.

An image flashed through her mind. That brief moment when he lowered his eyes and glanced away. The automatic defence of someone who is lying or being evasive!

He says he brought me here because I'm a writer, so I'll spread the word about the Work. Get past the flattery, dope-brain, it doesn't add up! I'm not exactly A-list. He draws from a pool of people from all over the world, and he's got big money backing him. No way I'm the only writer who could do the job. I can think of dozens who would jump at the chance. There's something else going on. Some other reason why I'm here. If I–

Olwen broke off abruptly. The tiny thing that had been scratching at the back of her mind, like a cat at the door, finally broke through. One of the photographs on the mantelpiece in Rose's den. It was in an oval frame. The image shone with light as if overexposed, but the subject was discernible: a young man in black leather with white-blonde hair to his shoulders. He held a small harp in his hands.

She caught sight of herself in the wardrobe mirror again. She looked dazed. *Fairy struck.*

The room had grown dim with twilight. Slowly, almost mechanically, she turned off her computer and stowed it under her bed. The primal urge to retreat inside a cave was overwhelming. The Great Unknown crouched just beyond her campfire. She closed the shutters of the windows against the coming night. Heaped more turf on the hearth. The waves of heat made her drowsy. *Put that head to bed.* When she opened the dresser drawer to take out her pyjamas, she caught sight of the red satin camisole set that William had bought her. What was she thinking when she packed it? The sudden longing for him was a physical ache. She put on the lingerie and crawled into bed. If only he were there to hold her, to make her feel safe. She rejected any thought of Dr Jack. He was a stranger, under suspicion. She needed, wanted the familiar.

Drawing her knees to her chest, she hugged herself tightly. The tears began to fall. Another night when she would cry herself to sleep.

CHAPTER TWENTY-SEVEN

FIFTH NIGHT: THE WILD HUNT

Olwen woke to the sound of tapping on her window. She sat up, alert. Not a sound to be heard. Had she imagined it? Or was it part of a dream? Her stomach felt queasy. Something she ate? No, she had skipped supper and cried herself to sleep. The room glimmered faintly. Moonlight seeped through the edges of the shutters. *There's a crack in everything. That's how the light gets in.* The air was stuffy. She got out of bed to open the shutters. She opened a window as well, the one that looked down on the courtyard. That was when she felt something brush her hand. With a yelp, she jumped back. The touch was light and furry, like a paw. One of the house cats? Could it climb that high? She looked quickly around the room. No sign of an animal. With a shiver, she closed the window and returned to her bed.

The sheets felt icy against her satin lingerie. She was growing colder by the minute. Her fire had gone out, only grey ash in the grate. She hugged her duvet around her, but it didn't help. Jumping out of bed again, she took down an extra blanket from the top of the wardrobe and threw it over the bed. But as she slipped back under the covers she felt it: something long and hairy, like an arm or tail.

With a screech of terror, she leaped out of bed and slammed on the light. There was nothing there. Nothing she could see.

Backed against the wall, she clutched her stomach. She was shaking violently. The clock on the mantel showed 3:00 a.m. The true witching hour. Was that when he used to come to her? Long after his wife and children were asleep? He knew where the babysitter's room was.

Get a grip. Calmate, chica.

Given the nature of the Work at Dunesfort House, she had to expect regression into her personal history. She couldn't, wouldn't let it tyrannise her. Years of therapy had convinced her she was more than her past.

I am an adult, not a terrified child.

She made a quick search of the room, including under the bed, and shook out both the blanket and duvet. Nothing. Turning out the light, she got back under the covers. She was determined to sleep.

Then the breathing sounds began.

Low and heavy, it was like sandpaper scrubbing brick. The sounds came from the direction of the window overlooking the courtyard. Was something sitting on the sill? Her heart pounded so hard it hurt. There *was* something there. A hunched shape. The more she peered at it, the bigger it seemed. Too big for a cat. More like a large dog. She fought the urge to dive under the covers and squeeze her eyes shut. Instead, she lay mesmerised, peering over the blanket. Better not to let it out of her sight. If it moved, she had to know where it went!

Slowly, surreptitiously, she stretched out her arm to reach for the bedside lamp.

A hoarse whisper rasped the air.

Don't...

She pressed the switch. No light.

...be a wuss.

She nearly fainted. Tried to scream. A squeak came out. Was she asleep? Was this a nightmare?

What did ye ask for?

His voice was unlike anything she had ever heard before. Deep and coarse, yet also musical, it echoed with other sounds like the rustle of leaves and the fall of rain. There was an undertone of something implacable. A bedrock of will. One thing she was certain. It wasn't harmless. As she acknowledged what it was, she was overcome in equal measure with both terror and delight.

Desperate for courage, she called up every scrap of strength she could muster. Her own indomitable will. With deliberate slowness, she sat up in the bed. She didn't want to trigger off any reactions on its part, any sudden leaps towards her. Gripping her knees, she pressed them against her chest, to help contain her fear. All the time she was straining to see, to grasp its form. It seemed inchoate, a moon shadow.

Have ye glimpsed me yet? Human eyesight, what good is it? If ye don't know what you're looking at, ye can't see it!

Her mind threatened to unhinge. Her sense of reality, her firm place in life, was shattered. No ground to stand on. Caught between the dimensions. Lost between the worlds.

Come closer.

Curiosity battled with terror. *Curiosity killed the cat!* Amazed by herself, she got out of bed and stumbled towards it. Her legs were like rubber. She felt dizzy and nauseous. Some part of her was screaming about a demon. Every part of her was demanding that she *flee*. But she continued to approach. She would not be defeated by cowardice. She would not be terrorised in her own bedroom.

The air around her was charged with electricity. Her skin tingled. She began to discern a shape. Something bearded. A little old man? But there were leaves and branches. A leafy bush? The spirit of a bush? Her eyesight kept blurring. She forced herself to put out her hand.

Something reached back. Was that a leafy branch or a furry paw?

The touch was damp, soft, warm and cold all at once. She couldn't stop herself from shuddering.

It shuddered too. Did it feel the same revulsion at encountering something so utterly different from itself?

She was shaking and sobbing and terrified and overjoyed.

"You...you're...real...you...exist."

It was still a struggle to see him, to allow her eyes and mind to grasp him. Leaves, paws, teeth. A cross between a bush and an animal with wild eyes. She turned her head and tried a sideways glance. Much better. He came into focus. A young face that was impossibly old. Ancient, in fact. And for some reason vaguely familiar. But how could that be? His skin gave off a dim glow, forest-green then golden-brown, then green again and brown. He wore a vest of woven leaves and leathery pants. Knickerbockers? Cloven feet. No, pointy shoes curled at the ends. No, shiny hooves. No, curly-toed shoes.

Have ye a tongue on ye? Would ye ever get a hold of yourself. Can ye talk?

She was literally gripping herself, arms tight around her body in an attempt to keep herself together. *You asked for this. You wanted this experience. You've wished for it all your life. See it through. Or suffer regret till the day you die.* She licked her lips. They were dry as parchment. She tried to swallow. A half-strangled gulp. At last she managed to force out a hoarse whisper.

"I...I'm...t-t-trying...m-my...b-b-best."

Then she burst into tears as the truth rang through her mind, like bells on Christmas Day.

They exist! They really exist! Fairies are real!

She was right in front of him now. He was no more than four feet in height. A small boy with an old face and pointed ears. Pan. Puck. *Púca.* Goaty-looking with horns. His eyes were the worst. She panicked every time she looked into them. They were so utterly and undeniably alien. It wasn't at all like looking into the eyes of an animal. These eyes had nothing in them that could reassure her.

He sat on the window ledge, legs crossed, a demented Peter Pan.

Where's your manners? Introduce yourself.

"I'm...Ol...Olwen."

Pleased to meet you, Ol Olwen, I am Goldhart. That's h-a-r-t. No h-e-a-r-t in me!

His last words were said with a wicked goaty laugh.

"N-n-nice name," she uttered.

Ye've found your manners, that's a start. But for fucksake, ye're not going to be blubberin' the whole time, are ye?

He folded his arms and pinned her with his eyes. They didn't blink. They were lidless. She had to look away. She couldn't bear the black depths of them. With a huge effort, she sucked back the sobs and wiped her nose with the back of her hand.

What's the bloody fuss? Aren't ye a believer? Forever telling stories about us?

"That's different...easier...me going into your world...in my imagination...belief isn't the same as experience...But this...you coming into my world..."

He made an impatient noise.

To'ing or fro'ing, same difference to us.

She was beginning to reach some semblance of calm, when the horns rang out – beyond her window, a wild tantara calling through the night.

Goldhart stiffened. Lifting his nose to the air, he sniffed loudly.

It's begun. The Wild Hunt. We must away!

He opened the window. She saw what was coming next. As he jumped out, his voice echoed behind him.

Bualaimís an bóthar! Go tapaidh!

He expected her to follow him! He had come for her! That was why she was able to see him. Why he had let her see him. But though she was thrilled at the thought and the honour of it, she was no less terrified. From years of research into Faerie, she knew the invitation was fraught with danger. There were so many taboos, so many transgressions to avoid. She would have to guard her tongue and watch her step. Ignorance of the law was no excuse. Faerie practised zero tolerance. And the consequences were always grave.

Be quick! Be nimble!

He shouted from the courtyard below.

She couldn't do it.

No wish or desire, no hope or dream could make her take that leap of faith. The window was hundreds of feet above the ground. She would either crash through the glass roof of the conservatory or land hard on the cobblestones. A wave of grief and despair washed over her. She had failed the test.

There must be another way!

She ran for the door. There was no time to dress, no chance to grab a jacket or sweater. It was now or never. In her red satin lingerie, she raced barefoot down the stone stairs of the broch and out into the courtyard. Not a sight or sound of him. Nor of the Wild Hunt.

She raced through the archway and out onto the road. Her skin was turning blue with the cold. Her teeth chattered. She didn't care. She had to find them.

The night seemed alive. Mist and moonlight mingled in the dark grasses. The roar of the sea echoed from the cliffs. Shadows moved around her, slipping in and out at the edges of her vision. Everything was in motion, yet invisible.

The horns wound again. So far in the distance! A cry escaped her lips. They had left without her. Then another sound rang out, from the stables behind her. A high-pitched neigh. *Epona.* The mare was calling to her!

Olwen raced to the stables. Lord Donn's stall was empty. Had he joined the Hunt? Or was Rose out riding him, late at night? Epona was nervy and restless. There was no time to saddle her. Without stopping to think, Olwen jumped onto her back.

And they were off.

It was an incredible journey, chasing after the tantivy that echoed through the night. Riding bareback, half naked, she felt the icy wind on her skin, the sleek hide and hard muscle between her thighs. She kept her seat with the grip of her knees and calves, her fingers enmeshed in the long mane.

Valkyrie.

Horse and woman galloped over the wild moors, in the shadow of the mountains, past craggy coast and hidden loch. There was a moment when they stopped on the verge of the road, towering over a car as it crept passed them. Two pale faces peered out from the windscreen, dumbstruck.

With a burst of speed, they were away again, traversing the night landscape of Lewis. *Leòdhas. Leogach. Marshy land.* Who whispered the words in her mind? The placenames as they went? *Gearraidh na h-Aibhne. Beinn Mholach. Tolstadh Ur.* Was it Epona? Or the land itself?

At last they caught up with the Wild Hunt.

Once again she had to fight to keep herself sane as the truth overwhelmed her mind. These riders were not human, not of her world. Somewhere in the dazzling flashes of light and colour, the living fireworks, she glimpsed limbs, flowing tresses, sculpted features and wings. And their steeds were as wondrous, with fiery manes and nostrils snorting flame.

At first they appeared indifferent to her, as if she were beneath their notice. She was happy not to draw their attention. In their presence she felt like a clod of earth, heavy and ugly. But after a while she grew aware of their antagonism. *Interloper. Trespasser.* And she suddenly understood. She wasn't supposed to be there! She hadn't been invited! It was Goldhart's fault. These were Scottish fairies, Lewisian fey. What was an Irish *púca* doing amongst them?

Getting her into trouble, that's what. She was caught in a web of Otherworldly intrigue. Perilous politics. And where was the culprit? Looking around, she finally spotted him. He had shape-shifted, but she recognised him: a great golden stag, standing apart from the others. He shook his antlers at her with a jaunty toss of his head.

Goldhart.

Before she could complain or accuse, the horns wound again.

And the Wild Hunt charged off!

Epona kept pace with the fairy riders, catapulting over the land like a missile. But Olwen soon felt the effects. Her skull rang with a high-pitched noise. Her teeth buzzed like a drill. Every cell in her body screeched with nervous energy. How could she possibly keep up? She was made of matter, not light! The others flickered and flashed around her, like lightning in a storm. They all carried weapons – tall spears, shining swords, and bows and arrows. She had nothing. Only now did she wonder, what were they hunting?

A great *ROAR* shattered the night.

"*No.*"

The word came out as a whimper, even as the buried memories erupted in her mind. A white labyrinth. The Beast.

The others raised their weapons and spurred on their steeds. The Hunt was in full cry.

Did Epona sense her distress? Or was it that Olwen had loosened the grip of her knees? The mare fell back as the other riders charged ahead. It wasn't long before the two were alone in the dark landscape.

"Thank you," Olwen murmured. "Let's go home."

She patted Epona's neck as they turned back for Dunesfort House. The mare didn't gallop, but kept up a steady canter. They had travelled far. There was no sign of the big house. Olwen was numb with cold. She thought longingly of the fire in her bedroom and the soft duvet on her bed.

Then she heard it behind her. A savage screech. And the sound of hooves striking the earth.

Almost fainting with terror, she glanced over her shoulder. He was charging down on her, with his thick bull-head and hirsute body, naked genitals protruding. His cloven feet kicked up sods of turf as he ran. The wicked yellow eyes were fixed on her.

"Fly!" she screamed to Epona.

But she knew it was hopeless. The Beast was too close; Dunesfort House too far away.

Then things got worse. Instead of fleeing, Epona turned her head and raced towards the monster.

You can't trust anyone.

With helpless horror, Olwen was carried to the Beast. His foul stench invaded her nostrils. Her stomach heaved. The awful hands reached out to grab her. She couldn't escape them. Skimpily clad in her underwear, she was too small and vulnerable, with no means of defence. If only she had more clothing. Some kind of weapon. Someone to save her.

Mum. Help me.

She closed her eyes, wishing it all away, knowing that she could do nothing to stop it. Then came a violent jolt and a dreadful squeal.

From the Beast!

Olwen's eyes shot open. Epona's head was snaking forward, teeth bared to bite again. A second bloody gash scored the monster's chest. Now the mare spun around to kick out with her hind legs. The blows landed with heavy thuds and the crunch of bones. The Beast crashed to the ground, bellowing with pain and rage.

Olwen clung to Epona's mane and wept with joy. Ruairi's words echoed in her mind.

She be foliar. *Nought can harm a true mare. She will fight off any evil that comes at ye.*

The monster rolled away from the deadly hooves and lurched to his feet. Maddened and roaring, he clawed at a huge rock half-buried in the earth. Could the mare fend him off once he had a weapon? Olwen wasn't about to wait and see.

"Fly!" she cried again. *"Seek sanctuary!"*

There was no need for urging. Epona sped away.

The Beast gave chase. Olwen could hear his heavy breaths behind her. The ground trembled underfoot.

Ahead on the moor, silhouetted by moonlight, a great jagged shadow rose up. It wasn't Dunesfort House. The shapes were separate and uneven, like giants striding across the landscape. She suddenly recognised the Callanish Stones. And with that leap of logic common to dreams and fairy tales, she knew they would be safe if they reached the monument.

The Beast seemed to know that too. His shriek of frustration was terrible to hear. She couldn't stop herself from looking back. He was charging down on them in leaps and bounds. In his hands was the huge rock. With every step he took, the distance between them narrowed.

Epona's flanks were drenched with sweat; her breathing laboured and wheezy. There was blood in her nostrils. She was killing herself to save Olwen.

A piercing whine sounded behind them. The mare veered so sharply Olwen almost fell off. The rock shot past. A near miss. But miss them it did, and the time the Beast had taken to stop and aim had given them more of a lead. With a last spurt of speed, gasping for breath, Epona galloped up the avenue of the Callanish Stones.

It was as if the monument embraced both horse and rider. In her mind, Olwen saw a tall Lady reach out for her Child and lift it high on her shoulder.

Sanctuary.

Behind them a wail died out in the night. The Beast was gone. Olwen collapsed with relief on the mare's neck.

"Thank you," she murmured. "*A stór*, my treasure".

Epona carried her to the heart of the Stones, to the central ring that encircled the burial pit. There, perched on the tallest stone – the one Olwen had dubbed the king-stone – was Goldhart. He wore the shape of a *púca* once more, and was smoking a pipe. The smoke trailed downwards instead of up and sweetened the air.

"You!" she spluttered furiously. "We could've been killed!"

Goldhart let out a goaty little laugh.

Ah, give yourself a rest. Ye survived, didn't ye? And ye can't be blamin' me. Ye were the one who asked to see us. Ye know full well it's not safe to play with the fey. But ye've made a friend or two on Leòdhas, haven't ye now?

He glanced at Epona. The mare was still blowing hard, flecked with sweat and blood. Olwen slipped off her, hoping the *púca* might help.

But Epona ignored both of them and lowered her head to the burial pit. She nickered quietly, as if speaking to someone or something. A liquid light began to seep from the earth, filling the pit like a pool. The mare took a long drink. In a matter of seconds, she was restored. Nickering more loudly, evidently pleased with herself, she moved away to graze on the long grasses.

Happier now that Epona was well, Olwen clambered onto the stone nearest to Goldhart. There was no use arguing with him. He was right about one thing. In the heel of the hunt, it *was* her first intention, her first hope and dream: to see fairies. She could hardly complain that her wish was granted.

The stone was icy under her bottom. She might as well have been naked for all the protection she got from her lingerie. But though she was shuddering from the cold as well as the aftershock of the monster's attack, she couldn't deny that she felt fantastic. It was great to be alive.

She spoke from the heart, words spilling out in Irish and English, as she told him of her joy and her gladness that she had met him.

The *púca* almost fell off his perch.

Ye've got spirit, girseach! I'll grant ye that!

He offered her his pipe. Carved from blackthorn, it had a pattern of leaves and antlers along the stem. She took a quick puff. There was a strong taste of blackberries, but the smoke was acrid and burned her throat. She coughed and choked. At the same time, a rush of heat coursed through her limbs, and her skin changed from blue to a rosy pink.

She drew her knees up to her chest. The great stones surrounded her like a queen's guard. The landscape shimmered with moonlight and starlight. In the distance lay a range of hills that resembled a female figure asleep on her back. Olwen was thinking about fairies. How she had believed in them all her life. They were so important to her when she was a little girl. The thought of them had helped to keep her mind off the hunger and the violence and the other things that had happened.

"You were always there, weren't you?" she said to him. "Not just in stories, but all around me."

He puffed on his pipe before answering.

We were. Like the willow trees ye loved and the white clouds in the sky when ye lay on the grass, and the rain and the wind that ye listened to at night.

"But you didn't help me directly," she said, with a sigh. "I guess you couldn't."

Didn't we now?

There was something in his voice, a sadness that was almost human.

I'm thinkin' we took ye away more than once, to keep ye from the worst. It's all we're allowed to do in the scheme of things...more's the pity.

A stream of red-gold infused the horizon; the herald of dawn in the eastern sky.

Goldhart's mouth widened into a big yawn.

The night is done and a good night's work it was. Ye' ve passed the test. I'm thinkin' ye just might be up for it after all.

"Up for what?" she asked.

The task ye' ve been called here to do.

She sat up straight. The truth at last! And from such an unexpected source! A hundred questions crowded onto her tongue, but he was already shaking his head.

Time for the leaba, Ol Olwen. Beddy-byes!

And with his wicked goaty laugh, he pushed her off her perch.

With a yelp, she fell into the burial pit below. But instead of landing on the grass, she found herself falling through moonlight.

CHAPTER TWENTY-EIGHT

SHIP OF SOULS

Olwen woke the next morning feeling extraordinarily well. *The strange workings of the psyche. You cry yourself to sleep and wake up feeling grand.* An image flashed into her mind. She and Dr Jack, their bodies entwined. *Omigod, can you not behave? What do you think you are, a bloody teenager?* More memories poured in. A wicked grin crossed her face. *I'll be old soon enough. It was fucking brilliant. And brilliant fucking.* She laughed out loud. *Je ne regrette rien.* The images entertained her for a while, until a less pleasant memory intruded. Her meeting with Rose. The suspicion of a conspiracy reared its head once again and with it, the question of whether she was going to leave.

Don't be a wuss. How could you possibly go now? This is the most exciting adventure you've had in ages!

She jumped out of bed, eager to start the day. Two things struck her with instant dismay. A glance at the clock showed she had overslept by hours. Not only had she missed breakfast, she was late for the first session. More disturbing was the fact that her lingerie was streaked with mud and she ached all over!

What the hell! Sleepwalking? But where did I go? What did I do?

There was no time to solve the mystery. She needed to catch up with the programme. Rifling through her desk, she found her copy of the schedule. Something called "Spirit Boat" was taking place in the Trance Room. Her curiosity was piqued by the title alone. She didn't stop to shower but washed as fast as she could, then threw on jeans and a T-shirt. Pulling her hair back in a ponytail, she raced out the door and charged barefoot down the stairs. God knows how she would function without her morning coffee, but her chief concern was to catch the boat.

When she reached the door of the Womb, she hesitated outside. The oval door was solid oak with a brass ring for a handle. Dare she go in late? Or was it forbidden, like entering a theatre once the show had begun? She pressed her ear to the door. A faint sound of music. The low beat of a drum. And was that waves crashing or was she imagining it? She was suddenly reminded of an illustration by Pauline Baynes in *The Voyage of the Dawn Treader*. The picture showed three children falling into a painting of a Narnian ship at sea. But the Trance Room made no effort to pull her in and the door stayed stolidly shut. She would have to enter on her own volition.

Still, she hesitated. Rose would be furious. He was a stickler for rules and proper timekeeping. Not that she gave a damn how he felt; her qualms were for the others. What if she disturbed them and ruined their experience? She felt the loneliness of the outsider. *Trespasser. Interloper.* But against all her fears and insecurities was the bottom line: she didn't want to be left behind.

Fuck this for a game of soldiers, I'm going in.

She pushed the door open and stepped inside.

A wave of sound rushed to meet her: mesmeric music accompanied by the crash of surf and the cry of seagulls. In that moment she was utterly confounded, truly at sea; for two realities confronted her, like a picture by Escher, both fighting for her acceptance.

On the one hand, she saw clearly the mechanics of what was happening. They were all seated on low, padded benches arranged in the shape of a ship – pointed at the bows and square in the stern. They had their backs towards her. Everyone was singing beautiful glossolalic chants as they rocked back and forth, like rowers in a galley. Some were shaking rattles and clappers. Rose was the only one standing, like a tillerman in the stern. Roy was seated beside him, beating a huge drum; a lambeg. The beat created a theta wave to fortify the trance music. At the prow, Elsie sat alone like an ancient figurehead. She held a carved staff that fluttered with the long white feathers of a swan.

Olwen felt a cool breeze on her face. It carried the scent of seaweed. She assumed the high windows were open behind the shutters. The light in the room was dim, pale blue and wavering, as if underwater. Images flowed on the curve of the walls: tides racing to shore, clouds scudding across the sky, waves crashing on the rocks.

It was an impressive sight, even at the level of ordinary reality, but Olwen also saw the Other: a different truth that flickered in and out of existence. A great ship sailed upon the sea, bow rising through the spray. A graceful caravel dancing over the swell. Mythic. Archetypal. A ship of souls.

Overcome with awe, she thanked the gods that she had come late. How else could she have seen it? If she were one of the crew, she would be lost in the experience, eyes shut tight, rocking and chanting. She and Rose were the only ones standing, the only ones with their eyes open. Did he see what she saw? He had yet to acknowledge her presence as he leaned on his cane, staring straight ahead of him.

She approached the ship slowly, as if moving in a dream. Only now did she see what lay at its heart. A mild ripple of shock. Thomas Tillman was stretched on a mat, his crutches on either side of him like sword and spear. She remembered the old man's courage in the Sweat House, and his heartbreaking grief for his daughter. Admiration and affection surged through her. Someone sat cross-legged beside him, a slender figure dressed in white, with black hair falling down her back. Suzume! Once again, Olwen was struck by the mythic resonance. King Arthur in his barge. The Lady of the Lake by his side.

The chant rose higher, arching overhead to form a cathedral of sound. Olwen sensed the power being raised. It swirled around the ship like an invisible current, propelling the vessel through space and time. She understood. The Spirit Boat was sailing to the Isle of the Blest, to seek healing for Thomas.

She yearned to be part of the voyage. She turned to Rose, eyes silently pleading. For the first time since she had entered the room, he glanced her way. With an almost imperceptible nod, he indicated an empty position in the bow, behind Elsie. Her bench-mate on the port side was Dr Jack.

Thrilled and grateful that she was allowed to board, she attempted to join the others. To her surprise and consternation, she found herself barely able to move. *What's happening?* Something pushed against her. An invisible force. She struggled forward. It was like wading through deep water. The more she tried to move, the more resistance she felt. One part of her brain registered astonishment and disbelief. The other accepted the obvious. The Spirit Boat had already left the earthly shores she stood on. She had to catch up.

She began to move her arms as if swimming. The air around her responded, allowing her to move alongside. Her vision blurred. She glimpsed the ship at the corner of her eyes, rising and falling on the waves. A tall mast rose overhead. White sails snapped in the wind. Was that an albatross circling the look-out?

But something heavy was holding her back, pulling her down, threatening to drown her. She had to try harder. Her arms ached. She was now more than halfway along the boat, but still far from her place. *This is insane. Like one of those dreams where you're stuck in one spot and can't move.* It was the reminder of a dream that inspired her. With a sudden fit of effort, she burst from the water in a shower of spray and leaped over the waves to reach the bow.

She scrambled onto her seat. Her T-shirt was drenched, her skin clammy. Sweat or sea water? She glanced over at Dr Jack. He was far away, in a trance, singing in a deep baritone. He was beautiful to behold. *My lover.* Her pleasure at arriving was short-lived. She let out a moan as a blinding pain struck the back of her skull. She grasped hold of her head and looked around for help. Everyone had their eyes closed, even Rose. Of course. They had all worked their way into an altered state while she had just dived in! The current they had created, the waves of energy propelling the ship, had struck her full force. Her ears rang with a buzzing sound. Her teeth began to vibrate. She feared her cranium might crack like an egg.

Humpty Dumpty had a great fall.

Despite the mind-numbing agony, she opened her mouth to sing. She was long past any rational reaction to the experience. Tears streamed down her face as she surrendered to the sweeping motions of the ship, the rising and falling, rocking and rolling. How long the voyage took she couldn't tell, but the pain slowly subsided and she began to enjoy herself. All around her rang the voices of her companions. Her shipmates.

The music began to fade. The drums and rattles stopped. Of one accord, they all grew silent. They had reached their destination. Their destiny. The Isle of the Blest. Did she catch the scent of flowers? In her mind's eye, she saw green hills suffused with light.

We have come for healing for Thomas Tillman. We have come for healing for Suzume.

A deep peace washed over her, followed by waves of love and compassion. She let out a sigh of happiness. All around her rose similar sighs from the others. Eyes still closed, she trailed her hand over the side of the boat. A gentle warmth. Was it light or water? She inhaled the sweet air and leaned back to tilt her face to the sun. Was that an echo of their own singing she heard overhead? The true nature of the welcome dawned on her.

This healing is for me also. This healing is for all of us.

She could have stayed there forever; but after a time, the big drum beat again. Slow sonorous tones. She could feel the ship turning. They began to chant once more, a different song for the voyage home – a livelier air, a sea shanty.

Some time later the drumming stopped, and then the singing. They had returned, bringing with them a cargo of health and joy.

CHAPTER TWENTY-NINE

SEX AND CHOCOLATE

Back in her room, Olwen lay on her bed. She was in floods of tears, drowning in her emotions. Her thoughts turned to Dr Jack. He was the first to hug her when the Spirit Boat docked. She had felt a surge of electricity as he pressed his body to hers. His response was an erection. They broke apart quickly, he with a grin and she, confused. There just hadn't been enough time to sort out her feelings.

Don't start obsessing. It gets you nowhere.

And what the hell was she doing? Yes, he was brilliant, beautiful and sexy, but it was as obvious as the aquiline nose on his face that he was a philanderer, a fox among the chickens, a divil of a man. In other words, both her type and her bane. Had she learned nothing from William? From any of them?

Stop thinking about Jack. Stop thinking about William. Stop thinking about MEN. Get a life!

She jumped off the bed and rummaged in the wardrobe for her stash. A stab of panic. She was down to the last chocolate bar! How to replenish her stock? No car. No shops. She would have to pace herself. Divide the bar into pieces to make it last. The plan was doomed, she knew. She was an all-or-nothing person. Maybe Morag or one of the staff could get her some on their next shopping trip?

She placed her last precious bar on the desk and set up her laptop. Rose had suggested they write about the Spirit Boat in their journals. He was obviously pleased with the session. Everyone else had been ecstatic, laughing and crying and hugging each other. Thomas had leaned on Suzume as he got to his feet, both he and she looking radiant.

After a time, Rose called them to order and announced a break until lunch. They were given the rest of the day off to assimilate their experience and to prepare themselves for the evening's Firewalk. There would be no supper. As with the Celtic Sweat House, fasting enhanced the ritual; but there would be a midnight feast afterwards.

The computer keys clicked noisily as Olwen typed.

I've come to love what we are doing at Dunesfort House. I AM SO GLAD I'M HERE! Today was the best yet. Real magic. Isn't that what I've searched for all my life? Isn't that why I write fairy tales? My chief desire has always been to find a way into the Other Realm, in whatever form it might take or whatever way it's presented. Now that I come to think of it, I totally reject Rose's assertion that my love of Faerie is a death wish. It isn't death I seek but TRANSFORMATION.

Olwen broke off writing for a moment to take a bite of her chocolate bar. Her pulse was racing. Once upon a time she would have reached for a cigarette.

I'm looking forward to this Firewalk ritual, though I'm a little apprehensive as well. I managed to ask Elsie about it before we left the Womb. We take turns walking over hot coals – OMIGOD – but she says it's much easier than it sounds. Think of a pattern in your life you'd like to burn away, she said. Just one? I said back. Oh Lordy, oh Lordy. I need to rest up for it. Maybe after lunch. I'm too wired right now. Wired to the moon!

Olwen leaned back to stretch. She felt restless and edgy. Before she could stop herself, she dived on the chocolate bar and took another bite.

So much for pacing.

Bar in hand, she flung herself on the bed. Her muscles twitched. She was jumping out of her skin. Images of Dr Jack danced through her mind. His magnificent physique as he stood on the shore in his briefs. The mat of dark hair on his chest. His body diving through the waves like a dolphin. His body diving into hers.

I want him.

Ignoring her own protests, she kept eating till the bar was finished. The fantasy that followed was no surprise. While the Canadian part of her was appalled by the political incorrectness, the rest of her swooned.

Dr Jack...made of chocolate.

She licked him all over till he was wet and gooey. He rubbed against her, covering her skin with a sticky brown film. A little nibble of his shoulder. A nip at his smooth belly. His chocolatey smell was making her faint. When she took his penis into her mouth, he melted in spasms and spurts. She fought the temptation to bite. The threat hung in the air: the hint of castration that heightens fellatio for every man, as he stands helpless and enthralled before the one who holds him in her mouth.

A memory seized her mind, a nature video on the mating habits of the praying mantis. She had watched, in equal parts horrified and fascinated, as the female bit off her mate's head in the throes of passion and continued to eat it, even as the remainder of his body humped away.

Chomp. Chomp. Chomp.

She couldn't stop herself.

Chomp. Chomp. Chomp.

OMIGOOOOOOOD.

Satiated, Olwen stared at the ceiling. She let out a groan of dismay.

"I am not a good person."

CHAPTER THIRTY

BAPTISM BY FIRE

By the time the gong rang to call them to the Firewalk, Olwen was more than ready for company.

Lunch had been a dull affair as Dr Jack failed to show. She did her best to hide her disappointment and to refrain from constantly looking at the door; but Elsie wasn't fooled. The old woman's look was both wry and sympathetic. After lunch, Olwen had headed for the stables. Both stalls were empty and there was no sign of the horses. Rose was out riding without her. Could that be where Dr Jack had gone too? The thought of the two men banding together and leaving her behind was infuriating.

She had walked along the cliff above the cove where she and Dr Jack made love. The tide was out. The sand glistened like gold dust in the sun. They hadn't had any real communication since that day. Was he avoiding her? Had he withdrawn? An old tape began to run, a recurring theme in the story of her life: rejection and abandonment. The crazy-making, heartbreaking indifference of the lover who could return to his life as if their union meant nothing. But was that true of Dr Jack? The last time she saw him was the Spirit Boat. He had reached for her immediately. She was the first person he embraced. And surely there was no truer barometer of a man's feelings than his erection? No, it was the programme that was keeping them apart and Rose was the one who was arranging it. Did he invite Dr Jack to ride with him just to keep him away from her?

Now you're being paranoid.

Really? What's the definition of a paranoiac?

Yeah, yeah, someone who has all the facts.

She had wandered aimlessly along the precipice, musing on the choppy waters of the loch. Was that a seal's head bobbing in the distance? Too far away to know for certain. By the time she had returned to her room, she was refreshed but no less restless. The fact that supper was postponed till midnight and she had no more chocolate only added to her distress. A shower helped to distract her. Then she chose her clothes for the evening – brown cotton pants that rolled up easily to the knee and a baggy yellow shirt. No need for shoes or sandals. They would be walking barefoot. For the final hours, she chose a book from the shelves, Herman Hesse's *Steppenwolf*, an old favourite from her college days. She was astonished to discover that Harry Haller, the main character, was only forty-nine. Her own age! She remembered him as an old man, stooped and grey. No wonder, as Hesse had written him that way. Did people age faster back then?

It was twilight when the gong sounded. She had already turned on her lamp. Putting down her book, she paused to take a deep breath. Was she ready for an ordeal by fire?

The others were already outside. Beyond the front lawn, on the tract of grass that bordered the precipice, two bonfires burned. They were fashioned of wooden blocks stacked in tiers and set ablaze like towers. Several figures stood dark against the flames, holding shovels and rakes: the guardians of the fire. Olwen spotted Dr Jack amongst them, deep in conversation with Euphémie. Irked by her own jealousy, she moved to a spot some distance from them.

A loose circle had formed around the two fires as everyone stood to watch. The flames crackled noisily, showering the air with red sparks. Overhead shone the stars and the white face of the moon.

When the tiers collapsed into red ruins, the fire-keepers raked the embers into a sparkling path. Torches were lit on either side to make a fiery avenue.

Rose stepped forward, leaning on his cane. As usual, he was dressed in black. His features looked strained, half lost in shadow. His eyes glittered darkly.

Necromancer.

"We have had a very successful week thus far! Today, the Spirit Boat proved the bonding of the circle. I am pleased. So, too, should you be. This work is not easy, and the power of the circle depends on each and every one of you. Tonight we move to the next level. Fire-walking is strong magic. Like the rituals used by hunters of old, we act out that which we wish to bring into reality.

"There will be three walks. The first is for yourself, for your hopes and dreams, and especially this week's intentions. The second is for those closest to you, your partner, family, friends, or whomever else you choose. The third walk is for the wider community, your nation, race, special groupings, animals, the Earth itself."

They began to queue along the edges of the fire path. No one spoke. Olwen's stomach tightened. Her palms were sweaty. Was she really going to go through with this?

Elsie was the first to take up position at the starting line. She wore linen trousers hitched up like a skirt. Her feet were small, frail, white, and veined. When she spoke, her voice quavered.

"I walk towards the moment when I forgive myself, so that I may live and die in peace."

Olwen's chest constricted. She forgot her own anxiety in her concern for Elsie. What tragic tale lay behind those words? What hidden pain? The old woman hopped over the coals like a bird, a magpie peering down at shiny objects. When she reached the other side, she let out a whoop and did a little jump in the air. A roar of applause rose spontaneously from the crowd.

Dr Jack stepped up next. Olwen felt her womb clench like a fist. He looked so handsome and dignified.

"I walk towards an understanding of my spiritual path and purpose."

Then he marched smartly across the coals with an almost military gait.

Again the others cheered.

Euphémie stepped up quickly to follow Dr Jack. Even in the dimness, her beauty shone. She wore a light sundress that reached her knees. Her arms and legs were bare. The nap of dark hair curved around a pale neck. Her doe eyes and red lips gleamed in the firelight. Yet she showed none of her usual confidence as she stood shaking.

"The writer Anaïs Nin say life shrink or expand *en proportion* to our *courage*. I walk for *courage pour ma vie*. Because I have much fear, no, *terreur*, that I lose my youth. I lose my beauty. I cannot lie about this. Not here. *Mais bien sûr*, I wish to accept what Thich Nhat Hanh, my teacher, say: that I am of the nature to grow old. I am of the nature to die. *C'est tout*."

Her honesty was as breathtaking as her beauty. Olwen's jealousy evaporated. Her heart went out to the young woman who flitted over the fiery trail like an elemental spirit.

Tenzin Dawa walked next. He had rolled his jeans above his calves and wore a sleeveless T-shirt. Though he looked calm, he clenched and unclenched his hands, the muscles in his arms twitching in response. His glossy black hair was tied back in a ponytail. His eyes flashed with excitement. Taking a deep breath, he joined his hands in the prayer position and bowed to the path. Then he chanted in a low voice.

"*Dag gi ji nye sag pay gay wa di, ten dang dro wa kun la gang pen dang.*"

Glancing up briefly, with a half-smile, he spoke aloud in English.

"Whatever virtue I may gather here, may it bring benefit to all transmigrating beings and to the Buddha's teachings."

Some of the onlookers gasped as he walked with studied slowness over the coals. Was it the bravado of youth or was he really impervious? He held his hands in a *mudra* pose, his face expressionless. But when everyone applauded as he finished, a shy smile crossed his features.

Euphémie moved quickly to tamp down the embers after the young Tibetan's walk. Then she stood near, leaning against him with a proud grin. He smiled back at her.

Suzume had been standing beside Christy, watching the others. Now she stepped determinedly to the front of the Firewalk. Christy hurried to the opposite end. Suzume looked anxiously at the coals, then ahead at Christy. He lifted his arms, like a father encouraging his child to walk. With a quick catch of her breath and not a word, she ran lightly along the path and into his arms. Everyone cheered and clapped. Olwen joined in, surprised by the strength of her feelings for the girl.

Christy moved to walk next. He cleared his throat a few times before he managed to speak.

"I walk towards a life lived with meaning and purpose."

Then he hurried across the coals, like a man late for work.

One by one, they took turns, male and female, most expressing their thoughts and feelings before they walked the fiery path towards their dreams. And as each reached the other side, he or she was cheered by the circle.

Thomas limped into place, leaning on his metal crutches. He wore old hiking boots on both real and artificial limbs.

"I walk towards acceptance of the fact of death and its place in life. As my old friend Alan Watts once said to me, 'Death is as much a part of life as birth, just like the tail is as much a part of the cat as its head.'"

Olwen was near enough to see the wry smile on the old man's face. She found herself holding her breath as he walked slowly along the path. The heavy boots protected him, but they also kicked up sparks that struck his bare leg. He faltered a moment as the hair on his calf was singed.

There were noises of concern from the others.

"I'm fine," he called out, without looking up, concentrating on the walk.

The applause, as he reached the end, was more like an uproar.

When it came to Rose's turn, an intense hush fell over the group. Instinctively Olwen leaned forward to catch what he said.

"Some may think that what I am about to say belongs more properly to the third round where we walk for community. But, like Thomas, because of my infirmity I will walk only once. At the same time, many of you will know that what I am about to ask for is, indeed, my heart's desire. My cherished hope and dream."

The very air seemed charged. Olwen, like the others, held her breath. What would he wish for?

"I walk towards a successful Rite of the Cailleach."

The response from different members was instant and overwhelming.

"Oh my God," cried Elsie. She held her hands to her mouth in astonishment and joy.

Savitri burst into tears. Roy let out a whoop and grabbed hold of Una to spin her around. Dr Jack nodded with a pleased look, but Olwen noted that he wasn't surprised. Had Rose told him beforehand? Many of the group were hugging each other as if they had been given a gift of incredible value.

Olwen was flummoxed. What did it mean? What was going on? *Rite of the Cailleach.* There was nothing on the schedule by that name. She would have noticed it. She was quite familiar with the word *cailleach,* having used it in one of her books. The same word in Irish and Scots Gaelic, it meant "wise woman", "hag" or "witch".

Witch.

Suspicions confirmed? Some kind of black magic cult thing?

Her mind was still spinning as she watched Dr Jack take Rose's cane. The Director lurched onto the trail of burning embers. Unlike Thomas, he didn't wear boots. He had rolled his trousers to the knee, revealing the lame leg that was twisted and scarred. His features strained with the effort to walk unaided. Halfway across the path, he faltered. His foot dragged in the coals. Muffled cries rang out here and there. Euphémie dropped her rake and moved to help him, but he gestured her back. They had no choice but to watch as he continued slowly, teeth clenched, muscles working in his jaw and neck.

When he reached the finish, the response was mute and awestruck. Some wept quietly. He nodded with a satisfied smile. The fire guardians moved quickly to rake over the many coals he had displaced. Dr Jack handed him his cane, then embraced him with a hearty thump on the back. They both laughed. Only then did it occur to Olwen that these two men were best friends.

She hadn't intended to follow Rose. In fact, she was having second thoughts about walking at all, but suddenly, somehow, she found herself at the starting line. She was reluctant to state her intention out loud. It was too private. Too absurd. But at the same time, she yearned to declare her deepest dream. She looked up at the stars. *Spéirbhean* was what she called herself. *Skywoman*. As a child, she had spent hours lying in the grass of summer or the snow of winter, gazing up at the sky. Above her now shone a full white moon with a halo around it. Something was happening inside her. She lowered her gaze. Before her lay a trail of fiery jewels. Everyone was watching her. She felt the weight of their eyes. Dr Jack took up position at the other end of the path. His teeth gleamed white against the darkness of his skin as he smiled at her. A rush of adrenalin coursed through her. She could do this. She was Sagittarian, a fire sign, this was her element.

She called out in a clear voice that didn't waver.

"I walk towards a vision of God."

Even as she lifted her foot for the first step, some part of her registered the reaction of the others. A shock wave ran through them and surged back towards her with joy and approval. But she had no time to think or wonder about it, as she left them all behind and stepped onto the coals.

It was a strange, oneiric experience. Each step was a marvel in itself, as the burning embers crunched underfoot. Whenever a spark flared against her bare heel or sole, it was like a hot kiss. She was not only astonished that it didn't hurt, but that some part of her welcomed the kisses. Time seemed to slow and stretch out, even as the fiery trail seemed to extend before her. Her mind expanded, she felt deeply altered, moving through another time and space, another way of being. She thought of what she wished the fire to cleanse: her fear of being lost, like Dante, in a dark wood at mid-life; her fear of ageing, illness, and loneliness; her fear of loss of love and passion. Consumed by the fire, her fears fell away, while each burning kiss enkindled a new ardour for life. The crunch of the embers brought to mind the crunch of freezing snow that once scorched her feet. When was that? When had she run barefoot through the snow on a frosty Canadian night? Ah yes, the time she had fled a drunken, violent lover.

Let that burn away, too. Let it all burn away, the inevitable mistakes and failures of a human life.

Reaching the other side, she stepped onto cool, damp grass. The moon and stars spun above her. Here was the larger life she craved! She raised her arms to the sky and let out a howl. The others roared with her. Then Dr Jack was gathering her up and swinging her around, as they both laughed wildly.

But the moment he set her back on the ground, she pressed against him and hissed in his ear.

"What's the Rite of the Cailleach?"

She felt him stiffen. He attempted to break away, but she clung to him all the harder, whispering again.

"Tell me! I've a right to know."

He looked around before he answered. His arms encircled her and his voice was low.

"It's a moon rite at the Callanish Stones."

A thrill ran through her, but also a shudder. An internal alarm sounded. Some dark thing she couldn't recall.

"What does it involve?"

He drew her away from the group, speaking quickly. "For Rose, the Rite of the Cailleach is the zenith of the Work, but it doesn't often occur. Many factors need to be in place before the ritual can happen – the time of year, the lunar cycle, the bonding of the circle..."

Though she couldn't read his face in the darkness, Olwen heard the reluctance in his voice. He didn't want to talk about it. Why?

Euphémie joined them. "You speak of the Rite? Exciting, *non*? I knew of the lunar event, *naturellement*, but when he say nothing I keep silence also." She patted Olwen's cheek. "It is because of you, *chérie*."

"What?"

"It's because of all of us," Dr Jack said hastily. "The energy must be right throughout the circle."

"*Mais oui*," Euphémie said, but the Gallic shrug said otherwise.

Before Olwen could question her, the Parisienne had slipped away to rejoin the circle. Olwen opened her mouth to question Dr Jack again, but he shook his head.

"Not here. Not now. I have duties to perform. We've got to concentrate on the Firewalk. Everyone needs the full support of the circle. All of this feeds the Rite. I'll talk with you later, sweetheart. I promise."

Sweetheart.

It was the word and the warmth in his voice that made her back off. But when she, too, returned to the others, she remained on the fringe. Suspicion and paranoia nagged at her. Disparate facts and incidents kept coming to mind: her talk with Rose and the conviction that he was hiding something; the many indications that most or all of the group were privy to something she knew nothing about; the confirmation from others, including Rose, Elsie, and now Euphémie, that she herself had a special part to play. And why was Dr Jack always disappearing? Where did he go? From the first day she arrived, she had sensed that some secret lay at the heart of Dunesfort House. Tonight, that mystery was finally named: the Rite of the Cailleach. But what did it mean?

Sacrifice.

The sinister whisper in her mind chilled her to the bone. She sidled up to Euphémie who had resumed her place by Tenzin Dawa.

"What did you mean," Olwen asked her quietly, "when you said the Rite has to do with me?"

"*Pas maintenant.* We speak of this later," the Parisienne assured her. "I promise."

Olwen wasn't satisfied. She turned to Tenzin Dawa.

"I know nothing of the pujas and practices here," he told her. "But we will know when the time comes."

Observing her distress, he regarded her curiously, but before he could say more she had moved on. By the time the second round was called, Olwen had attempted to question many of the others. Some were obviously thrilled with Rose's announcement.

"It's a dream come true!"

"I never dared hope that I would be here for it."

"Whether it succeeds or fails, we are honoured by the attempt."

But she made little headway beyond their initial reactions. No sooner was someone willing to talk than they broke off to cheer another fire-walker or to take their own turn.

The second walk was in honour of one's nearest and dearest. Most named their immediate family. Elsie walked for her children, grandchildren, and great-grandchildren. Penny Li walked for her parents and grandparents in Malacca, and for her late husband's family in Sarawak. Olwen felt her heart tighten when Dr Jack called out the name of his ex-wife and wished her health and happiness. Brother Aguerre walked for the priests and brothers of his friary. Others walked for ageing parents, a child facing exams, a cousin with MS, an uncle who was dying of cancer.

When Olwen took her turn, she called out the name of her daughter, Robyn, wishing her strength and courage as she set off into her life. The second walk was easier as Olwen knew what to expect. Her tread was lighter and slower and she savoured the fiery kisses even more. But the moment she reached the other side, she resumed her investigation. With some chagrin, she recognised that she was the only one who was not fully present. Nonetheless – and this only increased her frustration – it was clear that for many, Rose's words had added an extra charge to the Firewalk.

Elsie was the most amenable to talking, but Olwen's problem lay in pinning her down. Full of energy and excitement, the old lady seemed to be everywhere at once. Cheeks mottled, eyes sparkling, she chattered like a starling, dropping titbits of information as Olwen followed her around.

"The biggest thing is the timing of the moon...we should be so lucky...Euphémie can explain all that...the circle is also important... it must be exactly right...everyone has to match up...the energy, the balance, the flow...what the Work calls up and releases...an exact calculation...it can fail even if all the boxes are ticked, this we know."

The more Elsie told her, the more baffled Olwen grew. But at last a break, a whole paragraph she could understand.

"I've been here for the Rite a few times. Jack, too, and Thomas and some of the others. Many of the others, now that I come to think of it! We've never been successful, but every attempt is a rare and priceless experience. We got very close, two years ago. Close but no cigar, as my Chaim used to say. A last-minute glitch. *Oy vey.* It wasn't the poor girl's fault. You can't stop where your heart goes, specially when you're young."

Finally Olwen was getting somewhere.

"You mean one person can make the Rite fail? What did she do wrong? What is the Rite for?"

Elsie was about to answer, when the third and final Firewalk was called.

"I'm up!" she chirped. "Showtime!"

And in a flash, she was gone. By now, Olwen realised that Elsie, as the eldest of the circle, held the honour of beginning each walk.

The third round was an offering for the larger community, including countries, species, and the Earth itself.

Elsie walked for the peoples of Israel and Palestine, that they might find peace and flourish together. Harry asked that the Findhorn Community in Scotland continue to grow as a Fortress of Light. Savitri prayed for the poor of India, asking that they find the hope and strength to rise above their conditions. Tenzin Dawa walked for a free Tibet. Roy walked for the two communities of Northern Ireland and the ongoing peace process. Immediately after, Brother Aguerre walked for a peaceful resolution for the Basque nation. Penny Li walked for the forests of Borneo and the land rights of the native peoples who lived in them.

Olwen hesitated for a moment, unsure of what she wished to pray for. Something for the Earth or creatures of the Earth?

"I walk for all God's creatures, big and small, whose lives are threatened by humanity through hunting, vivisection, factory farms, animal cruelty, road traffic, and so on. I wish them safety and sanctuary."

By now the coals were cooling. The avenue of torches had died out. The dark blanket of night fell over them. The Firewalk was done. There was a murmur of happy chat amongst the participants.

Some embraced quietly, while others headed for the house.

Then Christy shouted suddenly for a fourth round.

"Let's walk for the pairing of *anamchara*! Soul-friends!"

There was a great cheer of agreement as he clasped hands with Suzume. The two ran across the path together. Other pairs began to form. Olwen looked around for Dr Jack. But he had already caught hold of Elsie and joined the queue behind Roy and Una. Even Thomas chose to walk again. He leaned on Savitri as they took their place in line.

Olwen had no time to regret that she had no partner. With a shock that bordered on horror, she saw that Rose was coming for her. There was no doubt of his intention. His hand was outstretched. She backed away. Every part of her cried *no*. She had to bite her lip to keep from screaming it at him.

His features stiffened as he acknowledged her response. He didn't turn away, but stood regarding her intently. Some of the others noticed what was going on. Olwen was too worked up to care. Was this the final piece of the puzzle? Something to do with her and Rose? Was this why she had been invited? What she had been groomed for all along? Whatever it might mean, she was certain of one thing: she wanted no part of it. No part of him.

Olwen turned on her heels and ran back to the house. She didn't stop to wash her feet in the basins left in the porch, didn't notice the trail of black footprints behind her. Her only thought was to escape. At last she reached her room. *Sanctuary.* Locking the door, she dragged the captain's chair over to prop under the handle. It was only the second time she had done that since she arrived, though it was something she always did in hotel rooms and B&Bs. Now she saw the sooty prints she had left on the white carpet. With a cry of distress, she sank onto the bed.

Her mind was racing with fear and paranoia. Did they expect her to match up with Rose? Was this what made her a key player?

Was she supposed to do something with him in the Rite ahead? The very thought made her ill. How did she get herself into this mess? More importantly, how was she going to get herself out of it? What should she do? What could she do? She had no car. Her mobile phone didn't work. She had no way to call Dr N. Might Morag help her? But the housekeeper was the faithful servant of Rose.

Oh, this horror film was all too familiar!

She used her counting technique to still her heart and slow down her breathing, then she went into the bathroom to wash her feet. Feeling a little calmer, she tried to clean the carpet. If only there was someone she could talk to. Someone she could trust. But everyone in the circle was suspect. Too many secrets had been kept from her. She gave up on the carpet and lay down on the bed again. She needed to figure out what to do next, but she was exhausted. First, she needed some rest. A last thought trailed through her mind as she slipped into an uneasy sleep.

I've got to get out of here.

CHAPTER THIRTY-ONE

SIXTH NIGHT:
THE LITTLE MERMAID

Olwen woke to the sound of someone knocking gently on her door. Groggy and confused, she sat upright in the bed and stared around the room. She had left the light on. Nothing was out of order. She was still dressed. Another knock on the door, a little louder this time. The chair was still wedged against it. Her heart began to pound.

"Who is it?" she called, trying to sound calm.

"It's me," came Suzume's voice in a loud whisper.

Olwen scrambled out of bed. Quickly removing the chair, she unlocked the door.

Suzume looked like a fairy who had wandered lost into the tower. She was dressed in the white gown she had worn for the Spirit Boat. The long sleeves trailed like wings. Her feet were bare. She wore a chain of daisies in her jet-black hair and another around her neck. Her almond-shaped eyes shone like black glass in the porcelain-pale skin. A nervous smile quivered on her lips.

Olwen's maternal instincts rose to the fore.

"Are you all right, pet? Is anything wrong? Is there something I can do?"

"I don't want to be alone. Will you come with me? I'm going outside."

"Of course. Just wait a minute while I get my jumper."

But even as Olwen turned to get her sweater, Suzume giggled behind her.

"You won't need it."

With a shock, Olwen saw what she meant. There on the bed lay Olwen's body, sleeping soundly. In that moment she remembered all the other dreams and visions and wondered briefly why she kept forgetting them. But she didn't dwell on the question. The night was calling.

Suzume had already skipped down the stairs of the broch, leaving a trail of laughter behind her. Olwen raced to catch up. She laughed, too. She had never seen the girl so happy and light-hearted. Together, they ran out the front door.

The midsummer night was balmy. There was a glow to the air, as if every particle was alive and spilling light. What was that exquisite sound? It seemed to fall from the sky like rain. The stars were singing! Directly overhead, the moon smiled like a white face in a dark sea. *An Cailleach.* Everything seemed charged with meaning. But what was the message? What was the night trying to say?

Suzume raced to the edge of the precipice. Her hair blew behind her like a scarf. She glanced over her shoulder at Olwen with a mischievous grin.

"Can you fly?"

And then she jumped.

Olwen let out a cry and ran to the edge. A peal of laughter greeted her. Like a feather on a current of air, Suzume was floating downwards to the cove below.

As soon as she landed, she called up to Olwen.

"Come on! You can do it! Let the kid out!"

Olwen froze. How many dreams had brought her to this point? Standing on a high wall or tower, on the edge of a skyscraper, in the boughs of a tall tree, she was forever being confronted with this moment. Though she knew instinctively she could fly, she had always backed away, lacking the faith to act.

Not this time.

Half terrified, half exhilarated, she jumped. There was a rush of wind and wings, dark sky above and gold sand below, and she landed in the cove.

"That was brilliant!" she said to Suzume. "I'm so glad you made me do it!"

Suzume's laughter trilled through the air. "Let's build sandcastles!"

The girl flung herself on the ground, digging in the sand like a puppy. Olwen knelt to join her. Only now did she notice that Suzume seemed feverish and over-excited. There was a strange glitter to her eyes. Olwen felt a pang of concern.

They worked together, sculpting heaps of damp sand into walls and turrets, moats and passageways. Gull feathers, pebbles, sea shells and seaweed decorated their creation. Despite the hour of the night and the wind blowing over the waves, neither felt cold.

"What do you think of Tenzin Dawa?" Suzume asked wistfully.

Olwen hid a smile. "He's a very handsome young man. Definitely what my daughter would call a 'hottie'. What do *you* think of him?"

Suzume ducked her head and giggled. She concentrated on the arch she was moulding and tried to sound nonchalant. "He's okay, I guess. Good dancer." She paused to gather a handful of small stones to make a pavement around the arch. "He's a *tulku*, did you know?"

"A what?"

"A reincarnated lama. Very important. But he ran away from all that. He wants to live in America as an ordinary person. That's why the head of his monastery sent him here. He asked Tenzin to do this one thing before he rejected his destiny."

"How do you know this?"

"I heard some of it from Tenzin and some of it from Euphémie. She likes him a lot and he likes her too, and not just because they're partners in the circle."

Suzume let out a little sigh.

Olwen couldn't stop a wry grimace. Apparently the charms of *la belle Parisienne* crossed the generations.

Meow.

"I never had a boyfriend," Suzume said suddenly.

Olwen's heart tightened. She remembered what Suzume had said in the small group sharing about the girls in her cult being drugged and raped. She remembered also how Suzume had screamed in her Breathwork session. What could Olwen say to her? How could she help?

But Suzume's dark mood fled as quickly as it had come. She leaned towards Olwen with flushed cheeks, giggling once more.

"Guess why Tenzin stopped being a monk in the first place. He wasn't an exile or a refugee in India. He lived in one of the last monasteries in Tibet, high in the mountains. One day he was sent on a journey to bring a message from his abbot to a hermit. Somewhere along the way he met and fell in love with a nomad girl. He tried to elope with her, but her family caught up with them and stopped the marriage. There was a big scandal and his heart was broken and his monastery had to pay compensation and everything." Suzume clasped her hands to her heart. "So romantic! That's why he left Tibet and ended up in Dharamsala where the exiled Tibetans live."

"Did Tenzin tell you this or Euphémie?"

"Savitri. She's like a mother to him. They both live in India. Well, she told Christy and he told me. Is it bad to gossip? We all know things about each other. It's one of the ways the circle bonds."

Olwen cringed. How much did the others know about her? Her face flushed as she realised that they probably all knew she and Dr Jack were lovers. She almost choked. Really, it was all too incestuous and claustrophobic. But she also felt a pang of regret that she hadn't got to know more of the circle. So many fascinating stories. But there was only so much you could do in a week with such a large group of people.

Suzume sat back on her heels to admire their work.

"My family never went to the beach," she said. "It's too crowded near Tokyo. But once we went on a holiday when I was very young and I played with sea turtles."

Her face lit up with the memory.

Olwen smiled. "This reminds me of a sand sculpture I made with my daughter, when she was about seven. We spent the whole day at the seaside, building the ancient city of Merv. I was reading about it at the time. People came by to admire our work, it was so amazing."

She had hardly finished speaking when Suzume reached out to touch Olwen's forehead. Their creation whirled in a miniature sandstorm and took on the shape of the one Olwen had just spoken about. And now Olwen was no longer looking at Suzume, but at her daughter, Robyn, at seven years of age. Her round face was tanned and freckled by the sun. Her raven-black hair fell in thick curls to her shoulders. Her eyes were full of laughter.

"Robby," Olwen murmured. She felt a swell of love and loss for the little girl she would never see again.

Suzume returned to her own form. "You love her very much, don't you?"

"She's the best thing that ever happened to me. The jewel of my life. The pearl of great price."

Suzume winced. "I wish you were *my* mother."

Olwen thought her heart would break. She reached out to stroke the girl's face.

"All mothers are flawed," she said softly. "All parents damage their children. It's one of the tragic facts of human life. Believe me, my

•

daughter has many complaints about me and they're all valid. I did a lot of things wrong. I made a lot of mistakes."

Suzume's eyes clouded over. She folded her arms. Her voice echoed from the depths of her hurt.

"My mother wasn't there to make mistakes. By the time I came along, she had already checked out. Addicted to rice wine and the pills our family doctor gave her. My father wouldn't let her do any kind of work, not even in the garden. I never saw her smile. I never saw her happy. I had a nanny who loved me and I loved her, but my father sent me away to boarding school when I was seven and I never saw my nanny again. My mother died when I was thirteen. An overdose of pills. I wasn't really sad. I never knew her. There wasn't anything to miss."

Olwen couldn't think of a thing to say. She just shook her head sadly.

Suzume gave her a shy smile. "Your books helped me through my childhood."

Olwen managed not to weep, but her voice was hoarse.

"Thank you for telling me that. The greatest honour I could receive. It's exactly what I say about C.S. Lewis."

A companionable silence fell between them. The only sound was the splash of waves coming to shore. Olwen had noted the creeping tide at the corner of her eye, but it was still some distance away. She was more interested in the things scattered in the sand around them. It was all the picnic paraphernalia she and Robyn had brought that day by the Irish Sea – plastic pails and shovels, butterfly net, and the old picnic basket with cheese sandwiches, hard-boiled eggs, crisp packets, and red lemonade.

"How did you do this?" she asked Suzume. "Can you read my mind?"

"It's not me. It's both of us." The girl looked thoughtful. "It's something the Master used to say. There's no separation between us.

Any of us. That's an illusion of life. We are all One playing the game of separation."

"The Master?" Olwen shuddered. "You mean the head of the cult?"

Suzume nodded. "A lot of what he said was very wise and true. He was a Buddhist, you know. Sometimes Tenzin Dawa says things that the Master said. He *was* a saint, I believe that, but then he...turned...crazy."

She looked sad and lost and hurt again.

"I know how you feel," Olwen told her. "Some very important men in my life were like that; when I was a child and then again when I was older. Even now when I feel anger or hatred against them, it's very confusing, because I loved them too."

"Yes! That's the biggest difference between books and real life. The bad guys in books are always pure evil and you can so easily tell them from the good guys and it's easy to hate them. But in real life it's not like that. The bad people can also be good and kind and that makes it all much harder and confusing."

Suzume's hands fluttered nervously as she spoke. She picked at the flowers in her hair, until they were strewn in bits over her clothing. The daisy chain around her throat had disappeared. A necklace of rubies now glittered there, like drops of blood.

The unease that Olwen had felt earlier returned. Something was very wrong. She chose her words carefully.

"Do you ever feel that this circle and Dunesfort House might be a cult?"

To her surprise, Suzume nodded readily. "It's very much like the way the cult was at the beginning, but even better. You see, the cult was like a family to me, the family I never had. The police psychologist told my father that I was typical of the kind of young person who joins cults. Because I was a loner and not interested in the things most girls my age were interested in, like boys, karaoke, fashion and shopping.

"My father wanted me to study science or business. I wanted to be an artist. That was the last thing he would ever agree to. The night before I ran away, I packed my bags and wrote him a long letter. I tried not to blame him or to make him feel bad. I told him I was on the shining path to happiness and liberation and that I wished the same for him.

"I knew he would come looking for me. The cult had communes all over Japan so I went to one far away in the countryside, where he couldn't find me. I worked in the kitchen, preparing the food offerings for the shrine and also for the other members. It was mostly vegetarian – soyabean burgers, rice, and ramen noodles. We were told to make the meals as tasteless as possible, so as not to encourage an attachment to food. I worked day and night, with other young women in the kitchens. Work work work until we nearly collapsed. But we had fun, too. Like I said, I felt I was part of a real family. When we were cleaning all the machines in the kitchen, the supervisor said to us, 'Clean them as if you were polishing your own hearts.'"

"And did you see the Master?"

"Once or twice a year he visited his communities. We would get very excited about his coming. Everything had to be extra clean and orderly. The kitchen staff missed most of the pujas, but we got to the late-night ones after the kitchen closed. I was always in the back of the hall, so I didn't see him up close. The Inner Circle sat in the front rows. But I felt his energy touch me, as if he were right beside me. It was beautiful."

Suzume's face lit up again. She seemed lost in her memories. Then her features darkened.

"That was before the Master changed and the police started to come and there were rumours of kidnappings and murders. People started to leave, like our supervisor. The new people in charge weren't as nice. From time to time we...the girls in the kitchen...were called up to the rooms where the Inner Circle stayed. Always just one at a time."

Suzume's voice started to fade. Her face was a mask, her eyes dark with confusion.

"Anyone called away was usually gone for a few days. None of us could remember anything even though we tried. If we asked about the others, we were told they were ill and being taken care of."

The night had grown chill. Water was seeping through the sandcastle, slowly dissolving it.

Olwen felt sick. She was trembling as much as Suzume. She wanted to protect the girl. To save her.

"Do you think Rose is like the Master?"

Suzume glanced nervously in the direction of Dunesfort House.

"Yes...no..." Her voice quavered. "He's like the way the Master was...Oh!" Suzume scrambled to her feet. She swayed, as if buffeted by wind. "We mustn't talk about him! He will hear! He will come!"

Olwen went cold with fear. Jumping up, she caught hold of the girl.

"Who might come? The Master? Rose?"

Suzume leaned against Olwen weakly. She was much smaller and slighter, fitting into Olwen's arms like a child. Her smile was sleepy as she looked up.

"You write fairy tales. I love fairy tales."

Olwen's fear was growing.

"Listen to me, Suzume. I'm leaving tomorrow. I want you to come with me. We can go back to the house and pack your bags and you can stay in my room. Will you come with me?"

Suzume didn't seem to hear. Her eyes had a faraway look and her voice took on a sing-song tone.

"My favourite fairy tale is 'The Little Mermaid'. Not the Disney version, that was stupid, but the true one. Do you remember the part about her human life, when she got her legs? She said it was like walking on knives." Now Suzume's voice echoed with naked pain. "Every day I live, every moment I'm here, *I'm walking on knives.*"

"You poor girl," Olwen murmured, weeping softly and holding her tight.

Suzume stiffened suddenly. "He's awake! He's coming for me! *No!* He mustn't find me!"

Olwen felt a rush of terror, but forced herself to stay calm.

"It's all right, Suzume. I'm here. I won't let anyone hurt you. Who's coming? Is it Rose? Do you mean Rose?"

But despite her words of assurance, Olwen felt a growing dread. Something was very wrong. Every instinct told her that the girl was in danger.

Suddenly, violently, and with surprising strength, Suzume broke from Olwen's arms and raced for the sea. Olwen raced after her. The ghost of the truth, some inchoate sense of what was really happening, rose in her mind.

"DON'T GO NEAR THE WATER!"

Suzume was younger and faster, but Olwen's legs were longer. Catching up with the girl, she reached out to grab hold of her. They struggled by the shore. Suzume seemed blind to whom she was fighting, and her determination gave her a greater strength. Breaking away once more, she ran into the tide.

Olwen followed after. But the moment her toes touched the water, she leaped back with an anguished cry. For in that second she had felt it: the utter disruption of her being, as if every cell in her body was being torn asunder. The shock was appalling, but she still managed to call out, pleading with Suzume to come back.

To no avail. Suzume was swimming away from shore, rising and falling with the swell of the sea. A song echoed over the sound of the surf. She sang like a mermaid under the moon, as she slowly dissolved in the water, turning to foam on the waves.

Olwen fought against her own horror. Looking back at Dunesfort House, she finally understood what was really happening. Running, climbing, then flying over the rocks, she screamed at the top of her lungs.

"WAKE UP! WAKE UP!"

CHAPTER THIRTY-TWO

CATASTROPHE

Olwen woke in her bed and bolted upright. She was wide-eyed with panic. There was no time to lose. No room for doubt. Dream or no, she had to act. She had fallen asleep in her clothes, so there was no need to dress. She threw aside the chair that still blocked the door. Racing down the stairs of the broch, she stopped at the second landing. Could she remember the way she had gone with Dr Jack? Past Suzume's room? Her rational mind drew a blank. Instead, she moved on instinct, like an animal stalking its prey. Her sense of dread increased with every step. Monstrous images haunted her mind. She screamed silently as she went.

Hold on, Suzume, I'm coming! Hold on!

The moment she arrived she knew she was too late. The door of Suzume's room hung loose on its hinges. It had been broken open with brute force. Muffled sounds came from within. Olwen forced herself to go inside. Her sight blurred. She was sweating profusely. An icy hand seemed to be squeezing her chest. The room was smaller than hers, but with similar furnishings. The bathroom was on her left. That door, too, had been shattered. Olwen lurched to the threshold, legs threatening to buckle.

The dark heart of the labyrinth.

Red, red, and more red. Splashes and splatters of blood over wall and floor. A wave of nausea struck her. Her mind seized up, paralysed by the horror of what she saw. Two men were hunched over a prone figure. Dr Jack and Rose. Between them lay Suzume, a drowned Lorelei. Her black hair was drenched, straggling over cold features. Her white dress was incarnadine with bloodied water. On the floor lay a dagger, its enamelled handle and silver blade stained with blood. Her throat had been cut.

Olwen gazed on the still face, so young, so beautiful.

Oh my child, my poor little one.

Something snapped inside her. Here it was. The secret agenda of the Work.

Sacrifice.

She started to scream at the two men.

"What have you done to her? Help! *Murder!*"

They turned towards her, shocked. Dr Jack's eyes were red and bloodshot. So were Rose's. The Director staggered to his feet. What happened next was all ajumble. Did they attack her or did she attack them? The room spun around her. There were fists flailing and too many arms, like an octopus. Blood stained her clothes. Hers or theirs or Suzume's? Her legs gave way beneath her. She was on her back, struggling wildly like an animal fighting for its life. Her arms and feet were caught in strong grips. The ceiling moved above her. She was being carried from the bathroom. Where were they taking her? Somewhere in the distance, doors opened and closed. Was that her voice shrieking for help?

More chaos exploded around her. People, voices, other cries and shouts. At her eye level, a black bag appeared. In the midst of the mêlée, a calm voice and soothing words. A doctor. Not Jack. A woman doctor. Olwen's eyes flickered open and shut. She had no control over them. Cool fingers were feeling her throat and forehead. Gently pulling at her eyelids. The scent of jasmine wafted over her. Savitri! In a dark blue sari. No, a dressing gown. What was in her hand? A hypodermic needle.

Olwen tried to fight her off, but more hands pinned her down. Rose was on one side of her, Euphémie on the other. A look passed between them. An unholy conspiracy. They *were* the enemy. Someone pulled at her trousers. She started to scream again, to struggle harder, but it was no use. A needle pierced her thigh. Her head buzzed like a swarm of bees. The ground opened beneath her and she was swallowed by the darkness.

Olwen woke in her own bed and let out a groan. Her head felt as if it might split open. She stared at the clock on the mantelpiece with incomprehension. How could she have slept so late? Memories of the previous night trickled into her mind. Suzume in the cove. No, in her bathroom. Blood everywhere. Her throat cut.

God, what a nightmare! The worst yet!

Lifting the duvet, she stared blankly at her pyjamas. She had not undressed for bed, she was certain of it. Her stomach churned. Images flashed through her mind like the red light on a police car. Blood on her trousers. Two women undressing her – Savitri and Euphémie. Did Savitri really give her a needle? Olwen pulled down her pyjama bottoms. There it was. A red pinprick on the skin of her thigh. Moments later she discovered the other one on her inner arm.

What the–?

She climbed slowly out of bed, too sick and dizzy to move quickly. She felt absolutely awful. Like the worst hangover imaginable. What kind of drug had they given her? Fighting back waves of fear and panic, she forced herself to take a shower. She needed to wake up, to clear her head. Whatever was happening, she had to keep her wits about her. If murder had taken place...

Oh, Suzume! Poor girl!

In the mirror, Olwen's face looked old and haggard. She dressed slowly, pulling on jeans and a white shirt. There was no sign of her clothes from the night before. The ones she had worn for the Firewalk. The ones covered in blood. And yet, despite such damning facts, some part of her clung to the last shred of hope that it was all a bad dream, the kind she had been plagued with most of her life.

Slowly, carefully, she turned the handle of her door, half expecting it to be locked from the outside. It wasn't. She opened it a crack and peered into the hall, suspecting a guard. There wasn't.

Paranoid Patty strikes again. It was just the usual night terrors.

Oh yeah? Explain the needle marks! And where are my fucking clothes?

Within moments of entering the dining room, she saw that something had, indeed, happened. Something terrible. There were only a few people scattered here and there at the tables, picking at their food. They looked like refugees. An air of catastrophe hung over all. Everyone seemed lost or in shock. Some were weeping quietly. There was no sign of Elsie or Dr Jack. She went up to Thomas Tillman. He sat erect in his chair, staring into space. His food was untouched.

"What...what's going on?" she managed to ask.

The old man looked at her strangely. "You don't know? But I heard you were..." He stopped, shook his head. His eyes were glazed with pain. "Suzume...she killed herself. The poor dear girl. If only we could have done more for her! If only we could have saved her!"

Suicide? Olwen rejected the notion. She was remembering more with every passing minute. The memory of herself and Suzume in the cove was equal in strength to the memory of finding the girl dead in her room. Her conversation with Suzume was particularly clear and the girl's terror of Rose. At the same time, all suspicions of a mass conspiracy were dispelled. Everyone in the room looked dazed and distraught, their grief too raw to be fake.

The police were holding interviews, Thomas told her. The circle was being called one by one into the front parlour to make a statement. Those who hadn't been called yet were in the Common

Room. She would have to go there first, then she could have lunch. That was how it was organised. The day's events had been cancelled. A question mark hung over the rest of the week. The course was most likely over.

Lost and confused, Olwen made her way to the Common Room. There were more people gathered there, all in varying states of distress. Some of the women held each other as they wept out loud. A group of men stood in one corner, talking in low tones. Penny Li sat on the sofa, arms around her stomach, rocking back and forth. Harry Rhymer sat with her, his face buried in his hands. Was it Olwen's imagination or did everyone react to her entrance? Did all eyes turn towards her?

She backed out of the room and ran down the hall. Without thinking what she was doing, she found herself in the corridor that led to Suzume's room. Yellow tape sealed off the area. The door was still unhinged. As she stood there helplessly, Dr Jack came out of his room.

He was unshaven and dishevelled. His clothes looked as if he had slept in them. But he brightened visibly when he saw her.

"You're up! I was just coming to look in on you. You were out cold the last time I checked. Savitri said you might sleep long as she gave you a second shot. She felt you needed it."

She stared at him in bewilderment. There was nothing in his look or tone that implied duplicity. Only deep concern. She fought to keep her voice neutral, but the question came out as an accusation nonetheless.

"Why did she drug me?"

Dr Jack's brow furrowed at her tone, but his answer was straightforward and without hesitation.

"You were given epinephrine for anaphylactic shock. You had all the signs of the kind induced by exercise. I agreed with Savitri's diagnosis. Quite frankly, we were both concerned about cardiovascular collapse, but one dose returned you to normal fairly quickly."

It all sounded so reasonable. Why couldn't she accept it? *Because of Suzume's fear of Rose, that's why!* Perhaps Dr Jack was innocent – she dearly hoped so – but that still left the Director under a cloud of suspicion.

"I need a cigarette," she declared.

Dr Jack frowned a moment as if about to argue the idea, then changed his mind.

"I'll get you one. Meet me in the porch. We'll go for a little walk, nothing strenuous. I need to be outside."

She knew what he meant. The atmosphere was suffocating. Dunesfort was a death house.

Olwen went back to her room to get her sweater. She buttoned it to the neck and regarded her reflection in the mirror. She looked pale and sickly, her eyes dark with fright. *A deer caught in the headlights.* Why was she so ready to trust Dr Jack? She knew the answer. She needed desperately to trust someone.

He was waiting for her on the front steps. He had two gold-tipped Russian cigarettes and a packet of matches from a jazz club in Paris. She didn't need to ask where he had got them. Her body shuddered involuntarily as she recalled the look that went between Euphémie and Rose as they pinned her down. Who could she trust?

"I just want one. Thanks."

He lit it for her.

"The other is for me," he said, with a rueful shrug.

They walked away from the house, along the road that bordered the moor. The sunshine seemed an affront, but it was also soothing. Dr Jack did most of the talking, as if he needed to unburden himself. She heard the deep weariness in his voice as well as the grief. She realised that, unlike her, he hadn't slept. And there was something else in his tone: guilt.

"Suzume was my patient. This wasn't her first attempt. There were others. Most recently last year. The early efforts were clumsy, but the last two times she almost succeeded. It was only sheer dumb luck in one instance and intense vigilance in the other that allowed us to catch her in time. This circle was a gamble, we always knew it, but we had to try. It was her last chance. Her options had narrowed to radical healing or life-long incarceration in a mental institution. Was I wrong not to condemn her to the latter? At least she would be alive today."

Dr Jack paused. A spasm of anguish contorted his face.

"The last few circles had been so promising, the match with Christy so strong! He was the good father she had needed all her life. Our hopes were high. Perhaps that in itself was our downfall. When she offered her place in the Spirit Boat to Tom – it was she who was meant to lie at the centre – I thought it a good sign. People in a depressed or hopeless state are rarely capable of thinking of others. How wrong I was. How wrong that analysis!"

Another spasm of guilt.

"I know now she was rejecting any further attempts to heal her. She had already given up, already decided she would die."

He stopped to rub his face with his hands.

"It's almost impossible to imagine the amount of pain she suffered in her short life. The unapproachable father who could never be pleased. The loss of the beloved nanny who was the only enlightened witness among the adults in her life. The addict mother who chose suicide just as Suzume reached puberty. Suzume was the one who found her. Then the gang rapes in the cult which she had embraced as her family. She had no conscious memory of the violations. They drugged her, as they did the other women, but her body and her unconscious knew what had happened to her. She suffered chronic nightmares and suicidal depressions as a result."

Olwen felt a wave of unbearable sadness.

Every day I live, every moment I'm here, I'm walking on knives.

Olwen linked her arm with his, keeping their bodies close. She needed the physical contact for support and was happy, in turn, to give it to him. Yet she was wracked with doubt. How could she believe him? Trust him? Though it all made sense, something didn't add up.

"What about Rose?"

He didn't notice how carefully she spoke.

"He's utterly shattered. Blames himself, of course. He's the Director. This is his circle. But the Spirit Boat and the Firewalk had convinced him she was safe, just as it had convinced me. He relaxed his watch on her, even as I did. She eluded him almost to the end and then it was too late."

His words only served to confuse Olwen further. She was afraid to say too much. She needed to know more.

"What will I tell the police?"

Her question took him by surprise.

"What do you mean?"

"Nothing," she said quickly. "I just...I wondered what the others were saying, and if there was an official line or something."

He gave her an odd look, but she clammed up completely. She had no intention of relating her dream. Her own feelings of guilt were mingled with fear. Even if he wasn't her enemy – and she didn't know that for sure – he would undoubtedly tell Rose.

Soon after they returned to the house, Olwen was called into the front parlour. Two policemen were conducting the inquiry, a young red-faced constable with a local accent and a grey-haired gentleman. The latter was introduced as a detective from Edinburgh. The young constable asked the questions, jotting down the answers in his little book: her name and contact details, profession, length of stay on Lewis, relationship with the deceased. The older man stood by the fireplace and listened and watched. It was only when she was about to leave that Olwen felt driven to confess.

"I think I was the last to see her alive."

The two men were instantly alert.

"Please explain, ma'am," said the detective.

"I...It was...This will sound strange but...It was a dream of sorts. We were together in the cove, last night, Suzume and I."

Olwen caught the look that passed between the men.

"You are understandably upset, Ms..." The detective paused and stepped forward to glance at the constable's notebook. "Mellory. Only natural."

"A cup of tea would do you good," suggested the constable.

Olwen nodded, her eyes tearing up. Of course it sounded ridiculous. But she had to try, for Suzume's sake. It was the least she could do.

She turned to the local man.

"Do you know much about the Director?"

He was startled. "Are you speaking of Mr Rosenthal?"

His tone said everything. It rang with deference and respect. The detective raised an eyebrow at him.

"He's well-known hereabouts," the constable said hastily. He directed his words more to the older man than Olwen. "He was in residence long before I was stationed here. I understand he restored the house some twenty years ago. Many local people work here and have done so in the past. There's never been anything said against him. Only good."

The constable's words were like a splash of cold water. The reality of Rose's life countered Olwen's irrational suspicions. Didn't Morag and her brothers work for him? Surely they knew him better than she?

"Do you wish to say something about Mr Rosenthal?" the detective asked her. He fixed her with a stern look. "Something about him and the deceased girl?"

Olwen bit her lip. She wanted to say that Suzume was afraid of Rose. The girl had shown terror at the very mention of his name. But Olwen had to admit it was only in her dream. Though she wracked her brain, she couldn't recall a single incident before that night.

"Only the dream," she said faintly.

The detective returned to his position by the mantelpiece. She was dismissed.

The rest of the day passed in a blur. The staff continued to serve meals in the dining room, though few sat down to eat. A heavy silence lay over the house, disturbed only by muted conversations and intermittent weeping. Many spoke of going home. Someone mentioned that Christy had left already, devastated and inconsolable. There was no desire among the rest to resume the Work.

Things fall apart; the centre cannot hold.

Olwen spent most of the day alternately wandering the halls as if in search of something, or lying on her bed staring at the ceiling. Dr Jack had disappeared again and Elsie didn't show for meals. Were they with Rose? Holed up in his lair at the top of the house? The Director had yet to make an appearance. Regardless of her own feelings towards him, Olwen could see how much his absence disturbed the others. Rudderless and adrift, Dunesfort was a ship without a captain. That observation led to more confusing thoughts. Could Rose really have caused this? Why would he want to break up the circle and sabotage his own Work? Nothing made sense.

On one of her wanders, Olwen ran into Savitri.

"Here you are at last!" The Indian woman's eyes were bright with worry. "I am looking for you all day! I wish to take your blood pressure and check your heart, if you please."

Olwen drew back instinctively. Images of being held down and drugged raced through her mind. Savitri seemed unaware of

Olwen's reaction as she gently propelled her down the hall and into her room. The air was pungent with the scent of sandalwood.

It was while she was being examined that Olwen heard more about Suzume's death. Once the interviews had ended and photographs were taken, the police had given permission for the room to be cleared. Mrs Macleod and her brothers took care of everything. Suzume's body was wrapped in a blanket and placed in the freezer in the basement. It would be flown back to Japan and cremated there.

"She planned it long in advance, poor child. The knife she used belonged to her mother. It is called a *kaiken*. Nowadays it is tradition to give this knife at weddings, but in the past it was used by the wives and daughters of the samurai for self-defence and – if necessary to keep their honour – for ritual suicide. This was always done by severing the jugular veins."

Olwen blanched, remembering what she had seen. At the same time, something inside her rebelled.

"Is it absolutely certain that she died by her own hand?"

"There is no doubt whatsoever. She left several letters, one in Japanese for her father and three in English – for Director Rose, Dr Jack and Christy."

Olwen was not convinced. Suzume could have been forced to write the notes; or something more subtle might have occurred, the kind of brainwashing and pressure typical of cults. As for the *kaiken*, who said it was her mother's? How could they know for certain? Rose had many unusual artefacts in his den. But even as the arguments crowded her mind, Olwen faced the one gaping hole in her theory. Why would Rose want this, his Work in ruins?

Savitri put away her stethoscope. She frowned at Olwen. "Your heart rate and blood pressure are normal, but we are left with the mystery of what brought on the shock. Contrary to popular belief, anaphylactic shock cannot be the result of psychological trauma.

It is normally caused by some kind of allergen and, in rare cases, it can be induced by physical activity. May I ask what you were doing before you came to Suzume's room? Do you exercise late at night?"

Olwen stiffened. She wasn't prepared to speak of her dream. She didn't feel safe enough. Against her natural inclination to trust Savitri was the fact that she hardly knew her.

I know none of these people well and now one of them is dead!

"I wasn't doing anything," she insisted. "I was asleep in my bed."

"But how did you come to be—"

"I must have been sleepwalking," Olwen said abruptly. "Sometimes I do. Thank you for looking after me. I wish to rest now."

She stood up quickly and headed for the door.

"Wait just a moment!" Savitri commanded. "Please!"

Reluctantly, Olwen turned. The older woman regarded her with grave concern.

"I will not pry, but let me tell you this. If the spirit walks separately from the body at night – what is called by some 'astral travel' – there are dangers that must be avoided. Most important of all is the manner of return. A sudden and violent entry can send the body into shock."

Olwen met Savitri's look without blinking. "And if this happens, one can recover from it?"

"Yes," the doctor replied, but her concern deepened. "However, you cannot let it happen again. Please believe me. I do not exaggerate. A second time would most likely kill you."

Olwen left without another word.

Back in her room, Olwen paced the floor. She wanted to accept the rational facts of Suzume's troubled history and premeditated suicide, but she couldn't overcome the overwhelming suspicion that there was more going on. Suzume had belonged to a doomsday cult in Japan. Could she have gone from one to another? *Before the Master changed and the police started to come and there were rumours of kidnappings and murders.* Was that why she had come to Olwen? To warn her? Or to ask for help? And somehow Rose found out? Was he the only sinister element here? Were the others pawns to be sacrificed in some fiendish moon ritual? Was he a necromancer? Didn't a necromancer need to raise a dead body for his purposes?

Olwen walked in faster and faster circles. Regardless of her overactive imagination and her propensity for paranoia, she kept returning to one hard cold fact. All the activities of the week, the myriad stories, and the strange hallucinatory experiences and dreams had culminated in a death. No matter where her thoughts went, she always arrived at the same point she had reached the night Suzume came to her.

I've got to get out of here.

CHAPTER THIRTY-THREE

THIS BIRD HAS FLOWN

Olwen had a plan. She would leave Dunesfort House that very night, in the darkest hours when everyone was asleep. She had found a map in a book on local history on her shelves. The nearest village was only a few miles away. The good news: she didn't have to take the steep road down the precipice. The bad news: she had to cross the moor. But she was counting on the full moon to provide her with light. All she had to do was walk in a straight line, keeping the house at her back, and she would eventually reach the village. There she would call Dr N to come and get her.

Her last hours in Dunesfort House were spent staring out the window, waiting for nightfall. At last it was time to go. She was taking only her knapsack with a few clothes, and her handbag and laptop. The laptop was heavy, but she had no intention of leaving it behind. Everything else was packed in her suitcase to be collected later.

She opened the door a crack. No one in sight. But she had only stepped into the hall when she heard another door open. Retreating quickly, she caught a glimpse of Euphémie hurrying past. The Parisienne was clearly upset. She wore no make-up and her face was streaked with tears. Was she wearing anything beneath that short silk dressing gown? Her legs and feet were bare. Olwen couldn't help but notice that she was heading for her own room, having come from Tenzin Dawa's.

Isn't that interesting.

Not your business! Focus!

Olwen waited until she heard Euphémie's door close. Eyes and ears alert, she crept into the stairwell and down to the ground floor. The murmur of male voices trailed from the direction of the front hall. Had Rose posted guards? That left the back door as her only exit. There were too many rooms nearby. And what if there were people in the courtyard? She should have checked from her window before she left the room! *Idiot.* Her heart pounded against her ribs. Was she trapped?

Then she remembered the door in the basement, the one she and Dr Jack had used. She tiptoed down the staff staircase, into the bowels of the kitchen. She had to stifle a cry. A gaunt figure stood at the open hearth, stirring the cauldron that hung over the fire. It took her a minute to recognise Mrs Macleod. The housekeeper was making the porridge for the morning meal. The smell of cooked oats filled the air. *At this hour of the night?* Stranger still was the tame sparrow perched on her shoulder. It bobbed its head and fluttered its wings as it chirped in Morag's ear. Though she didn't turn round, Olwen suspected that the older woman knew she was there.

Whispering a farewell in Irish, Olwen slipped past her and into the passageway that led to the back door. When she reached the walk-in freezer, she paused a moment and bowed her head. Her heart ached for Suzume. Then she hurried past and out of the house.

The night was cool and windy, but thankfully dry. After a harrowing dash across the courtyard – no one there! – she was through the archway and out into the countryside. *House at your back, walk in a straight line.* Just as she had hoped, the moon lit up the landscape with an eerie grey light. She stepped off the road into the tall grasses of the moor. She was glad of her walking boots though she would have preferred wellies. She had to look out for bog pools and soft muddy patches where her feet would sink. Wasn't that how the Isle of Lewis got its name? *Leòdhas. Leogach. Marshy land.* Now how did she know that? Did she read it in a book?

All the time she walked, Olwen tried her mobile again and again. Though there was still no signal, the blue light was reassuring. Knapsack on her back, bright moon above, and the occasional call of the midsummer cuckoo in the grasses helped to buoy her sense of optimism and adventure. She would reach the village in no time.

When the weather changed, it changed suddenly and Olwen wasn't prepared. She hadn't spotted the storm clouds racing in from the loch. As the sky darkened, she struggled to pull the hood of her jacket from its pouch at her neck. Too late, the rain lashed down and soaked her head. With the storm came a wind that battered her mercilessly. Worst of all was the loss of light as the clouds cloaked the moon. Each time she looked back to check the position of the house, it seemed to retreat further into the murk. Soon it disappeared altogether. She had lost her marker and all sense of direction.

She tried not to panic. Hood up, head down, she staggered over the moor, opening and closing her phone to make a fitful flashlight. The way grew steadily more treacherous. She splashed through bog pools and stumbled into hollows. Then came the moment when she tripped on a rock half buried in the ground and crashed to her knees. Her cry was a mix of pain and anguish as the phone went flying through the air. She scrambled after it, pawing through the mud and brackish water. There was no hope of finding it. She was blind in the dark and the rain. Sitting on the wet ground, she bawled like a baby.

After a while she stopped. The rain appeared to be letting up. She dragged herself to her feet, chilled to the bone, covered in muck, drenched and exhausted. Worse still, she was ravenous. If only she had eaten more supper! She tried not to think of the hot shepherd's pie with marrowfat peas and thick brown gravy.

Stop it.

She forced herself to move. One foot in front of the other, one step at a time, desperately ignoring the fact she was utterly lost.

What the fuck are you doing? Are you out of your fucking mind? Who with even a modicum of sanity would attempt to cross a bog by night without the most basic equipment like a flashlight, rain gear or a bloody compass?

The madness of her actions cast serious doubt on her previous reasoning. She began to review the thinking that had led her to this predicament. Why did she question Suzume's death when everyone, including the police, accepted it as suicide? What gigantic head stagger had allowed her to believe that everyone else around her – including people she had previously liked and admired – was suspect, wrong, or deluded, while she was not? What were the facts on which she based her conclusions? A dream. No, her interpretation of a dream.

The rain stopped at last, but now Olwen was tormented by self-loathing and disgust. This wouldn't be the first time her imagination and paranoia had run riot to ill effect.

You make interesting mistakes, a professor of Latin once remarked to her.

The story of my life, she had replied. *I'll have it carved on my tombstone.*

The flicker of humour brought some relief. Well, if she didn't die of exposure, it would make a good scene in a book one day.

Having come full circle in her mind, Olwen allowed herself some wishful thinking about a rescue party from Dunesfort House. If someone came to her room – Savitri or Dr Jack – and found her missing, might they come looking for her? Perhaps Morag would sound the alarm, given how bad the night had turned. Olwen tortured herself briefly with the image of the housekeeper coming to her room with a tray of fresh scones, home-made jam and a pot of strong tea. Oh to be back in her tower with a fire in the hearth! New tears pricked her eyes. Could she be more miserable?

Suck it back. You're in survival mode.

She no longer knew if she was moving away from the house or towards it. Could she be going in circles? Moonlight and starlight flooded the moors once more. There was even a faint trace of light in the sky. Dawn? But what good would it do her? There was no sign of Dunesfort House in any direction. Despite her efforts at humour, she knew she was in trouble. She had been walking for hours. She felt weak and feverish. How long could she last?

When she first saw the lights, she thought she was hallucinating. Then she thought they might be will-o'-the-wisps, jack-o'-lanterns, or the more horribly named corpse candles. Nonetheless, she decided to go in their direction. After a time she found she was treading more solid ground, crossing patches of heath. Then she spotted the jagged shapes in the distance. They looked like a troop of giants marching towards her. With a burst of joy, she realised where she was and what she was looking at: the Callanish Stones!

Shadowy figures with flashlights moved amidst the Stones. A fire burned at the heart of the inner circle. Olwen's mind spun. A shiver of her old paranoia returned. Was the Rite of the Cailleach going ahead? How did they get here before her? Did they know she'd run away?

"May I assist you?" a voice asked behind her. "You look the worse for wear, I'm afraid."

She yelped in surprise and wheeled around to confront a friendly-looking gentleman with grey hair and a beard. His accent was well-educated English. He wore a big rain coat and carried a flashlight. She had never seen him before. He wasn't from the Dunesfort circle.

Taking her arm firmly, he led her to the Stones where a small group was encamped. There were tents pitched here and there. Though most of the campers were sleeping, the inevitable late-nighters sat around a small bonfire. Someone put a blanket over her shoulders and someone else handed her a mug of hot soup. Her teeth chattered against the metal rim of the cup. She was shaking all over.

"The fire will warm you up," one of the women assured her.

It was surreal to be sitting amongst the great stones around a fire at dawn with total strangers. They were a mixed bunch, though all had come to view the lunar standstill due the following evening. Some were amateur astronomers. The English gentleman was one of these. Others belonged to a pagan sect who had come to hold rituals for the unusual conjunction of full moon, summer solstice and lunar standstill. There was also a scattering of old hippies, young backpackers, and adventurous tourists. In total they numbered less than fifty, but hundreds were expected the following day and night.

It was the pagans who caught her attention. Outwardly they looked no different from the others, in rain gear and plastic ponchos, but their talk was of ancestral magic, geomancy and the Great Mother. The High Priestess was an intense young Scotswoman with pierced eyebrows and tattoos. She reminded Olwen of Una. While most of her company came from the mainland, she herself was a native of Lewis.

The High Priestess pointed to a range of hills in the east.

"The moon rises from there. Some call the ridge 'the Sleeping Beauty', but in Scots Gaelic it's *Cailleach na Mointeach*, 'the Witch of the Moors.'"

"*Cailleach*," Olwen murmured.

The High Priestess warmed her hands at the fire. Her voice rang with excitement. "The moon skims across the horizon, like a stone skimming over the waves. She is so close to the Earth it looks as if she is walking on the land. This happens every nineteen years or so. I was six the last time it did, on the 2nd of December 1987."

"December 2nd!"

The hairs rose on the back of Olwen's neck. Her birthday!

"My parents brought me," the young woman continued. Her smile was wry. "It was a family outing to break up the winter. Little did they realise they were setting me on my spiritual path. I was caught that night. By moon magic."

"Do you know of the prophecy?" one of the other women asked Olwen.

She shook her head.

"When the moon walks on the land, the Shining Ones will return."

Olwen shivered and felt suddenly breathless.

"Who are the Shining Ones?" she asked.

The answers chimed from all around her.

"The ancient deities."

"Ancestral spirits."

"God and his angels."

"Aliens!" The young backpacker's grin was faintly mocking. He strummed his guitar. "This is an ancient launching pad."

Some of the younger pagans glared at him, but the older women just rolled their eyes and laughed.

The High Priestess smiled and gave a little shrug. "Ancestral spirits. Ancient gods. Elementals of sky and land. Perhaps the immortal energies of the Stones themselves. Everyone has a different interpretation, but no one denies that something happens."

"The scientists see the moon," another woman added. "We see the Moon Goddess."

Olwen was enjoying their company. The hot soup had revived her and they offered her tea and sandwiches as well. She was grateful that no one asked how she had come to be there. With every passing minute, her fears seemed all the more ridiculous. But there was no point wallowing in regret or self-blame. She would just have to withdraw from Dunesfort House with as much grace as possible. She would rest until daylight and then borrow someone's phone

to contact Dr N. The two of them could collect her things at the
house. A wave of shame and embarrassment washed over her. She
was mortified at the thought of facing the circle.

I'll think about it tomorrow.

You do that, Scarlett.

The backpacker started up a song on his guitar. Everyone knew it
and they all joined in.

I'm being followed by a moon shadow.

Moon shadow, moon shadow.

People began to drift away to their tents. Olwen was nodding off.
One of the pagans offered her a spare sleeping bag. She spread it
out near the campfire and climbed inside. In no time at all, she was
curled up like a foetus, fast asleep at the heart of the Stones.

CHAPTER THIRTY-FOUR

SEVENTH NIGHT: A MIDSUMMER NIGHT'S DREAM

Was she awake or asleep?

Her body felt heavy and rooted to the ground. Only her eyelids moved, opening and closing on the scene around her. The campfire seemed to have grown immense, showering sparks into the night sky. The Stones towered above her, crowned with the stars overhead. Where was the moon? It was nowhere in sight.

She wasn't alone. Shadows danced in the firelight around the Stones. Naked women. She recognised the High Priestess, tall, glorious, straight as a spear. Her long dark hair cascaded down her back. Her skin was painted with blue spirals. The other women had decorated their bodies with ash from the fire. They were singing as they danced, to the music that seemed to echo from the Stones themselves.

I will light a fire in the darkness,
I will smear my face with ashes,
I will dance in the place of my ancestors,
I will sing to the stars and my mother, the Moon.
Teach me, O life, to rejoice in everything!

Was she awake or asleep?

The pagan women were gone. A scorched kettle sat on top of the campfire. Someone sat opposite her. A young man in black leather that gleamed in the firelight. His white-blond hair fell over his shoulders. He cradled a harp in his lap, strumming as he sang. His face was marked with spirals of ash. Dark eyes watched her like a cat. The words he sang were strange. At first she couldn't make them out. Then she realised he was singing in Danish. Her mind began to translate.

I will light a fire in the darkness,
I will smear my face with ashes.

Was she awake or asleep?

She was with Mrs Macleod. The housekeeper was transformed. She was no longer Morag but the giantess MAGOG, ancestral mother of the Celts. And Olwen herself was a tiny bird perched on the titan's shoulder.

Magog was stirring a gigantic cauldron with a spirtle the size of an oar. When Olwen peered down into the massive pot, she saw a mess of star stuff – suns and moons, stellar clouds and planets, swirling galaxies. The turbulence was shocking and magnificent to behold.

Magog hummed a tune as she stirred. The tune inspired Olwen to sing her own song and she trilled like a blackbird.

I want to know there is a God or some Source of Love that cares for
*   the world.*
I want to know there is a reason why everything exists, that life is not a
*   random array of matter.*
I want to know that the suffering and sorrow woven into the very fabric
*   of life is not meaningless, but serves some good and noble purpose.*
I want to know that evil, like suffering, also serves the Good.
I want to know that humanity is more than a chance occurrence, that we
*   are here for a reason.*

I want to know that my life, regardless of whether it is a success or a

failure, is of value in and of itself.

I want to know that I am not here by accident.

I want to know that I am loved by life.

All the time she sang, she sensed the Mother listening with a boundless intensity of love. Other beings moved around her, tending the fire on which the crucible stood. They, too, were singing to the music of the spheres and it seemed that Olwen's small refrain was part of a Great Song.

At the heart of the universe, we sing of a life lived in matter.

CHAPTER THIRTY-FIVE

TURNAROUND

Olwen woke in the central burial chamber, curled up inside her sleeping bag. The campfire was ashen. Wisps of smoke curled in the chill of the morning air. Her head was resting on a stone as if it were a pillow. The glare of the early sun made her blink. The day was already promising to warm up, might even get hot. She stood up shakily. Her body ached from the hard ground. The area around her was littered with abandoned sleeping bags and rain sheets. A blackened kettle sat on a rock. The sight of a guitar case made her frown. Shouldn't it be a harp? She looked around quickly, half expecting to see the young biker. A vehicle pulled up in the car park nearby. The Dunesfort jeep. She wasn't really surprised when Rose got out.

Doing her best to tidy herself up – her clothes were caked with mud from her falls on the moor – she collected her things and made her way towards him. Her companions from the previous night were breakfasting in their cars and vans. The High Priestess called out to her to join their group. They had set up a table under a green canopy and were feasting on porridge, scones and coffee. Olwen smiled her thanks but declined. New arrivals were filling up the car park. Some local people, dressed in sober black suits, handed out tracts about keeping the Sabbath sacred. It was Sunday, she realised.

Rose waited for her by the jeep, leaning on his cane. As usual, she couldn't read his expression.

"I've brought your things," he said quietly. "I'll drive you to wherever you wish to go. Stornoway or perhaps where your friend is staying."

She stared at him a while. Everything had changed, changed utterly. Some part of her noted that he no longer seemed to tower over her. They were, in fact, the same height.

"How did you know I was here?"

He returned her gaze without blinking. "I dreamed it."

There was nothing she could say to that. She suffered a moment of uncertainty. She wanted to apologise, but didn't know where to begin. To her surprise, he beat her to it.

"I am sorry," he said, and he sounded sincere. "We...I...should have looked after you better. I should have come to you after Suzume..." He choked on his words. Grief and guilt ravaged his features. "Things fell apart. *I* fell apart."

Her own grief and guilt rose to mirror his, and with it the added pang of shame and embarrassment. How could she have let her fear run so rampant?

He opened the passenger door for her.

"Is the course over?" she asked, as she climbed in.

Her luggage was in the back.

"There will be a meeting this morning to decide. Christy has called it. He wants us to hold the Rite of the Cailleach."

"I thought he left?"

"He came back."

She sat in silence as Rose walked to the driver's door. Her throat felt constricted, but she had to say it. He needed to know. As he climbed into the jeep, she spluttered out the words.

"I'd like to go back myself. I'd like to attend that meeting."

His body juddered visibly. He nodded, apparently unable to speak.

They were quiet for most of the drive. Olwen was too exhausted to talk. It was only when they were in sight of Dunesfort House that Rose finally spoke. He indicated the moor that stretched beyond them, wreathed in mist.

"You may know already, in Denmark when it is like this we say *mosekonen brygger.*"

"No, I've never heard that expression."

A smile twitched at the edges of his mouth.

"It means 'the witch of the moor is brewing.'"

She couldn't help but smile as well.

When they arrived at Dunesfort House, they found Ruairi waiting for them in the courtyard. Olwen knew it was him because he didn't utter a word, but only grunted as he lifted her luggage from the jeep. She was about to follow him into the house, when Rose stopped her a moment.

"Thank you for returning. I cannot express the depths of my gratitude."

His eyes had a peculiar look. His voice quavered. She found the strength of his emotions too overpowering. Nodding quickly, she hurried away.

No sooner was she in the back door than Mrs Macleod was there. After wiping her own hands on her apron, Morag grasped Olwen's. A broad smile lit her face.

"Ach, it is good to have you back, *dawtie*. You are in time to break your fast. Go and wash. I will have your meal ready for you."

Entering her room, Olwen felt a sense of homecoming. Her luggage stood in the middle of the floor, as it had on her first day. The windows were open to let in a warm breeze. A vase of moorland flowers sat on her desk – purple thistles and sunny marsh marigolds. Mrs Macleod had known she would return.

After she had showered and changed, Olwen headed downstairs

to the dining room. It was awash with sunlight. Most of the others were finished their breakfast. Many smiled over at her or nodded in greeting. She felt a little shy and awkward. Both Elsie and Dr Jack jumped up to embrace her, Elsie beaming through her tears.

"I was worried sick," Dr Jack murmured in her ear. Then he stood back to survey her clinically, to reassure himself that she was fine. "Rose said he knew where you were and that you were all right."

Both the concern and relief in his face were unmistakable. How could she have imagined he would wish her harm? How could she think that any of them would? She was shamefaced and painfully discomfited. Her tablemates saw this and didn't press her with questions.

Mrs Macleod arrived with scrambled eggs, orange juice, toast, and tea. Olwen attacked the food like a gannet.

"The porridge has all been eaten," the housekeeper said, with a little wink. "But there will be more tomorrow."

Dr Jack and Elsie stayed with Olwen as she ate, making small talk about the weather and Mrs Macleod's cooking. Olwen was just finishing her last slice of toast when the gong rang out.

"We're gathering in the Meeting Room," Dr Jack told her. His tone was grave. "It's crunch time."

They sat in a circle as usual. There was no talk as they settled into their places. Rose sat also, hands resting on his cane. He didn't have a clipboard.

"It is time to speak of Suzume's death," he said.

His voice was low and sad as he spoke of the young woman who had been part of their circle for just over three years.

"She suffered more than most, and struggled valiantly until she could do so no more. Alas, all our efforts to help her heal herself failed. Each of us, in his or her own way, has to deal with that failure, even as we have to deal with it as a group. Many of you have come to me to say you wish to leave. Others have requested that the Work continue. The circle must decide whether we finish today or proceed to the Rite of the Cailleach this evening. We will take as much time as is needed for each of you to have your say. Those who do not wish to speak are under no obligation to do so."

They sat in silence for a while, then Thomas Tillman spoke up. He looked wan and distraught. His voice was almost inaudible, as he kept coughing and choking on his words.

"I...leave...today...never to return...the error...mine...the Spirit Boat...for her..."

It seemed as if every syllable had to be forced from his throat.

"Even if...the Rite...I...don't deserve..."

Some of the women wept as they listened to him. Olwen was appalled by the depths of guilt he revealed. How could he possibly think it was *his* fault?

Though the circle normally refrained from commenting on each other's words, Christy spoke up in reaction to Thomas. The Irishman looked haggard. His face was gaunt, his eyes dark and terrible; yet it was also apparent that some kind of peace had come to him, some extraordinary acceptance of what had happened. Olwen wondered briefly if he, too, had crossed the moors last night.

"It's not on, Tom," he said bluntly. "You can't take the blame. It's not yours to take. We've all got our cross to bear in this, but I can tell ye now, she wanted ye in the Boat and she wouldn't have agreed to anything else. God love her, she was many things and one of them was stubborn. 'Twas that strength that kept her alive for so long, but I'm thinkin' it also carried her to her death. Once she made up her mind, she was not for turnin'." Christy waited a moment to let Thomas absorb his words, then he continued. "I know everyone here believed that I was supportin' Suzume. The truth is, she was supportin' me. She was me chance to have me darlin' daughter back. She eased the pain in the place where Bernie's loss was most deeply felt." Christy pressed his hand to his heart for a moment. Then he turned again to Thomas. "We've the ghosts of our own daughters here, Tom, as well as Suzume. This is the pain you and I must bear in this life until we pass over to join them. And neither Suzume nor your daughter would want to hear ye say that you've no right to be healed. They'd wish it for ye, of that I've no doubt. Ye can't pass up a gift if it's offered to ye. It'd be wrong and that's the truth of it."

One by one various others spoke. Some expressed their love for Thomas and Christy as well as Suzume. Others revealed their own grief and guilt which Suzume's death had triggered.

It was Elsie's story that caught most by surprise, though not Rose or Dr Jack. She sat stiffly in her chair, like a dowager queen. From time to time she slapped her thigh to emphasise what she was saying.

"I've made no bones about the fact that I got a secret and that I didn't intend to share it with the rest of you. But death has a funny way of stripping things down...like pride and secrets. In the face of death, there's only the truth. And one thing I know for sure is that the strength of this group – just like the strength of anyone in it – rests on the truth.

"I'm not going to beat around the bush and I don't want any sympathy or comments. I'm just going to say it, for my own sake and for the sake of the circle. Suicide is not something that happens to everybody. It has happened in my life. I helped my beloved Chaim to die by his own hand. It's what he wanted. It was his own choice, made in sound mind though not in sound body. He was dying of cancer, but it wasn't physical pain that drove his decision. All of you know the stories of the camps. I don't want to talk about them here; but maybe not all of you know that the survivors live with a guilt that nothing can erase. Many choose suicide at the end of their lives even though, like Chaim, they are already dying. They don't allow themselves a natural death in memory of all those whose deaths were unnatural."

She paused a moment. Her eyes were dry. She had shed all her tears long before this day; but there was no question of the fact that she was suffering.

"I was against it. As far as I'm concerned, it's another victory for the Nazis, another death they caused; but I couldn't stop him and I wouldn't let him do it alone. I've carried the knowledge of his death and my role in it for the most part alone." She glanced at Rose and Dr Jack. "It's important to me that my children and grandchildren never come to know of it. But today I share my secret in Suzume's name, so that her death has some meaning, if only for me."

Those who wanted to weep for Elsie fought against it, out of respect for her. It was not their place to express a grief she contained herself. The room remained silent for some time.

Then Euphémie spoke up. She wore no make-up. Her face looked white and worn. All glamour had fled. Her voice was barely audible.

"I do not wish to say much but, like Elsie, I am called to speak in the name of Suzume. When I am in my first year of college, my younger sister, Véronique, die by suicide. She was merely sixteen. It was not something my family could see to happen, but then we are not a family of emotion. Like my father, I study science, and there I find no *confort*, no consolation. I seek an answer in many place and I find it in Plum Village, where I meet my beautiful teacher, Thich Nhat Hanh. With the death of Suzume, I live again the loss of *ma soeur*, the guilt I feel and the sorrow. Tenzin help me very much. He is like Thay. That is all I say."

Tenzin Dawa was beside Euphémie. He bowed to the circle to indicate that he would speak next. Olwen was surprised. The young Tibetan rarely shared his thoughts or feelings. She heard the change in his voice. Something older, much older, echoed there.

"I spoke with Suzume the evening she died," he said quietly. "I am telling you this because you need to know. From my talk with her, I understood that she believed the Rite of the Cailleach would be a success. *More than the day of our death, we fear the day of our healing.* This is what she rejected when she ended her life. There is no blame on Suzume and no blame on the rest of you. There is no blame to be apportioned, only karma to be lived. As she was a Buddhist, I have begun the prayers for forty-nine days that will assist her in the bardo and into her next incarnation."

Olwen hadn't intended to speak, but Tenzin Dawa's words made it impossible for her not to. As simply as she could, she described the last night she had shared with the girl: the knock on the door, the race down to the cove, castles in the sand, their conversations, especially the mention of 'The Little Mermaid', Suzume's fear of Rose, and, finally, her last run to the sea.

"At the time I thought she was running away from the Director, because she was afraid of him. I've come to realise that she was running away...because he was coming to save her."

When Olwen finished, there was a profound silence broken only by muted sounds of grief. Rose bowed his head towards her. No one else spoke. All that had to be said, had been said.

Then Rose stood to make his announcement.

"It is up to each of you to decide if the week ends here, or if we are to hold the Rite of the Cailleach this evening. Depending on numbers, the ritual may or may not go ahead. There will be no show of hands, no pressure on anyone, no recriminations. The choice must be freely made and without doubt or hesitation; for the Rite cannot succeed otherwise. I will give you an hour to reflect on your decision. For those who wish to leave, transport will be provided. Please gather in the courtyard with your luggage in an hour's time. Anyone not leaving, I would ask you to return here to the Meeting Room at that time and we will see if it is possible to proceed."

Without waiting for questions or comments, Rose left the room.

....

An hour later, Olwen's alarm went off. She pulled herself from the bed where she had been napping and staggered to the window. Below her in the courtyard was the Dunesfort jeep and beside it the minibus. Between the bus and the jeep stood Rose, leaning on his cane. He looked a forlorn and solitary figure, but there was also something heroic about him, like the statue of the unknown soldier. She felt a momentary compulsion to go down and stand beside him. How many would leave? Were there already people in the vehicles? She couldn't see from her vantage point.

After a quick splash of water on her face and a brush through her hair, she ran downstairs to the Meeting Room.

The first thing she registered was the number of people. A good-sized crowd had gathered. More were still arriving. Everyone milled around, glancing at their watches. She checked hers. It was just over an hour since Rose had made his announcement.

Dr Jack left first. Christy followed after him. The gong rang out in the hallway like the toll of a bell. The room was utterly silent. Everyone looked solemn, their eyes shining. By this time the truth was obvious. They were all there. No one had chosen to leave.

When Rose walked into the room, with Dr Jack and Christy just behind him, there was a spontaneous outburst of cheers and applause. Caught off guard, he ducked his head. Olwen suffered a moment of disorientation as she suddenly saw him in a new light. He wasn't aloof and unapproachable, he was *shy*! How could she have missed that? Didn't he tell her he was an introvert?

There was a slight tremor in his voice as he addressed them. It was the only indication that he was deeply affected. His features remained typically controlled and impassive.

"There will be a change of programme to accommodate the Rite. The original timetable lists Walking the Labyrinth and Farewell Feast. The Rite was not scheduled, of course, although some of you knew of the upcoming lunar event." He glanced at Euphémie.

"As too many variables come into play, we can never know in advance if we can hold it. But now that we are going ahead, I feel the circle needs to increase its *chi*. There has been much soul loss from the trauma of Suzume's death. We need more energy to hold the Rite. If you are all agreeable, we will do another session of Breathwork."

Everyone nodded vigorously. There was nothing more powerful. Olwen agreed with the others. Beside her, Una was whispering to Roy. He raised his hand and called out.

"You'll need facilitators. Una and I put ourselves forward."

There was instant chatter in the crowd as the various pairs of Breathers and Watchers conferred with each other. More volunteers would be needed. Olwen kept silent. She had too little experience to even consider the role. When she glanced over at Dr Jack, she saw that he was talking with Elsie.

"Count me in!" the old woman chirped loudly. "I should be so lucky. I get all the good of it without working too hard."

A ripple of laughter met her words. No one believed what she said.

Rose thanked the volunteers, then dropped his bombshell.

"I will not be a facilitator myself. I will participate."

Olwen felt the shock strike the group. There were gasps and spontaneous cries. She sensed delight, excitement, and even traces of fear.

Behind her, Savitri whispered in her ear, "He has never done this before. He has always been a facilitator. It means he believes this circle can hold him."

From all sides came impassioned offers to be paired with him. Astonished, Olwen had to make another adjustment to her viewpoint. It was something she had glimpsed earlier in their support, but had failed to fully recognise. They *loved* Rose! They were devoted to him!

The Director gave a brief smile that was almost a wince and held up his hand.

"It is all right, thank you, but the matter has been settled. As Dr Jack will facilitate in my place" – he hesitated a moment before he finished – "I would like Olwen to be my partner, if she would agree."

All eyes turned in her direction. There were looks of surprise and gratitude and the odd flicker of envy.

Elsie clapped her hands and lifted them high in the air.

Only Olwen showed no emotion. She held herself rigid.

Over my dead body.

CHAPTER THIRTY-SIX

ANGELS AND DEMONS

It was a long walk across the room to where Rose and Dr Jack stood surrounded by well-wishers, but Olwen crossed it with the speed of fury. They had obviously cooked this up together. How *dare* they? Without consulting her! On that basis alone – before she even considered the other welter of objections – she intended to put an instant stop to the idea. But she had no sooner reached them than Dr Jack caught her by the elbow and propelled her out of the room. Rose followed close behind. Before she knew it, the three of them were alone in the front parlour with the door shut behind them.

"You should have asked me!" she exploded, before either could speak. "You had no right!"

"It was all last-minute," Dr Jack rushed to explain. "Rose thought the whole thing was over. He expected at least a third of the group to leave. The Breathwork was Christy's idea, concocted in the hallway just before we entered the room. You were already inside. We couldn't get to you. It all just happened."

Rose kept nodding in agreement to Dr Jack's words. Both men looked genuinely contrite, in fact, like two schoolboys caught out and in trouble. A giddy sensation came over Olwen. She had to suppress a laugh. Crossing her arms, she struggled to hold on to her righteous indignation.

Rose seemed unable to speak. Yet again, she saw him from an

unexpected angle. He was vulnerable, no longer in command. Events had overtaken him. He was adrift and at sea.

The last of Olwen's anger dissipated. She was the one calling the shots. The sudden feeling of power was heady. She reined it in. It wasn't appropriate. There was too much at stake, too many others involved. And she realised something else. There was a sense of rightness in the unfolding of events. This was meant to happen.

A shudder ran through her as she considered the idea of being partnered with him. There was no denying the unease she still felt in his presence.

"I'll do it," she said at last, "but on one condition." She addressed him directly. Her tone was unapologetic. She knew what she could and couldn't do. "I'm not comfortable with the idea of you being my Watcher. I want Jack. But I will be *your* Watcher."

A look of relief crossed Rose's features.

"I will tell the others," he said. "The first session will begin in half an hour. I will breathe in the second session, if that is all right with you?"

It was her turn to be relieved. She was in no hurry to be paired with him. When Rose left, Dr Jack turned to her, arms wide.

"Don't," she said quickly, backing away from him. "I've agreed to this, but it's all seriously freaky. I need to be alone. To deal with it."

He dropped his arms. "I understand." He smiled at her proudly. "See you in the Womb in half an hour. I'll have everything ready for you."

She almost ran to her room in the tower. Diving under the duvet, she hugged her knees to her body and closed her eyes tight.

What have I done?

As soon as she entered the Trance Room, Olwen felt the buzz. Change was in the air. Rose stood quietly with the other facilitators. Christy was in charge.

Olwen settled down on her mat with a quick nod to Dr Jack.

"Ditto the last instructions," she told him, "except I don't mind if Rose comes to help."

Dr Jack regarded her thoughtfully. "You'll go far. You're clearly at the wheel."

"*Rotha Mór an tSaoil?*" She grinned at his puzzled look. "Irish – the Great Wheel of Life."

When the room had settled into silence, Christy addressed them. He turned around slowly to take all of them in.

"Well, dear hearts, aren't we a bit surprised to find ourselves back here?" His smile was gentle. Everyone smiled back, some already in tears. "We're out of our depth and don't we know it. We're swimmin' in her shadow, beyond the safety of the shore, into the currents of the deep. We must rely on our faith to guide us, the belief – no, the *knowledge* – that each of us has an inner navigator, a greater Self, a spark of the Divine that knows exactly what we need to heal ourselves. Breathe your way to that guiding star. Breathe your way to that inner pilot. Breathe for your life.

"To start us off, I'm going to read a few lines from a poem by my favourite poet, a Dubliner and Northsider like meself, Paula Meehan. The poem's called 'She-Who-Walks-Among-the-People.'"

The people will endure.
They are scattered
over the face of the earth
like those stars above you
over the face of the heavens.
Our dreams are as clear
as water from a good well
...and we mind each other.

Olwen lay flat on her mat. Without mask or scarf, she simply closed her eyes. As soon as the music began, she took the deepest and longest breaths of her life.

The initial resistance surprised her. An invisible weight seemed to push against her. She felt as if she were pinned to the ground. She kept trying to move, huffing and puffing like a grampus. Fragmented images floated through her mind. Flotsam and jetsam. It seemed ages before a whole vision emerged: a huge crater in the earth. Before she knew it, she was sucked into its maw, diving downwards into an underworld of mudflats, fungus and primal slime. Choking, lungs heaving, she gasped for air as she struggled against feelings of suffocation. Then, slowly but surely, she clawed her way out through a bloody gash.

Dazed and bewildered, she pulled herself onto her knees. Eyes still closed, she felt the first blow to her ear. It knocked her down. As she scrambled up again, she was aware that she was small and wearing a dress. Her hands clutched the edges of her hem. She was crying, because she was in trouble and afraid. *Smack!* She fell to the floor again. *A good box in the ears.* And again. And again. The side of her head ached. Her ear was swollen. Here was the source of her chronic earaches! Each time she was knocked down, more memories assaulted her, images from her childhood and one of her love affairs and, then, from her marriage: a blow to the stomach, a slap across the face, head hitting the wall, blood gushing from her nose. *Stop it! Stop hitting me!* She was crying and falling and falling and crying, sometimes with the voice of a little girl and other times with the voice of a terrified woman.

Then came a time when she fell down and refused to get up. Curling into a tight ball on the mat, she wept her heart out. A powerless child. A defeated woman.

Time passed. All her tears were shed. She lay still and quiet, as a deep peace enveloped her. With it came the slow seep of strength.

I survived it all.

She was on her knees again, but now her back was straight, her arms raised, her fists clenched. She lashed out. Her right hand made contact with something soft. She followed up with her left. Then she exploded, striking furiously with no thought of who or what she was hitting. Blow after blow landed as she roared at the top of her lungs.

"PICK ON SOMEONE YOUR OWN SIZE, YOU BASTARD!"

Eventually, her rage was spent. Satisfied and thoroughly pleased with herself, she let her body relax. King of the World, she sank back into the mound of cushions behind her. Without opening her eyes, she signalled imperiously for a cup of water and drank deeply. When she was finished, she handed the cup back with a courteous wave to the one who had served her.

It was time to lie down again. Time to breathe some more. She had bigger fish to fry.

Her breaths were quick and sharp. She needed to move farther up and further in. The speakers were pumping out a loud, pulsating beat. She sped up her breathing to match the pace. A burst of white light flashed in her brain and she was suddenly elsewhere.

The dome-shaped structure was made of glass. There were video monitors everywhere and men in white coats who were in charge. It was some kind of station with ramps going downwards into an underground area. Curious, she went below. It was like a car park with many levels, but there were also shops and buildings. The streets were crowded. Uniformed police and military were everywhere. A major bust was going down. People were being held at gunpoint, some on their knees, others up against the wall or over the bonnets of cars. One of the policemen waved her away from the arrests. She gave them a wide berth, walking in a half-circle towards a stone wall.

There she found the child: a little girl in a ragged grey shift that was barely a dress. Her face was dirty. Her lank hair straggled over her shoulders. She was hunched on the ground. Olwen hunkered down beside her. The child stared straight ahead with glazed eyes. She appeared to be reciting a poem.

I was raped.

The first line was followed by a string of words like pearls, beautiful and powerful, but in no language that Olwen recognised.

Then the child repeated the one comprehensible line.

I was raped.

Followed by more exquisite and incoherent words.

Then a third time.

I was raped.

Olwen reached out to comfort her, but the little girl was oblivious to her presence. Here was form without content. A shadow of the past. A body without a soul. The vital essence gone. Olwen would have to search for it. With that decision, the dome collapsed. The glass shattered. Olwen breathed more intensely, more urgently. She knew what had to be done. A soul retrieval in a Breathwork session!

Music swelled around her in grand orchestral harmonies, epic and heroic. Now she found herself surrounded by a web of black lace. It seemed alive. Was she caught inside it? Or was this her home? Something lay beyond the web. Something horrible. It was coming for her. She gulped back her terror. Let it come! A shadow fell over her. A great eye blinked, yellow and malevolent. It had her in its sights! Then came the smell. Nauseating and overpowering and all too familiar. The stink of the demon. He was bearing down on her. Every part of her wanted to scream and run. But she held her ground. She had to face it. And even as her lips cried *no, no, no* her mind mirrored the sounds as *know, know, know.*

The demon tore away the net, laid his body on top of hers. The weight and stench were overwhelming. His fingers invaded her mouth. His lips tore at her chest and sucked out her heart. Now he forced her legs open. And even as she suffered the horror, she caught slivers of memory: the original abuse, an adult bearing down on her, the terror and powerlessness, and the final surrender that heaped more guilt and shame upon her.

Waves of nausea struck her. Just a hint of the true memory was more awful than any demon. Oh god, the child's terror. Oh god, the child's revulsion, at an adult male using her sexually. The tearing. The pain. A hand clapped over her mouth to stifle the screams. The suffocating, smothering, physical horror.

Oh god. Oh god.

Olwen retched over a basin, vomiting violently bile and blood.

"Do you need help?" a voice murmured, as if from a great distance.

But she was already gone, falling back on the mat, chest heaving as she gulped great breaths into her lungs.

There was a little girl to save.

She was adrift in the black night, a female body floating amongst the stars. She had given birth to a baby, an orphaned star, but it had already disappeared, shooting away like a comet. She called out her name, sensing that the child was on the far side of the universe.

OOOOLLLLWWWEEEENNNN.

How could she possibly find her?

She paused to gather strength from the music and the others around her. In that moment she understood the exact nature of the Work. The individual energies released in the circle could be harnessed by all to release even greater resources in a chain reaction that was both personal and cosmic. There was more than enough power in the circle to propel her across the vast inner spaces she needed to traverse.

Through zaarahs of darkness and deserts of light, under architraves of immense constellations and clouds of glittering dust, whirling planets and blazing suns, across galactic seas and eternities of twilight into nascent realms newly quickening to life. Out beyond height and width and depth, she plunged over the abyss into brighter boroughs even more mysterious that swam in black oceans like serpents swallowing their own tails. It was a voyage of exquisite and breathtaking proportions and all the time she journeyed, she cried out her own name across the void.

At last she found her, standing alone on an asteroid like the Little Prince. No longer in a ragged shift, the child wore a fairy costume with gossamer wings. In her hand she clutched a starry wand. Olwen held out her arms. The little girl jumped eagerly into them, clambering over Olwen's shoulder to ride piggy-back. She was small and warm, like a little lamb or a golden fleece.

Olwen started to laugh; but the laugh was cut short as the child whispered in her ear.

"*You will have to kill him for me.*"

Olwen shuddered with dread, but she knew it was true. She had to banish the demon once and for all.

Now she stood before the white labyrinth under the night sky. She wore silver armour: helmet, breastplate, greaves, and gauntlets. In one hand she carried a tall spear, in the other, a shield emblazoned with the moon on a black background of stars. *Spéirbhean. Skywoman.* The child on her shoulders had turned into a wolfskin. And there was something else on her back. With a shudder of joy, she acknowledged the weight of the great feathered wings that almost touched the ground.

Though her mouth was dry and her heart beat wildly, Olwen strode through the winding passages of the labyrinth. For good or ill, this must be done. A tortuous cradling had brought her to this. Her life had been lived in the shadow of a nightmare. She could feel the anger burn in her blood, course through her veins. All those years blighted by the foul deeds of another. She nursed her rage, stoked it higher and higher, till it was fashioned into a weapon of white-hot metal: her backbone, as straight and steely as the spear in her hand.

She stalked the demon. He was somewhere ahead. His roars echoed through the night. She raised her shield.

It's only a memory. Something I have already survived. Time to banish it forever. Time to kill it.

She caught up with him at the heart of the labyrinth, in front of his lair. He was huge, with barrelled chest and thick arms and legs rough with coarse hair. His genitals hung exposed. His face was brutish, the eyes cold and dead. Worst of all was the smell of him, both the foulness of his breath and the stink of his sweat. Her stomach heaved as she grappled with his flesh, soft and corpulent. She was fighting the demon and she was fighting the memories. Waves of nausea threatened to overwhelm her; but there was no question of retreat. Her cause was just, her rage pure. She fought with a grim and deadly determination.

The battle was short and swift and terrible. At last her spear plunged deep into his vitals and he shrieked in his death throes.

The demon lay vanquished at Olwen's feet. She wasn't surprised that his features bore some resemblance to her abuser. Uncle B had never shown remorse for what he did to her, nor what he did to her siblings and even his own children. Whatever circuits were crossed in his brain – sociopathic or psychopathic – he was an unrepentant paedophile to the day he died. She remembered meeting him years later. How affectionate he had been towards her. She also remembered how he had looked at her daughter, only three years old at the time. There was no question of forgiving him. He had never asked for forgiveness. He had never sought it. He was now long dead. That part of him that was good had already left on its own soul's journey: the man who had taught her songs to sing; who had played with her in the park; who had wooed her as a child. A lonely child who longed to be loved. That man was gone and the thing that lay at her feet was the demon in him. In the end, she had slain it without hatred or bitterness, but with the rage that was needed to expel it from her body and mind.

She was suddenly aware of the others beside her, two angelic figures, shining with light.

"The deed is done," Ruairi said.

"And it was nobly done," Calum added, with a smile.

Olwen smiled back. Then she saw the great host of winged beings behind them, her brothers and sisters.

"It's insane down here," she told them. "So many of us go mad and do terrible things to each other. Vast numbers are lost in the forgetting."

But they already knew that. She could see it in their eyes, dark with pity.

"It is all part of the journey," Calum said.

"There is a purpose," Ruairi agreed. "Everything serves the Good."

But she already knew that.

She fell back on the mat with a sigh.

She was finished.

CHAPTER THIRTY-SEVEN

SHADOW PLAY

Olwen sat up on her mat. She felt thrilled and invigorated and ravenous.

"I'm done," she said to Dr Jack. "Let's blow this pop-stand."

Several of the Breathers had already left the room, but most were in the throes of bodywork, screaming or weeping. The din of a battlefield. Olwen looked around with a keen delight. Like many a veteran of the wars, she was almost sorry to leave it behind. Here was the suffering of life met full-on. Here was the crucible, the heart of the furnace, the fires of healing stoked to a roar.

"Hold on," said Dr Jack. "I'll get a facilitator."

His voice shook. Only now did she notice how bad he looked. Her session had been hard on him.

When he returned with Elsie, Olwen beamed at the old lady.

"I don't need bodywork. Just food. I'm grand."

Elsie frowned. Her sharp bird-eyes studied Olwen.

"Get Rose," Olwen said. It was almost a command. "He'll clear me."

"Sure thing," said Elsie. A smile flickered over her face. "But you stay there on your keester till I get back."

Dr Jack sat beside Olwen. He looked ill and shaky. She reached out to touch him, but he stiffened. She withdrew her hand. His reaction didn't affect her. Euphoric, she felt sympathy for him and some regret that she couldn't ease his pain; but everything was unfolding as it should. Everything that happened was good.

They sat in silence until Rose arrived. He went down on one knee and stared into her eyes. She returned his gaze with a cheeky grin and a clear challenge.

He smiled with surprise and nodded. "Well done." Then he turned to Dr Jack. "She can go."

As soon as they entered the conservatory, Olwen headed for the tea station to grab a slice of chocolate cake.

"The usual. One of everything," she said to Dr Jack, her mouth full. Then she stopped a moment to consider the half-eaten cake in her hand. "Bizarre," she murmured. "Matter consuming matter."

She headed over to a place where the ivy trailed down from the glass roof. She was eager to paint. Dr Jack brought her a tray heaped with goodies. She helped herself to a cup of Earl Grey tea. He poured himself a mug of coffee. His face was ashen, his eyes red. He looked as rough as he had on the day of Suzume's death.

"Was it too much for you?" she asked. "The violence? The abuse?"

He sipped on his coffee. "I stopped taking child clients years ago. I had to accept I just couldn't detach. The suffering of innocents is too…"

He stopped. Anguish contorted his features.

She refrained from reaching out for him. Instead, she returned to her painting.

"You were right about this work," she said quietly. "The years of therapy I did helped me to deal with what happened, but it was still all there in my body and my psyche, still affecting how I lived my life and my relationships. The Breathwork allows us to physically exorcise the demons." She grimaced at the literal truth of her words. She considered how best to convey her experience and, if possible, to help him. "It deals with the bigger questions too. The great *why* of suffering and evil. Everything serves life. *Everything* serves the Good."

He jerked back, as if she had struck him. His body went rigid with anger. He pressed his lips tight, biting back the harsh words he wanted to say. He didn't have to speak. She knew the arguments. She had voiced them often enough herself.

Don't give me that New Age self-serving shite! It's all very well for you to say these things when you are well fed and housed and your worst suffering is linked to the need for more money, not physical or psychological survival. What does that bullshit mean to the parents who have lost their child, to the people of Darfur or Iraq, to the woman being raped, the man being murdered, the child being abused?

But the truth had nothing to do with facts or words or thoughts or even reason. It was something she had come to know in every cell of her body.

"For an immortal, even a lifetime of suffering is experienced as worthwhile."

"That's arrant nonsense!" he burst out, unable to contain himself any longer.

He was struggling wildly with his emotions. This was not how a Watcher should act. Then he caught sight of the clock on the wall.

"I'm sorry," he said, suddenly calmer and almost businesslike. "Would you mind if I went? Can you manage on your own? This is wrong of me but…"

"It's all right," she assured him. "Go. Please. I'd prefer if you did." Her smile was genuine. "You're raining on my parade."

He wasn't able to smile back; in fact, he ran away. She was relieved that he was gone. The peace she had gained from the session was precious. She knew instinctively that it would inevitably leave her. All too soon the veil of forgetting would fall, an integral part of the play of existence.

The taboo against remembering who we really are.

….

An hour later, Olwen went to the dining room in search of more substantial food. She had spent the entire time on one painting and, happy with the result, left it in the conservatory to dry.

There was no gong to announce meals. Schedule and routines had gone with the wind. An all-day buffet was laid out on the sideboard, continually replenished with hot and cold foods. As always, Mrs Macleod anticipated their needs.

As soon as she stepped into the dining room, Olwen felt the current of triumph. Both Breathers and Watchers were all smiles and shining eyes. The session had been powerful for everyone. Elsie waved to her from their usual table. No sign of Dr Jack. She would talk to Elsie about him.

Moving along the buffet, she piled her tray high. She was heading for her seat when a burst of loud laughter drew her attention. It was Euphémie. The young woman had just entered the dining room with Dr Jack by her side. He was leaning over her in a flirtatious manner, whispering in her ear. A few eyebrows were raised by those around them. Some of the glances were directed at Olwen.

Olwen's equanimity was shattered with a stomach-churning, all-too-familiar dismay. She continued to her table, eyes cast down. The items on her tray rattled. Her hands were shaking. She had been here too many times before. She wanted to run away and hide.

Was that a frown on Elsie's face as she greeted her? Or a look of sympathy? Olwen was unable to judge, unable to speak. She was in a fug, a fugue state. Her mind had short-circuited. Her whole system was shutting down. Too many buttons pressed or maybe just one big one. Head down, she started on her soup.

I will not cry.

Elsie maintained a companionable silence, allowing Olwen to collect herself. By the time Dr Jack joined them, she had regained some equilibrium. Her voice was calm, though edged with anger.

"So what was that all about?" she asked him. "Are you trying to punish me? For triggering off your stuff? For having my own answers? Is that how you make yourself feel better and to hell with how I feel?"

His eyes widened, as if with surprise, but she could see in their depths that he knew exactly what she was talking about. Something flared in response to her words, before his features settled into a professional mask.

"You have to be careful with this kind of work, Olwen. It brings up the shadow and old unresolved issues. It's vital that we refrain from casting projections onto others."

His tone was measured, almost superior. No doubt the voice he used when his clients got shirty. It infuriated her all the more. Elsie snorted beside her. Olwen took that as encouragement.

"Projections, *my arse*. I'm pulling you up on this, so deal. My session triggered off some pretty big stuff for you and then what I said in the conservatory upset you even more, enough to make you leave. Are you trying to tell me that it's only a coincidence that you're suddenly treating me with contempt and deliberately trying to hurt me by carrying on with Euphémie right in front of me?"

His face flushed. He drew back in his chair. The force of her attack had caught him off guard. The smooth mask slipped. There was naked fury in his eyes. With visible effort, he composed himself. An icy tone crept into his response.

"You're being hysterical. It's not unusual after a powerful session. But I don't have to listen to this. I'm not responsible for your feelings. You are."

She felt the blow in her gut. It might have defeated her, if she hadn't heard Elsie gasp beside her. The old woman looked furious. He *was* being a prick.

"Really?" Olwen retorted. "And are you refusing responsibility for your own behaviour as well?"

He was out of his chair in an instant. She blanched automatically, fearing a physical blow. But there was no question of that. Though he stood shaking with anger, his arms hung at his sides, fists unclenched.

"I can't do this right now." He turned to Elsie. "You talk to her."

And he strode out of the room.

Olwen felt as if a bomb had exploded around her. What had happened? What had she done?

"Was that my fault?" she demanded of Elsie. "Am I in the wrong?"

Elsie stared thoughtfully at the door through which Dr Jack had just barged.

"Something big happening there. 'Bout time." When she spoke to Olwen, her tone was frank and without judgement. "Did you two have sex?"

After a moment's hesitation, Olwen nodded guiltily.

"Well, that was a no-brainer," Elsie murmured to herself. And then to Olwen, "You needn't worry about Euphémie, then. He's not that much of a *putz*. But you hit the nail on the head. That's how he makes the pain go away. He doesn't use drink, drugs, money, or religion. He uses women. And ain't he the man-whore. Sugar baby for the ladies. They can't resist him and he can't resist them. This is his wound from the mother. All women must love him and he needs to know they do."

"Oh god," said Olwen wryly.

"Your pattern?"

Olwen grimaced. "I used to think it was beautiful bastards, but as I got older – though evidently not any wiser – I began to realise every one of them had serious issues with their mother. Bloody Freud was right. Oedipal wrecks. And that made them misogynistic or promiscuous or both."

"So, what are you doing in that picture?"

The question was gently put. Olwen smiled sadly. "A perfect match. My wound comes from a violent father and a male abuser."

She reflected a moment. "But what about Jack's wife? He was obviously dedicated to her and he would have been a faithful husband if – "

Elsie's snort was loud and clear. "He picked her, didn't he, knowing what she was like? She didn't do sex. For this he loved her. And that's the basis of a healthy relationship? But she was the exact opposite of his mother. So now he could lay all the blame for the failure of their marriage on her, while telling himself he was perfectly capable of loving a woman if only she let him. Do you know what Mr Smoothie had the brown balls to tell me about the women who fall for him? *They're adults. It's their choice. I make it clear from the start that it's not serious and we're just having fun.* Did you ever hear such self-serving horse shit in all your life?"

Olwen was confused by both her words and her tone. "I thought you and he...?"

"Are best buds? You bet. But to truly love someone you've got to acknowledge their shadow and accept them regardless. That's Jack's. He takes no responsibility for his beauty and his charm. He has left a trail of broken hearts and broken women behind him. And though he denies it with every intellectual tool at his command, he's taking revenge on women for what his mother did to him. *Physician, heal thyself* never applied more. You watch yourself, honey-bun."

"I've already withdrawn to some degree." Olwen sighed ruefully. Not for the first time in her life, she wistfully recalled her childhood intention to be a nun. "But that doesn't mean I'm inured by any means. And still, I'm worried about him." She glanced over at the door. "He looks like he's coming apart at the seams."

"He is," Elsie agreed. "And good thing, too. He's been holding that show together for far too long. You're dynamite, *bubbeleh.* You've got two men moving who've been stuck for too long. But don't you worry about our Jack. I'll take care of him. He's my partner, too, remember. It's the other one we need to talk about right now.

Will you come for a walk with me? I have to tell you things that'll be hard to say and even harder to hear. We need to be outdoors, in the open air."

Olwen felt her stomach flip. Her row with Dr Jack had allowed her to forget what lay ahead: her duty as Rose's Watcher. She glanced at the clock on the wall. The second session was in less than an hour. She had intended to have a rest in her room. After the intensity of her own session, she needed to muster her strength. But it seemed she wasn't going to get the chance. Didn't C.S. Lewis say in one of his Narnian tales that if you accomplish a great task your usual reward was to be set another?

"Okay, but let me get my sweater," she said to Elsie. "I'll meet you in the porch."

CHAPTER THIRTY-EIGHT

HEART OF DARKNESS

They strolled along the edge of the cliff overlooking the loch. The water shone a silvery blue in the sunlight. A sea breeze wafted over the waves. Olwen buttoned up her sweater. Elsie wore a dark red tracksuit zipped to the neck. She linked her arm in Olwen's.

"There are things I must tell you about Rose before his session. He has given me permission to speak of them."

Olwen felt a chill of foreboding.

"Goldfarb is my married name," Elsie began. "I was born Ilse Schoenberg in Copenhagen in 1927."

Elsie paused to let Olwen draw the connection to Denmark and Rose. Olwen's imagination went further. She remembered the scene she had witnessed between the two of them. Was Elsie his mother?

"Do you know the story of the Danish Jews in the Holocaust?" Elsie asked her.

Olwen thought a moment. "Was there something about the Danish king wearing a yellow star?"

Elsie made a little noise. "Urban legend. It should be so good. But like all myths, it points to a bigger truth. Denmark was invaded by Germany in 1940. A day I will never forget. The end of my life as I knew it. It was April. A soft spring day. I was in school. I had just turned thirteen, an only child in an affluent family. My father was a music teacher at the university and my mother, a well-known cellist in the national orchestra. We had a fine house, a big garden, and servants. My parents had their problems, chiefly arguments over my mother's absences and her dedication to her career. The servants raised me, really, and my father. I was his princess. It wasn't perfect but it was a good life. I was happy."

Elsie smiled a moment in memory.

"The invasion seemed unreal. We knew there was a war going on but we had seen little of it, except for the occasional refugees. But that day the skies were black with bombers, and the streets were crowded with truckloads of soldiers and uniformed Germans on motorcycles. The noise was shocking, all the more so because we were silent. Dazed and silent. There was resistance, but not very much. There was no point. Our country was too small, the invading forces too big. And it's no lie there was a brotherly relationship between the Danes and the Germans. So the king and the government, the police and the army – all agreed to do nothing.

"There were about eight thousand Jews living in Denmark at the time. Most of us were Danish, but there were also some refugees from Germany and Eastern European countries. For the first three years of the occupation, our lives didn't change. Though the Nazi authorities kept pressuring them, the Danish government refused to make Jews register names or property and refused to make us wear yellow stars or armbands. Even the synagogue stayed open. A few times a gang of riff-raff along with German soldiers tried to burn it down, but the Danish police stopped them. Denmark was providing a lot of food and war products to Germany, so the Nazis didn't want to upset things too much.

"The atmosphere changed in 1943 when it was beginning to look like Germany might lose the war. Danish resistance grew stronger. There were strikes and acts of sabotage. The Nazis clamped down and tried to set up military courts. The king and the government resigned. Overnight, everything changed. The king and the crown prince were put in prison. Word came that the Jews would be arrested and deported.

"This is the part of the story many people don't know about. It should be shouted from the rooftops! The Danish resistance began to hide Jews, intending to get us out of Denmark. Once the rescue got under way, the police and authorities and the Christian churches joined in. Next thing there was help from people all over the country. The plan was to get us across the channel to neutral Sweden. The fishermen offered their boats, but they could only take a dozen or so at a time. We had to hide until we could get on a boat. Though it was only a half-hour voyage across the Sound and even less in some places, the seas could be rough. Also the Germans were patrolling the waters. Some boats were captured. Some were lost with all lives on board."

Elsie paused a moment.

"My parents were on such a boat, though I didn't know this till after the war."

She paused again.

"I had got separated from them in all the moving about. Sometimes we would wait in a place for hours and then suddenly there would be a big rush into cars and trucks. At first I wasn't afraid. I was with neighbours. They assured me they would look after me until I was reunited with my family in Helsinborg. There were about thirty of us, hiding in a church in a little village outside Copenhagen. We had no possessions, only food parcels, so we wouldn't overload the boats. The villagers brought mattresses and blankets for us to sleep on. There were children crying and I was nervous about the boat ride and missing my parents. But I knew everything would be all right the next day.

"Late in the night, we woke to the sounds of breaking wood and hammers smashing through doors and voices yelling in German.

Then began the nightmare of my young life. To go so quickly from hope and the dream of safety to such terror and the likelihood of death, you can't imagine. We were pushed into trucks, mothers with infants, pregnant women, elderly people. We were screamed at, kicked, beaten. All crowded together, we were driven through the dark of the night. No one to help us. Afraid to cry out loud. At the train station, there were more trucks, more people, more shouting and hitting. We were pushed like cattle onto railway cars, hundreds to a car, no food or water.

"Most of us had some food hidden in our clothes, so the first part of the journey wasn't the worst. Then the food and water ran out. Sometimes you could see farmland through the slats of the rail cars, other times towns or cities. We had no idea where we were going. People whispered about slave camps and worse; but these things are not possible to believe until you experience them. No ordinary decent person could think of such a thing as real. It was like ghost stories to scare children.

"Days later, we arrived in Terezin in Czechoslovakia, what the Germans called Theresienstadt. It was originally a little village with a prison on the outskirts, but the Nazis built a high wall around all of it and turned it into a ghetto camp. We were crowded into cell blocks with thousands and thousands of other Jews from all over Europe. It was a special camp, not a killing centre. A propaganda tool. The place the International Red Cross was allowed to inspect. They made a movie about it. 'Hitler builds a city for the Jews, to keep them safe.' We didn't wear uniforms and they didn't shave our heads. They sent Jewish war veterans there, and famous artists and intellectuals. Many artists – musicians, poets, writers, painters.

"There were no gas chambers, but there were crematoriums because thousands died there of starvation and disease. It was also a transit stop. Countless numbers passed through Terezin on their way to Auschwitz and other death camps."

The old woman grew quiet. Olwen was glad they were outside. She was having trouble breathing and her stomach hurt.

Elsie made an impatient noise. "I want to tell you Rose's story, not mine!" She pursed her lips as she sifted through her memories. "One of my neighbours, one of the women in the group that I was captured with, was Mrs Rosenthal. She was pregnant and her time had come. Her husband had put her in the car with my group to make sure she was safe. All our men did this. They gave first place to the women, children, and old people and then went last in whatever was left, even horse-drawn carts. Sometimes they walked. This is just the irony of life. She would have lived if he had let her wait with him." Elsie shrugged. "But what use is thinking this way.

"Mrs Rosenthal gave birth in Terezin and died shortly after. There were doctors and nurses among us but no medicine. Conditions were hopelessly insanitary. They could do nothing for her, but the baby was healthy. There were nursing mothers who offered to share their milk. This was when we first arrived, before the scarcity of food took its toll. The Council of Elders, Jews appointed to run the camp, assigned extra rations to nursing mothers; but the food was not sufficient to keep an adult healthy, let alone an adult feeding a baby. One woman's milk dried up. The others eventually refused to feed the orphan child, in case their own babies starved. Can you blame them? All the time in the camps, terrible decisions had to be made. Decisions no human being should ever have to make.

"I don't really know how or why I took charge of him, a sixteen-year-old girl with no experience of children, not even younger cousins. Maybe because I liked Mrs Rosenthal. She was part of my past and everything good I had lost. I had no family there, no relatives, only a few neighbours whom I didn't know very well. I clung on to him as if he were my little brother. Years later I came to see that he gave me a reason to live. As long as I could keep him alive,

I would survive myself. He must have known he was in danger and that his right to life was precarious. He was very quiet and placid. It was easy for me to mind him. If he had been a difficult baby, I might not have done it. I might not have kept him. Who knows. It was hard enough to do. I started to pester the mothers and begged them for milk. Sometimes they would agree, just to get rid of me. I tried mixing my ration of milk with water, but he was too young to digest it. He threw it up. Someone told me if I could get yoghurt, it would be better for him."

Elsie stared straight ahead as she walked.

"The guards had yoghurt. The prisoners didn't. I was young and pretty. Just think, the dreams a young girl has of romance and first love. Imagine that traded for sex with a stranger to get food."

Olwen's throat was so tight she couldn't swallow. Her eyes filled with tears she refused to shed. This horror was Elsie's and the old woman wasn't crying.

"He was a Czech guard, not a Nazi. He brought the yoghurt from his mother's farm. It was good. The baby thrived. He was not a bad man, much older than me, but not a brute. He brought food for me as well and clothes for the baby. And he protected me from the others...for a time."

Again a long pause, Elsie looked out over the sea, the Scottish sea, as if to remind herself that she was far from Terezin.

"The Nazis were diabolically clever. They knew human nature, knew that goodness always rises like wildflowers through concrete. They kept changing the guards to prevent them from getting too close to the prisoners. It wasn't love I felt for that man, nothing like it, but I missed him after he went away. When he was there, I was safe. After him, there were other guards...and Nazis...I would never feel safe again."

They were walking more slowly now, and Elsie leaned heavily on Olwen's arm.

"I worked in the laundry. It was how we survived the winter, the baby and me. It was the only place that was warm. I was allowed to keep him with me most of the time. At night it was good to have him beside me in the bed. My little dolly that kept me warm, that kept away the worst of the loneliness and despair. I think, too, he was my lost innocence that I held so close to me, like a hidden treasure.

"There was one time I woke up in the middle of the night. The dormitory was dark and silent. The quiet was unusual. There were always sounds of coughing and moaning and muffled weeping. The beds were wooden bunks with scratchy blankets, one apiece. I don't know why I woke up, maybe I was cold, but I was suddenly aware that I was being watched. I looked down to where the baby was close to my chest and I saw he was awake and staring up at me. His big pale blue eyes gazed at me without blinking. I gazed back at him and something very strange happened.

"It was like his eyes were speaking to me. *Isn't this incredible?* they were saying. *Here I am a baby and you, a young girl, and we are together in this madhouse. Isn't this absurd? The whole thing? Like a crazy joke?* I can't put exactly in words the feeling and the meaning, but neither of us was who we were – a baby and a teenage girl – we were something much bigger and more powerful playing out a bizarre tale and the whole thing was just insane and ridiculous!

"I don't know who started to laugh first, the baby or me, but it went on for quite a while. We woke people up, not because we were loud, but because laughter was never heard in that place. No one told us to be quiet. I think they all lay there listening, maybe smiling to themselves.

"We were in Terezin for two years. It seemed forever, a lifetime. We had no idea if it would ever end and no hope of it ending, except in death. Yet here is the strangest of things. Though we were crowded beyond belief, sometimes tens of thousands in buildings suited for only a few thousand and so little food and so many sick, still there were many marvels that showed the wonder of humanity and our ability to survive under any circumstances. We had a rich cultural life! Can you believe this? Concerts, theatrical performances, artworks, poetry readings. At one time there were two full orchestras in the camp, as well as numerous chamber groups and even jazz ensembles. Thousands of artists were sent there, and philosophers and scientists and doctors. There was a library of Hebrew texts. Lectures were given regularly on art, medicine, and economics.

"Because there were so many children, the Council of Elders decided to house them separately and to assign people to look after them. They had some of the finest teachers in all of Europe! I began to leave little Ulf with them for a few hours a day. Did I tell you that was his name? His mother named him before she died; it was her husband's name. He was very happy with the other children, especially when he began to walk and run. There was laughter in that block and no other. Not loud, as even the smallest child knew it was important not to draw the attention of the guards or worse, the Nazis. All those children..."

Her voice broke and she stumbled. Olwen reached out to catch her. When Elsie spoke again, her voice was older and wearier.

"They were sent away, too. I saw the figures once. Fifteen thousand children. That's how many passed through Theresienstadt. Most died in the death camps. We lived under that dark shadow. Behind the hardship and the cultural life were the deportations. We clung to the belief that people were being sent to labour camps and to the mines to work, but deep inside we knew. Why else did we hope and pray not to be chosen? We knew our fellow prisoners were being sent to their deaths. And still, we clung to the illusion, all of us did, that if we worked hard enough and obeyed our German masters they might let us live.

"I'm not sure when we began to realise that the Danish Jews were never sent away. From early on, parcels of food and packages of clothing arrived from the Danish Red Cross and the Danish authorities. Later we discovered both had made constant enquiries about us and persistent requests that we not be deported to the killing centres. There can be no doubt that this is the only reason no Dane was sent to a death camp. Fifty-one of us died in Terezin – from malnutrition and sickness – compared to the millions of other nations' Jews who died in the Holocaust. The majority of Danish Jews survived because our people and our country did not abandon us."

Elsie grew quiet. The two had walked some distance from the house. With unspoken agreement, they turned and retraced their steps. Olwen was perplexed. She had understood that something terrible lay in Rose's past. As soon as Elsie began to tell her story, it seemed obvious that it involved the Holocaust. But while Elsie's experience was horrific, the same did not appear to be true for Rose.

As if she could read Olwen's thoughts, Elsie shook her head. The bitterness in her voice was shocking to hear.

"To think the best part of that child's life was a Nazi camp!"

"What?"

Olwen felt a sliver of ice pierce her heart. There was a darker tale to be told?

Elsie continued. "In April 1945, the Nazis allowed the Swedish Red Cross to free the surviving Danish Jews. We were taken from Terezin in trucks and buses bound for Denmark, traumatised and half-starved, but alive. I was eighteen, and I had a little two-year-old on my lap.

"It was only in the strange and unreal days of freedom that I discovered my parents were dead. I had long feared it, but how much worse it was to have it confirmed. Instead of being overjoyed to return to my home, I wandered through rooms forever empty of their presence and their music. In some ways it was harder because the house looked as we had left it. Our truly Christian neighbours – like so many all over Denmark – had cared for our property. Even Aniki, our cat, was still there! But I was an orphan. I had some relatives, the ones who had managed to escape to Sweden. All of them offered to take me in. But I wanted a new life, far away from the Europe that had aided the Nazis to slaughter Jews, or stood by and done nothing. I was sick of the old world and wanted a new one.

"It was a simple choice back then – America or Palestine. I knew very little about either country, but I had some distant relatives in New York so that decided it. One of them agreed to meet me and put me up until I got on my feet. My family in Denmark collected funds for me and my uncle promised to sell my parents' house and send me on the money. And so my new life began. It was in New York that I met my beloved Chaim. Against the loneliness, the despair, and the shadow of death, against the Nazis who had blighted my life, I was happy and eager to marry and have a family."

Elsie came to an abrupt halt. Her face was white and she was shivering.

"You're cold!" Olwen said, concerned. She pulled off her sweater and wrapped it around Elsie's shoulders. "Come, we'll hurry back. We can finish this inside where it's warm."

"No!" Elsie cried, and it was almost a wail. "It's not the cold. It's the thing I must tell you! The thing I don't want to say out loud. We can't be trapped indoors! We must be outside where there is air to breathe and an open sky."

Elsie's body shook violently. Olwen was trembling too. Something unspeakable was coming. She put her arm around the old woman, guiding her along, like a nurse with an invalid. Below them the waves crashed on the rocks.

"What happened to the child?" Olwen asked gently. "Did someone take him when you returned to Denmark?"

Elsie nodded mutely. She gulped at the air.

"I wanted to say he was mine, but I couldn't. The others knew his family name and who he belonged to. They took him away from me. Oh how he cried as they carried him away and I cried too, like a mother robbed of her child. He was collected by relatives. Distant relatives who lived in Sweden." She looked stricken.

"To this day, we can't be certain who they were. Post-war records and administration were fast and loose. They may have forged the papers. They had that kind of power. No other family came forward. Mr Rosenthal had died during the war in the most tragic of ways. He had made it safely to Sweden but when he found his wife wasn't there, he set off to find her. The madness and loyalty of love! He was never seen again. He must have been killed somewhere on that journey through the hell that was Europe."

Elsie straightened her back. Her voice was stiff and matter-of-fact. What had to be said had to be said.

"Like the same evil that thrived in the Nazis, there is an evil that rises in times of calamity. Where there are natural disasters and wars, where law and order break down, women and children are not safe. Vultures descend to prey on the weak. The couple who claimed little Ulf were deviants. Sick and depraved. They belonged to a circle of paedophiles and perverts – wealthy businessmen, judges, politicians and the like. Powerful citizens of many nations.

"From infancy he was used and abused – drugs, torture, rape, mutilation – and photographs of his abuse were shared within the circle. He grew up in a warped environment, in a fortified mansion in the countryside. There were occasional moments of happiness, as life will inevitably provide, usually involving the workers around him. The staff were constantly changed, mostly illegal immigrants. This ensured that if anything was discovered, it would not be reported. When he was ten, there was a boy of his own age whose mother was a cleaner in the house. He and the boy played soccer in the tennis court. They let him enjoy that for a time...then they destroyed his leg with instruments of torture.

"He tried to escape when he was twelve. He did not get beyond the grounds. That is when he got the scar on his face. He tried again when he was fourteen. This time he managed a night of freedom out in the countryside, but again he was caught. I will ask you to consider what is the worst thing they could have done to a fourteen-year-old boy, for I cannot say it."

Olwen was shaking her head and gulping for air, as Elsie had done. Her whole body was clenched like a fist. Her muscles screamed at her to flee. Why was this harder to hear than Elsie's story? Why was it harder to believe?

"I...I can't..." she said.

"You must!" Elsie gripped her by the arm. "You must hear it and accept it! For his sake. You must have the courage to bear witness. I know what you're feeling. Disbelief and denial. It's only natural, only human. It's one of the reasons I left Denmark after the war. I tried to tell my family what had happened to me and I saw no one could hear it. Even though reports were coming out and the survivors were speaking up all over Europe, no one could believe it. No one could absorb the truth of such depravity. Not for a long, long time could people hear it. When I went to America it was the same. Not even the Jews there could listen. We soon learned, we refugees of the camps, to talk only among ourselves." She made a sad little noise. "That is how I met my Chaim. That is how he came to love me. I could hear the terrible story of Auschwitz. His story."

Olwen drew herself up. She had to get a grip on herself. Elsie was right. This horror had not been inflicted on *her*. She was only being asked to acknowledge it.

"Please continue," she said.

"Good. You have heard the worst. You might think that this would have defeated the boy, but it did not. He believes now – and I agree – that despite the depths of darkness and suffering, the buried memory of his earliest years kept his spirit alive. He made a promise to himself: that he would keep on trying to escape as long as he lived, no matter what they did to him.

"Though they had warped his body and mind, he had a keen intelligence. He convinced them he was resigned to his fate at last. Over time their guard relaxed. Then one day it came, the opportunity he was waiting for. A simple thing. A delivery truck with a door left unlocked. He hid inside and was gone before they knew it.

"He wandered through the cities of Europe, living on the streets, prostituting himself to men. He soon learned to find clients who would care for him. He discovered the astonishing fact that he was beautiful, and that his beauty had a monetary value. But he was afraid to stay too long in one place. He had to be careful not to fall into the hands of any authority. He knew the couple and their circle had powerful connections. He knew they were looking for him and would murder him if they had to, to protect themselves. He learned to live in the shadows, to be invisible.

"By the time he was twenty-five, he had a new name and identity. He had also got an education and a degree in film-making. Around that time, a wealthy client died who had loved him. The man left him a large sum of money. Perhaps you will not be surprised to hear that he became the most notorious producer of pornography in Scandinavia. The early 1970s saw a growing climate of tolerance and sexual openness; but while others were exploring erotica, Rose – as he now called himself – was exploring sado-masochism and perversion.

"By his early thirties, he was rich and powerful, yet still clandestine. He located copies of some of the films made of his own rape and torture. He hired people to search for the couple. What kind of people, you can imagine. He intended to have them murdered. But there was no trace of them. The house where he was imprisoned had been sold over a decade before. The couple may well have been killed by the people they served. He never found them, but he didn't give up searching until his life changed.

"Towards the end of his career as a pornographer, Rose teamed up with the wife of another film-maker, another Dane, Soren Christiansen. Christiansen's wife, Madeleine, had starred in her husband's films but she was driven by darker urges. She and Rose started their own company, making short films that were increasingly more brutal, the violence always directed at her. Madeleine's desire for pain fascinated Rose. I suppose you could say he fell in love with her, but 'love' is hardly the right word. They mirrored each other. Her background was one of excessive abuse also."

Olwen felt dizzy and nauseous. It seemed an abomination to hear such things from the mouth of an elderly woman she had come to love and respect; yet this same old woman had been the victim of abominations herself.

Elsie stopped a moment, as if to catch her breath. Her lips pressed together in a thin line.

"You know, whatever the arguments about free speech or art or sexual tolerance, Rose once told me this: he never met a single person in that business – the business of producing pornography – including the men who made their riches from it, who wasn't damaged. Pornography is a soul sickness, a perversion of something that is natural and beautiful."

She continued with her story. "The last film they made together involved a form of Chinese torture called 'a thousand cuts'. It was agreed that Madeleine would die on camera. He began cutting her and filming it. There was no one else there. But something happened. As Madeleine approached her death, she went into a kind of trance. An altered state. Her face shone with a strange light. She started to beg him to save himself. She told him he was a great soul with a great destiny. And she looked at him with such unconditional love, that it shattered the concrete casing in which he lived.

"He was utterly undone. For in that moment, he saw another face, that of a dark-haired girl gazing at him with love."

Again Elsie stopped. There were tears in her eyes and she smiled.

"That was when he remembered me. His mind flooded with memories of the first two years of his life, and the young woman who had cared for him and loved him as if he were her own. He remembered the songs I used to sing him, the Yiddish lullabies, and the games we used to play and all the times I held him and kept him close. But the pain those memories brought – the experience of goodness and love and the agony of their loss – was worse than the pain he had suffered in his childhood. It drove him mad.

"He brought Madeleine to the nearest hospital and left her there. Then he returned to his studio. He set fire to it, intending to die in the flames. He was broken wide open, do you see? And he couldn't bear the weight of his feelings. But it was not his fate to die. Rescued from the fire by a heroic passer-by, he spent more than a year in a burns unit. When he was released, he went into a monastery in Germany where a famous mystic lives who became his first teacher and mentor. When he left the monastery, he bought a motorcycle and set off around the world."

Elsie glanced at her gold watch.

"Oh dear, there's so much more I would have liked to tell you! The countries he visited, the many teachers he met, the secret initiations, the abilities he unlocked, the *siddhis* or powers he achieved...and the early days of the Work when the first circles camped out in the ruins of Dunesfort House."

Again she looked at her watch. She let out a cry of frustration.

"Too late! Too late! No time to tell the best tale of all, how he and I finally found each other. For though I had my own family, I never forgot the first child I loved. As soon as my life allowed it, I began to search for him, long before he began to search for me. That story will have to wait for another day; but truly the moment when we were reunited – and this I could never tell my husband or any of my children – that moment was the sweetest of my life."

They had reached the house. As they entered the front hall, they heard the gong ringing out for the next session.

"Do not ask for whom the bell tolls," Olwen murmured.

Elsie raised an eyebrow.

"I know, I know, I'm a drama queen."

The old woman smiled and shook her head. "You're an Irish warrior-queen." Then she was serious again. "You had to know these things to be his Watcher. So that you can hold the space where he will release his pain. But remember, you are not alone. There are a few of us who know his story and those who don't, have intimations of it; for there is no one here who hasn't suffered deeply." She heard her own words and smiled wryly. "There's no one *here* – on this planet – who hasn't suffered, eh?"

Olwen bit her lip. "What about Jack?"

"Don't you worry about him. Jack must face what he must face. The walls are down. He can no longer hide behind his profession. This is the big crunch. For all of us. Trust the process. Let it play itself out. Trust the journey."

"Everything that happens serves the Good?"

"You got it."

CHAPTER THIRTY-NINE

THE HEALING OF MEN

The Trance Room was almost full. Most of the Breathers were already lying on their mats, eager to begin. The facilitators had also arrived and were beginning their rounds. There was no sign of Rose.

"Might he change his mind?" Olwen whispered to Elsie.

"All bets are off. Anything's possible."

The old woman scanned the room with a pensive look. Her features hardened as Dr Jack came striding towards them. He held himself stiffly in an attempt at control; but it was obvious he was rattled and that his debonair façade was cracking under the strain of internal pressure.

Avoiding Olwen's eyes, he spoke directly to Elsie. "Christy tells me I'm not facilitating?" His voice quivered with anger. "And Harry has replaced me?"

"That's right," said Elsie. "It's my decision. I'm in charge. You need to breathe. And don't go bothering Rose about it. He's got enough problems of his own, he doesn't need yours as well. Do as you're told and don't make a fuss. It's not a perfect match, but it'll do. You and Penny Li know each other well enough."

He opened his mouth to argue.

Elsie folded her arms. "It's not open for debate, Jack. This is about you, but not only you. I'm considering what's best for the circle. Now go lie on your mat and suffer. That's what you're here for."

Again he opened his mouth.

"Go!" she ordered.

He seemed to diminish in size. Turning slowly, like someone in shock, he walked over to Penny Li who was waiting for him.

Olwen was taken aback by the exchange and more so by the steel in Elsie's voice. No longer a little old lady, here was the young woman who had survived the Holocaust and kept a baby alive against the odds, the grown woman who had supported a deeply wounded husband and with him raised a healthy family, and the same woman who had suffered the anguish of helping that husband die, bearing the burden of the secret alone so that her children and grandchildren would not suffer.

Elsie caught Olwen's look of awe and admiration.

"Hard love for a hard man," she said. Tears welled in her eyes. "My heart breaks, but I can't do his work for him. He needs this as much as Rose."

"If Rose doesn't come, I can be Jack's..." Olwen began.

She stopped, aware of the sudden change in the room. It was as if an electric current had charged the air. She knew what it meant, even as she acknowledged how closely attuned she had become to the others.

Rose had arrived.

He wore black as usual, loose trousers and a long-sleeved shirt of martial art design. He walked slowly, leaning hard on his cane as if stooped with pain. He kept his head lowered, avoiding eye contact with anyone.

Olwen saw several people move towards him. She hurried to reach him first, warning them off with a stern look.

"This way," she said quietly.

She linked his arm and guided him to an empty mat. He followed her directions meekly. She took his cane and helped him to settle down. He didn't speak, but he nodded gratefully when she showed him the signals she and Dr Jack had used. She was just finished when Elsie came over.

Kneeling down beside him, the old woman cupped Rose's face and gazed into his eyes. Olwen caught her breath. The depth of love that passed between them was humbling to behold. When Elsie left, the other facilitators came over, one by one. Most didn't speak, but merely touched him gently or clasped his hands.

When it was Christy's turn, the Irishman embraced him heartily. "My king, my king."

Some of the Watchers and even a Breather or two attempted to approach, but Elsie shooed them away.

"Too much," she said, shaking her head. "He knows. Support him in the Work."

But when Dr Jack lurched forward with a pleading look, she let him pass. He went down on one knee beside Rose, head bowed towards him. Rose bowed his head also till their foreheads touched.

"Journey well," Dr Jack said quietly. "Oh captain, my captain."

For the first time, Rose spoke.

"You too, my dearest friend, my right hand. Let us keep faith in the dark."

With a glance and a nod to Olwen, Dr Jack left.

Olwen was shaking inside. She had been distracting herself with details, making certain Rose was comfortable, arranging the cups, water bottles, cushions, and tissues. Now she felt sick and wanted to run. As far away as possible.

Harry was the last facilitator to arrive. After he had wished Rose well, he drew Olwen aside.

"You're the one securing this space for him. It will be painful, you know that, but keep in mind we're also here, securing the space for *you*. Neither he nor you are alone. We've got your back." Harry was about to leave, when he paused. "I heard you were an officer in the Canadian military? Is that true?" he asked.

"When I was young," she said, with a little smile. "Naval reserve."

He came to attention and saluted her.

"Fair winds and following seas, ma'am."

Her smile widened as she saluted him back. "Lock and load, Harry."

She returned to Rose with a straighter back, deeply grateful to the former soldier. He had reminded her of her pride in her training so long ago and the ideals of honour and courage that she had been taught.

I can do this. I've slain a demon. I'm the fighting Irish.

Elsie was calling for Breathers and Watchers to conclude their agreements. Olwen sat on a cushion near Rose's head. He opened his eyes and turned to look at her.

She spoke her mind. "You took a chance choosing me. I could've refused, like at the Firewalk."

A hint of a smile touched his lips. "I believe in you," he whispered. Then he frowned. "If you find you cannot do it...if you must leave... I'll understand."

"I'm not going anywhere," she said, with more confidence than she felt. "Bring it on."

Harry called the room to attention as Elsie cleared her throat to read a poem.

"This is the epigraph to the 1999 edition of *Yosl Rakover Talks to God*. It's said to be an inscription found on a cellar wall in Cologne by Allied troops written by Jews who had hidden there during the war:

I believe in the sun,
Even when it doesn't shine,
I believe in love,
Even when I don't feel it,
I believe in God,
Even when He is silent.

As the music seeped through the room, Rose began to breathe deeply. Arms at his side, features frozen, he lay utterly still, except for the rise and fall of his chest, inhaling and exhaling with slow, precise effort. Like Dr Jack and Olwen, he didn't cover his eyes but simply kept them closed. Time passed. The other Breathers began to erupt with emotion, but he continued to lie without moving. He was deathly white, like a corpse. He seemed to have stopped breathing. Was he holding back? Afraid? Perhaps he couldn't do it? Would his session fail?

When the change came at last, it was sudden and shocking. His body began to twitch. His face contorted with pain. He let out a low moan. Both of his hands went rigid. Each finger jerked violently and twisted into a crippled curl. With growing horror, Olwen realised they were being broken – one by one. *At what age?* She didn't want to know. She grabbed a towel and pressed it to her mouth to stop herself from making any noises. This was only the beginning.

His head began to jerk from side to side. His mouth opened in a rictus of agony. A silent scream. The scar on his cheek reddened, as if inflamed. She knew what it meant. He was back there, being cut. Without an anaesthetic. *At what age?* Did Elsie tell her? But she couldn't think straight. Her body was mirroring his spasms.

A child's voice broke from his throat.

Please. Please don't.

Olwen bit down on the towel, smothering her sobs. She felt her mind shutting down. Disbelieving. Rejecting. Denying. The childish pleas continued.

Please. Please stop.

She needed to get away. No, she needed help. Panicked, she looked around the room. It was like one of Goya's paintings of hell. The music had reached a raucous cycle guaranteed to push everyone over the edge. All the facilitators were busy. Several Watchers glanced over at her, anguished. They couldn't help her either. Their

Breathers were in distress. All the Breathers were in distress. Rose's pain was charging the circle, driving everyone to the heart of their deepest hurt. She didn't know what to do. She couldn't place his needs above that of the others. And he hadn't given her any signals. He had yet to ask for help.

I believe in you.

He must've known this would happen. If ever she needed faith in something greater, some reality beyond damaged humanity, this was it. All those strange experiences she had had throughout her life. Those wild fairy flashes. Those scented angelic moments. Those wells of sudden peace in which a still, small voice whispered: *All shall be well and all shall be well and all manner of thing shall be well.*

She steadied herself.

There was worse to come.

His lame leg trembled. Now it began to twist around, slowly, impossibly. They had used some kind of instrument. His entire body was juddering as he cried and begged.

Her mind threatened to break.

She steadied herself.

There was worse to come.

His legs jerked open, as if pulled apart. His pelvis began to vibrate, every cell objecting to the violation. The cries were that of an older boy, but they soon reached such a pitch they were a child's again.

Then a whining sound that was almost inhuman.

Olwen put her hands to her ears to block the sound. Then she sat on her hands so she wouldn't block it. She was his witness. His Watcher.

The whine stopped abruptly. The silence was all the more shocking as his body continued to spasm. Olwen knew what was happening. The boy was gone. He had left his body behind. Instinctively she looked up at the ceiling, half expecting to see him there.

And now she remembered something Rose had said at the beginning of the week: that the past was malleable, that it could be changed. He had argued that the Work traversed time, that it allowed them to return to their past and support themselves through their trauma. As a result, post factum, they would recall a buried memory of a benign presence that had aided them throughout.

And now she understood what was happening. Rose was not simply reliving the trauma he had endured in the past. He was actually back there, aiding the child and the adolescent and the teenager; supporting himself through it. Along with the core memory of Elsie's love, here was another reason he had survived. Another reason he hadn't tried to kill himself. He had known, throughout his youth, with absolute certainty, that he would escape one day. He had told himself so.

And now she realised, also, the significance of the session and why the others had been so excited about it. This was the first time Rose was able to heal his own story. This was the first time he was able to use the Work for himself.

The music began to change again. Concertos by Debussy and Brahms to bring an ocean of peace. The room grew quieter, though resonant with weeping as Watchers held their Breathers. Here and there new cries of pain erupted, as the facilitators began the bodywork.

A faint colour had entered Rose's cheeks. His breathing grew normal. When his eyes opened, he gazed at her without speaking. There was a stillness about him that was wondrous.

"Thank you," he said softly. "I am finished. I will leave now."

She hesitated. Awe for what he had done inclined her to defer to his authority.

"One of the facilitators must clear you first."

"I'm fine," he insisted, sitting up. "Can you not see that?"

He did look well. She hesitated again, remembering her own clarity earlier.

"No," she said, though she was uncertain. "You...you must wait until a facilitator says you can go."

She looked around the room. Both Christy and Harry were with Dr Jack. They were holding him down as he roared in rage and despair. But the cries were not that of a warrior. They belonged to a young boy. Another truth to accept, so obvious in hindsight. He, too, had been abused. Her heart ached for him; but he was not her charge. She had to concentrate on Rose. With relief she saw that Elsie was just leaving a Breather. Olwen stood up to wave her over.

Elsie responded quickly, though she looked exhausted. It had been a hard session for an old woman who refused to spare herself.

Olwen helped Elsie to get down on her knees beside Rose. Gnarled fingers cupped his face as she studied his features.

"I'm good," he told her, almost matter-of-fact. "I'm finished."

"Not just yet, my little *boychik*."

Her tone was the opposite of the sternness she had used with Dr Jack. Infinitely soft, infinitely gentle, she spoke as a mother would speak to a small child.

"Some bodywork, first, *min skat*. Just a little, nothing harsh, I promise."

She took his right hand in hers and kissed it. Soft little kisses. Then she began to stroke it with gentle touches, first the palm, then the back, then each broken finger. As her hands moved slowly up his arm, Olwen's eyes filled with tears. It was as if Elsie were bathing him, a nurse with her patient. No, a mother with her baby. She moved carefully to the other hand. Then the other arm.

Rose's eyes were clenched shut. A vein worked in his neck. It was as if he were being tortured again. A single tear trickled down his cheek. Now Elsie began to rub his back, gently, lightly, barely touching him, as if he were too fragile to touch, too frangible. And all the time she murmured terms of endearment in Yiddish and Danish. Tremors shook his body. His limbs moved fitfully.

The room had grown strangely quiet. There were no screams or shouts. Dr Jack had stopped fighting and was sobbing like a broken child, held between Harry and Penny Li. Most of the Breathers were finished, but no one had left. Along with their Watchers, they sat cross-legged, eyes closed, in meditative position. Supporting Rose.

Elsie had moved to stroke his feet, still slowly, still gently. She signalled to Olwen to go behind him. His eyes were shut tight, his face drenched with tears. Olwen sat at his back and put her arms around him. His body shook against hers. He began to sob, great heaving sobs that she feared might break him.

When he cried out loud like a wounded animal, she cried with him.

And when his cries turned to howls, she howled too, rocking him back and forth.

Elsie stood up slowly and gazed down at them. Now it was Olwen who held Rose as a mother holds her child, even as she once held her own daughter after a nightmare, soothing and shushing. *It's all right, my darling. It's all right, my baby. They're gone. It's over. You're all right now. They're all gone. It's all right, sweetheart. You're all right, my baby.* She was the Sorrowful Mother and he, the Wounded Son, and she held him and rocked him till he fell quiet against her breasts.

Looking up at last, she met Elsie's smile. The old woman nodded and left them alone.

The others began to leave the room. Rose was sleeping peacefully in her arms. Various Breathers and Watchers bowed on their way past. She continued to hold him for a long time.

In the conservatory, humming to himself as he worked, Rose painted a child-like picture of boys playing soccer. One had just scored a goal and was punching the air with his fist. Though he hadn't requested food, she brought him a hot chocolate with a marshmallow on top. He was delighted. She sat back in her chair and smiled as she watched him. They didn't speak. Nothing needed to be said.

When he was finished, he invited her to look closer. She stood up and leaned over his shoulder. He had transformed the soccer game. It was taking place in a night sky sprayed with stars. The players were painted in silver and gold, and the pitch was awash with the shimmering colours of the Northern Lights: the Cosmic Game.

"Like the ending of your last book," he said, with sudden mischief, and he started to laugh.

A young, carefree laugh. His face was beautiful. Radiant.

CHAPTER FORTY

INTERLUDE

Olwen rested before supper, then took her time to shower and get ready. The word had gone round that they were to dress for a celebration. Remembering her earlier paranoia about sacrificial blood rites, she wondered with a grin if she ought to wear white. Her wardrobe offered her a few possibilities, but she settled finally on a lilac-coloured gown and silvery shawl. An amethyst necklace and earrings completed the ensemble, along with purple pumps on her feet. She brushed her hair to fall freely over her shoulders, applied make-up lightly and a spray of perfume.

"Ye fine t'ing ye," she said to her reflection.

Her thoughts went instantly to Dr Jack. Would he like how she looked? Was he all right? She had lost track of him after the Breathwork session.

The first thing she saw when she entered the dining room was the great oval table. The peculiar shapes of the original tables were finally explained. They all fitted together to make a single whole. Olwen smiled to herself. *The Round Table.*

The second thing she noted, with a pang of regret, was that Dr Jack was missing. A few people were, including Rose. She hurried to join Elsie. The old lady looked like an empress in blue and gold brocade. Her white hair was coiffed in a French roll.

"You're only gorgeous," Olwen told her. "Love the hairdo."

"Euphémie did it." Elsie patted her hair. "You can't beat the Parisians for style."

The table was set for a banquet with lace cloth, candelabras, and antique china and silverware. The cut-glass vases were filled with white lilies that exuded a sweet scent. But the meal itself was light. Olwen was glad of that. Her stomach fluttered nervously whenever she thought of the Rite. No doubt the others felt the same. Most nibbled frugally on the offerings of fresh fruit, miniature breads, cold meats and cheeses. Some sipped on glasses of red or white wine, but most reached for the carafes of sparkling water.

The talk was also light and low. There was an overall sense of courtesy and decorum. They were like knights on the eve of a great quest.

"Is Jack okay?" she asked Elsie.

"He's more than fine. He had a great session." The old woman glanced at her jewelled watch. "He's praying now, or getting ready to."

Olwen fell back in her chair as the penny finally dropped. All the times *he* had glanced at his watch or at the clock. All the times he had disappeared.

"He's Muslim."

"Yeah." Elsie shrugged, nibbling on a fig. "I'm soul-matched with a towel-head, go figure."

Olwen remained silent as she absorbed the information.

"You didn't know?" Elsie looked surprised. "He's a private person, but it's no secret. You have to admire it. Five times a day without a miss, no matter what he's doing or how he feels. And it's not easy this far north. With sunset so late, the evening prayer isn't till midnight. Then he's up at 2:00 a.m. for the one before dawn. That's some commitment."

"We shared a lot of stories," Olwen said, "but I guess there's only so much you can say in a week. We didn't go near religion."

Elsie studied her a moment. "You'll hear about it, I'm sure. Islam made a man of him."

There was to be a last gathering in the Meeting Room. The gong would let them know when, but people were already drifting in that direction.

"Coming?" Elsie asked as she rose from her seat.

"I'll follow in a bit."

Olwen reached for a slice of apple and munched on it pensively. She was hoping for Dr Jack to arrive; but there was something else as well. A reluctance to face the final act. Was she really ready for this Rite involving god-knows-what? And were these last lingering doubts to do with her role? The old threat of sacrifice?

He was waiting for her in the hall. The dark sheen of his skin glowed against the white open-necked shirt and jacket. She couldn't help but be awed by his beauty; yet it was more than that. He had always looked handsome, even when he was angry or falling apart, but he was changed now, changed utterly. The golden mask was gone, the spell of glamour, that shiny carapace of charm that had covered his pain. Now there was a rich warmth and a lightness of being.

She smiled at him.

"The beauty of the man."

He chuckled deep in his chest. Then he took her hand and pressed it to his lips.

"Oh divine Irishwoman. You've forgiven me?"

It was more a statement than a question. She didn't bother to answer, at least not in words. She leaned towards him and kissed his mouth, lingering there. He opened his lips in response and pulled her against him. Her arms moved under his jacket and over his broad back.

They were both vaguely aware of others passing by, but they made no effort to stop.

It was a while before they broke apart. The hall was empty. One of the doors of the Meeting Room had been left ajar.

"'Once more unto the breach'," quoth Dr Jack.

"'Dear friends'," she responded, "'Once more.'"

CHAPTER FORTY-ONE

THE WARP AND THE WEFT

They entered the room together. Various people smiled over at them. Elsie had kept two seats beside her in the circle. Many of the soul partners were deep in conversation with each other. Rose sat beside Christy. Some seats were still empty.

Tenzin Dawa was the last to arrive. His head was shaved, and he wore the crimson and saffron robes of a Tibetan monk. Euphémie stood up to greet him, her face wreathed in smiles. She wore a black evening dress with a red stole. He walked over to her, smiling also, and bowed with his hands joined together. She bowed back. Then they both burst out laughing and embraced.

When everyone was settled, Rose addressed them. He remained seated, looking refreshed and at ease. He was dressed in black as usual, but his shirt was embroidered with Native American designs. His hands rested on the silver handle of his cane.

"I will not, cannot, say much about my session. I am still overwhelmed. But I want to thank you...all of you...and especially Olwen."

There were teary smiles all round. As applause broke out, Olwen bowed her head in acknowledgement.

Christy spoke next, his hand placed over his chest.

"Me heart's burstin'. I've never seen the like of what was done today. If only me darlin' girl could've been here." His voice caught in his throat. He took a moment to collect himself, then gazed around at them. "I won't be goin' with ye's tonight. It can't be helped. I've no soul match in the circle and I'd only throw the balance off; but I want to wish ye's the best. For me, it's enough that I had the honour and blessing of serving today. It was a labour of love. So I'll say good luck to ye's in the bit of Irish I have. *Go dté sibh slán agus go luaithí Dia dhuibh.* May you have a safe journey and God speed."

There were more tears. Savitri, who sat on the other side of him, put her arm around his shoulders.

There was a moment's silence after Christy spoke. Then Tenzin Dawa signalled that he would speak.

"Firstly, I wish to express my appreciation to Euphémie for her friendship. It is of great value to me. I also wish to express my gratitude to all of you. As I told you when I arrived, I did not want to come here. I was very surprised that my teacher sent me. He does not normally approve of the practices that are called New Age. I have since discovered that he and the Director are good friends." Here Tenzin Dawa bowed towards Rose, who bowed back. "I myself have come to see the value of what is being done in Dunesfort House. I was pleased that I was granted the freedom to breathe or not. When it was my turn to breathe, I chose to meditate. In the presence of so many doing the Work, it was very powerful."

He paused a moment and his features were so serene, so infinitely equable, that Olwen caught her breath. Then he continued in the same measured tones.

"In Buddhism, we say that all beings are streams of energy in the universe. The goal of meditation is to develop, in the body itself, a link between the ordinary deluded mind and the universal Buddha-nature within each of us. Once achieved, this is a stepping stone to further levels of consciousness and compassion, and to the development of *Abi-buddhi*, the Supreme Wisdom or Complete Enlightenment. My experience with the first level, here in

Dunesfort House, has inspired me to return to the precious path to which I was born in this lifetime."

Tenzin Dawa paused again. A slight smile played at the edges of his mouth as he turned to Christy.

"I wish to invite you to participate in the evening's puja. My knowledge of my past lives allows me to balance more than one."

A ripple of astonishment ran through the circle.

Christy grinned with delight. "Gowan, ye good t'ing ye!" he called out to the young lama.

Peals of laughter broke out.

One by one they spoke, presenting their last epiphanies. Olwen could see how each offering wove truth and emotion together to knit the circle tighter. Penny Li thanked Harry for reminding her that she was first and foremost a gardener. Through her long talks with him, she remembered her love for growing and planting. Her activism would take a different route. After her husband's murder she swore she would never go back to Borneo; but now she intended to return, to work on tribal reclamation projects.

Harry, in turn, spoke of the unexpected thrill of facilitating the circle. Everything he saw around him – the horror and the heroism – was all so familiar. At one point he felt as if he were truly in a field hospital in wartime. In that moment he saw that war itself was part of the scheme of things, part of the great opera of life, and a deep wound inside him was healed.

When Dr Jack began, he was hesitant at first and kept his eyes lowered; but the more he spoke, the more his confidence grew and by the end he was looking around at all of them.

"'*Physician, heal thyself.*' The problem with clichés is that they are usually rooted in the truth, but they make that truth mundane and hence easily ignored. Honesty is crucial to healing. First and foremost, self-honesty. I know this, it's part of my training and my profession, and yet I have not practised it. I have not been honest these many years."

He sighed, shrugged his great shoulders.

"Better late than never, as I tell my own clients. I gave you all as much of the truth as I was prepared to give – of my childhood. It was painful enough, but I have never spoken of my adolescence, when the worst damage was done. I was in trouble as early as ten, petty crime and fighting. By the time I was twelve, I was involved in drugs, not using them but acting as a courier for a dealer. That put me in juvie a year later, for the first but not the last time. I was an angry kid, ready to act up and out. And that brought the inevitable backlash. The violence was bad enough, but the..." he paused and cleared his throat, "...the rapes were the worst. I wasn't the only victim. At that time, abuse went unchecked in juvenile detention centres, orphanages and residential homes. When the scandal broke in the 1990s, most of the perpetrators were protected by their union or by political connections. I'm still deeply angry about that. It's one of the reasons I haven't returned to Canada.

"When I reached seventeen, I was no longer a juvenile and began a series of stints in adult prison. I suffered racism from the guards, but the sexual abuse had stopped once I was big enough to defend myself. I was prepared to kill and they knew it. I was still angry and rebellious, got in a lot of fights, did a lot of solitary. Then one of the older black men took me under his wing. Marcus had got education and religion in prison. He told me about Malcolm X, Angela Davis, the Black Power Movement...and he introduced me to Islam.

"I was nineteen when I converted, a Sunni like Marcus, like Malcolm X. It was one of those life changes from which you never look back. I completed high school through prison programmes and once out, never returned. I tried my hand at a few different things before I decided to go to med school and into psychiatry. It wasn't easy. I accepted cases others were unable to handle, where the levels of abuse had been extreme..."

He paused again.

"But I couldn't treat children or adolescents. I couldn't separate from their pain. I should've noted the warning signs, should've known what they indicated. But denial is a powerful thing. Most, if not all, in the caring professions suffer from it."

Savitri and several others nodded their heads.

"I was forced to face this truth after my *two* soul partners ganged up on me. Hard love and hard lessons for a hard man."

He grew quiet as he considered something.

Olwen held her breath. Some bigger truth was coming.

"This last session showed me a lot. It was bad enough to see how my profession enabled me to hide from my own pain. Can you imagine how big a revelation it was that the Work did the same?"

Many looked surprised at this, even shocked. Only Rose nodded in agreement.

Dr Jack continued. "I see now that I used the Work like a drug, to achieve ecstatic states, to get out of my body and my mind. The compulsive desire for transcendence can be another kind of addiction, another means of escape from old pain. In that last Breathwork session, I saw in the depths of my rage and hurt that my stated wish – to unite with God – was a lie. The truth is," he paused again, "I wanted to kill Him."

A silence fell over the group. Dr Jack looked around the circle. His sudden smile had a hint of laughter.

"I have said again and again that my intention was to unite with God. For a Muslim, this is nonsense. We *surrender* to Him. That's the meaning of the word 'Muslim'. *To surrender to God*. My intention now and until I leave this life is to heal myself and help others, especially children and young people. That's what I'm here for."

There was a loud round of applause and a few whoops. Dr Jack laughed happily.

Olwen frowned. She was the last to speak. A great reluctance had come over her. She was afraid if she started talking she might never stop, yet she felt she had to say something. Everyone had given their gifts to the circle. It seemed miserly to withhold her truth.

"I can't say I've been in denial about the stuff that has happened to me. I've spent most of my life in recovery – from poverty, alcoholism, physical, and sexual abuse. I've joined 12-step programmes, read hundreds of self-help books, done therapy, counselling, meditation, yoga. I've practised several religions, read spiritual books and depth psychology. It's one of the reasons I came here. I've always been ready to explore any avenue that even hints at an answer to my questions. A dear friend once sent me a card with a woman frowning at a stone on the ground. The text said: *Did I turn that one over?*"

Everyone laughed.

"My recovery has been long and slow. Despite all my work, I have proved incapable of having happy or healthy love relationships with men. That is the great sadness of my life." She didn't look at Dr Jack as she said this, but she could feel him beside her in silent support. "I know I sounded flippant the first time I shared in the circle, when I said that maybe I'd get a book out of this. That was bravado. I was terrified of what I might have got myself into. But there was a grain of truth in the remark. I've always said there are three pillars to my life that have kept me here, on the planet, that is – AA, my daughter, and my writing.

"The last few years have been a nightmare. My daughter grew up and my role as mother shifted to part-time. That meant a big chunk of my life's purpose was gone. At the same time, I embarked on several years of revision of old work for American publication. The decision was based on financial concerns, but also a desire to improve the books that I felt had epic potential."

She stopped for a moment, shook her head.

"I don't regret it, they are superior to their originals, but at the same time I was drinking from an old stream and my Muse was dying of thirst. When I arrived here in Dunesfort House, my cup was dry."

She stopped again. Her heart began to beat faster.

"'*What I do is me.*' Gerard Manley Hopkins said that. My writing *is* my soul's work, my life's project. It has nourished my belief in a meaningful existence, in magic, in the hope that there is something more than material reality. Only that belief can make suffering and evil bearable. This past week has been one of the most glorious weeks of my life. I've been given back my belief in magic. I've been given back my soul."

She looked across the floor at Rose. They stared long and hard at each other.

"I *will* write a book about this," she promised.

Her words were met with loud cheers and clapping. She ducked her head shyly.

"Good on ye, girl!" Christy shouted.

When the noise died down, Rose addressed them. "The hour approaches when we leave for the Rite. I would like to ask Euphémie to say a few words about the lunar event which fuels the ceremony. Then I shall speak of the Callanish Stones themselves. Euphémie?"

The Parisienne beamed a beautiful smile at everyone before she began. She was almost breathless with excitement.

"The astronomer and the interstellar physicist work always with the computer image. But many of us enjoy to take the telescope from the machine and look upon the night sky with the human eye.

"In ancient time, they make their own machine to watch the sky. The great stone calendar is in many *civilisation*. It mark the movement of the sun and the moon, and many event like the equinox, solstice, lunar standstill, and eclipse.

"The Callanish site is one of these calendar. It mark the northern moonrise and the summer solstice sunrise. Most especially, it mark the 18.6-year moon cycle caused by the *précession* of the lunar orbit plane.

"At the cycle peak – we call it major standstill and it happen last in 1987 and now it happen this night – the full moon near the summer solstice reach only 3.5 degree over the horizon, from the place of Callanish. More north, there is no moon at all! But from Callanish, this moon seem to walk along the ground. *C'est très beau!*"

Euphémie finished speaking and Rose took over.

"That is the science of it," he said. "And there is good argument that the lunar and solar calendars were related to the seasons and the planting and harvesting of crops. However, there are those of us who believe that the stone calendars had sacred purposes also.

"Mrs Macleod tells me that the word 'Callanish' is derived from the Scots Gaelic *cianalas*, meaning 'sorrow' or 'longing'. She also tells me there is another name for the Stones – *Tursachan*. This word, too, refers to sorrow, and roughly in English means 'place of sadness'. For this reason, I believe that healing was at the core of the ancient rites once held at Callanish. The Stones are made of local Lewisian gneiss, crystalline throughout and three billion years old. They are truly Old Ones, ancient grandmothers and grandfathers.

"Shortly before midnight tonight, as Euphémie has said, the moon will rise just above the horizon. From a viewpoint among the Stones, the moonrise occurs over a range of hills called in English 'the Sleeping Beauty' and in Scots Gaelic *Cailleach na Mointeach*, the 'Witch of the Moors'. Depending on where you are standing, the moon sets in the pregnant belly of the Sleeping Beauty or between the northern avenue of the Stones. Then, after a time, depending again on where you are standing, there is a moment when the moon appears to rise at the very heart of the Stones in the central circle.

"This event occurs at Callanish approximately every nineteen years, in keeping with the 18.6-year wanderings of the moon. There can be no doubt that the Stones, as Euphémie said, were designed specifically to celebrate this event. The last time it occurred was 2nd December 1987."

"My birthday!" Olwen whispered to Elsie and Dr Jack.

They both raised their eyebrows.

"The next will be 11th June 2025," said Rose.

Olwen did a quick calculation.

"I'll be sixty-eight," she hissed.

Elsie snorted. "I'll be dead."

Rose continued. "There is historical support for the notion that the Callanish Stones were built for this purpose. Eratosthenes, chief librarian of the Great Library of Alexandria in the third century BC, wrote of 'a winged temple in the Hyperborean lands'. Hyperborea was a term used by the ancient Greeks for the most northerly point. The lines of stones that extend east and west from the inner circle could be seen as wings. More fascinating is the account of a first-century BC Greek historian called Diodorus. He describes a northern island where the moon appears close to the Earth, which has a temple 'where a god visits every nineteen years.'"

The more she heard, the more excited Olwen grew. In the depths of her psyche, a lunar wind was stirring.

When the moon walks on the land, the Shining Ones will return.

Rose stood up. "There is nothing more to be said, no more preparations to make. You have done the Work these past seven days. We will go now to the Stones. The ritual is simple. Each of you, in silence, will go to a standing stone and take up position beside it. There is no need to be anxious about this. Your stone will call to you. Then you need only wait. Wait till the moon walks the earth. Do not fear success or failure in this Rite. We are asked only to be present to the Mystery. *Whatever happens is good.*"

They rose together.

The time for the Rite of the Cailleach had come.

CHAPTER FORTY-TWO

EAST OF THE SUN

They filed silently through the hallway and out the back door, into the courtyard. They were a strange sight, everyone in evening dress, like a party of lords and ladies setting out on an after-dinner lark. It was twilight. The shadows of dusk softened the contours of the stone walls and greenhouse. The fountain splashed quietly. An antique bus waited in the yard. It was dark crimson in colour with gold wings painted on the sides. Ruairi sat in the driver's seat. Rose stood by the open door to usher them in. Mrs Macleod was beside him, shaking hands with all who boarded and wishing them well. Olwen and Dr Jack were the last in the queue.

"You're coming with us!" Olwen said to the housekeeper, delighted.

Morag shook her head. "There is no need. I and my family are of the Stones. It is given to us to see."

Before Olwen could ask what she meant, Mrs Macleod had reached for Dr Jack. Now Olwen understood what Morag was doing there.

She's blessing us.

Olwen turned to Rose. "There'll be a crowd at Callanish tonight. How can we hope to do this with so many around?"

"The place will be empty," Rose answered, "when we get there."

Boarding the bus, Olwen saw that all the soul partners were seated together, except for Elsie who was with Christy. At the very back, Calum sat alone. Olwen was struck by the notion that he was the tillerman, even as his brother manned the wheel. Her impression of a ship's company increased when Rose took up his position, standing behind Ruairi.

Oh captain, my captain.

Dr Jack nudged Olwen into a window seat and sat down beside her. She was grateful to be with him. While everyone else seemed happy enough, she was a bag of nerves. And with good reason. When the others were queuing to get on the bus, Dr Jack had drawn her aside for a quick word.

"I want to explain why I'll be matched with Elsie for the Rite."

"You don't have to. I understand. I'm Rose's soul partner...for this."

"He says he has spoken with you about the nature of the Work?"

"It's a kind of human alchemy, isn't it? Our suffering is spun into gold, into healing, and the healing of the individual charges the healing of the group."

"Nicely put. I like the alchemy analogy. And tonight we bring that healing to the Stones. They have their own energy which is particularly charged at full moons, equinoxes and solstices. Some believe that is why they were built. Euphémie jokes that they're ancient particle accelerators. Their energy mirrors and magnifies ours. There's the potential to go right off the scale. It can take us anywhere."

"Omigod. Do we dare?"

"Why not? It's our inheritance. We're children of the universe, as the 'Desiderata' said. At the same time, it won't be easy and it can be dangerous. With so much power unleashed, the circle has to keep its balance. The centre must hold. And that centre is Rose and his partner. Elsie is the closest match to him, but given the age of her body, it would most likely kill her. She's all for it anyway – no surprise there – but Rose forbids her. I, too, am a match for him, but we've found that the polarity of male and female works better. Over the years, various females have attempted to partner him, though he never felt safe enough in the circle to do Breathwork with them. The closest match was Euphémie.

"What I'm about to tell you is not gossip, because you need to know. It was obvious to some of us that she had fallen in love with him, but we chose not to interfere. That was our mistake. At a Rite held during the summer solstice two years ago, her feelings emerged and threw the circle off. We were all in danger for a time – to put it mildly, our brains were nearly fried – but Rose, Elsie and I managed to steer the circle back. No one blamed Euphémie. Who would hold love to blame? And it is her wound, like so many of us, to love the unattainable. I was pleased that Rose invited her back for this session. It's a sign of his great respect for her; but of course he feels no love for her. He's incapable of that kind of love in this lifetime. He's too damaged. He has accepted that truth."

Olwen bit her lip. "Are you telling me this because you're worried that you and I could throw the circle off?"

"Yes. I've only known you for a week, Olwen, but it's the nature of the Work that we get to know each other intimately in a very short time. And we've been brought together by a highly skilled matchmaker. I feel things for you I've never felt for anyone, not even Mercedes. It's all very new and exciting and I'd like to explore it further if...Am I right in thinking the feeling is mutual?"

"You have to ask?"

His smile was dazzling. "But of course this is precisely the kind of thing that's a danger to the circle. Potent, glorious, divine, it breaks the chain and sends everyone flying."

"We're adults, not teenagers, Jack. We should be able to contain ourselves for the greater good."

"I was hoping you would say that. It's my opinion, too. But Rose is concerned. For our safety, as well as everyone else's."

"Well, thanks for letting me know all this. No pressure."

On the bus, Olwen stared nervously out into the night. She was reminded of the old nightmare of finding herself on stage, in the lead role, without script or rehearsal. It was her task to hold the centre with Rose. What the hell did that mean? And what if she screwed up? Could she really guarantee a lid on her attraction to Dr Jack? Her libido wasn't something she had ever been able to control. It had always got her into trouble.

She started to chew on her thumb. If only she had some chocolate.

Dr Jack put his arm around her and drew her close. He kissed her forehead. "You'll be fine," he murmured. "You're a star."

She relaxed against him. He withdrew his arm and took her hand in his, weaving their fingers together. Only then did she notice that he wore no ring.

They had only gone a short distance from the house when the bus turned off the road and bumped onto the moor. After the heat of the day, a haze hung over the long grasses, mingling with a mist that issued from the earth like a damp breath.

"*Mosekonen brygger*," Olwen called out to Rose.

The Director glanced over at her and smiled. Dr Jack raised an eyebrow.

"The witch is brewing on the moor," she translated for him.

Night was falling. The stars began to shine. There were no lights on the bus, not even headlamps. They were journeying into the heart of darkness. She wasn't afraid. Ruairi was at the helm and Calum at the tiller. She trusted the twins absolutely. The bus rocked gently as it lumbered over the rough ground, like a ship on the waves. A ship of souls.

The landscape outside was lost in shadow; a lonely stretch of bog and hollow. There was no sign of the moon, only a faint shimmer of starlight. She was beginning to feel drowsy. Many of the others had fallen asleep. Dr Jack stared ahead, as if in a trance. The low roar of the engine made its own music. Somewhere in the sound she heard the skirl of bagpipes, the beat of drums and the clatter of bones. A sweet scent wafted through an open window – burning leaves and peat smoke. She caught sight of her reflection in the dark window. The face looking back at her was fey and dreamy-eyed. Journeying into the uncharted night, who was she?

As her eyes grew accustomed to the darkness outside, she began to see things in the shadows. When she spotted a woman stumbling over the moor, she was about to call out for the bus to stop. Then she recognised the woman's clothing, the knapsack on her back, and the way she held her phone in front of her like a flashlight. When the woman tripped and fell, Olwen heard her cry out.

"You'll be all right," she whispered to herself. "All will be well."

A short while later she heard the sound of a motorcycle. Fair hair flying behind him, harp strapped on his back, the young Dane quickly overtook the bus. He didn't even glance at her, but she caught the trail of his song as it echoed in his wake.

Jeg vil danse på min fædrende jord.
I will dance in the place of my ancestors.

She tightened her grip on Dr Jack's hand. He didn't move. It was as if he were no longer there. Her hold on reality was unravelling. She felt both terror and delight.

The winding sound of a horn rang out. Hooves thundered over the turf. Her heart raced wildly. Would she see them? She peered into the mist, searching every corner, but no matter how hard she looked, there was nothing to see. Then, suddenly, in the distance, for the merest second, she caught sight of a silhouette towering on the horizon: a great stag, antlered and golden.

Or was it a goaty-looking Pan blowing a long horn?

The bus trundled on into the night.

Now came the strangest sight of all. A small group of men – or the vague shapes of men – walked in procession. They carried a canopy above their heads supported by tall poles. The canopy was a black cloud of ash that swayed and undulated, shedding bits of darkness into the air. Though the men appeared to be moving in slow motion, they kept pace with the bus. The vision affected Olwen in a way she couldn't explain. She found herself murmuring words from a favourite poem by Wallace Stevens.

These are the ashes of fiery weather,
Of nights full of the green stars from Ireland,
Wet out of the sea and luminously wet,
Like beautiful and abandoned refugees.

At last they arrived at Callanish. The Stones loomed dark and solemn. Only now did Olwen understand what Rose had said to her and the slight emphasis he had used.

The place will be empty when *we get there.*

There was no sign of the Visitors' Centre or any human structure for miles around. The bus drew up on a level place where a car park would be built one day. Overhead, the ancient sky was a midnight blue, speckled with stars. But no moon. The landscape looked surreal. Mist whispered over the ground and around the great stones. In the distance rose the black shadow of hills.

Olwen's shoes sank into the soft earth. The hem of her dress was soaked. She slipped out of her pumps, felt the cool moist ground underfoot. *Delicious.* The others removed their shoes and socks too. Moving silently, they fanned out amongst the Stones.

Olwen wasn't surprised to see Rose stride towards the king-stone; the one the fair-haired biker had caressed and that Goldhart had perched upon. Elsie and Dr Jack followed quickly after him, to stand by the stones on either side. Others were moving confidently to take up position inside the megalith. Some leaned against their stones in a friendly manner. Others greeted them like long-lost friends. Una put her arms around hers, murmuring through the darkness.

"*Oh precious one.*"

Did the Stones shine like beacons to call out their partners? Or did they whisper their names? Olwen had no idea. She was staring around her, trying not to panic. She saw nothing, heard nothing. Fighting back her dismay, she looked for Calum or Ruairi, hoping they might help. But they had vanished along with the bus.

Barefoot, her gown flowing against her legs, she wandered through the monument. Once inside, all fear and anxiety fell away. The others acknowledged her as she passed by. Many bowed their heads. A few of the women curtsied. Christy gave her the standard Irish nod and a wink. She greeted each in turn, lifting her hand gracefully, like a queen in her court.

She felt free to move in any direction.

She was present to the Mystery.

Now she stood on the threshold of the northern avenue. Two lines of stones stretched before her, forming a wide path. A low humming sound rose around her. Was it the humans who sang or the Stones themselves? Or both? She gazed down the avenue towards the burial chamber at the heart of the monument. She was suddenly afraid. *There lies suffering. Sacrifice. Death.* But the song encouraged her and sustained her and bore her up.

She walked slowly to the burial chamber. Darkness welled in the shallow pit, like a pool of black water. She caught her breath. This was it. This was the part she had to do alone. This was her duty. Her dharma.

All of nature waits for us to achieve our full potential. The universe itself holds its breath in anticipation.

She stepped into the chamber. The darkness flowed around her. She began to sink. There was a moment of pure panic and terror.

She was drowning.

She was dying.

CHAPTER FORTY-THREE

WEST OF THE MOON

The dark water was everywhere. She was choking and panicking and gasping for breath. Submergence. Suffocation. The weight on her chest was agony. A voice cried out. Was it Dr Jack? But he had another name, her husband.

"She proves her innocence! Raise the stool! For the love of God, raise the stool!"

Oh yes, yes, please let her breathe! Please let her live!

A stern, officious voice replied. It was Rose, but he, too, had a different name, the magistrate who had both accused and condemned her. The man who hated her because she had married another.

"It is God's will. Suffer not a witch to live. Only if she drowns does she prove her innocence."

Elsie's voice screamed in anguish.

"My daughter!"

The raucous cheers of the onlookers. So many of the circle. Enjoying the spectacle of her death.

She was no longer in the water. She was lying on her back at the centre of a great ship. It wasn't moving. Not yet. The night was dark. Men stood over her with flaming torches. A dead man's body lay beside her. Rose: but he had another name, the Viking chieftain who was her master, even as she was his thrall. They both lay on a pyre.

Her hands and feet were bound. Standing over her was an old witch-woman, wielding a great knife. The Angel of Death. *Elsie!* Olwen began to scream as the knife descended. Her cries of agony were drowned out by the man who beat his sword against his shield. The greatest warrior of the clan. The one who had loved her in secret. She saw the sorrow in his eyes as he set the pyre alight.

These are the ashes of fiery weather.

How many times did she live and die with these same souls around her? Drowning in the darkness, in the tomb and the womb, dying and birthing, again and again.

She felt the pall of the world-weary woman.

How many times must I turn on the wheel? When will I be free?

She was buried under a weight of soil and stone. Was this her cairn? Another tomb? But no, it seemed she was waking from a great sleep. She was vast. Her body rose and fell like mountains. She was countless years old. A mother of the earth. She was the Sleeping Beauty. The Witch of the Moor. Heavy with the torpor of matter, she stretched her limbs.

The first pangs shot through her. She contracted with pain. Was this birthing or dying? She was heavily pregnant! Her stomach was round like a great hill. Now a crevice opened. Something emerged from her womb. An orb of pale gold.

My daughter! Most precious, most beloved daughter!

The moon-child crawled over her body, slowly, so slowly. Those big alien eyes looking at the world for the very first time. They were an eternal pair, these two. The Mystery at the heart of Eleusis. Mother and Daughter.

Am I dreaming?

Isn't this life but a dream?

Am I waking?

She struggled to get out of the burial chamber, to get out of the black well at the centre of the Stones. *Get out of the water!* She was drowning, not waving. A stray thought moved to soothe her. It came from one of her stories. One of her turns on the wheel. The voice of a woman helping another woman who was lost in addiction.

Surrender is not a feeling or a decision. It's not something you do in your head. It's an experience. Accept it. Let it happen. Surrender to win.

She let herself sink into the darkness, into the hills, into the bog. And her moon-child sank with her. Falling into time. Falling into matter. Surrendering to the Great Mater. A dizzying, disturbing, even revolting sensation. *How can a being of light exist in matter?* She was utterly disoriented. Her memory confused. Who was she? What was she? Was there a briefing? A briefing for this descent into hell? Her mind threatened to unhinge.

How can a being of light exist in matter? Surely it would be driven insane! Unto what is the journeying? What stitches the weave of the warp and the weft? What lies between the layers of every moment?

She found herself standing at the top of the avenue, looking towards the heart of Callanish. She had come full circle and she was not the same. The great Stones were light-filled and luminous, so bright they could not have been viewed with mortal eyes. She and the others were transformed. The Work had made them pure. There were no dark twists. No secrets. They stood like white candles in the night.

When the moon walks on the land, the Shining Ones will return.

She walked slowly down the avenue, greeting each as she passed, aware of the love they exchanged with her and each other. When she reached the centre of the Stones, she glanced a moment at her body asleep in the chamber. Her eyes turned to Jack. The love she felt for him rose up, even as it had for the others; but this feeling was different. He was special. Countless lives had been shared with him as father, mother, son and daughter; but most of all, as lover. Her eternal beloved.

His arms opened. Without hesitation, she stepped into his embrace. Desire flared between them. *Love is all that matters.* They began to kiss, falling into the heady pleasures of passion. All thought of the others was obliterated. Any notion of consequence gone. They were driven by that imperious urge that creates life itself.

Somewhere around her Olwen sensed the dismay. There was no judgement, no anger, no effort to change her mind. Only a deep disappointment. The moon was about to rise again and the Queen was not at the centre, where she should be. She was away with her lover.

Love is all that matters.

She stiffened in his arms.

But not at the expense of others.

Gently, deliberately, they loosened their hold and broke apart. As they bowed to each other, both struggled not to grin. They had almost ruined the Rite, but who could blame them? The nature of sex was anarchic and free. When they sensed the amusement of the circle, as well as its relief, they allowed themselves a laugh. A cosmic giggle.

She returned to the centre.

He was waiting for her there. The Fisher King. The Enchanter. Glimmering with a stern beauty. The great moment was upon them.

The moon rose for a second time that night, at the heart of the Stones in a blaze of glory. Mother and Daughter and Cailleach in one. Lunar light charged the Stones. The explosion was nuclear. Macrocosmic. Microcosmic. *As within, so without. As above, so below.* The blast nearly felled them all.

Instinctively, Olwen reached for Rose. *The centre must hold.* They clung together as the stream of power surged around them. The rest of the circle linked with each other and with the Stones. The streams of energy began to fashion a chain, like ancient knotwork.

The ecstasy was a challenge in itself. They were all swooning in the rapture, lost in the bliss of *remembering* who and what they were.

Beware, Rose whispered in her ear. *The serpent will rise. The shadow will fall.*

She felt the uncoiling at the base of her spine. The snake at the root of the Tree of Life. The primal urge, fire and passion, the original desire to surge into matter.

Her body began to shudder violently. An electric current tore through her. Throwing her off balance. He gripped her tightly so that she wouldn't fall. His touch inflamed her desire.

There was a time when the Goddess mated with the King to grant him sovereignty of the land.

Her lips brushed his mouth. *The taste of mortal existence. A drop of honey on the tongue.* She sensed his opposition. He was not her beloved. She tried to understand, to remember a smaller story, but even as she recalled a name, he changed in her arms. Now she embraced the young Dane, his hair flowing with light.

Desire flared again, her attraction to Rose, buried so deeply she had no awareness of it until now. Fragments of memory taunted her. The Turkish Delight in his den. Riding together across the moor. The morning he came for her. *Mosekonen brygger.* The time she clasped him in her arms as he lay broken. Their laughter in the conservatory. From the very first day, when she sensed his history of violence, there was the inevitable attraction beneath the revulsion – to the dangerous man. The original wound of the father.

You are mine, she heard herself say, as she pressed her mouth to his, taking him captive.

He did not draw back, but his surrender was stained with a dark grief. As they locked together in an ardent embrace, the energy streams around them began to erupt. The chain was breaking apart. Cries of pain rang out from the others.

A male voice was heard, a gentle baritone gently reminding her.

He's incapable of that kind of love in this lifetime. He's too damaged. He has accepted that truth.

Had the voice expressed anger or jealousy, she might have rebelled; but there was only compassion for both her and Rose.

This is not a coronation rite. The King is mortally wounded. He has come for healing to the Lady of the Lake.

Now compassion rose in her also. The nature of her embrace altered profoundly. She grew in stature, even as Rose diminished, and she lifted him high on her shoulder for all to see.

Behold, my child, my beloved child!

The chain of the circle was forged anew, all the stronger for having been tested. Fire and light wove together in a cosmic embroidery. The circle was spinning outwards, radiating like a spiral galaxy.

They were falling...

flying...

here...

there...

then...

now...

The blood tide of Fate is loosed upon us. We plumb the river where the currents of existence flow. We walk in the shadows of the sun. We are asked The Question. We say yes! We all say yes. We wouldn't be here if we did not say yes. Yes to the wonder! Yes to the horror! Yes to the joy! Yes to the sorrow! Yes to the whole catastrophe! The taste of mortality is a drop of honey on the tongue. We fall willingly into matter. So very young and so very old, we go to seed and run wild in the world. The countless forms it offers. The infinite dance. To life we wake from the long-forgotten dream, the beautiful mystery, from where we came and to where we go. Many of us go mad! Still, we serve the life force in all its expressions. Whether it is willed we live or die, suffer or be joyous, we accept what happens.

At the heart of the universe, we sing of a life lived in matter.

We are servants of creation.
We are servants of life.
Yes.

Her first thought, when she began to remember herself, there at the heart of the universe, was that she would find a Great War. Some eternal conflict being waged between good and evil, light and darkness. She was prepared to fight. Her army was all around her, winged and shining with light.

But there, at the heart of all that is and was and will be, she grasped a Great Truth.

There is no evil.

Out in the boundless reaches of infinity, deep in the boundless heart of life, there is no evil.

What was the force that welled all around her? What was the origin? Unto what is the journeying? What stitches the weave of the warp and the weft? What lies between the layers of every moment? Beyond the fragmented eye, the fragmented I, beyond the great divide of spirit and matter, beyond all this and that, what is it?

We swim in an ocean of love.

She fell into her body. *Wet and luminous and gloriously wet.* She stared at her arms, rubbed her hands together, stroked her own face. It was a moment that was physical and spiritual and erotic and sensual all at the same time. *The time falling bodies take to light.* Everything was excruciatingly beautiful and exciting.

Just to be *alive.*

Just to be human.

Just to *be.*

Thank you, she kept saying, *thank you, thank you, yes, thank you, thank you, yes, thank you, yes, yes, yes, thank you.*

They fell into time, as the Rite came to an end. A shower of stars falling in the night sky, plummeting to the earth, towards the Stones. Below her, she saw the star gazers, the tourists, the visitors and locals, their faces upturned, stunned by what they saw.

The Scottish High Priestess raised her white arms. "The Shining Ones!" she cried. "The Shining Ones have returned!"

But even as Olwen came back to herself, she wished the Priestess could have seen what she saw.

As above, so below.

Those who looked up in wonder shone with the same light as those who fell.

OMEGA

Olwen sat up in her bed. What time was it? She glanced over at the clock. She had slept so soundly and so late, she had missed breakfast. *Ah, but what delicious dreams.* The last sparkling trails glittered in her mind. She practically smacked her lips.

She jumped out of bed, naked as a newborn babe. She laughed, remembering how she had shed her clothes, as a snake sheds its skin, to slide under the cool sheets. Now she danced a little jig. Her limbs tingled. She felt exquisitely alive, bursting with energy and ideas and plans and hopes and dreams. So much to do, so much to think about, so much to write.

She showered at her leisure, enjoying the rosy scent of the soap as she lathered her skin. The clothes she picked to wear were loose and bright; a long flowing skirt with a flowery print and a silk blouse. A straw bonnet would have suited it, with cherries on the brim, but she didn't own such a thing. *Yet.* She slipped into her sandals. Chose dangly earrings. No make-up was needed. Her cheeks glowed, her eyes shone. She let her hair fall freely over her shoulders.

The house was strangely quiet as she strolled through the hallways. Not a sound to be heard. When she entered the dining room, she found only the serving girls clearing up. They smiled at her. A single setting awaited her at her usual place by the window. There was a vase of wildflowers on the table, surrounded by a heap of gifts and cards. She accepted, then, that everyone had left. Gone home.

She had no sooner sat down than Mrs Macleod arrived with breakfast. The porridge was newly made, sprinkled with brown sugar and drizzled with cream. It was better than any she had ever tasted. There was a moment when she peered into the bowl and caught a glimpse of suns, moons, and stars. She cradled the mug of brewed coffee, savouring its aroma before she sipped it. A sudden reminder of a much-loved film: *Wings of Desire.* Then came scrambled eggs with smoked salmon and toast. The perfection of the morning.

When she asked Morag about Rose, she wasn't surprised to hear that he had left for the Continent along with Elsie. She knew where they were going. She wished them well on their journey.

She took her time to sift through the cards, notes and gifts. *Bravo! Well done! Take a bow!* Savitri had left her a Kashmiri shawl. The hand-carved prayer beads were from Tenzin Dawa. The jewelled hair clip from Euphémie. Christy's note was in English and Irish, both badly spelled, giving his address and phone number and an invitation to Sunday dinner with his wife and family. Penny Li left her a jade bracelet and a wallet-sized photograph of herself. *Don't forget me, kawan saya, adik saya.* Harry's card came from his community – *Expect a miracle!* – and included their website. Dr Jack's personal stationery showed an address in Carmel, California. A generous hand had scrawled over the half-page: *What's an ocean when we've crossed the universe together?* She smiled to herself. So romantic. Then a frown of suspicion. She turned the page over. *Once you go black, you never go back.*

She laughed out loud. Kissed the paper. Let out a sigh.

She was glad it was like this. She couldn't have borne the weight of their gratitude and affection in person. And really, it was nonsense to give her so much credit, when she was simply the last piece of the puzzle. In a game of chess, even the most powerful queen has no role if the other players aren't engaged.

Morag returned to tell her that her friend, Dr N, had called and would arrive by noon. A lunch would be provided for both of them.

"How can I thank you?" Olwen began. "You and your brothers –"

The housekeeper raised her hand.

"It is not the custom of our clan to accept thanks for what we do."

Olwen nodded. She knew this tradition.

"May I thank Rose?" She indicated the gifts and cards. "Even as they wanted to say something to me, I feel the need..."

"I think you know what he would like," Morag said quietly.

Olwen nodded again. "I'll send him a copy as soon as it's readable. Perhaps," She hesitated, suddenly shy to ask. "Perhaps he might invite me back...in 2025?"

Morag smiled.

When Dr N arrived, she stared intently at Olwen.

"You look different. I can't wait to hear the story."

"It's a book."

"Excellent!"

After their lunch, Ruairi carried Olwen's bags to the car. Calum stood in the shadow of the greenhouse and raised his hand in salute. Morag was under the arch.

Olwen was about to get into the car, when she stopped.

"Could you wait a minute?" she asked Dr N. "A last farewell."

But she found the stables empty. No sign of the horses. She was sad. She would have liked to have seen them one last time.

The car wasn't long on the road when she spotted Lord Donn and Epona grazing on the moors. The horses galloped to meet them and raced alongside. Olwen rolled down her window to shout her love and thanks.

"I'm getting shivers and goosebumps," said Dr N. "I'm guessing it was truly magical?"

"Every minute of it."

"Did you hear what the wonderful Morag called out as we left?"

Olwen shook her head. "I didn't catch the words on my side. Was it Scots Gaelic?"

"It certainly was. *Gus an coinnich sinn a-rithist.*"

"Which means?"

"Until we meet again."

Olwen smiled to herself.

Until we meet again.

....

PERMISSIONS

ABOUT THE AUTHOR

O.R. Melling was born in Ireland and grew up in Canada with her seven sisters and two brothers. Her home is Bray, Co. Wicklow, a small town by the sea, but at present she is helping to run a Tibetan Buddhist Centre in the Irish countryside. The latter work has brought her to Outer Mongolia and across the Gobi Desert.

Melling has a BA in Celtic Studies and an MA in Mediaeval Irish History. Her award-winning books have been published worldwide and translated into many languages.

www.ormelling.com